Love &
Mu

GW00362934

Lover, Husband, Father, Monster

A novel in two voices

Elsie Johnstone

Elsie Johnstone

Graeme Johnstone

Lover, Husband, Father, Monster

A copy of this publication can be found in the National Library
of Australia.

ISBN: 978-1-921791-16-1 (pbk.)

Published by Book Pal
www.bookpal.com.au

Dedication

For children everywhere who suffer because of the choices their parents make.

Her Story

Chapter 1

The photo jumped off the screen. The sparkling smile, his hair a little lighter than I remembered it and longer than most men his age would wear it. Sitting at a set of drums, he looked almost the same as that day a whole lifetime ago I flew out of Heathrow back home to Dublin, heartbroken and melancholy, to reassemble the shattered pieces of my fragile existence. He had used me, abused me and discarded me and now, all these years later, here he was having the temerity to ask me would I be his Facebook friend?

My stomach lurched. I thought I was well and truly over Tommy. And I was! I had a successful husband, a wonderful home and three beautiful children. Tommy could never have given me anything like that. He was still a drummer, for God's sake!

'Jennifer,' I inwardly counselled, 'do not go there. It was the hottest of loves but it had the coldest of ends, so just leave it where it is. It does no good to stir up ghosts from the past.'

'Tea, darling?' inquired Stuart, suddenly appearing at the doorway with cup and saucer in hand. 'I'll just be going up to the church. They have a meeting on about Heritage Week, but I don't expect there'll be many there. It'll be just the Reverend John and me making all the decisions so I wouldn't be thinking it will take too long.'

There he stood - my Stuart, the pillar of the Church, sturdy and reliable. My husband, the very successful insurance salesman. My man, tall, fifty three years old, with a defining shock of greying hair and a comfortable but not fat body, handsome in a very ordinary sort of way.

His clothes looked well on him because he took great care of himself and he was particular about what he wore - a conservative dresser with impeccable taste. His suits were personally tailored by Louis Copeland & Sons in Capel Street and his Italian leather shoes were always shone to a bright sheen. Shirts and casual gear were bought off the peg from either Copeland's or the House of Fraser at Dundrum. He ran at six o'clock each morning before he began his day and worked out three times a week in the gym near his business.

My Stuart was a man who gave off an air that was affluent not flashy, stylish not trendy. He was calm and controlled, the reassuring type that people tend to trust. You cannot be successful in the field of insurance if you do not market yourself, and to do that you need to monitor every part of the process.
'Buy insurance from me and you won't need to worry,' was his mantra. 'Nothing bad will happen to you and even if it somehow does, my company will put it right. Just sign here and pay me, and I will take care of things for you. I provide solidity and certainty in an uncertain world.'

In retrospect, I was just like one of Stu's satisfied clients. When I agreed to marry him I willingly gave over personal autonomy for a warm feeling of security. I exchanged me - with all my faults, foibles and slightly harum-scarum approach to life - for the safety and insurance of a well presented husband, a good home, a reliable income and a family that would never want for anything. Stuart was older and wiser than me and made enough money to pay the considerable mortgage, send the kids to good schools and take us all abroad on a family holiday each year.

They say every person has their price. That was the down payment on the price I was to pay.

'Cheerio,' he said, handing me the tea, exactly as I liked it – black, weak, half a teaspoon of sugar and just a smidgin of cold tap-water to cool it down. 'I'll take Molly with me for the walk. Is there anything I can pick up while I'm out?'

'No thank you, Stu,' I said, staring at the screen. 'I'm just looking up a recipe for dinner. I'll head up the road myself when I find out exactly what I need.' This wasn't entirely true but Stuart didn't approve of me being on-line 'living in that lah-lah world', his description of social networking sites.

I smiled to myself as I turned around to watch him and Molly walk hand-in-hand out the door. 'What a wonderful picture they make, father and daughter, and how lucky am I to have three beautiful children,' I thought. After all, for a long time I had thought that the god that governs the universe had different plans altogether for me.

Then I turned back to look at the photo on the screen. 'Hmm. I bet Tommy the drummer wouldn't be making his little wifey a cup of tea before heading up the hill to see the vicar!' Things had certainly

3

changed and I had changed with them. Best to leave it at that.

I reached for the mouse, clicked it, and Tommy and his sparkling smile, his slightly long hair and his drums disappeared.

Chapter 2

My life was like a pond. Once there had been great excitement and activity, with different and wonderful and sometimes scary things happening down in the depths, up on the surface, along the banks and by the shores. Now things had settled. The mud had ceased its churning and lay on the bottom, vegetation had grown up to prevent too many ripples on the surface, and a rhythmic, seasonal and predictable pattern had evolved. I had reached that stage in my life where there were no surprises any more.

Here I was - Jennifer Mary Hoare, formerly O'Brien - forty eight years old, wife and mother, mellowed and stable, with everything nicely in place. Stuart Junior, our eldest, was fourteen years old and just wonderful, still very much a boy - and every mother knows just how beautiful they are. 'What's for dinner, Mam?' he would call out as he came in the kitchen door, bouncing one form of sports ball or another in front of him. 'Junior, wipe your feet and leave that outside please. You know how much it annoys your father when you bring a wet ball inside!'

'Okay! Okay! Gotcha! What are we having for dinner, Mam?'

Life for Junior was simple - sport, food and school.

Richard, at twelve, was younger than Junior in years but seemed older in the head and more of a worrier. He was an astute people observer, in touch with what went on in the family, who said what, where did they go, what happened to whom? He listened to conversations rather than letting them go over his head and knew all the news and gossip. He was what you would call a people person. Rich was in tune with me and seemed to instinctively know if I was upset or unhappy. He loved to take his little sister Molly outside on the grass to play and always included her in his games. She in turn happily tagged along with him and his friends. 'I love playing with Molly,' he told me one day in confidence, 'because she thinks I am really clever and I can teach her lots of things. But Junior, well, he always teases me and says I can't do things properly.'

Rich possessed a high degree of emotional intelligence, something that Stu saw but didn't like in him and so had made it his mission to make him a man. Poor Rich did his best to please, but a lot of the time he just didn't shape up.

'Let him be,' I'd beg, 'he's only twelve. He's just a little boy trying to keep up with his big brother and sometimes that is pretty difficult. He still needs a cuddle and so do I. Just allow him to be himself.'

'He's soft,' Stu would say. 'You're making a sissy out of him. You'll turn him into a homosexual. That's what happens when a boy gets over-mothered. Get him out from under your petticoats.'

As for Molly, our beautiful little girl, Stu wanted her to be named Moira after his mother. 'But Moira is such an old fashioned name,' I begged. 'She won't thank us for it.' I managed to hang out against him until I got my way, one of the few times in all our years together that I asserted myself. In retrospect, perhaps I should have stood up for myself more often. Maybe if I had done that in the beginning then things would have turned out very differently.

He treated Molly as if she was a precious porcelain doll. 'She's beautiful,' he'd say, 'but I feel as if I will break her.' In some ways it was understandable; he'd had very little to do with girls, big or small.

'Best you see to her until she grows up a bit. I'll see to the boys,' he'd add. So that is what happened.

I just knew my Molly would have a magnificent future and that she was going to grow into the best of Irish women - intelligent, capable, happy, optimistic and chatty, a great communicator. The world was her oyster and I was eager to enjoy the journey with her. She would be me, but ever so much better.

Chapter 3

Do we ever entirely forget our first love? It is like the first-ever taste of ice cream on a hot summer's day. The mother runs her finger through the soft, sweet stuff and proffers it to her baby to suck. The little one has no idea of the treat that is in store until the icy sweetness tickles the tongue and the cooling, creamy flavour explodes onto the palate. There is no going back after that. The little one pleads for more; the tiny hands are held high, demanding. Eventually, mother relents, hands over the whole cone and baby gobbles it down. There will be other hot days with other ice creams, but they will never quite be the same.

As I sipped the tea that Stuart had given me, I wondered about Tommy's life journey in the more than twenty years since he and I were lovers. Almost everything about me had changed, that was for sure. What about him? I hadn't thought of him for such a long time but now my memory had been jolted and, seeing as the house was quiet, I allowed myself time to indulge in the guilty pleasure of reflecting on the past.

It had been a long, long time and many, many things had happened since my days of being a young, carefree Cambridge University student known as 'Jobby', an acronym from my initials, Jennifer O'Brien.

Jobby, the energetic redheaded, green-eyed, much loved daughter of Seamus and Mary and adored baby sister of the entire front row of a rugby scrum. Jobby, another girl in another era when I was in the prime of my youth and having the time of my life. Jobby, newly released from the restraints of her strict Irish Catholic upbringing in Dublin and with the world at her fingertips.

My father had come from Killarney in County Kerry. The saying goes, 'Once a Kerry man, always a Kerry man,' and it was back to his home county we would go for family celebrations and the like, affairs that were always loud and boisterous. As children, we spent most summers with family in the Kingdom. 'God's own country,' Da would say as he stood gazing at the mountains, deeply breathing in the country air. 'Sure, it's good to be home where we all know each other and there's no pretendin' or puttin' on airs. I thank the Good Lord for landing me on this glorious piece of earth.' He said the same thing every time.

We knew our Kerry relations well as they always stayed over at our home when they came up to go to Croke Park for a GAA match or simply to do a bit of shopping, so I grew up feeling secure and connected.

'Be careful of Uncle Brian's legs, he's a diabetic you know, and we don't want to be causing him any trouble by knocking them,' Mam would warn me before the Kerry onslaught. 'And whatever you do, don't go mentioning your cousin Liam to your Aunty Agnes, she's very upset with him and we don't want

9

to make her cry. And Jennifer, make sure that Dermot gets some food in him before he pours himself a drink, it calms him down and we won't be all sufferin' later on.' That was the way it was in my big extended family. We were all talkers and were all mad in one way or another. It was just in the genes. Life was for living and we had fun.

Then suddenly, school days at Dominican College were over and the simple predictability of the daily rules and rituals that had made my time there so happy and secure was a thing of the past. No more prayers before class, no more piano practice, no Angelus bells at noon, hockey matches or Irish dancing lessons. I need never speak my native Gaelic language if I chose not to. Old Sister Madeleine would never again shake her head as I chattered away in class, clucking her tongue in lament and declaring, 'Ah, Jennifer O'Brien, will you not give it a rest then? I swear if you were left all on your own in an empty room, you'd be talking to the stones in the wall. Do you ever stop, girl?'

The friends from my childhood had all dispersed and gone their own ways. My uniform had been cleaned and pressed and passed on to young Maeve down the road and my old books had been bundled up and taken to a charity shop. School had been fun and I had enjoyed it, but it was a rite of passage and now it was done. My whole life spanned out in front of me.

I had been a diligent student who enjoyed learning and had passed my Leaving Certificate well enough to obtain a place at Cambridge, studying

Law. 'Jayzus, will you look at that?' said Da. 'Our little girl's off to England to study!'

But his enthusiasm didn't come without a warning. 'Now don't be bringing back an English-man to marry,' he added. 'Remember, we have the best men in the world here on our little island. You can't go past them!'

My mother and father willingly gave me the opportunity and support to study abroad and I was lucky that my brothers had paved the way for me, ironing out any wrinkles and sorting out any problems that my parents might have had. Each had left home to study, had succeeded in varying degrees and happily returned home to roost. Mam always quoted the text, 'If you love something you should let it free and then if it truly belongs to you it will return.' Mam and Da were happy for me to take my chances on English shores and although they knew they would miss my presence in the home, I think they also were secretly pleased to finally have some time for themselves after all their child-rearing years.

There were five of us; me and four older siblings - Patrick, Daniel, Brendan and Kevin. I loved them all but it was Kevin, the next brother in age to me, who became my best buddy. Being the only girl, I was everybody's princess but he and I shared a lot of things when we were growing up and came to be great friends as adults. Kevin saw himself as my playmate, my protector and my confidante. We played together with the other children in our street, not coming inside until half nine on summer nights; we rode our bicycles around the streets, lanes and parks of our local area; we got up to harmless fun and mischief.

Within the family we were an island unto ourselves, 'the little ones', as we were called, and the chores and responsibilities that all the older members shouldered somehow never landed at our feet. So we had a carefree and happy childhood, a lot of it spent on the handball courts the local kids had crafted out of the walls at the end of the cul de sac. I was as good as the boys until I began to worry about breaking my fingernails.

It was Kevin who was to be with me on that awful day that would change my life irrevocably. He was the unwitting witness to the terrible thing that would forever have both of us unable to close our eyes at night for fear that we would relive it once again in the narrow isthmus between consciousness and sleep.

Chapter 4

The whole family accompanied me to the airport the day I left Ireland for Cambridge - Mam, Da, my brothers, their wives, my nieces and nephews. There was much teasing, jesting and many hugs and after a teary farewell, during which Mam told me that it was 'my time in the sunshine' and that I should enjoy it, we said our goodbyes and I headed for the plane.

'I will really miss those crazy dudes,' I thought as I adjusted my seatbelt. 'But best get on with it though and enjoy the journey.'

I comforted myself with the thought that they would all still be there when I came home, wiped the tears from my eyes, and flew across the Irish Sea to the student life, where things would never be the same.

Settling in at Cambridge was not difficult. Three of my brothers had been residents at Robinson College, then the newest and most modern of the university's many halls of residence and I carried on the tradition. It was a little removed from the centre of things and not quite as snobby as the others, and so many foreign students assembled there. Evensong at Kings didn't interest us much and neither did the niche specialty men's clothiers like Ede & Ravenscroft that occupied many of the little shops fronting the cobbled streets leading to the university.

As I carried my red suitcase over the drawbridge which formed the main entrance, my assigned senior, Hannah, who being an Australian was a long way from her home, touched me on the arm and welcomed me in her native twang. 'G'day Jennifer!' she said heartily. 'Don't be nervous. Here at Robinson we're all in the same boat, mostly undergrads in foreign territory, and it is all new to us. So embrace it and learn and, most of all, have fun. Come on and I'll show you to your digs.' We walked and chatted together through what seemed like miles of passageways until we came to the end of a corridor.

'This is it,' she said. 'Number 102, where you can put down your swag and lay your weary head, and this is your room mate.' She motioned towards a gorgeous, gentle girl standing opposite. 'Rhani, I'd like you to meet Jennifer, you two will be bunking in together. I'll leave you to get acquainted but feel free to call me any time you need help. Take care now.' With that she gave a little bow and a laugh and left us to it.

I put my suitcase down and smiled at my new roommate as she put out her hand to take mine. 'Welcome,' she smiled, 'I only got here myself an hour ago, but isn't this all lovely? Take a peek out the window at the garden. It's gorgeous, so English and so different from Thailand where I come from.'

I was to quickly learn that Rhani's delicate Asian beauty and quiet demeanour belied the fact that she had the brains to be studying Medicine at one of the world's top universities. She said she had never been to my home country and I had to look up an atlas to determine exactly where Thailand was situated in the world, so we had much to learn about each other.

Over many nights, lying on our beds when we should have been studying, we talked and laughed. She shared with me some of her traditions and beliefs and I came to understand her and her culture. We discussed my cloistered convent school education versus her exotic Oriental upbringing, marvelling all the while at the fact that we were both there in Robinson College, Cambridge, an oasis brimming with culture and learning where all the nations of the earth were represented and where the possibilities were endless. 'Isn't this exciting?' I'd say.

As the semester progressed Rhani and I also began to spend more time off-campus together. The ceaseless tolling of the Cambridge bells punctuated every activity in the famous university town. We explored narrow laneways, leafed through old books at David's Second Hand Book Store, tried on clothes at Edenlilley's Department Store and ate delicious cream buns at Fitzbillies' Bun Shop opposite the Fitzwilliam Museum. We loved the regular market in the square where they sold all sorts of produce and trinkets, Rhani saying that next time she went home to Thailand she should bring back some of the local crafts and sell them.

A couple of times we took a punt on the River Cam, but that lost its shine the day I got my oar stuck in the mud and toppled into the water. Being Irish, I don't swim very well, but fortunately a group of gallant young men rescued me and returned me dripping, embarrassed and flustered to my college. Rhani doubled over in laughter, clutching her sides, barely able to move.

The first time I ever saw Tommy, he and other members of Amnesty International were using mime in the village square to highlight the injustices that were happening in Argentina at that time. While his face was painted white like all the others and he was wearing the same theatrical prison costume, he stood out from the rest with his stage presence, the artistic skill of his lithe moves and his obvious fervour for change. Of the group, he was the one who captured the most attention.

But, important as their cause was - the Dirty War, I think it was called, in Argentina - Rhani and I soon turned away. We were more fascinated with a long queue of people nearby who were patiently waiting to use a fascinating new device called a bank flexi-machine where for the first time you could get money from a 'hole in the wall'.

Coming from Thailand, Rhani was a Buddhist and the more I got to know her philosophy, the more I admired her and her outlook on life. 'Buddhism is not a religion; it is a way of life,' she would tell me. 'There are no absolutes and everything is open to debate. The only essential for being a Buddhist is the belief that change is possible.' This free thinking philosophy was completely at odds with my dogmatic Irish Catholic background where every-thing was set in stone and not to be flouted.

Perhaps that's why Buddhism appealed to me so much. In many ways it sat well with my Irish culture – Irishmen love a good discussion, our Celtic background was heavily involved in the spirit world, and many of us believe in supernatural things such as banshees and the little people. Rhani introduced me to her meditation groups and the world of Buddhism. Young, enthusiastic and thirsting for knowledge, I embraced this ancient philosophy and so, although I was on campus and part of university life, I gradually became separated from the student mainstream. Rhani, me and our Buddhist friends developed a subgroup within the whole.

It was on a meditation group one weekend, on the east coast of Scotland near Portsoy, that I first said 'hello' to another member of the movement - Tommy. For the next five years, he was to be the love of my life.

Chapter 5

Tommy was beautiful in a delicate, exotic sort of way. His mother was Thai and his father English and their union had melded the two sets of genes to produce an amazing, universal creature that delighted the eye. He was strikingly different, the perfect representation of Eurasian chic. Oriental, but at the same time English; small boned but manly; polite, but extremely outgoing. He had been educated at the best of English schools, so he combined excellent manners with that indisputable self belief of the British upper class. Tommy was exotic, golden-skinned, doe-eyed, lithe, smart and funny. And he wore all this as a magnificent, colourful, eye-catching robe, as only a person who is completely happy in his own being can do.

I don't think he really noticed me much at first, except in passing. The connection was that his mother, Leah, had sponsored Rhani to study at Cambridge. Their families had both come from the same poverty-stricken Thai village and Leah had heard of Rhani's potential when she was home visiting. 'Without Leah's patronage,' Rhani told me more than once, 'I would have had hardly any education. In fact I would have been lucky if I had been able to read. I probably would have ended up getting married young and helping run the family's food stall in the village market.'

Rhani said that Leah had been a fabulous mentor and support for her and her family all through her school years. 'I really feel that I have to do very well to thank her and to make her proud,' she said. 'She's a lovely lady.'

Tommy was at the meditation weekend with his mother, but the link between me, Rhani, Leah and him had little to do with how things panned out. It was a case of me being drawn by an irresistable magnetic force to this opposite being. He was so different to me. He would do anything for fun and he exhibited a charisma that swept people up with him. His confidence and sense of self propelled him towards being naughty, anti-establishment, a rebel. He seemed to be dancing through life like there was no tomorrow, living each day as it came, not worrying about the future, having a ball.

Being Irish, that take on life was hard for me to understand. As a nation we believe in reparation for sins committed and reward for sins avoided. We believe in Heaven, Hell and Purgatory, that place where you go to suffer so you can make up for the good times you had on earth before you are free to look for all eternity on the face of God. We chant the mantra, 'Sure, suffering does you no harm at all; in fact it can be good for you because if you suffer in this life you are sure to be elevated in the next. There's nothing wrong with having a good time but you'll surely have to pay for it in the end.' From an Irish cultural perspective, even if things are bad, they are never so bad that they can't possibility get worse. Our nation wakes up every morning expecting it to rain, and if it doesn't, we're quite certain that it will rain tomorrow. At the end of the day we pour ourselves a drink and listen to sad songs about things that went wrong and which could have turned out better.

Another thing we Irish don't like is people who get above themselves and flaunt the good times they are having and the successes they may be enjoying. 'Ah, Mary McNamara, will y'be takin' a look at her!' some local will say sipping his Guinness when Mary walks into the room looking resplendent in a new outfit. 'Does she not she think she's Lady Muck? Just because she's a lawyer in the city. All those airs and graces! But did y'know her mother was in one of the Magdalene laundries, run by the the nuns for the orphans? Now here's her Mary strutting about as if she's the bloody queen of England.'

As a race we are bitter-sweet and naturally seem to take the pessimistic, melancholic view. Perhaps that's why, at the end of the day, we like to party - if we're going to be ruined, and it is almost certain that we will be, then it is best that we enjoy ourselves while we can. But to be sure, we will pay, one way or another.

Tommy was the antithesis of all this. He was never negative, always believed in himself and optimistically loved life. On the surface he had everything - money, friends, style and an engaging smile. He was always very visible on campus and seemed to be a part of everything cool that was going on, having an enviable ability to sit comfortably in a variety of social situations. One of these was as the drummer in a rock band that did regular lunch-time gigs in the main courtyard. They were pretty good, too, performing a lot of their own stuff as well as the popular covers of the time.

The time they did an open-air session of African drumming drew a courtyard full of undergraduates, pounding out the beat on anything that was available - our books, our bike helmets, our bags, whatever - jamming away like there was no tomorrow. Some of the professors even felt compelled to join in. Anyone who was there that day would remember it; the whole quadrangle was alive with the beat. As the drummer in the band, Tommy led the rhythm making, his charisma carrying the day. Many of us went home that night with hands all red and swollen from beating too hard and too long.

Whichever way you looked at it, Tommy was Mr Cool. All of which captured my heart almost instantaneously. I wanted to be cool, just like him. I was a shy little Irish girl who had jumped out of the constrained shallows of her own little pond and was struggling to keep her head above the rolling waves of the big bad world. I wasn't part of the cool group. Redheads just weren't cool!

As well as the meditation group, Tommy was also into student politics, sitting on the Student Representative Council as spokesman for the fledgling Green lobby. When he spoke of things Green, I began to listen and I agreed mostly with what he said and, because I wanted to be where he was, I got involved. He often spoke out on the causes espoused by Greenpeace which was, at that time, an embryonic organisation operating out of dingy little offices above a gym in South London.

'Our precious planet is being destroyed by the excesses of big business and compliant politics and this has to be stopped,' he would declare. I got involved initially by doing small things like handing out pamphlets around the campus or setting up an information counter in Cambridge itself, but as time went on I became very active on several fronts. It was the major campaign to halt the French nuclear weapons testing in the Pacific that caught our imaginations - and brought us together.

'We have to let the French know that they are being watched,' said Tommy one day to a small group of us in the café. 'By letting bombs off underground they are cracking and destroying the atolls.'

'What are we going to do?' someone said.

'Greenpeace aims to prevent the detonation of bombs by placing boats in their way. I'm going out there to do my bit. Does anyone want to join me?'

I can't remember if I put my hand up or murmured 'yes' or simply nodded, but I know my stomach was churning with anticipation and my response was almost instantaneous. And that is how I found myself during the long summer break of 1982 with Tommy and a few other like-minded souls aboard a ship that was part of a flotilla near Muroroa Atoll in the Pacific Ocean.

Perhaps it was heat of the tropics or the perceived danger and excitement of our mission or maybe the beauty of our surroundings, I don't know, but our feelings smouldered - a touch, a look, a glimpse, a word - until one night while we were both on watch we reached for each other and entangled ourselves helplessly and irretrievably amongst the sheets of both the boating and bedding kind.

I gave myself entirely to Tommy and in so doing fell hopelessly and madly and head over heels in love with him. We couldn't take our hands off each other. I would have gone to the end of the earth and back for my Tommy. Although we prevented a bomb being exploded while our flotilla hung around, as soon as we sailed off, the French let one loose anyway. But it didn't matter. He was my first love. I started out on that expedition a virgin and came home a woman in love. I had found sex and I loved it.

On our return, the news spread around the campus, the Buddhist circles and the music scene, 'Hey, did you hear about Tommy? That little Irish girl is his new girlfriend!'

I still lived in my student digs but little by little I began spending more time at his shared house with his band mates. It was a cool party place, with lots of comings and goings and life never, ever being dull. Although Tommy's band was not big time, many of the other musicians and groupies that came, strummed, drank, smoked, crashed and left, belonged to popular bands of the time. And so we were always going to gigs, making music or just doing wild and zany things - things that you can only get away with while you are still young enough to escape the consequences. I was cool at last! The shy little redhead from Dublin had made it. We were the coolest couple on campus.

With this newfound lifestyle there came a down side. I was not a drinker. I didn't like the way it made me feel. I still don't. But there was a lot of pot being smoked in Tommy's house and little by little I began to indulge. At first I'd share a puff as the joint was passed from one to another, then I began rolling my own. Later I began procuring supplies for my friends and me until, in the end, I was so spaced out I ceased going back to my bed at Robinson and hardly went to university at all.

Tommy had certainly introduced me to his hedonistic world, the one that I had aspired to so much - the world of parties, music, politics and recreational drugs - and I had jumped right into it. We sometimes attended classes but most times we were too busy getting over the previous night's buzz or preparing for the one ahead. We made love and were in love. There was no world except the one in which we existed. That semester and the next, my study habits were erratic and for the first time in my life, I failed to achieve my academic goals.

'What is going on, Jennifer?' Rhani asked me quietly on one of the rare mornings I turned up at our shared room. 'I do not understand. Your grades are suffering. This course should be so easy for you.'

I had no real answer, and I had no real worries either, because I was in love and as long as Tommy was with me, I was happy. Life was grand. It was our time in the sunshine and we were enjoying every minute of it. It would not have mattered to us if

World War 3 had broken out; we were enthralled in our own little world where tomorrow, with all its needs for study, exams and a career, seemed eons away. We danced through each day as it came.

I took up with Tommy boots and all, neglecting my own friends and hooking myself into his network. His friends became mine. My birth family had taught me to trust and that is just what I did. I loved wholly and with my all. I had been brought up to look after my man and anyone else in the vicinity who may have needed nurturing. It was never an even relationship.

Chapter 6

While Tommy was virtually my whole world, he did not rely entirely on me for company or intellectual stimulation. He had his music, his student politics and by now was becoming an important spokesman for the ecological movement, often being asked to comment on all things Green. He also happened to be at university, but that didn't worry him too much. He passed some subjects but, by and large, he was a 'professional student'; he came, he enjoyed and he crammed at the last minute for exams.

Sometimes he absorbed the right stuff and achieved acceptable grades, sometimes he didn't and he failed. When summer arrived, he would charm his way through the usual committee evaluation of his efforts and turn up the following term flashing that engaging smile, set for another year as Mr Cool. His father kept paying the bills on the share house and he always seemed to have enough money to do pretty much as he liked. It looked like he was going to stay at Cambridge until he was thirty.

I was soon to learn that while Tommy may have enjoyed all the material comforts throughout his childhood and study years, what he did not have was domestic peace. Leah, his beautiful Thai-born mother, had met and married his father, an English barrister, when she was studying and working in London as the court stenographer on a murder case in which he was involved. But the bubble soon burst, the marriage didn't work out and after years of argument and vitriol they separated when Tommy was twelve years old.

Tommy went to live with his mother and from that point on, saw his father only on monthly access visits to the new love nest, presided over by his stepmother, Janine. She was in her early twenties when she came on the scene, not much older than Tommy, and deliberately made things difficult so that the visits were miserable. 'I never feel I belong there,' he told me one day after yet another unhappy journey up to London. 'I positively hate going because Janine is always on my back about something. And I just can't stand the way she flirts with Dad as if I wasn't in the room. It makes me sick when I see them together.'

He felt he was an outsider looking in on the cuckoo's nest that had been vacated by his betrayed mother. There was always tension between him and Janine, between his father and Janine and between him and his father. It was the price his father paid for taking a second wife young enough to be his daughter. Later, the couple had twins and the only difference it made for Tommy was that he was now practically banished from his father's life altogether.

Sleep deprived nights tending two babies made his step-mother tired and even more irritable so that she constantly spat venom at him, making it almost impossible for him to be in the same room as her. She resented Tommy, didn't want him there and made this quite clear. She wanted her husband for herself and her children. Ultimately, his father acquiesced. It was almost as if he did not want to be reminded of his previous failed marriage and the son that it had produced.

However, the old man was happy to keep writing the cheques because as far as he was concerned, Tommy could have as much money as he wanted as long as he didn't show up at his home and annoy his young wife and their two daughters.

The other personal cross Tommy had to bear was that his mother, Leah, was busy trying to get on with her own life but with little success. She seemed to be permanently unlucky in love. Across the years she had had a conga line of lovers, none of whom respected her or treated Tommy well. She had the knack of attracting the apparently unobtainable, only to find herself being discarded when the target of her affection finished using her as a plaything. Tommy hated this and could not bear to watch it happen.

Once I went with him to his mother's place for Christmas dinner. It was a very quiet affair - Tommy, me, Leah and her partner at the time. This one, a fat surly builder/developer, had drunk too much Christmas cheer the night before and was hung-over and grumpy. Despite Tommy's best efforts to get conversation going, we ate in subdued silence.

Although she had been living in London since her student days, her roast chicken still tasted of the spices of her native Thailand. And instead of potatoes and roast veg she served fried rice and stir-fried vegetables. She and Tommy enjoyed a side dish of hot chilli but my taste buds could not cope with that. For sweets she made banana fritters and ice cream.

'Did you like what Mum cooked? No potatoes?' Tommy whispered anxiously as we washed the dishes together in the tiny kitchen.

'I certainly did,' I said. 'The whole meal was just like you. Exotic, enjoyable and so delicious!'

Afterwards we went for a walk around the common. Leah's grumpy sidekick didn't come, as he wouldn't pull himself away from the warm lounge and television. By herself, away from the tension of the house, Leah was talkative, humorous and loving towards Tommy and me. It began to snow as we were heading home and she held her hands out wide and ran around trying to capture the snow flakes in her palms. She was light hearted and free and so we copied her, laughing as we ran. As soon as we went back indoors, Leah became a subservient little Asian woman again, tiptoeing around her over-bearing Englishman and trying to please him. It was demeaning to watch and I realised then how it made Tommy feel. Her humiliation was his and he didn't want to be there.

We didn't stay the night. Instead we cut the visit short and went back to the share house after tea. Despite his outgoing confidence, Tommy was torn between two worlds and it bothered him. He was protective and paternal towards his pretty mother but he needed his distant father to finance his lifestyle. In one way, he was a free spirit but in another he was a prisoner of his childhood.

Because of that, he found it difficult to give himself entirely to me, as there was always an element of distrust lurking in the background. In a private world to which I did not have access, he always kept a part of himself for Tommy only. He said to me once, 'Don't ever expect me to marry you, Jen, because I won't. I will never marry anyone. Marriage? It's all a sham. People say they are going to love each other forever but they don't.'

Another time he stated, 'I will never marry and I will never bring a child into this world, a place where everybody tells lies and everything is such a mess. Besides, it will all blow up soon, just look what they are doing in the Pacific.' When he went on those melancholy rants, he would always add, 'But, Jobs, I do love you; you're my sweet, little Irish leprechaun.'

Did it worry me? Well, I was young. Marriage was definitely not in my plans at that moment, anyway. So, I took it all with a grain of salt, not thinking about it, just enjoying being with him.

After we had been together for more than three years, at my mother's insistence, I persuaded Tommy to come with me to Dublin for Easter to meet my family. We flew with Aer Lingus and there they all were, waiting at the airport, faces glowing with anticipation - my mother, my father, my four brothers and their wives and partners and by now, a growing cluster of blue eyed grandchildren. Customs officers delayed Tommy and went right through his bags, no doubt because of his pop star looks and cheeky demeanour. I emerged a good ten minutes before he did and walked out to a huge welcome.

Everyone was so pleased to see me and they all were talking and laughing at once and passing me around to be hugged and kissed. The noise was unbelievable as we chattered furiously while waiting for Tommy. It was grand to be home!

I turned and said, 'Oh, there he is,' as he emerged through the door, and I ran to take his hand and bring him into the fold.

The talking stopped. It was like a pause in a film. Several seconds of silence elapsed while this vision of a cool dude Asian rock god amiably sauntered towards them.

And then, just as suddenly, it started again, with everyone all talking at once. He was not what they had expected at all. He was too petite, too beautiful, too exotic, too 'out there' in his clothing and attitude.

They were expecting someone like all the other men in our family - big, silent, blue eyed, sporty types who stood solid and firm. When Tommy materialised before them they were a little taken aback. But he didn't care, he needed no one's approval and he was very happy in his own skin. And so he greeted them in his casual way, giving high fives to all the kiddies, shaking hands with my father and brothers, kissing any female face that came near him, and giving my mother a huge cuddle. Then, he put his arm around me, planted a kiss on the top of my head and told Mam that she had done 'a pretty good job here, Mrs O! Jobs is way cool.'

Well, that was it. Give them their due, once my mob realised what they were dealing with and got used to the idea, they embraced Tommy and gave him a big Irish welcome that secretly frightened him to pieces. For the next few days he became one of us and was privy to all things family. Nobody ever stood on ceremony for long in our home and Tommy was soon sitting comfortably at the kitchen table drinking tea and joining in the yarning and singing.

While they thought he was exotic, he was in turn entranced by my mad mob because he'd had never seen anything like it. It was so far from his experience and concept of family that he was gob-smacked. Based on his cold, fractured experience, he couldn't believe what he was seeing. 'The talking, the eating, the cups of tea, the pints of Guinness that they are able to consume,' he said to me later. 'They never stop. They never leave the kitchen table!' It was a whirlwind of tales, talk, bagging, teasing, laughter, singing and occasionally scolding.

Throughout all this, the kiddies came and went - a drink here, a scone and jam there, sweets galore and plenty of hugs and teasing. They'd be in and then out to play in the street again with all the other kids. It didn't matter in whose kitchen we were sitting there was always other children in the street to play with - soccer, football, bikes, roller skates or hide and seek. They ran and ran and only came inside for sustenance or if the rain was pouring.

Sometimes one of the men would go out to check on them and to kick the ball around a bit. Tommy did more than his share of this as I think at times he preferred playing with the little ones than trying to keep up with the witty exchanges that went on inside the house. The kids loved him as he seemed to have a natural ability to play. After all, he had played pretty much all of his life, and to him, life was all a giant game where it was simply enough just to take part. It wasn't about winning. He had been around music and show business for a long time, so he knew how to entertain, and that is what he did. When he went out to play there was great merriment in the street and cries of, 'Tommy, Tommy! Kick it here, kick it here!'

He showed the neighbourhood kiddies his magic tricks from his busking days and organised drumming jams using any rhythmic objects they could find to beat. One night he had twenty or thirty adults and God knows how many children pounding away in my eldest brother's lounge room. It was so much fun. My brothers embraced Tommy even though he wasn't their football playing type and my sisters-in-law adored him. Women just did.

He enjoyed the applause. But while he loved it and envied me the fact that I always knew my family stood shoulder to shoulder behind me, supporting and loving me unconditionally, I also think he found it hard to cope with the rowdy familial intimacy which could lead to a lack of privacy and down time. When the moment came to return to England, after all the tears, smiles and goodbyes, I think he quietly breathed a sigh of relief to be returning to a place where nobody expected anything of him.

Chapter 7

That was the one and only time Tommy met my family. Not long after we returned from Dublin, our romance started to fall apart.

Perhaps it was the trip back to my home territory, with all its noise and laughter and silliness, that began our demise as a couple. But I think it was simply the circumstances, the time line and the events that were about to unfold. When we got back to the share house the place was ablaze with the news. Tommy's band had been asked to be a support act for the Rolling Stones on tour. They had played a gig in support of a Greenpeace initiative and a talent scout had seen them and decided that they were good enough to open for the Stones but not good enough to outshine them. Everyone was excited but there was little time to be lost as they needed to rehearse hard so that everything was note perfect when they went on the road in six weeks' time.

'This is it, Jobs!' Tommy would say excitedly as he'd head off for another practice session. 'This is it!!! Our big chance. The break we've all been dreaming about!'

You couldn't blame him. Tommy and the boys had been working towards a chance like that for more than three years. Opportunity was knocking and he was answering that door, there was no question about it. This was his moment for glory and nothing was going to get in his way. Not even our relationship, if it came down to that. If he did think that perhaps he might miss me, he certainly never verbalised it.

I assumed that I would go along with him and said, 'I'll defer, just for this semester, and go on the road with you so we can be together. Besides, I've never been to any of those places. It'll be fun.'

'This is my gig, Jobs,' he said solemnly, 'and really has nothing to do with you. It's for me and the boys and we're not paying for any of the accommodation and stuff so I don't think hangers-on will be welcome. Best you stay here.'

'But you'll be away for months!'

'It won't be long before we'll be back together. And I'll phone you every night, promise.'

'Great …'

'Jobs, this is something I have to do on my own. You understand, don't you?'

Deep down I could see his point so I agreed that, painful as it was, we would do our own thing - he tour with the band while I took the opportunity to clean up all the academic odds and sods that I needed to get my degree finished.

That tour was the beginning of the end for us. The Stones had more than enough groupies hanging around for themselves and all other comers, and apparently a good time was had by all. I am not saying that Tommy was unfaithful, but it opened up a world of possibilities to him that he had previously only dreamed about. The whole thing was a success and out of it, Tommy was eventually singled out by a record label and offered a job as a studio drummer.

People generally tend to underestimate the importance of the drummer in a group of musicians, but he is essential to the shape, soul and depth of the music. Lousy drummer, lousy band! The record company understood that. 'The rest of your crew are shit, man,' they told him on the side, 'but you've got talent.'

The final gig of the tour was in Glasgow. The good news was that as soon as it ended Tommy was able to hitch a ride down south, rather than having to wait to return in the band coach with the entire entourage, so he suddenly turned up at home earlier than I expected. We had missed each other terribly. The reunion was wonderful and we rejoiced in each other, unleashing our passion until we were spent.

In order to save a bit of money and as I was a one-man woman and had no intention of having sex with anyone other than Tommy, I had stopped taking the pill while he was away. I had remained celibate while he was on the road and although I started taking it again immediately he came home, I was one day late. The deed was done. When my period didn't turn up on time I freaked out and immediately made an appointment at the women's health clinic on campus. It didn't take long. They confirmed my pregnancy.

As one of their counsellors went over the options with me, my emotions were mixed. I was half terrified and half thrilled. I didn't want a baby at this time of my life and yet I did want Tommy's baby. I felt a sense of loss at the thought that I was losing my independence but a sense of excitement when I walked into Mothercare in High Street and lovingly looked at the baby clothes and the toys and the prams. I could imagine our beautiful baby - 'And he will be beautiful,' I'd say to myself, 'just look at his daddy' - all wrapped up and snuggled within. In my Irish way I was thinking, 'Whatever will be, will be, God knows what is best for me,' while deep down in my heart intuitively knowing that Tommy would not be thrilled when I told him the news.

He wasn't.

First came the anger. 'Pregnant! What do you mean, you're fucking pregnant? Why did you go and do that? Can't I even trust you to take a fucking pill?'

Then came the mistrust. 'Are you sure it's my baby? I know, you're just doing this to make me marry you, aren't you? How do I know that you weren't fooling around with some other Joe while I was away?'

And finally, the self-interest. 'What about my drumming career?'

He angrily fired the questions at me like ball-bearings shot from a cannon.

I had certainly expected shock and maybe a smidgin of disbelief, but never dreamed that he would doubt my faithfulness to him or accuse me of deliberately getting pregnant. I shot back with my voice raised. 'What I mean, Tommy, is that I am pregnant with *your* baby, not anybody else's baby, *your* baby. I have never had sex with anybody but you, so it can't belong to anybody else but you. And if you had phoned and let me know that you were coming home early instead of turning up on the doorstep all horny as hell, I would have started up the pill again before you got home. Besides, it was about time you started using a condom because by telling me you don't trust me, that tells me something about you! I don't know where you've been. So don't go getting on your high horse and telling me that I tricked you into it. It takes two to tango, you know, and you're in this right up to your ears with me. Instead of accusing me, start talking rationally about where we go from here. I'm the one carrying your baby and I want answers!' By the end of the diatribe I was hysterical and crying.

But if I thought that I might have struck a sympathetic chord somewhere, I was wrong. Tommy looked at me coldly, with absolutely no love or compassion. He made no move to comfort me. 'I don't want a baby, Jobs. Not now, not ever. I have told you that many times. I'm not cut out to be a father.'

Then he uttered the phrase that seared into my soul. 'I will get you the money for an abortion and I don't want to hear anymore about it.'

I ran off into the bedroom and slammed the door. The message was loud and clear. We couldn't have a baby together. He had a career that was just taking off. A child just couldn't be countenanced and that was that.

The next night he came home with a wad of notes in his pocket, a steely look in his eye and little love in his heart. 'I got the money you need from Dad,' he muttered.

'The money *I* need!' I said. 'You mean the money *we* need. We're both in this, you know.'

'Yeah, well, it wasn't easy. I went to his office so he wouldn't make too much of a fuss in front of his staff, but that didn't stop him. Oh no. He went absolutely crazy at me for not wearing a condom and said that this was the first and last time I could stuff up. You know what? I think he thinks he's too young to be a grandfather.'

'Pretentious old prick.'

'Don't speak about my father like that, Jobs. Here, take the money.'

He peeled off a dozen big ones from the roll and threw them at me. 'Fix things up and let's pretend that this never happened. It'll all be over in a day. It's just an embryo so it's no big deal.'

I supposed I should have resisted. Weighed up my options and made my own decision. Instead, exhausted, shocked and confused, I did what he wanted. I had my baby aborted. I thought it would save our relationship. I was wrong.

Without the calm and loving support of my friend Rhani, I don't know what I would have done. 'You are not on your own,' she said, hugging me when I tearfully told her my story, 'we will do this together. I will come with you and I will stay with you until you are okay.'

True to her word, she came with me to my appointment in a dank, nondescript building in the middle of town on a cold, forlorn day in November. One lone protestor stood outside limply holding a pro-life banner.

'Ignore him, it's absolutely none of his business,' whispered Rhani as she hurried me past him to the solid red door which was locked. We pressed the brass button and waited in the drizzling rain to be buzzed inside. After I had filled out the paperwork I took the bottle they proffered and disappeared into the toilet located under the stairs to produce a urine sample. The nurse examined it, did some routine medical checks on me, and informed me that I was about eight weeks pregnant. Then she sent me off to speak with a counsellor who outlined my options. She gave me the chance to change my mind if I wished. I couldn't. I had no choice. I declined.

I returned to Rhani and sat down nervously in the waiting room with a group of about twenty other women, only a couple of them with accompanying partners. It seemed that we were like divers about to embark on our maiden journey into the depths. We had received our instructions and, with very little training, had thrown ourselves overboard. Now we were nervously waiting for the instructor to take us one by one to the dark bottom of the ocean so later, having travelled to the depths, we would be returned to the surface, changed forever, but somehow still the same.

The mood was tense at first, but it gradually eased and we began to talk, as women do. We all knew why we were there, but we only discussed non-personal things like celebrities and fashion, our real mission to this place being the elephant in the front room of the old terrace. That subject was never actually brokered, each of us having our own personal story that we held tightly within and which would become a permanent part of us from that day on.

Although the vacuum aspiration part of the procedure took only a minute, the pain was intense. They then scraped clean the lining of the womb and it was all over in less than five minutes. It left me feeling weak and shaky. Armed with some painkillers, antibiotics and a few photocopied pages of relevant information, I was free to go with Rhani to a hotel that we had booked especially for the two days of recovery.

That first day I did nothing but sleep, but the next we tuned into some chick flicks on the hotel system, got some take away and spent the day with our feet up. After that Rhani dropped me home at Tommy's and apart from suffering cramps for the next couple of weeks, physically I was great. Emotionally I was a mess.

As for Tommy, he seemed to think that it was all over and done with from the moment he handed me the cash. My once warm and caring lover suddenly became a cold and self-obsessed stranger, living with me in the same room but emotionally existing on another planet. Time and again I broached the subject, trying to tell him about my feelings and hoping that he would tell me that it would be all right and that he would look after me. That was not to be the case.

'For Christ's sake, give it a rest, Jobs,' he'd hiss, 'you just go on and on. If I hear any more about that baby thing, I am going to puke, so just let it go!'

'Baby thing? It wasn't a *thing*, it was our baby, yours and mine, and they sucked it out of me!' I answered hysterically sobbing.

'For fuck's sake, get a grip, it was only an embryo, right? We didn't ask for it, we didn't want it and it couldn't have lived by itself in any case. So, just shut up about it. I'm sick of hearing baby, baby, baby!'

'Tommy!'

'Jobs, listen. I just don't want to be around you anymore! You're too morbid!'

Underneath the chirpy, swaggering exterior was a heartless, selfish little man. I needed him to hold me, to tell me that it was all going to be okay, but he wouldn't do that. He pushed me away and no longer wanted me in the same way as he had done before. I was now, apparently, damaged goods and getting in the way of his music career.

I should have left then, but I didn't. We stayed together simply because we were used to each other and I wouldn't let go, so I muddled through this awful time in his company but without his love or support. My mood swings went from feelings of great relief to those of absolute self-loathing, fear and anger and then on to frustration, confusion, sadness and finally heartbreak. It was the beginning of the end.

The pivotal moment came when he heard there was going to be a massive demonstration in Berkshire, at Greenham Common RAF air base, where a women's peace camp had been set up protesting against the nuclear arsenal located there.

'We should go down there,' he said. 'It'll be a blast, and it'll be good for us. Please, Jobs, let's put all this other thing behind us and go.'

But I had no desire for it at all. I just couldn't go, my legs were lead, my stomach churned constantly, I was always so tired. I felt like I was stuck in a dark, hollow chasm and was unable able to shake myself out of it. I just wanted to sit in a corner and cry.

'I don't feel like it and I don't want you to go and leave me here alone. Help me to get through this, Tommy, please,' I said.

'Fucking hell, Jobs. You used to be so much fun! Now all you do is mope around the house and carry on about that fucking baby,' he spat at me. 'Why can't you just give it a rest, forget it all happened and get on with your life? And I'll get on with mine.'

Tommy went anyway and from there we drifted apart until I had no choice but to face up to the harsh reality that as far as he was concerned, I was a dead weight, dragging him down, getting in his way and preventing him reaching the pinnacle of his musical ambitions.

'Just leave it, okay?' he said one day. 'We had a good time, we fucked things up, let's move on. It's no good any more, Jobs. We do each other's heads in. Let's leave it here, now, while we still have some respect for each other. I'm through trying to fix it.'

I was shafted. I finally realised that Tommy had been nowhere near as committed to our relationship as I had been. It had always been about 'him'. He had never factored 'us' into his decision making. I considered myself beyond pity. To my Irish eyes, I had done the worst thing a woman could do; terminated the life of her own baby. It haunted me then and still does to this day.

Not that I enlisted support or told anyone at home! I just couldn't speak to my mother about such a thing. I know that she would have feigned surprise that I, an unmarried girl, had been having sex in the first place, followed by her disgust that I had an abortion. Rosaries would have been said, Masses offered and novenas made for my soul. I could not have coped with that. You have to be brought up Irish to understand. We are not always strictly honest about things. We prefer things to be as they seem and find it difficult to accept them as they actually are. In my mother's generation of Irish culture there were unwritten rules and unspoken understandings. Some things had to be seen to be done, while other things were done but never to be seen. What the neighbours thought was important. If anything bad or unacceptable occurred, you just didn't go there, you never said a word and you pretended that it hadn't happened.

And that is what I chose to do. I suffered by myself, because this awful thing that I had done was too terrible to tell even my own mother. It was my dreadful secret and it had to stay that way, locked away forever in my psyche, in a dark, deep place somewhere inside me. It was only when Stuart and I were having trouble conceiving years later, and the medico asked me straight out if I had ever had an abortion that I verbalised my secret to anyone other than my friend Rhani. It was only then that I owned up to the fact.

With my baby now gone, my lover out of my life, and my heart weighing heavily, I worked like a woman possessed to complete my study and pass. With my tail between my legs, I brought myself and my new Law degree back to Dublin and my family, got a marketing job with the newly-established Ryanair, set up in a tiny flat in Temple Bar and retired hurt to secretly lick my wounds.

My family welcomed me with open arms and drew me within their noisy bosoms. But they remained totally unaware of the sadness and turmoil that visited me anytime I was alone.

Jobby, the happy-go-lucky university student, was no more.

Chapter 8

When I came back from England, Dublin was a new city to me. Although I had been brought up in Blackrock, I had spent all my post-school life in Cambridge and had only made rare excursions home for Christmas and special occasions such as my brothers' weddings. I'd fly in, go to the celebration looking pretty gorgeous as young women do, and fly out again. It was almost as if I did celebrity gigs.

Mam and Da absolutely loved having me home to complete the family circle, all together again, just like old times, falling back into our designated roles. Mam and I would be in the kitchen with the sisters-in-law making sandwiches and brewing tea, spreading the gossip and laughing, washing an endless round of dishes. Amy and I enjoyed the catch-ups and reverted to the cosy friendship we had enjoyed at school, now without the complicating factor of her lust for Kevin which had been dampened by the familiarity of marriage and a child.

The brothers and Da would be talking business and sport, all the time bantering with each other, sometimes in the front room watching a game on the television, or other times in the backyard or out in the street playing with the kiddies. There was always a pint or two imbibed. Every now and then Da would make an appearance, cuddle the nearest woman or dance her around the kitchen, saying something like, 'Ah, but it's grand to have our

Jennifer home.' One sister-in-law or the other would be sitting on the 'good chair' in the corner, breast feeding a baby and being waited on. In fact, call me bitchy if you like, but I always suspected that that was why Patrick's wife, Kathy, had five children. She saw the breast feeding as a perfect excuse for never having to do anything in the kitchen.

The nieces and nephews idolised me because I was young and pretty and always came with a gift for each one of them. They lapped up the attention that an adoring aunt lavishes when she knows that in a couple of days she'll be off again, never to be seen for months, and that now is the time to create those memories. They'd line up to have lipstick on, sit at the kitchen table drawing and colouring with me and loved to get the cards out for a game of Pairs. My brothers were very proud of their young sister who was doing better academically than they did; they loved to have a drink with me at the pub with their spouses and mates.

Of course, in the days before we broke up, I was always torn as I missed Tommy and wanted to get back to him because when he was not with me something was missing. I now realise that that is not the basis of a healthy relationship, that I was totally dependent on him for my feeling of wellbeing. Eventually, when his love was taken away, I was like a shark that had had its fin removed and been returned to the water. I could swim, but only just, and it was a languid, listless attempt that kept me moving helplessly in a meaningless circle.

A city only is truly yours if you have walked its alleyways in the early hours looking for fun and laughter, ridden your pushbike over the cobbled streets to a friend's house when you needed solace or taken the first train of the morning home after an all night session. These are the things you do when you are young and free and that is when you etch city life indelibly into your genetic footprint.

I knew all the main drags of Cambridge intimately - Kings Parade, Trinity Street, Silver Street and Quayside, and a lot of the subsidiary roads as well. I doubt that I could find myself lost in it. I danced through its streets with Tommy and our mates, going to gigs, eating at cheap student places and supporting artists in my ever expanding circle. Sometimes we even went to classes!

That was why Dublin was not 'my city.' I had left it as a girl and returned a woman, and so it was there for me to discover. Now aged twenty-four, I had to learn its streets, its moods and the way it worked.

I felt old, used and dispirited. To my desolate self, Dublin appeared to be exactly like me - old, used and dispirited. We soon melded together in the greyness of the streets and the bleakness of the weather. For that first twelve months I don't think I laughed out loud at all.

Mam instinctively knew my inner spirit was badly damaged and guessed that it was simply my breaking up with Tommy that made me so sad, but like all good Irish mothers she didn't bring this up directly with me. Instead she alluded to it, saying things such as, 'Jen, my darling, lighten up now. Don't go fretting after that Tommy boy. It would never have worked. He was English and you know they're just different. There's a good Irish man waiting out there; you just haven't found him yet. I'll burn a candle for you at Our Lady's altar, she always listens to me.' No doubt she had a few Masses said for my intentions as well.

The last thing in the world I wanted was for Mam to guess about my abortion. My God, that would have set her doing novenas for the rest of her life. Poor woman would have never been out of the church! She would have been praying for me so that I would repent and see the evil of my ways; down on her knees for the little soul dancing around in Limbo who was never ever going to see the face of God; asking God for forgiveness for her own dereliction of duty in failing to bring me up to know what was right and what was wrong; interceding on behalf of the soul of the doctor who performed the deed, hoping that he would see the light and begin to use his skills for good rather than evil; lighting candle after candle at the altar of Our Lady, the Blessed Virgin, Patron Saint of all Mothers and Babies. There'd be no end to it.

She also employed other, more worldly tactics in order to find me a new partner. She would cross-examine my brothers' unmarried mates, asking what they were up to and whether they had a girlfriend. She would buy me a pretty dress to add to my wardrobe in the hope that I would wear it out and dazzle a prospective husband with my elegance and beauty. She tried to feed me up and tempt me with her Irish stews, her mashed potatoes and her roast pork with crackling that positively crackled. She cooked up jam and cream sponges and sat me down with the ubiquitous cup of tea.

Of course, I was Irish too, so I knew what was expected of me. Better to leave things alone and not dredge in murky waters, stirring up the banshees and nasty spirits from the past. My solution was to pretend that everything was grand. Irish women are supposed to be resilient, happy and unselfish, so that is what I appeared to be. Inside I was numb with disappointment and grief.

I had gone against my conscience and done the unthinkable and even though I had done what I thought I needed to do to save our relationship, it was all in vain. I had lost my love and I felt dead inside. More than anything I was disappointed in Tommy and how he had let me down, choosing his drumming and his music over me and our baby.

In typical Irish mother and daughter fashion, we both pretended that everything was all right and that my melancholy state was just a case of a broken heart. Mam was certain it would mend as soon as the sun came out.

Chapter 9

It took me a long time to pick up the threads of my life, but as one year back in Dublin merged into two and the second into the third, I simply put the Tommy thing behind me and got on with it.

My law degree stood me in good stead even though I didn't actually take up a job with a legal firm. I eventually left Ryanair and found a very satisfying role with a fledgling company at the cutting edge of the new Information Technology revolution about to be set loose in Ireland, heralding the era of the Celtic Tiger. As their business developer/company lawyer, I helped draft policy, explore initiatives and look after the growing company's legal interests. Challenging work, but exciting.

I was working with a bright young group of 'nerds', all a few years younger than I was, who really didn't care about the way they looked and who all had an individual approach, a zany sense of the ridiculous and an expanded world outlook. They were cool because they were so uncool. Just what I needed, stimulating company in an alternative environment.

The internet had been around academic circles for fifteen years but was just beginning to make its presence felt in mainstream commercialism and culture and its future was rosy for those of us in the know. In those days it was not so much about the money. It was about the democracy of the internet, the excitement of exploring unknown territory, the maniacal highs obtained from giving birth to new ideas and processes, the knowledge that we were at the forefront of a new and exciting age, the uncertainty that what we were doing would ever amount to anything, and the satisfaction of finding and sharing new knowledge and building on blocks of previous work. Everything was fluid and there were no rules. We were free to fly.

My colleagues and I were at the cutting edge of a whole new world, exploring untapped frontiers. It was an exciting and stimulating time. We set our own rules and had our own language, our own in-jokes and our own way at looking at things. We were all in it together. Many a time we worked all night to get the job finished. If we were onto something we just kept pushing forward, working co-operatively with other nerds in the US, Europe, Australia, India or even Fiji. It was fresh, thrilling and all consuming. I could sit at the computer and before I knew it ten hours would have gone past.

Although we weren't into making money per se, it somehow came our way and before we knew it this jolly band of nerds was accumulating all the badges of wealth - driving new, flashy cars, buying inner city apartments and eating out at good restaurants. At that time, and in my state of mind, this really suited me.

Work became my new love; a demanding lover that sapped all my time, energy and consciousness. I lived to work and my workmates filled any need I might have had for other human beings. Tommy retreated into my past and the busier I became, the less I reflected on him and what he did to me, until one day I realised that I hadn't given him a thought for three whole weeks. 'Jennifer,' I said to myself in the mirror one morning, 'you are over him. Good girl.'

Work, work, work! That's all I did and that's what I had become. My spiritual dimension had been eclipsed.

Then I awoke one day knowing that I needed more. Tommy had gone from my life, but the urge to re-develop my personal spirituality still burned within me. I knew I had to start all over again, to rekindle my Buddhist spirit. After looking through a few alternative newspapers and making some calls, I came across a group that adhered to the Celtic form of Buddhism. Ireland had been a pagan country before St Patrick brought Christianity to its shores and remnants of that paganism still hold root in our culture. Celtic Buddhism incorporates many aspects of Irish culture quite seamlessly, and so I was drawn to it. With some like-minded souls, I began to explore my consciousness and inner self.

I suppose it was because of my depressed state of mind that I became heavily involved in self-help groups to the extent that, outside work, they almost took over my life. Sometimes, I wondered if this was good for me. We were all lost souls, searching for an elusive opiate to soothe our battered egos, at the same time affirming each other's manias while sinking deeper into our lonely bogs.

The lawyer and business person in me saw the opportunities that this New Age era was opening up for those of us in on the ground floor. There were many people out there just like me - self absorbed and obsessed with desire for affirmation. We were children of the 60s, brought up with fluid boundaries and looking for something to guide us through life. I took advantage of this mood, coupled it with the internet, and a business was born.

I wrote a series of small booklets, each with about twenty pages of platitudes and New Age thoughts - *The Inner Me, Finding the Inner Me, Accepting the Inner Me, Forgiving the Inner Me, Re-inventing the Inner Me, The Inner Me and Others*. I borrowed sayings from Confucius, Ghandi and the Prophets; I even threw in some Oscar Wilde and Brendan Behan. Some realisations I came to myself, but wherever these notions came from, they seemed to hit a chord. There were an awful lot of lost souls out there willing to buy my books.

Weekends found me on tour at a variety of old Celtic stone sites in the west country, running seminars and leading others through deep mountain mists and across territory for which I didn't even have a map myself. Often my fellow travellers saw me as some sort of guru who knew all the answers. Little did they know! People were happy to pay for this, and although I wasn't exactly wealthy, for the first time in my life I had the financial freedom to do what I wanted. I bought a nice little terrace in Harold's Cross near to where I worked and between my Buddhist projects and my day job I was happily busy and affluent.

These seminars were also a way of meeting members of the opposite sex and so I finally put myself back on the market in search for perfect love. I had a long term relationship and several short ones, but I discovered there was absolutely no future in any relationship where two people were purely obsessed with their own emotional journey and wellbeing.

Although I was searching for love, I didn't enjoy the physical side of things. I had changed. Those relationships were never about the sex for me because I had lost my lust and my lustiness. Sure, appropriate noises were made and sighs released at the correct times, but that was the actress in me. I hated the closeness of intimacy and regarded it as an invasion of my personal space. I just endured it and waited for the act to be done.

This, of course, is no way to conduct a relationship. It's simply no fun to make love in a vacuum and it didn't take long for my partners to realise that for them it was all give and no take, and that the relationship was an empty shell, much like I was myself. And so, one after another, they moved on.

Sin and reparation were part of the culture and social fabric into which I was born and this was very firmly instilled into my very being. I couldn't help but see my lack of libido as a punishment for what I had done to my own unborn child.

'No more satisfying sex for you, my girl,' God was saying from his heavenly cloud, shaking an omnificent finger in my direction. 'You had your ration when you were a girl and you squandered it. You have sinned and you have to be punished. Go forth and be a barren old maid for the rest of your life. Be gone!'

It was as simple as that. Accepting my sex life was over, I continued the search to find myself. You could say I was pretty much an emotional cripple. It is only when you stop blaming yourself and accept that your past is just that, you can move on.

One day at a Buddhist camp, I met Wendy, a little New Zealand dynamo, who became the sister I never had. Over the years, I came to rely on her heavily for advice and support. As my mentor and confidante, she consoled and jollied me through the broken relationships and the self doubt and the recrimination with a jangle of bangles and a waft of perfume.

With her I could bare my soul because she was non-judgmental and accepting and very easy to be with. Although she hadn't quite worked it all out for herself, that didn't stop her, and she engendered in me the confidence and self belief that I sadly lacked. She could always make me laugh.

Eventually, when I did think of him at all, I began to hate Tommy and what he had put me through. I only thought of his selfishness, his shallowness and his lack of support and loyalty. Of the way he had so thoughtlessly been prepared to consign me and his baby to the waste paper basket. I was moving on.

No one hates quite like us Irish and no one hates like a lover scorned. My hate for Tommy was now as passionate as the love I had previously had for him. I was getting back on track. My hatred was sustaining me. I had a real reason to get on with things.

Next thing I knew, I was thinking life was pretty good. I began to laugh again; I slipped back into my crazy ways and began to get the old skip back into my step. I was over him and thank God for that!

Chapter 10

Funny how you come through these things and suddenly find yourself bathed in the light at the end of the tunnel. Sure as hell it wasn't Irish sunlight, though. There is no such thing! I began to think that I could actually make something of my life as my old biological clock began to tick, tick, tick away. By the age of thirty you begin to realise that time is passing and you have only a decade and a bit to get on with it and reproduce yourself.

Armed with the self knowledge I had acquired, and encouraged by my good friend Wendy, it dawned on me that in terms of the heart perhaps I needed to adjust my thinking and settle for something else. Not less, but different. To put it in internet language, I needed to change my search criteria. Out with the frivolous, passionate, exciting, pleasure-seeking hedonist! No more searching for heart-pounding, ear-fluffing, body-melting, joyous love. It just wasn't going to happen.

So I set down my conditions. Into my personal search engine I typed 'decent' (didn't want him to have diseases or a police record); 'reliable' (broad shoulders to lean on); 'professional' (must have a good income to support me and my children); 'intelligent' (at least I could enjoy a good conversation); 'patient' (even I had to admit that I could be difficult to deal with at times); 'sturdy' (stable and stoic enough to balance my out-there ideas); 'easy on the eye' (after all, he would be the father of my children); 'ability and means to provide a good home' (not poor); 'for a growing family' (desire to have children); and 'kind to his mother' (a man will treat his wife the way he treats his mother).

Men like that don't come along every day and when they do, they often have so much baggage that you need two airport trolleys to carry it all. I soon found out that an honest, reliable, good looking man without a load of life-time luggage is indeed a rare and beautiful creature.

Where do you meet him?

Certainly not in a pub. By and large, the pub clientele consisted of either married men escaping domesticity for a few hours by having a pint or two with their mates or professional drunkards who spent all their money on booze and the punt. So I scrubbed that one off the list.

I was too old for concerts. Call me an old fogey if you like, but they didn't excite me any more. By that time, I didn't know most of the bands that turned up to play in our fair city. Time had moved on and I hadn't moved with it. I was still into Sting, Michael Jackson, Whitney Houston, the Smiths and the Eagles. The bands that were touring at that time were U2, Pearl Jam and a wonderful Australian outfit named Frente with a gorgeous singer who just happened to be redheaded. But the ticket prices were astronomical and I didn't know the words. Truth was I would rather spend the money on a night out to the theatre. No chance of a chat up there, either! One had to be quiet.

Okay, how about the supermarket? Rumour was going around at the time that the frozen food aisle was the place to pick up, so I rugged up with my scarf and gloves and hung around looking at the peas and beans and commenting on the free range chickens. After a while I realised why this was not proving successful. It might have worked if I was gay!

Family and friends, maybe? Legend has it that friends and family are a wonderful way of meeting like-minded members of the opposite sex. Truth was that my family had given up on me, to the point that by that time the nieces and nephews were vying for my favour as they regarded me as the maiden aunt most likely to leave them a hefty inheritance. My coupled-up friends were cosy in their relationships and I suspected the women were looking suspiciously at a young, single, loose cannon in their midst, while my single friends were getting as desperate as I was. Not much hope there.

Internet chat rooms? I knew about chat rooms and dating sites as I was working in the IT industry. In the privacy of my own sitting room, I would burn the midnight oil scrolling down lists of prospective partners, making contact, chatting in meaningful one line sentences until finally, when the deal was about to be closed, withdrawing from the hunt, too scared of what I might have raked up. It all seemed too quirky for Jennifer Mary O'Brien, convent educated child of Eire. I would have hated anybody to know I was that desperate.

Dating agency? I spent good money putting my name down, filling out the forms, enduring the interview and checking out the names they listed for me. It appeared my profile matched exactly with all the men in Ireland who wore bad wigs, were painfully shy, stuttered at the thought of a woman or had a minor genetic defect. Call me callous but I never had it in me to be therapist for those lads.

Now, speed dating! That was great craic. I actually did that four times because I loved the adrenalin rush that it gave me. We'd all go into a large room, sometimes in a pub, or at a shopping centre or elsewhere. There'd be tables and chairs lined up in the middle, not unlike parent-teacher interview sessions from school days. The process itself was a like a cross between Musical Chairs and Team Tag. Men would line up on one side and women on the other. At a given signal we'd begin talking and we had exactly three minutes to inter-view the other person and vice versa. You kept a score pad something like in a Yahtzee game and at another given signal moved from your chair onto the next fellow. It was fun in its own way but nothing ever came of it for me. Mainly because my follow-up was appalling - in fact I never quite got around to reconnecting with anyone. I just enjoyed the sport of it.

So I as good as gave up altogether. And that's when it happened.

Chapter 11

Sometimes these things come along when you least expect it. When all seemed lost and I was settling into the life of the maiden aunt, I met my Stuart at a funeral.

It was a very sad event, that of a fourteen year old boy. The young lad was the son of a school friend and childhood neighbour, and I was there because I had been visiting my Mam and she had asked me to go with her. 'It's far too sad a business for me to go alone,' she said. 'Put on your coat, Jen, and please come with me. I can't be walking into the church by myself. It will only take an hour. Come on, do it for your dear old Ma.'

How could I refuse? I wasn't the most appropriately dressed in the congregation that day - a bit too fancy for a funeral, particularly one like that - so I endeavoured to keep a low profile, hovering close to the food. I was starving as I hadn't had time for breakfast and it was one of those cold, bleak Dublin days.

Stuart was at that same funeral because it was his Mam's cousin's child and so, you could say, we met over a plate of sandwiches. He looked every inch a man of the world in his tailored suit and expensive shirt and we got talking. He cut a fine figure and I was impressed. Somehow it all began from there.

I seem to remember later going to a wine bar nearby and must have given him my number although I can't recollect doing so. It's not the usual thing you do after a funeral, is it? He phoned and we met for coffee after work. Stuart was always the cautious one and would never have jumped feet first into dinner at a flash restaurant. Instead he opted for the less intimidating and less expensive coffee-and-cake on the way home from work after which we went for a walk around the beautiful grounds at Trinity College.

It was a still, warmish night in May and the streets of Dublin were busy with people just getting out of the house as it had rained non-stop for the previous six days and everyone had cabin fever. It is indeed a lovely city when the sun and the people are out and it was grand to be out walking and enjoying social interaction with a mature, good looking man. We just naturally clicked and I quickly realised I was the yin to his yang. My New Age thinking, work in the new technology and light hearted attitude was the absolute opposite to his conservative and thoughtful approach but we seemed to get along on an intellectual level and had plenty of things to talk about.

'I don't get it,' he said. 'On the one hand you are into Buddhism, which to me is a pretty airy-fairy sort of concept, and on the other you are up on the latest internet technology. That's amazing, the two things are so far apart.'

'Oh, I don't know,' I said, 'they are both based on the belief that anything's possible. And believe me, with the internet, it will be.'

He was a bit baffled when I began to talk about the future possibilities for IT. He just didn't see the potential. But he was quite taken with the fact that I pretty much knew how to take a computer apart and put it back together again adding, 'Even though you are a woman,' a statement I was generous enough to let go unnoticed. The computer was almost a closed book to him. 'My secretary, Doreen, knows all about that,' he said.

In turn I loved his apparent solidity, his style, his maturity and his faith in himself. He was in his late thirties and so had lost the awkwardness and selfishness of youth and in its place had obtained maturity and a certain urbane charm. I instinctively knew I had found the man I was looking for.

I don't think we kissed on that date, but things progressed from there and we started meeting up for lunch and then dinner until we were seeing each other every day. Within the month we were in bed. The foreplay was excellent. A nice meal, the theatre, perhaps a music concert, the cinema or a game of golf. Stuart was a man of the world and wonderful company as well as being a caring and considerate escort. He had excellent manners, and that impressed me. He was well spoken and he could converse with anybody on most topics. He was a pretty straight shooter, said things as he meant them. Like me, he wanted a family.

My mother and father thought that even though he was a Protestant, he was just too good to be true and that I was the luckiest girl, at my age, to be thrown a lifebelt like Stuart.

I discovered that Stu was clean and methodical in everything, including his approach to sex. Although the world didn't exactly move off its axis for me, it was not the unpleasant experience that it had been for the previous few years. In so far as the actual execution of the act of love, he was not what you would call polished. He was too quick out of the blocks by far, but he maintained that that was my fault. 'Jennifer, you are far too sexy for me,' he said. 'You turn me on.'

I figured his premature ejaculation was also probably due to his inexperience as I don't think he'd had too many opportunities to practise his skills in this department; he was a bit shy and unsure of himself around women. But that didn't worry me. I had experienced several unfulfilling encounters in the preceding years to the point where I thought that I had grown too old to enjoy sex. Volcanic eruptions were no longer on my agenda. Clean, clinical and mercifully brief was quite acceptable.

Wendy pointed out one day, 'Jen, sometimes it is less painful to be loved than to love.' And so I thought I could unobtrusively and gradually teach Stuart a thing or two and make this element of our relationship as classy as the rest of it was. Only it would take time.

I had long since given up on the notion of pure love and was happy to settle for a decent man with a good bank account who lived well, looked good and would give me the children I had always wanted. Stuart more than filled that bill. He was all the things I now wanted in a man, plus he had no baggage at all, if you discounted his lonely childhood growing up in an Army family that moved house every couple of years. As an only child, he hardly had any family and no really close friends. When I came along he thought all his Christmases had come at once.

He fell completely and totally in love with me. To be loved so unconditionally is an aphrodisiac in itself and I must say Stuart swept me off my feet. It wasn't long before our lives became intertwined. Summer changed to autumn and I began spending more time at his place, a spacious condominium in central Dublin, than I did at my own, which in comparison seemed tired and shabby and in need of a makeover and a paint. He was a man of the world with all its trappings - excellent job in insurance, classy SAAB sports car, comfortable apartment in a good block. In fact, he was impressive.

I liked his certainty, his strength and his solidity. He was someone I could lean on. He had many of the attributes that I, with experience and maturity in my corner, considered important in a man and he ticked most of the boxes. I couldn't do better than that.

There were moments in those early days when I found myself thinking that I had done a complete about turn. My head was ruling my heart and I had sold out. But I put that thought to one side. My clock was ticking and I yearned for children. Stu could give me that. He loved me. I would be happy.

Chapter 12

We had known each other less than six months when Stuart proposed to me.

To some people that might sound too soon, but we were both mature adults who knew what we wanted. Stu was looking to settle down and have a wife, a mortgage, a family and all that that entails. The way he put it to me was, 'I am thirty-eight years old and it's time I settled down. But until you came along, my darling Jennifer, I had seen absolutely nothing out there that would persuade me to give up the bachelor life.

'I have never found anyone I vaguely wanted to call "wife". But once I saw you I knew instantly that I wanted you more than anything in the world. I want you to be the queen of my home, the mother of my sons and my soulmate. Without you I am unfulfilled as a man. I am a shell and I need you.'

The way I saw it was that we were both on the same page.

Things were going along so swimmingly that he asked me to go with him to Cork for a holiday long weekend. He had a judo competition on the Saturday and he thought we could do a bit of sightseeing on the other two days. He had booked a B&B at Kinsale, about half an hour's drive south of Cork.

It says a lot about the man when you hear that Stu loved judo. It was his kind of sport. There is a certain amount of aggression, strict rules of conduct, much tradition to adhere to, and a lot of polite bowing and scraping. He had earned a yellow belt, which I gathered was pretty low on the pecking order, and was working towards the next one up. We drove down to Kinsale on what we Irish call a soft day. There was no wind but the rain formed a continuous mist so that the earth and the sea melded together into a soft grey landscape. Under the misty stillness, the hills and valleys formed a rolling green carpet.

When the cloud that was enveloping us moved to the east and the sun suddenly emerged, we were dazzled. Ireland is the most wonderful place on earth when the sun shines. And it shone for the two glorious days we spent in Kinsale. The bay stretched out, its sparkling blue waters lapping the emerald green grass on the surrounding shores and hills, its waves crashing against the forbidding grey forts that had stood stoically for hundreds of years keeping watch for foreign invaders.

The little town was pretty much as it had been since the 1601 invasion by the English, with multi-coloured houses and buildings of odd shapes and sizes looking anxiously towards the sea and abutting the narrow, winding streets which climbed the hills from the port. The quaint little yellow B&B could tell a thousand stories if it could talk, and the bed darn near did. Every time we moved it creaked, and so we thought, 'To hell with it,' and gave it a real working over. We were sure that at breakfast the next morning our fellow travellers gave each other knowing looks.

We walked the hills, explored the old forts, stopped for a pint at The Bulman Pub and meandered through the old cemetery on top of the hill in the grounds of St Columb's, wondering out loud about the lives of the townspeople and sailors who were remembered there in stone. It was grand and we felt good together, safe and happy.

That night we ate fresh seafood at Fishy Fishy restaurant and then climbed the hill to The Spaniard Inn where we listened to traditional music by the open fire and, while the musicians were taking a breather, sang old sea shanties with our fellow drinkers. On the way back to the B&B, right out of the blue, Stuart suddenly proposed to me. Initially I thought he had fallen over but on closer examination in the gloom, I discovered that he was on one knee, making a pre-prepared speech. 'Jennifer O'Brien', he recited, 'ever since you came into my life at that funeral you have lightened my whole existence and made me a happy man. I now know that I can't live without you and that we will be good for each other. I want you to be my wife. Will you become Jennifer Hoare? Please marry me.'

Without the slightest hesitation, without taking time to evaluate the pros and cons, without considering whether it would be a good decision or a bad one, without asking time to consider, I accepted there and then, on the spot. 'Oh, Stuart, of course I will, darling,' I said. 'Of course I will.' I don't know who was more surprised, him or me. We didn't notice, or care, how loud the bed creaked that night.

The next day we packed our things into the car and went for one last stroll around the village, going into a midnight blue jeweller's shop where I chose my engagement ring. I was pleasantly surprised that I managed to find one that I really liked in such a little, out of the way town. The jeweller, whose name was David, was a Welsh silversmith and had two or three one-off pieces that he had crafted. One of these was just perfect; it had one large diamond and four smaller ones in an asymmetrical arrangement that represented the Bay of Kinsale and its surrounding islands.

'Stuart, if I had ordered this myself it could not have been better,' I said. I loved it then and I still think it beautiful today.

We went away on that trip as friends and lovers and came back engaged to be married, much to the joy of both Stuart's and my own families. Everyone was delighted. They never thought they'd live to see the day when either of us would marry and settle down.

So began the charge towards marriage and our life together.

Chapter 13

Mam and Da were over the moon. In Stuart they saw a man whose steadfastness and conservatism provided exactly the foil I needed to steady me down. I was far too new age for their personal preferences and they constantly worried about my out there beliefs, acquaintances, clothes and attitudes. They felt Stu was the perfect match for me. He would calm me down while I, in turn, would lighten him up a bit. They thanked God that we had found each other. All Mam's rosaries and novenas had been answered.

'Ah, the good Lord works in mysterious ways,' she said. 'I always knew that the Blessed Virgin Mary would not let me down. I had my own dear Mam, plus all the family that has gone before, up there in Heaven interceding for me with the Holy Mother. She just couldn't ignore them.' My Mam could now die a happy woman!

Stu's family was ecstatic as well. His father, Richard, liked me even though he thought I was a bit of a flippety-jibberty. He often compared me to his own long dead Ma, saying my red hair and slim build reminded him of her. 'Ah, now she was a beauty,' he would reminisce, 'there was not one lad in Wexford County who would not have thought her the greatest prize of all. And she was a great home-maker! She did everything for us. My father never even had to polish his own boots.' I discreetly made it clear to Stuart that I had no intention of aspiring to those lofty heights but acknowledged that by comparing me to his long dead Ma, his father had certainly complimented me.

Stu was always a bit nervy and on edge when he was with his father as he never quite knew whether he was doing things right and up to his expected high standards. Although he respected Richard he never totally relaxed in his company. I think they were very alike in personality and that sometimes caused difficulty.

His mother buzzed around Stuart like a busy bumble bee pollinating the flowers, making sure that he was fed, happy, comfortable and that he had all his washing done. Clearly she adored him and he happily basked in her adoration.

Moira and I got along well from the day we met and, as the years went by, came to love and respect one another. She delighted in the knowledge that Stu was ready to marry and settle down at last, as she never thought that it would happen. Although things were always quite formal in their household I still seemed to fit in, probably because I didn't take much notice of their rigid outlook.

They would often discreetly shake their heads at each other when I surprised them with my apparently frivolous nature and unconventional way of looking at things. But they saw me as a part of the package that Stu had brought to the table and accepted me as I was. In fact, Moira was secretly delighted to have another woman in the family. 'I've lived in a man's world for so long, Jennifer!' she confided in me one day. 'I've been longing for the day I would have female company, especially on family occasions. Not just to share the work load but give a feminine perspective on things. You know men. They're convinced that what they say is the only thing that goes.'

Having unity and support on both sides was going to be of great help in overcoming our next challenge in planning our summer wedding. With my family Catholic and Stuart's staunch Church of Ireland, there needed to be diplomatic negotations. As I was Buddhist and not tied to any church, the logical thing would have been for us to get married in the Church of Ireland. However, this posed quite a dilemma, as my mob would have absolutely detested my marrying in a Protestant church. 'Darling,' I said, 'I don't think many of them will even turn up.'

After some lengthy discussion, I came up with a viable solution.

'Why don't we go with my Buddhist philosophy?' I said.

'What?' said Stuart. 'Get some Tibetan monk to do it?'

'No, no. We can get a civil celebrant, so that will make it legal, but can make it a Buddhist inspired ceremony. After all, Buddhism is not a religion, just a way of living.'

Slowly but surely, I managed to convince Stuart and everybody else that Celtic Buddhism was Irish enough for us both, even though some members of our families laughed openly at the concept.

Originally we planned to be a small party consisting of just our family members and a couple of close friends. Stu had one mate from his boarding school days and I just had my dear friends Rhani and Wendy. While we naturally invited my immediate family - my four brothers, their wives and my numerous nieces and nephews, my living grandparents on both sides and the uncles and aunties and cousins, many of them from County Kerry – we figured that as it was to be a night wedding in the middle of a field in Roscommon, the numbers would naturally cull themselves.

That didn't happen. They all came in force, overwhelming Stuart's small contingent, consisting of his mother, father, uncle, aunt and cousin, Mary, plus a couple of business acquaintances and his old school mate. My mob all dressed for the occasion in their Celtic layers, some in bright colours and some in the tonings of the earth. I was so proud of them. They knew that this would be different and so they did as they were asked on the invitation and came prepared to party.

Stuart and I were married in the forest on the night of the full moon closest to the Summer Solstice - June 23rd, 1991, at 8 pm - using our native Celtic Gaelic language for the ceremony. I dressed in the palest shade of green silk in a simple but flowing gown with strappy flat sandals and flowers in my hair. Stuart wore a suit.

We had no attendants as such but we asked all the children to dress in green for the occasion and to accompany Stuart and me as we walked down the moonlit path to the rocky area overlooking the River Shannon where a celebrant conducted a simple but moving ceremony. We all carried candles although the moon was bright enough to light our path.

Even my mob, who had been quite sceptical and who I know made jokes about our choice of time and venue behind our backs, were impressed and quietly reflective on the walk back to the courtyard of the renovated manor house with its old stables and servants quarters where we were all staying en masse in the outbuildings. A fire burned brightly giving off warmth and light, while tables laden with food and drink stood waiting for the celebration.

Traditional Irish music sounded into the night and first the children and then, after a few drinks had been imbibed, almost everyone jigged the night away. Even Granny and Pa kicked up a leg. It was a wonderful Celtic Irish celebration. Near to dawn there was still a few of us sitting around the fire singing the old songs. We had experienced a deeply spiritual and happy start to our married life and the future looked rosy.

We didn't consummate the marriage that night as we both fell into bed knackered. That happened the following night in a Dublin hotel where we stayed before catching an early flight to Stuart's surprise destination, Bermuda, where we honeymooned in the sun. Stu loved the beach and all the activities that were on offer but with my red hair and Irish skin I got badly burnt on the first day and had to spend most of my time indoors. Still, it was a happy time away from the everyday grind. The world seemed a wonderful place.

Chapter 14

We returned to set up home in Stu's Dublin apartment, which was perfect for a married business couple like us. It was centrally located in Ballsbridge, didn't need much maintenance, was light and spacious and in amongst the action. But I don't think Stu really liked having me there.

He reluctantly reorganised his clothes and gave me exactly half of the wardrobe, he avoided mixing his and my music on the same shelf, and he objected to me bringing in my kitchen utensils and knick-knacks. He liked everything the way he liked it and generally was a little possessive about 'his place.' One day when he was out, I rearranged the lounge room. You know what men are like; they go for the utilitarian rather than the aesthetic. He had the television dead bang in front of the balcony doors and so it was a battle to get outside as you had to step over cords and shimmy behind the set.

With the help of Wendy, I spent a good couple of hours rearranging the place. Afterwards we put on some meditation music, sat back, had a cup of latte and admired our work. We were pretty pleased with the result and I was sure the room would work much better. But the upshot was that we took ourselves off to see a movie and when I got back Stu had been home and had shifted the room back to the way it had been.

He was doing a slow boil. This was the first time I had seen it. I did not know it then, but it certainly was not going to be the last.

'Can you just tell that Wendy friend of yours to stop her interfering and to leave my things alone?' he fumed. I knew then that we would have to get 'our' place quickly, as the flat was still 'his' place.

A week or so later we were at a dinner party at my brother Kevin's house and we got talking about real estate, as you do. One of the guests, Darra, was an estate agent and he suggested that it was a really good time to buy in at the top end of the market. It was by then the early 90s, when house prices had yet to recover from the crash of 1987. I could see Stu was a bit unsettled about this, so when he was in the bathroom I took Darra's card and quietly asked him to come and have a look at our two places - Stu's in Ballsbridge and mine in Harold's Cross - and to give us a price on them. He obliged and when Stuart heard what sort of money we could achieve, we were on our way.

House hunting can be stressful, particularly when two people can't agree as to what they really want in a home. Stu was really keen on a new development at Rathfarnham, one of those gated communities. 'I love the concept,' he opined, 'the gates will keep out the riff-raff and low life. Besides, the house will be brand spanking new, so we will not be inheriting other people's problems or mess.

'And the best part,' he concluded, 'is that only people like ourselves will be able to afford to buy in, so we won't have to put up with noisy, uncouth neighbours.'

I took his point but felt uneasy about cutting our future family off from what I considered the real world. I had been brought up in Blackrock, knew it well and that was where I wanted to buy. It was a great area - well established, with lots of character, a variety of housing and a cross-section of the community, plus all services and good, regular public transport. There were traditional schools, excellent shopping and some lovely restaurants and pubs. Also, we would be near to Mam and Da who still lived in the family home there.

Eventually it was Darra who came up with the house that we bought and which became our home. Not in Blackrock, but not far away in Dalkey. Sometimes a house chooses you rather than the other way around and I think that this one screamed out to Stu and me, 'Buy me because I can give you the class and stability that you have always craved and your family will be safe and secure. You will be happy here!'

It was a beautifully proportioned house standing back from the water in a private cul de sac, with good neighbours and brilliant sea views. Properties like that didn't come up very often in Dalkey because they were tightly held, but this was a deceased estate and so we were lucky.

Stu came around to my way of thinking the minute he saw it. There was a castle near by, a beautiful local shopping strip with three or four good restaurants and you could buy lobster and crabs fresh from the little pier down the road where the seals came in to feed and which would delight our children for many years to come.

'And look at this, darling,' said Stuart, 'there's a Church of Ireland just a walk away further up the hill.'

We knew there would be things we would have to do to make the place ours, but it had good bones and from the minute we moved in it became our home. Stuart loved that house. It was his castle and he was always making improvements, fixing this, adjusting that and building up his arsenal of power and other tools. He could wander up the road to the church to attend meetings, practice on the organ or chat to the Vicar. The city was close and the surrounding dining scene was excellent, a detail that Stuart especially appreciated.

Because I am vegetarian and really could not stand the smell of meat in the house, I never cooked it. Stu loved a slab of meat so a couple of times a week we would walk to one of the local restaurants and he would order a steak and I would have the fish. I took an interest in the garden, particularly the kitchen garden where I grew fruit trees, herbs and many of the vegetables that the family consumed.

Overall, the house in Dalkey was perfect in all respects, and because we bought at the bottom of the market, it was remarkably good value for the money we spent. I could say I was happy there, but content is probably the best word for it. I loved the area and once I had children they completed me as a person and my world was at peace.

Expanding our family, however, was not as easy as it sounds. When children didn't immediately come our way, I panicked. I had married Stuart because I wanted to be a mother, but at first it did not seem that that was going to happen. After two years of trying, I started looking for solutions. And the first place I looked was dark and grim.

My Irish superstitions had me believing deep down that my barrenness was God's punishment for doing the awful thing I had done to my baby all those years before. My Buddhist beliefs would not countenance this dreadful thought but I was torn and deeply depressed about the situation.

I could never tell Stuart the reason for my anguish, as I had never dared open my heart to him regarding my affair with Tommy. He knew nothing about it at all.

After all else had failed and I put our name down for IVF, Stu turned out to be a real rock. He supported me as we went through all the physical and psychological testing to determine why we weren't conceiving. He subjected himself to every indignity, every test, every challenge. It was not his style, but he did it for us and I was grateful. That's because we both really wanted a family. He saw children as an extension of himself and of our relationship.

My friend Wendy, perhaps the least maternal person I have ever known, couldn't quite understand my inner yearning for children and our determination to conceive via any means. 'Relax, forget about it and it will happen,' she'd say over a cuppa in the kitchen. 'Now, what do you want to get up to while Stu is out?' Once I did conceive, though, she became a fantastic 'Aunty Wen' to my children, never babysitting them but often coming along to give me a hand or playing with them when we went on our meditation walks. She still had a lot of childlike qualities herself and so she got on famously with my little ones.

On the second phase of the IVF process, the egg took and I became pregnant with Stuart Junior. We rejoiced. When he was born and we brought him home we realised that we were now a real family; that our house had become our home; that our neighbourhood had became our community. And, well into their seventies, Stuart's parents had become grandparents for the first time. They doted on their grandson and we were happy.

Richard followed only eighteen months later. No IVF needed. He was conceived naturally.

'See,' said Wendy, 'there you go. You've both chilled out a bit.'

Stuart was delighted to have boys because they would carry the family name forward and, in his mind, to be the father of sons was to be the head of a clan. He loved that notion and took them under his wing and moulded them in his likeness. He was a stern but loving parent. There was nothing he wouldn't have done for his boys. It was a busy but happy time and the home rang with the sounds of small children.

Seven years later, out of the blue, came our crowning jewel, my little Molly. I say 'my' Molly, because a daughter was foreign territory for Stuart. He had named and owned the boys but he gave me the pleasure of naming Molly after my mother, Mary. She and I became a pair. My world was complete.

After that, the sex dropped off. I never fell pregnant again, but I was happy. What could be more wonderful than being the parent of three healthy and happy kiddies? I busied myself with the children, the kitchen garden, our neighbours and the community, doing everything I could do to make my children's lives happy and fulfilled. I volunteered as a reading Mum at the school, went as an extra helper on school excursions and trips, worked tirelessly on fundraisers and any other projects and ferried the children backwards and forwards to all their events. Stuart was a busy man so it was my job to keep track of the domestic things.

Come the weekend, work permitting, Stuart took the boys to their sports. He gave them fatherly advice and insisted that they behave like gentlemen. He taught them those things that he thought a man should know - how to mow the lawns, change a washer, use a hurling stick, throw a rugby ball, tie knots, open a door for a lady, all those things that are passed on from father to son. I suppose you could say that Stuart was in charge of the way in which his sons lived their lives. He always kept a keen eye on their progress at school and in his meticulous way left nothing to chance as he had a grand plan for them both and was determined to lay down a solid foundation. He would often quote the Jesuits, 'Give me a child until he is seven and I will show you the man,' and adopted it as his philosophy.

The children loved him and did their best to please him. They rejoiced when he came home from work and loved it when he took them to their sports or to the park with a ball. He was the font of all knowledge and they adored the ground he walked on and would turn themselves inside out to try and please him.

At work Stuart was an important man, part owner of the business, a well-respected leader who had received many accolades from his colleagues and industry associates. I am sure that along the way, he must have made some enemies, as he could be a very hard marker. To be fair, he never expected anyone to do any more than he did himself and he ran a tight ship where everyone in the office knew they had to perform. If they didn't like it, they left.

Stuart's work fulfilled him in the same way as our children and my Buddhist philosophy fulfilled me. He was pleased with the choices he had made in his life. He had a pretty wife who saw to his every need and who was a great hostess when he needed one to further his professional ambitions. He had a house that was suitably impressive for a man of his standing. He was proud of his children who were well behaved and smart. He drove a luxury car and played golf at a prestigious club.

At the end of the day, Stuart saw himself as being happy at work, happy at play and happy at home.

Chapter 15

I can't exactly pinpoint the moment when I looked around and realised that my marriage was no longer a joint celebration of our love but rather a day-to-day trial, with Stuart as the all-powerful judge and me the permanent prisoner in the dock. There was probably no one defining moment or single instance, rather an ongoing combination of comments, discussions, events, conflicts, attitudes, arguments and rows - sometimes isolated, sometimes interconnected - that slowly grew and grew in their content, acidity and vitriol, strangling the life of out of me and pushing me further and further into submission.

I do, however, recognize that things started changing very early in our marriage. The first indicator of the real Stuart - the more selfish, controlling Stuart - appeared the day Wendy and I re-arranged the furniture in his flat and he came home and immediately put it all back. I thought he would appreciate our endeavours and accept our gift of a new, more orderly living space with love and perhaps a dash of humour. But I was wrong. So, so wrong. His slow burn that day was only a mild indicator of what was to come.

That first flush of marriage also changed the way I presented to the world. Or should I say, the way I was allowed to be presented to the world. We were only a couple of weeks back from our honeymoon when I came home after an intense think-tank at work to find most of my clothes had been yanked out of the wardrobe and neatly laid out on the bed. 'Stu, what's all this?' I asked gaily, 'are you throwing me out already?'

'Of course not, my darling, I'm not throwing you out, I'm sorting you out. I've been thinking about the clutter in our wardrobe and the tension it is causing.'

'Tension? What do you mean tension?' That had me worried.

'Well,' he said patiently, 'your clothes are slowly taking over the apartment while mine are getting crushed into a tiny space. So I have a solution.'

'Oh yes, and what would that be then? Will you be buying a new closet for the spare room so you can move your clothes in there?'

He looked at me with a slightly pained expression. 'No, I've done my research, observed women in the street and read a few magazines, and I believe that there are clothes on that bed that are not suitable for you now that you're married. You just don't need them, so I thought we'd send them off to a charity shop. What do you think?'

Shocked at this sudden critical evaluation of my dress sense, I started to pick them up piece by piece and defend them, stating why I needed to keep this or that. Admittedly, my clothes had always been a bit out there, a trifle zany, but I was comfortable in them and thought they reflected the true me. My style had been developed during my years at Cambridge when I would buy pieces from charity shops and put them together in a different and creative way. It became further defined by working with my colleagues in information technology - people who had a whimsical approach to fashion. When I returned to Dublin I began to buy from the boutiques and student designers around the Temple Bar area, so while my selections became a little more upmarket, they were still quite distinctive.

I picked up an outfit. 'Stu, I love this skirt, it twirls when I walk. It's warm and looks great with those purple pants and top and this mauve leather jacket. I have even got the green bag and shoes that go perfectly with it. And you want me to send it all to a charity shop? It cost me a fortune! It will do me for years, I'll never get sick of it.'

But I was talking to a brick wall. Each attempt to save my signature items was met with a wry shake of the head and the reply, 'I don't think so, Mrs Hoare!'

'The time has come my lovely Jennifer, to move on from the foibles of youth,' he said, putting his arm around me and drawing back so that he was looking into my eyes. 'You're my wife and I want you to look elegant and affluent. You can't do that in those clothes. They make you look like a tinker. We'll go shopping and buy you a more grown-up wardrobe, quality classic pieces that you can wear anywhere.'

I thought, 'Well, perhaps he's right. Maybe it is time to move on.' So I relented. Only a few of my clothes escaped the purge. The next weekend we went shopping, Stu and I together. We bought ten quality items that could be mixed and matched and which cost the entire budget of a small third world country.

They were nice, and they were quality, and they were classic fashion. But they weren't really me. I had been styled! Made over. By someone else. Whether I liked it or not. When I walked into the office the next Monday I was met with much frivolity and teasing about my new look. 'You'll not be staying much longer with our little operation then,' laughed Danny the nerdiest nerd, 'it'll be Mary Robinson's job you'll be doing next.'

The funny thing was that they all soon got used to my more mature look. It seemed to engender a new and higher level of respect from both my colleagues and my business associates. After that, I never joined in their Friday night drinks; it just didn't seem appropriate. The old, carefree Jennifer had gone and was now existing under a new regime.

I had come to the marriage as a domestic dyslectic, with very few skills for running a household. Everything had been done for the little princess when I was growing up at home with Mam and Da. And of course when we lived the student life in Cambridge, domestic issues were at the bottom of the priority list. But once we moved to Dalkey and the daily management of the house became my full time role, I soon realised that Stuart would get upset at coming home to a messy space. I had to consciously and quickly learn how to keep house to his high standards. Everything neat, everything orderly, no dust on the mantelpiece.

After a disastrous clothes wash in the early days, when Stuart's crisp white shirts all turned pink and little balls of lint decorated his golf tops, he went ballistic. This was yet another side to Stuart that I had not seen before. Angry, red-faced, furious.

I stepped back and waited until the storm passed over, and then cajoled him about how wearing pink shirts might attract a whole new wave of customers. 'The gay euro is a much sought after market,' I said. How wrong was I to go down that path.

When he finally calmed down, he instructed me on separating the whites from the colours, hanging the wash out to dry on hangers not pegs, and using the correct ironing procedure so that the end result was well pressed pieces of clothing which were to be hung at three inch intervals in his wardrobe. 'All facing left,' he commanded, 'with the hooks on the hangers pointing towards the window.'

The task of setting me right on the routine of ensuring a well laundered product must have been terribly frustrating for him as, to be honest, I really needed the guidance. I was simply not used to men's clothing and always sought the easy way out for my own. I had always looked for the 'No Iron' label on an item before I considered buying it. To me, ironing was a waste of time and only contributed to the destruction of our precious eco-system. All my clothes had been machine washable, the shake and store kind. If, when I perused myself in the mirror before stepping out, I looked a bit ruffled then I had a marvellous trick of applying a fine spray of lavender water to the clothes I had on and letting my body temperature do the rest. This was certainly not Stu's style and he let me know that!

As the years went by and children came along, the mood of the house would tighten if Stuart came in from work tired and grumpy. It was in all our best interests to placate and humour him, and that is what we strove to do. As far as he was concerned, the children and I belonged to him. We were the perfect family about whom he could boast to his colleagues and customers and it irritated him if we failed to reach perfection in any aspect. Sometimes I thought he expected too much from our two little boys but he disagreed with me. 'Zero tolerance is a very effective teaching tool,' he would say. 'You have to set boundaries and make sure they stick to them.' Molly tended to cling to me and was somehow off his radar, escaping his strict scrutiny.

He worked long hours to provide the money that made our comfortable lifestyle possible, so he was an essential but vague figure, probably of more relevance to the children than to me. He liked to spend quality time with them, but not an excess of it, our holidays often providing a little too much face-to-face contact for his comfort. Each year we'd get away to the sun, usually in Spain or Portugal, but by the end of the fortnight Stuart's patience with the kiddies would be wearing very thin. He would easily get stressed if his routine was broken. The best thing for me to do was to take the kids off to the pool or for an outing in town and leave him to check his investments in the newspaper while he sat in the sun.

It was better all round that way; we had a fun time while he got his required amount of peace and quiet.

There was no denying that Stuart loved me, sometimes to the point of suffocation. I often wished he would realise that I was not the person he had placed on his pedestal. I was a living, breathing being who had thoughts and feelings and a mind of her own. He had another vision for me.

When the sex started to go out of our marriage, I used to worry about our lack of intimacy and the fact that we hardly ever talked or made love anymore. God knows I didn't really deserve the adoration he poured onto me, as I never reciprocated his feelings with the same intensity. But that did not seem to concern Stuart too much. He loved me as his wife and the mother of his children.

I knew, however, that this love was totally conditional upon one thing, me toeing the line. When I would unwittingly step over it, he would go into a violent rage and seem to lose all reasoning. Disagreements were like foreplay to him and his preferred method of reconciliation was to demand sex. After a while, it seemed to be the only time we ever made love, and as I was feeling so hurt I often couldn't raise any interest. I didn't even want to kiss him and would withdraw into myself. This only made him angrier. 'For Christ's sake, Jenny, you're my wife,' he'd roar. 'It's your duty to let me make love to you. I am the victim of a sexless marriage, plain and simple as that. You've changed but I should have known. You're a bitch, just like your mother.' Apparently, it was always my fault - or my mother's!

Then he'd go ahead, riding me like a Hereford bull, lording it over me, taking all and giving nothing and making me feel used and upset and teary.

Being a quick learner, it soon became a place I chose not to go. It was better to avoid confrontation at all costs and so I worked hard at living peacefully with Stuart, treading on eggshells in order to predict his moods and navigate around his demands.

Married and family life changed the rules I lived by. If I was going out I had to check with Stuart and he would let me know if it was okay, as he liked to have me to himself on the weekends. 'I married you so that I could be with you, so let's just go out to dinner together,' he would say. Or to the movies, or a show, or a business function, whatever. If I did manage to get out on my own, I was always conscious that he would be home waiting for me, ready to grill me on what had happened, screening every response I gave, prepared to pounce on a word or phrase that might hint that I had had too good a time or encouraged the attention of other men.

Despite my making the changes he demanded of me, I still seemed to have the ability to transform Stu from the calm, cool fellow he normally was when things were going his way into a raving lunatic when they were not. If you likened him to a recipe, he was the slow to warm up dish that, over time, sat on simmer, gradually became heated, reached the boil and then exploded untidily all over the cooker.

Even his mother was wary of his temper. 'Oh, he can be a hot head,' she'd tutt-tutt, 'always has been. He'll never give up until he's got his way. He's been like that since he could walk. Like a dog with a bone, as territorial as can be. My advice to you Jennifer my love is to give him what he wants first up. It saves a lot of grief, as you'll never win. I never did!'

As a naturally untidy and disorganised person, I learned very early on that crumbs on the kitchen bench or discarded clothes on the bathroom floor or magazines casually strewn on the coffee table could trigger one of Stuart's manic rants. On reflection, I should have left that first time when he threw the iron at me because I had left it and the ironing board set up in the lounge room of his apartment after doing his shirts, but I didn't. I ducked and let it smash into the plaster behind me, allowed him to have sex as a way of making up, and even made light of the incident afterwards by making a joke about 'ironing out our problems'. I accepted his contrite apology. 'I'm so sorry, Jen, I don't know what came over me. I'll never do anything like that again. Promise!'

Of course, he did. I rationalised it like this: he is an only child, he has been a bachelor all his life, he runs his own company, he is a man of the world and is used to having what he says goes. I could work around that. It was not hard to consider his timetable and his wishes. Over the years I learned to duck and weave, working around his moods and outbreaks because when Stu was a happy pappy all was well with our world and the children and I were safe.

But you never knew when things were about to explode. There was the time I went to a neighbour's 40th birthday party in our street. Stu couldn't come as the babysitter had cancelled at the last minute, so he said he would stay home with the children. That seemed okay. I was out by myself, the kiddies were safe and snuggled up in bed with Stu looking after them, and I knew he would enjoy being home with the television and a glass of red wine as parties weren't really his scene. It was a surprise party, the mood was good and it turned out to be one hell of a hooley. We were all young parents and it was grand to be out having fun. The music was ours and it was loud and pumping. It was getting close to midnight and I was dancing with no one in particular, just enjoying the ambience. Next thing I knew, Stu was standing next to me. 'Molly's upset, you need to come home,' he said. I quickly said my goodbyes and left in a hurry with him.

We got home and everything was quiet and, of course, I panicked. Quiet is not good when you are dealing with a sick baby. I went to race upstairs but suddenly Stu turned me around, pushed me back against the wall and began hissing at me, 'You are a dirty, filthy slut. You are *my* wife and I will not tolerate you dancing and flaunting yourself about like that. You're like a bitch on heat gyrating in front of everyone and making *me* the laughing stock of the neighbourhood.'

This attack came from nowhere and I just couldn't believe it.

'That's simply not true Stuart,' I sobbed, 'all the women were dancing. It was a party for God's sake, what were we supposed to be doing? Screwing in the back room?' That just made him angrier so he pushed me harder against the wall.

I was sobbing hysterically but he kept speaking at me, steadfastly talking me down, telling me that I was his wife and the mother of his children, that he loved me and that it hurt him to see me dancing like that, and hadn't he told me to be home by 10.30 pm?

I couldn't believe that he was setting curfews for me like I was a schoolgirl. I was confused. In my mind I hadn't been doing anything wrong but the way Stu told it, I had been disloyal to him and to the family. I pulled myself free and went up to bed. Stu slept on the couch that night because I locked the door to our room. Next morning when I came down ready for battle, he had the kiddies dressed and breakfasted and sat me down, as nice as pie, to the strawberry pancakes he sometimes made on a weekend. You would think that nothing had happened. I relented and let it pass. But I sure as hell didn't go out dancing again.

Another evening we were at a presentation night for Stu's work, an event he had organised and for which he was master of ceremonies. This meant that even though we sat together, he was distracted and busy up on the stage and I was left on my own and at a bit of a loose end. So I joined the table of a group of salesmen who I knew pretty well, as I had entertained them at home on several occasions. I had a fun night and the evening went very well, but Stu was very quiet on the way home in the car. I was driving as usual, as I never drank, so I didn't take much notice. As soon as we had let the babysitter go, he pushed me back against the wall, shouting in my face, banging my head back and forwards against the solid brick, accusing me of infidelity with one of the salesmen.

'I was watching you from the stage,' he screamed. 'You were giving him the come-on, you bitch! You were all over him! Practically sitting in his lap.'

He was red with rage and I had absolutely no come back. I just had to stand there and take it. I believe he would have killed me that night had not the babysitter rang the door bell because she had left her study book behind and needed it for school the next day. Stu answered the door and spoke to her as if nothing had happened. I made my escape upstairs to the spare bedroom where I jammed the chest against the door. He simply went to bed and next day said in a menacing way, 'If I catch you flirting with my colleagues again, your life won't be worth living.' He meant it and I took it as having been told.

Stu and I didn't always agree on parenting styles either. He was much too strict for my liking and it began to get to me. He and the boys were out in the garden one Saturday afternoon after the sun had popped its head out from between the clouds. Overcome by joyful anticipation of a good summer to come, the boys had been helping him. God knows they were working hard for little lads, but he was on their case all the time.

'No, hold it this way, Junior, that's not the right way to do it,' he said. And on and on it went. 'Come on, hurry up there, winter will be here again before we get this done.' 'That's not how we plant flowers.' 'You're bloody useless.' 'Give it to me, you're just getting in the way.' 'When I was your age, I was mowing the lawns by myself.' It was a tirade of negativity.

I felt sorry for them; they just couldn't get it right. They would never measure up as far as Stu was concerned; whatever they did would never please him. But the poor little mites still tried! After more than an hour of this, I couldn't help it. I put my oar in and said, 'For God's sake, Stu, go easy on them. They're only lads and they're doing their best. Try a little praise for a change; castles were built one stone at a time.' To diffuse the situation a little, I picked up the broom and, using it as a microphone, started to sing the old Bing Crosby song, 'You've got to accentuate the positive, eliminate the negative, latch on to the affirmative, don't mess with Mister In-Between.'

The kiddies loved it, but the clouded look came across Stu's face and he was fuming. He didn't say anything then but later when they were in bed he read me the riot act. His went so red in the face his blood pressure must have reached 180. Shaking his finger at me, he roared, 'Don't you *ever* question my authority in front of *my* children again! You made me look silly out there in the garden today and I don't like it. You are bringing them up to be Mammy's boys. They're to live by my rules in my house and that is it.' And so it went on. I had been told. I was wary of giving my opinion regarding father/son relations again. That night we watched television in silence, him impervious to my humiliation and powerlessness and me sitting there close to tears and feeling hurt and miserable.

Then, the following day, everything in the garden was rosy, as if the previous night's blow-up had not existed! He played with the boys at the park in the morning and had half the neighbours' children with him and they all thought he was grand. I realised I had married Jekyll and Hyde - when he was good, he was very, very good and fun to be with. But when he was bad he could be frightening.

Stuart harboured other issues about me that he didn't like and which could make him very angry. He hated me wearing bright red lipstick even though that had been my trademark in by-gone days and was one of the things he'd noticed about me when we had first met. 'Wipe it off, you look like a trollop,' he told me more than once. Even though I began to dress in modest, classical lines, following his direction, he would often suddenly deem that my skirt was too short, my top too low, the material too clingy or the cut too sexy. 'Change that,' he would snap. 'I'm not going to be seen in public with a slut.' It was difficult to get my look right for him.

'How do you cope?' Wendy asked one time after she happened to witness a classic Stuart 'I can never find anything amongst all this mess!' performance. He had an army of secretaries and underlings at work that made sure that his day went smoothly and without hitches. At home it was different. There were three small children in the house, so things did not always land in their right spot or go to plan. Stu was actually quite hopeless, always mislaying things, and this day he'd lost his diary. The tirade began and soon escalated. I was at the sink peeling potatoes for dinner, so I kept doing that, knowing that he would eventually find it himself. He did and he stormed off. 'Oh, I ignore it,' I said to Wendy, 'I used to rush around helping him but I have learnt now to let him play that game by himself. He eventually burns out.'

Although he tolerated my Buddhism, Stu certainly didn't celebrate it. He thought it all mumbo-jumbo and couldn't quite get his head around it, but to give him his due he left me to my personal spiritual journey. I belonged to him, the children belonged to him, but my spiritual enrichment was my concern.

To keep the peace and for family unity, on a Sunday morning I usually accompanied him to Anglican Mass, taking the children with us. This was not hard for me to do because the Catholic Mass that I was familiar with was not so different and it made him happy that we worshipped as a family. There we'd all be, lined up in the front pew, the perfect Irish family, the boys looking smart in good shirts and trousers and Molly decked out in pink. To be honest, I quite enjoyed the social and community aspect of the outing. Having people around me in a situation like that made me feel good, perhaps even secure. It meant that I was not alone with Stuart and the potential target for another flare up.

After church on Sundays we'd all pack into the car and go for a lunchtime roast at Stu's parents, who he always treated with the utmost kindness and respect. But if I or the children put a foot wrong he would glare at us and on the way home the grey clouds would descend again and I would be treated me like the enemy because I had let him down in front of his father. Not that the children would have realised; the way he did it was just for me and him to know. I found it menacing, but like him, I avoided having a scene in front of the children. After all, we were happy families, weren't we?

These things happened often and it was times like that that I needed the counsel of my friend Wendy who would say, 'Don't put up with it. Take your rightful place as an equal partner in your relationship.' She'd often end, 'Do you want me to come over and kick him in the balls?' Which, of course was the last thing I wanted, but at least it made me laugh.

With the passing of time, the arrival of children, the diminishing of our sexual relationship and the limits on my freedom, our differences escalated. If I broached the subject of us growing apart he simply put it down to our busy lifestyle with three young children, assuming it would get better at a later date. For me our relationship was fast becoming like one of Ireland's bogs - a top layer of plants, flowers and wild life that looked beautiful to the outsider, but for anyone who stepped on it, under the surface it was wet, cold sludge.

Why did I stay? I had three young children who loved their father; my confidence was low and my self-esteem all but gone; I thought the situation would somehow get better; I feared the shame of failure, the damning public exposure of not being able to make our marriage work; I just didn't have the gumption to leave; and if I had, an enraged Stuart would certainly have come after me and brought me back. All things considered, it was better that I keep the peace and learn to do things the way Stu liked them done.

Was Stu controlling when we married? Or did that come with the children? Hard to say, because at first I did love him in a grown-up, adult sort of way, and we did have the same wonderful vision for our life together. I had no doubt that Stu still loved me. I was his pretty little wife who did his bidding and saw to his comfort. But did I return the affection? I certainly loved his children and the best thing I could do for them was to love their father.

If he loved me why did he strip away my own self and replace it with his alter ego? It didn't seem right. I pondered and meditated upon these things, searching for the answers.

Chapter 16

During the daytime when all the husbands and partners were at work, a group of my old school pals plus a few young mothers in our neighbourhood would meet for coffee. We would talk about anything and everything as a group of women will do. There were always babies and young children everywhere - at the breast, on the knee or in a high chair making a mess of a biscuit. Nothing was sacred and there was always lively conversation and laughter. 'Holy mother of God,' someone would say, 'you'd never believe what happened!' And then she would tell you.

These girls came to know Stu as a dutiful, predictable husband. They knew how he liked to make lists; how he was frightened of the possibility that his sons might grow up gay; how he would lecture the candidate for the local council elections to the point where the poor man wouldn't want his vote; how he'd get so uptight if my lipstick was too red; how he thought I was trying to have an affair with every new young gun salesman at his insurance business when all I wanted was a good night's sleep; how I had to turn in receipts of my weekly spend so he could reconcile the accounts; how he rang me four times a day on the dot to see what I was up to; how he didn't like to change Molly's nappy because it embarrassed him to see a little girl's bottom.

With these girls a cappuccino and a chat was much better than therapy. However, I never told them the whole story about his explosive temper that lay dormant ready to erupt if things didn't go his way. That stayed within the family.

It was my coffee friends who introduced me to the social phenomenon that is Facebook. In the winter months the numbers at those get-togethers would always be smaller because one child or another would have to be kept home sick with a bug. On one such occasion, Annie, one of the younger mums, suggested we should all become 'Facebook friends.' She brought along her laptop and showed us how we could keep in touch on the social net-working site even if we were housebound. The added attraction was that we were able to share our photos and videos. We all took to it like ducks to water. It was a great way of communicating for busy young mothers and was certainly quite addictive.

Let's be frank. Facebook.com is a great time waster. You turn on the computer, log on, and before you know it, an hour has disappeared. Don't get me wrong, I loved it and after years of child rearing where I barely had time to turn around, I quickly discovered that I was enjoying it.

I had come to that stage in my domestic life where there was beginning to be a little light at the end of the tunnel. There seems to be a magic moment around the third birthday of the last baby in the family when he or she moves on from being highly dependent to being a separate little person. Almost overnight, mother ceases to be the sole mainstay of baby's existence and other people, such as the Montessori teacher and the baby gym instructress, suddenly attain credibility, influence and respect. This had now happened with our youngest child, Molly, and even though I mourned the passing of her babyhood, I looked forward with pleasure to what was to come for the family.

Suddenly I had time for things like the internet and it became a normal part of daily life to chat on websites, find recipes to cook, research children's ailments, plot out a journey - all these things and more. Even though I was pretty savvy with technology and computers, to me this was a revelation. It was years since I had worked professionally and that is a long time in computer land.

I could just lose myself and I loved it. If one of my friends was online we'd have a conversation of sorts and it was a grand way of keeping contact. Even old school friends sometimes popped up and I'd have a word or two with them. It gets to you. Barely a day went by that I didn't log in to Facebook and check what was happening 'in the hood.'

It was all pretty innocent. But Stu didn't like it at all. In fact he positively abhorred it. He didn't like it because he didn't understand such things and he knew he was being left behind. He was a technological dinosaur who could barely turn on a computer and had practically no keyboard skills. If it weren't for the email and Stock Exchange pages that his secretary pulled up on screen for him first thing each morning, he would have been totally electronically isolated. This frustrated him and he thought that the kiddies and I spent too much time looking at a screen. 'It is an energy drainer,' he espoused, 'and it takes up all your time and attention and never gives anything back. You are selfishly keeping yourself away from me and the family by spending time on the computer.'

He had a bigger theory, too. 'It is anti-social,' he expounded. 'In twenty years' time no one will be communicating directly face to face. We'll all be robots, chained to a computer and seeing the world through electronic eyes.'

Bearing in mind what might have been the consequences, I began to limit my online communications. Wendy was angry. 'You have a right to do exactly what you want with your time,' she insisted, 'particularly once the kids are in bed. That time is your own, nobody else's.' Although that was true, she didn't have to rationalise this with Stu, so I tended not to go online when he was at home. It was better to do as he asked and take my opportunity when he was out playing golf or at a Lions Club dinner or attending a church meeting.

When I first began using Facebook, it would amuse me when somebody would request to 'be my friend.' I found that really funny and would click 'agree' with a smile on my face. As time went by I realised that there were some wierdos out there who asked perfect strangers to be their friends and I learned to click them off my page and into the nether world.

One day out of the blue I saw a post pop up. 'Rhani would like to be your friend,' it said. Well, there could only be one Rhani, my dear sweet university friend, the Rhani who had seen me through happy days and tough times at Cambridge and who had been at my wedding by the Shannon. Once the children started coming and she moved back to Bangkok to lecture and do research at a university there, I am ashamed to say, we lost touch. She was busy and so was I. It happens!

But here she was again and we could communicate. I clicked her in and she became my seventeenth Facebook friend. I was excited to be in touch again and so checked her Home Page to find out what was happening in her world.

It seemed that she had married or, at least, had partnered another Thai. They had two nut-brown, smiling faced little boys whose grins filled the screen. I wrote her a notification telling her how great she looked and filled her in on the years that had passed since we last saw each other. I was pretty thrilled that I had made contact again because she and I had shared a great deal when we were young and held a good bit of each other in our hearts.

She felt the same way and we slipped back to the firm friendship that we had enjoyed so many years before. She related how she had returned to Thailand at the end of her studies and initially had practiced medicine in her home village. She had recognised the damage that tropical diseases were causing in her community and had developed an expertise in that field so that now she was researching and lecturing on the subject at the university. 'You should come to my homeland one day, Jen,'

Rhani wrote. 'It is a beautiful country, but we have a lot of things to fix.' In the next months we communicated two or three times a week, sending photos, talking about our families, discussing our lives and exploring the Buddhist philosophy that we both shared.

Inspired by this, Wendy and I joined an online group of like minded souls who believed in Buddhism and who were willing to exchange spiritual thoughts and bring about change. It was good for my soul. Sometimes I would print off a wise thought one of them had forwarded to me and tape it to the kitchen window over the sink so that I could meditate as I prepared the meals. I introduced Rhani to this group and she, in turn, invited other practicing Buddhists of her acquaintance. This was fulfilling as it was rare in everyday life to have the opportunity to interact with so many fellow believers, chatting and exchanging ideas and thoughts with people all around the world. There were regulars and then there were people who only came online once or twice and you'd never hear from them again. This newfound dialogue with my internet Buddhist friends developed us into a tight group of like-minded souls exploring our spirituality together.

In Buddhism, you are able to choose your own spiritual adviser. It doesn't have to be a member of the hierarchy and it can be a person of either gender; it can be simply someone who is compatible and who is on the same journey with you. Generally, it would be somebody older and wiser than you, but this is not always the case and as life goes on it becomes increasingly more difficult to find a suitable guru.

I was lucky. Through the online group I found my perfect match and, as fate would have it, she was Irish, although not of Irish blood, and lived reasonably close to us. Her name was Karena and she had been born and bred in Ireland of a Danish mother and a Kenyan father, who had brought her up in a home steeped in Buddhism. She was ten years younger than me, but had a heightened spirituality and ability to listen, think and discuss that is born in only a select few people. The Buddhist philosophy was deep within her soul and very being and she lived her life according to her conscience, so she was an excellent sounding board. She was intelligent and extremely well educated, and Wendy and I were just overawed by her and sought her counsel on many occasions.

Over the next two years Karena became our mentor, which meant that we could call on her for spiritual advice anytime and organize to go to places of meditation and learning with her. She lived in south west Dublin and so sometimes when the boys were at school, Karena, Wendy and I, along with Molly in her pushchair, would ramble the walking tracks of the Wicklow Mountains, seeking peace and quiet by the beautiful waterfalls in the rolling, green countryside near her home. Sometimes we would talk, sometimes we would just be at one with nature; either way I always felt renewed after such a day with her. Her calming thoughts and forward thinking ideas keep me focussed to the point that I looked forward to connecting with her each day, however briefly. She was great for me in many ways and often calmed me when I needed it.

'Nothing is permanent but change,' Karena quoted to me one day when I finally bit the bullet and confided in her about the oppression I was experiencing from Stuart. 'Jenny,' said Karena, stroking my hand after I simply could say no more, 'you have to change.'

Well, that threw me a little. Always being the one on the receiving end of the punishment when things got out of hand, I figured that maybe Stuart might be the one who could do with some changing.

'No, no, no, Jen,' said Karena. 'You need to hear this. You can't change Stuart. Try as you will, that will never happen. The only person you can change is yourself. If you change, then Stuart will treat you differently. From your change will come his change.'

'Karena, I *do* try to modify my behaviour, even though it is a hard pill to swallow,' I said. 'But I am always resentful because it is me who has to do the accommodating. You don't seem to understand how I feel.'

She in turn quoted admired thinkers and philosophers, pointing out, 'It is your subservient behaviour that is allowing Stu to act the way he does. And the way he acts destroys everything he values. By changing yourself, you will be doing him a favour.'

She looked deep into my eyes. 'Jen, you have to respect yourself before you can command respect from others.'

So there it was, the key to it all. Respect. Respect? Respect for myself? That had been all but destroyed all those years before when I had succumbed to Tommy's wishes and aborted our baby. There was rarely a day that I did not look in the mirror and feel ashamed at what I had done.

Karena snapped me out of my thoughts. 'Jen,' she said, 'it is up to you to find peace within yourself. Meditate and take yourself to a place where Stuart cannot control how you think. You are on a journey towards spiritual enlightenment and, difficult as you find it, your liaison with him is a valuable part of that, as it will teach you those things you need to know.'

She was right. I had to renew my belief in myself. That's where it had to start. Stuart would never believe in me if I didn't believe in me.

'So, with the assistance of others, I am going to help you do it,' continued Karena. 'You need more than just me. We will establish an online support group for you.' And that is what she did. She put the word out on our Buddhist site asking people from England, Ireland and Scotland to volunteer to help me change my life. Like me, they all had things deep inside themselves that they were working on and so our mantra became, 'One small change a day.' It may not have sounded much, but we were there for each other, and that was important. Each night at 9.30 pm we would all log in and report what we had done that day. This was a journey we were all sharing, one step at a time.

To do this, I had to introduce a change to the carefully controlled daily timetable of Mrs and Mrs Stuart Hoare. The first night we were all due to report in, I was shaking with nerves. I had to assert myself and tell Stu that I was not going to watch television but work on the computer for half an hour at 9.30. He didn't like that at all. 'Jennifer, this is *my* time for watching television with *you*,' he declared.

He forbade me to do it. He was angry. I felt scared but, with the re-assuring words of Karena in my head, I quietly stood up, went into the study and turned on the computer. I could feel the waves of fury emanating from the lounge room. I expected him to appear at the door at any moment and berate me. But, for some reason, he left me alone. He must have found something on the television that had grabbed his interest. Maybe he was just too tired to start a fight. I don't know, but I had my first nightly session with my newfound support group uninterrupted. I was elated. I felt great. I had won the battle! Although, as I was to soon find out, I was just beginning the war.

The next night, I did it again. And the next night. And the next. The 9.30 sessions annoyed Stu no end but rather than start a fight about them or try and stop me, he chose the well-worn path of sarcasm and ridicule. 'Sitting up all night sprouting mumbo jumbo to all and sundry,' was how he would put it. 'Do yourself a favour and come back into the real world. You can't communicate with a bit of machinery.'

I took this all on board and thought about it, meditated on it and did much soul searching. Karena introduced me to the perfect place for such inner reflection - St Colmcille's well at the foothills of the Dublin Mountains, a beautiful place of retreat by flowing water that is said to have healing powers for the eyes. It can, they say, make you see things more clearly.

'Go to that place, wet your hands and forehead with the holy waters and meditate, then come back and tell me what you know,' Karena commanded.

On many occasions when Molly was at Montessori, I would drive up the Oldcourt Road, park my car and walk up the hill to the well. Crossing the little footbridge over the stream, I would sit on the seat near the statue of the saint and think about my life. 'Where have I disappeared to in all of this?' I would ask myself. 'I had been bright, vibrant, successful, professional. A woman who knew what she wanted and went out and got it.' I felt I was being slowly suffocated and there was little I could do to get my breath.

Stu never knew about my trips to the well, but he certainly knew about my connection to Wendy and Karena and he knew that they were part of my Buddhist community, and he disliked them intensely. Wendy was all he hated in a woman; noisy, funny, disrespectful of institutions and authority, straightforward in her opinions. He reckoned that whenever I was with her I would change, that a different woman would emerge.

'What is she doing in Ireland anyway?' he once hissed. 'What is she running away from in New Zealand? They won't have her in her own country and now she is over here putting weird ideas into your head and interfering in my life. I loathe the woman.'

Because of the way he felt towards Wendy, I tried to protect them both by holding our meetings away from home and only on week days. Only very occasionally did I ask her around to our home. But Wendy being Wendy, would often turn up unannounced and uninvited on her way past, simply to say hello or to drop off some produce from her garden or a cake she had made. She'd burst in and brighten up my day. If Stuart happened to be home, it made me uneasy. I knew I would get the lecture or the silent treatment after she had gone.

He didn't like Karena either. Not that he'd given her much of a chance as he'd only met her once or twice when she had called to collect me for a spiritual gathering. Generally I picked her up in my car as we usually headed out to the countryside, which is where most of our Celtic Buddhist gatherings were held. 'She's black and she gives me the creeps,' was his blunt assessment of the holy, gentle and spiritual Karena. So I could never really include her in our family life either. That is probably why I spent so much time on the computer. My online support was essential to my well being.

The spiritual guidance I obtained from Karena balanced the happy-go-lucky approach to life that Wendy gave out. They were the yin to my yang and with their support and wisdom I appeared content with my life in the suburbs with a grumpy, unpredictable but apparently well meaning husband and three beautiful children full of beans. Content, but hollow.

Chapter 17

I couldn't help but notice one day that one of Rhani's Facebook friends and fellow Buddhist travellers was someone called 'Tom'.

'Hmm,' I thought. 'Rhani, Cambridge, Buddhism, Tom …'

Could it be that this 'Tom' was in fact, Tommy, my first and greatest love? I hesitated a moment or two, then cautiously scrolled down. Sure enough, the profile and the picture leapt off the screen and said it all. It was him. My heart jumped, whether out of devotion or revulsion, I couldn't really say.

The more guidance I had been given by Karena and the more help from her online support group, the more I was realising that in order to attain true peace and move forward I had to forgive myself for what had gone before. And to do that, I needed to forgive Tommy.

In many ways, it probably would have been better if I hadn't gone there. But eventually I did. And in doing so I opened a can of worms. A few days after my Facebook discovery, and when Rhani was online, I took a deep breath and nervously tapped in a question. 'I see Tommy is one of your Facebook friends. What's he up to?'

I pushed the chair back from desk, shocked at what I had dared to write, and waited for the answer to appear.

'Jen,' eventually came the reply, 'I'm a bit surprised that you would ask. But if you really want to know, this is what I can tell you. I still have regular contact with his mother, Leah, because, as you know, she came from my village and sponsored me through school and university. She comes home to see her ageing parents every year and we always spend some time together. I don't think she sees much of Tom, as he now prefers to be called, as being in the music business he works vastly different hours to the rest of us. He disappoints her because he still lives the Bohemian life, has never married and has no children. She would love grandkids. She treats my boys like the grandchildren she never had. That is all I know, but I can find out more if you want.'

I immediately wrote back, 'No matter, I just saw his name, that's all. Let's leave it at that.' And as far as Rhani was concerned, we did. But it must have played on my mind, as I soon found myself telling Wendy about my experience and asking her advice.

'So, you had an abortion?' she asked slowly and carefully after I had told her the whole story. 'You. Jennifer O'Brien. You did that?'

'Wen, you had to be there!' I replied. 'I was only a kid. I didn't know what to do. He didn't want me or the baby. And I certainly couldn't tell my parents.'

'No, no, Jen, wait. Please, listen. I'm not blaming you. I'm saying that this all makes sense to me now.'

'How do you mean?'

'Jen, I've known you for years. The happy-go-lucky Jen, the devil-may-care Jen, the good mother Jen. The Jen that we all love to see. But I always suspected, always felt, that underneath there was the Jen that you did not want us to see. Not just the unhappy Jen because Stuart was going off his rocket, but the Jen that was harboring a deep, dark, hurtful sorrow. And now I know Jen, and I now I feel so sad, and I feel so sorry for you that you have carried that with you for all these years, and it makes me love you even more.'

She came over to me and we embraced and in the silence, tears flowed. Eventually Wendy pulled back and stared me straight in the eye.

'So,' she said, 'has he contacted you at all?'

'No,' I said.

'Then just leave it rest, Jen,' she advised. 'Let it go. He obviously doesn't want to be in touch and you don't need to go opening old wounds. With every love you have, a scar is left on your heart. You say you hate what he did to you, so just don't go there! You don't need hate in your life. Forgive him and move forward.'

That seemed to be wise counsel and after some thought I took her advice. However, in moments of quiet at home or in the garden, I found my mind wandering back to those carefree days of my youth when I had loved so unconditionally. Now, it was finally occurring to me that in those early, glorious days neither Tommy nor I had set conditions for our love; we had simply fallen for each other without thought or concern for the future. We had lived in the now and the plans we made were purely for that day or the next. We hadn't ask for changes from each other, in the way we looked, the way we thought or the way we acted. We had just accepted each other for what we were. Our love had been pure and unconditional. Looking back on those university days, I realised that we were innocent, idealistic and hedonistic. I was naïve and unsophisticated, as I had been lucky enough to have been brought up in a family who nurtured me, shared everything they had with me and allowed me to believe that I was the centre of everything that happened in their lives.

Mature love with Stu was so different. We had both made a deliberate choice to be in love, a physical and economic decision. We both had our own agendas; me because I needed to have children, and he to extend himself to a wife, house and family and to placate his mother who felt it was time for him to do those things. From the very beginning, our love had had a set of conditions attached. In return for family, respectability and wealth, I lived by Stuart's rules and had come to accept them as my own. When I thought seriously about it, I realised that I was always holding my tongue, altering my actions, keeping my thoughts to myself or dressing and grooming in a certain way just to appease Stuart. He was a man who knew what he wanted, did what he wanted and got what he wanted by manipulating and changing those around him.

Tommy, on the other hand, was cynical and afraid of any sort of commitment. His early family life had been abruptly disrupted and because of those circumstances, he came to feel an outcast in his father's house and a voyeur in his mother's. He was an island and when the water surrounding him became turbulent he simply retreated within himself until the storm passed.

I never really knew how our baby's abortion had affected him as we had never talked about it. Perhaps we were so young and innocent that we just didn't have the appropriate tools to communicate meaningfully. He wanted to concentrate on his drumming. I had busied myself with finishing my studies and was so distracted with my pain and hurt that I couldn't talk to anyone. It had all happened right at the time Tommy's career was just beginning to open up. He was being noticed by the big wigs in the music industry, his dreams were coming true and he was excited. My pregnancy posed a huge threat to his plans and his reaction to it was exactly the same response that his lawyer father had always demonstrated to him when confronted with a problem. 'Here, take this money, fix it, and then stay out of my life.' Perhaps Tommy didn't do what he did to me out of hatred or evil intent. Perhaps it was just a learned response?

It was the first time in more than twenty years that I had allowed myself to reflect upon these things from the past. It was new territory for me, a place I had never dared transgress before, so I found myself going back to it, remembering and wondering.

Stu noticed that I was distracted and more than once commented on it, suggesting that I should bring myself back into the real world and stop all 'this meditation nonsense.' He even proposed that I go and see Doctor Steve, our local physician, to have blood tests as my energy levels seemed to be lagging.

Of course, I talked about these things with Karena and, to a lesser extent, Wendy. They realised that I needed to debrief and so let me talk, hardly ever giving advice, just listening. I gradually began to confront what had happened and it was a blessed release. By having refused to deal with my past, I had stunted my personal development and I was festering inside. 'Forgiveness always frees the one who forgives,' Karen kept telling me. And by forgiving Tommy and therefore freeing myself I could close the book on our love.

So, I did. I looked at myself in the mirror one day and I forgave him. I even whispered the words, 'Tommy, I forgive you.' I forgave me, too. I wiped the tears from my eyes. I went downstairs. I kissed Stuart on the top of the head as he sat in his favourite chair reading the business pages. He looked up, somewhat confused, as I went outside and inhaled the distinctive salty breeze blowing up from the sea. I looked around at my beautiful garden. I smiled. I had done it. I had released my soul from the chains that had bound it. I could finally move on.

I became a much happier person and this flowed on into family life. For a time Stu and I re-found each other and instead of arcing up against him I snuggled right up to him and he was pleased. Our relationship entered a new phase, one of neautrality, but at least we were not warring. I didn't resent the intimacy so much and our lives improved.

Chapter 18

Life throws up some surprising challenges and it was right at this time, just when I had dealt with my demons from the past and attained a new domestic harmony with Stuart that everything began to crumble.

Tommy had seen my profile as Rhani's friend on Facebook and wanted to make contact again. Hence the message: 'Would you be my friend?'

Despite all my misgivings and the new-found inner peace I had discovered, the moment I saw it, my heart began to pound like that of a teenager who is about to meet her idol. I couldn't believe I was reacting in that way. I stood up and moved away from the computer and went into the kitchen and got myself a drink of water. I felt sick in the stomach, but it wasn't the nauseous kind. It was a sickly, 'Oh my God, this can't be happening to me, but I like it,' feeling. What a blast from the past! I thought I had escaped the pull of those times with that person. But I could feel myself being drawn right back in. I thought that I had put this all behind me and now here I was feeling like a schoolgirl waiting in the corridor to see the headmaster. My stomach lurched. I sat down.

The magnetism of the past was affecting my decision making. Deep down I knew that it was a dangerous thing that I would be doing, but I rationalised that my relationship with Stuart was now strong again and it wouldn't hurt to put a bit of colour into my life. 'What harm could it do?' I thought. 'After all, it would be just a Facebook friendship, it would mean absolutely nothing, no physical contact or anything like that.'

As well, I had moved on. I no longer wanted to hurt Tommy for hurting me. I had forgiven him, even though he didn't know it. Now, here was a chance to let all grudges go. To finish it once and for all! There could be no harm in it, surely. I clicked on the notification.

Less than ten minutes later the conversation bar popped up and he was online.

Hi Ya, Jobs,

Is this the one and only red headed, green-eyed, pocket rocket, Jennifer Mary O'Brien from Blackrock in Dublin? Is this the girl who stole my heart and then hotfooted back to Ireland, dropping it overboard in the English Channel so that it became soggy and wet and I never got it back?

If it is not, please disregard this silly note, it is of no consequence.

If it is, please write me a long, long letter and tell me everything that you have been doing while I have spent my whole life in sackcloth and ashes, sleeping on a bed of nails, pining for you, wishing you were here with me.
Yours ever,
Tom.

How the historian defines how the history is told. Here was Tommy telling me that *I* had broken *his* heart! When he was the one who had shattered not only my heart but my hopes, my dreams and my whole being! He had taken my sweet, innocent, young love and bashed it ruthlessly against his big bass drum so that it fragmented and frayed. He had taken my spirit and locked it in the past. I just could not believe it. In my mind, I had done the right thing and forgiven him. Now I was thinking that I should take that forgiveness back.

I walked away from the computer. I couldn't deal with this without thinking it through. I still had to consider whether such drivel warranted a reply. I did, however, know that deep down the spark was still flickering. Otherwise why would I feel like a seventeen-year-old who has just danced with Bono? I had to take a moment.

I went out, turned on the hose and began watering the veg patch. It might have been a soft day, no wind, just misty rain like lavender spray from the heavens, and the garden didn't need water. But I sprayed it anyway. As a range of conflicting thoughts ran through my brain, I noticed that because summer had been fleeting and quite cool, my aubergines had withered on the bush. My courgettes had been productive but the cold was causing them to rot. And it didn't look like my tomatoes would ripen this year. Autumn had come and the harvest was disappointing. My spring garden that had held so much promise had given only a little and in the end had failed to deliver on its potential. A bit like my life really. Maybe it needed something else to make it flourish.

I went back inside and typed, *'It is I,'* hit the Enter button and waited.

It wasn't long before the reply came.

'I am so excited,' came quickly up on the screen. *'I have never stopped thinking about you. When you left, you took my heart with you. Have you still got it?'*

Now it was my turn.

'What!!! You sent me away. You talk about your poor little heart. Tommy, you had my entire body in your hands and you squeezed it and squeezed it until there was no Jobby left, only the shell. And that is what I have had to live in since.'

I pressed Enter, turned off the computer, stood up and walked away. It was time to pick up the kiddies.

Chapter 19

Then all hell broke loose in our house. Stuart Junior had been picked as part of an under age representative hurling team to play at a two-day competition at Croke Park. This was a huge achievement and he was very excited about it. As soon as he came home from school, he phoned Stu to tell him the news but couldn't get onto him. 'Sorry, Junior,' chanted his PA, Doreen, 'he's in a very important meeting and cannot be disturbed, but I shall tell him you phoned.' He rode his bike over to tell his Nan and Pa the news and, of course, they promised to make the journey to Croke Park to watch him in action. He phoned his Grandma and Grandpa, and his uncles, and even Aunty Wendy.

He called his grand-uncle down in Kerry, where there was great excitement all round. The clan from the GAA-mad Kingdom were all so pleased and proud of him, promising they would try to make the trip up for the big match. He even went down to the elderly neighbours at the end of the street, his hurling stick under his arm, and came back home with a grin from ear to ear. He was a happy lad and apart from being unable to tell his father, he was walking on air.

When Stu didn't phone in as usual that evening, I started to get concerned, but I was busy with the children, so put it to the back of my mind. At about 9 pm, Junior was about to go to bed and as Stu still wasn't home, he sat down and wrote a note for his father containing his good news. He left it on the kitchen table. Stu hadn't made his usual phone calls that afternoon and that was just not like him. We had an understanding between us that I would not contact him at the office unless it was an emergency and so I hadn't. But I was a bit worried and I waited.

At about 9.45, Stu came in looking dreadful. His complexion was as grey as the colour of his hair, his tie was askew and his shirt was hanging out. He looked old, tired and worn down. It had been a day of hell at the office, he said. The American sub-prime meltdown had started to affect Ireland and things were going terribly wrong. The Irish economy was like a house of cards relying on foreign capital and the prosperity of the American multi-nationals to keep it steady. They were faltering and on the brink of collapse. It would have been bad enough had his firm been dealing only in their core business of insurance, but they had diversified into financial services and property development. This was now all in jeopardy and some of their investments had come to a grinding halt. The banks were on their case and many of their clients stood to lose a lot of money.

He had been talking to people all day and was knackered. He didn't eat the dinner that I had cooked for him, but instead poured himself a whiskey, swallowed it and went straight to bed. I felt sorry for him, even though he read Junior's letter without commenting or really taking it all in.

Stu was up early next day and off to the office to get organised and get some paperwork done before everyone else got in. He said that it would probably be another day like the previous one and he was dreading it. I made the appropriate 'there, there' noises but once he had gone I got the kids out of bed and went about my business as usual. Even though he had yet to tell his dad personally about his success, Junior set off for school as happy as Larry with his hurling stick in his bag. After dropping the other two off, I went home, cleaned up, hung the washing out and turned on the computer.

However, I wasn't going to get online that day. In fact, weeks would go by before I had time to turn around. Just as I was about to log in to Facebook, the phone rang and I immediately answered it thinking it was Stuart. But it wasn't. It was St Columbus' phoning to say that, not to worry, everything was all right, but Junior had been in an accident. 'Could you come and get him and take him to the hospital for x-rays?' said the voice on the line.

I hot-footed it down there to discover, to my horror, that my lad had been struck by a reversing car - one of those big four wheel drive things that is so high off the ground that there are many blind spots where you just can't see little ones. It should never have been backing in a schoolyard while the kiddies were playing. The principal, the office lady and the first aider plus the physical education teacher, Mrs Ward, were all there fussing over Junior who lay on the bed in the sick bay looking pale and shocked. The poor lad was putting on a brave face, but as soon as I walked in the door he dissolved into tears. It hurt and he was just plain scared, but the thing that upset him most of all was that he was worried that he would miss out on playing for the county in his hurling team.

Mrs Ward, who was driving the car at the time of the accident, was a nervous wreck and when she saw me she also burst into tears. She explained that she had been loading equipment into the car to take to the sports day.

'I'm so sorry, Mrs Hoare,' she said. 'I thought I would move the car just a foot or two away from the doorway that it was obstructing. I just didn't see him.'

Junior should not have been where he was, as it was a restricted area. He was on his way to share his good news with Paddy Hewat, the school's hurling coach when it happened. Fortunately, the car had been going very slowly and Mrs Ward had pulled up immediately, but the damage was done.

I felt sorry for her, as I know how easily these things happen but, all the same, I hoped it taught her something. Junior had been knocked off his feet and was not able to put any weight on his left leg.

'It's probably best to get an ambulance to take him to Accident & Emergency,' said the matron in charge of the sick bay. 'I've given him some painkillers, but he's sufferin' something awful every time he moves.' An ambulance was duly called and I climbed in the back with Junior and spent the rest of the day at Mater Hospital. They took some x-rays and decided that, as the injury was a green break, they didn't have to operate to put pins in. He would just need to have his leg plastered for six weeks and he should be as good as gold.

My heart bled for my poor lad. The previous night he had been so happy and now he was so disappointed. I was almost as sad as he was but, at the same time, pleased that the injury was not worse. It was just a broken leg and it would heal. Poor Junior cried tears again for lost opportunity and I consoled him the best I could.

I phoned Stu several times but couldn't get hold of him as he was on-site at a property development in Tallaght. So I left a message with Doreen, telling him we were at the hospital, and not to worry as it was all under control but could he please get in touch with me as soon as possible. I then telephoned my sister-in-law, Amy, asking her to collect Richard from school and to drop him off at judo practice at the Community Centre. 'Hopefully, either Stu or I will be able to pick him up from there,' I said. I arranged for my Mam to collect Molly from Montessori and to keep her at her home until I could get there.

Come 5.30 pm, half an hour away from Richard's collect time, and still no word from Stu. Where was he? The man that usually phoned me four times a day was nowhere to be found when I really needed him. I phoned Wendy who agreed to do the pick up on her way from work and to wait at home with him until somebody got there. I was too concerned about Junior to worry much about Stu. I simply worked around him, as I so often had done in the past.

It was nearly ten o'clock that night when Junior and I limped in the front door - he on crutches and me worn out from a challenging and emotional day. I was not one to dwell on what might have been but I was aware that things could easily have been much, much worse. In spite of several attempts to reach him, I still had not been able to contact Stu so I had to leave my poor fallen soldier alone at the hospital while I took a taxi to the school to collect my car and then return to the hospital to put him aboard to bring him home.

Stu had beaten me home by a few minutes, long enough to be briefed about Junior's accident by Wendy and to send Richard, who had been taking full advantage of Aunty Wen's lenient nature, off to bed. By now Wendy had gone and so I phoned Mam to give her a report and to tell her to keep Molly for the night and that I would pick her up in the morning.

I returned to the kitchen where Stu was sitting at the table with his head in his hands. I assumed he was upset about Junior so patted him on the back, made some more 'there, there' noises and set about making a quick meal of rashers and eggs for us all, telling him about our day, never asking about his. I settled Junior into bed, cleaned up the kitchen and then dragged myself up the stairs to bed.

Stu must have come later. I didn't hear him. I assumed poor Junior's devastating news, that he had been in a county team and now, through no fault of his own, was out of it, was upsetting him. How wrong I was.

Chapter 20

The following few weeks went by in a blur. Children cope with these things far better than we adults do. Junior healed well and got used to his crutches to the extent that he could move around on them like a stick insect. Eventually he all but discarded them, hopping from room to room around the house. I was always picking them up from where he left them lying, so no one would trip over them and we would have to take another journey to the hospital.

After the first few days Junior returned to school, but had to be driven, so that was an added complication to our morning routine. Of course, the school treated him with kid gloves because they were frightened of being sued. It surprised me that Stu was not more upset about the circumstances, but he didn't rant and rave at all. He continued to be pre-occupied with his work. Junior's mates had great sport decorating his plaster cast and he became a bit of a hero both in his class and in his hurling team.

The coach insisted that he come along to practice as before and gave him the job of collecting statistics about the team members, which kept him busy. He weighed each of them, took note of what they were eating, how they were training, their practice match performances, their strengths and their weaknesses. The coach would come and take a look at his sheets and earnestly discuss the figures with him. Junior made individual and team graphs and although he would rather have been on the field he was well in his element as the club statistician, just like his father would have been. He was good at maths and found himself enjoying the challenge.

'It'll help quell the disappointment,' the coach said to me. It was great for Junior as he still felt very much part of the team. But it was not good for me as they were training three nights a week and I had two other children to care for. However, I was grateful to the coach for accommodating Junior so well and was happy to do the extra running around.

In all of this, Stu was nowhere to be seen. He was spending more and more hours at the office and I suspect would hardly have known that Junior had his leg in a cast if it were not for the crutches he regularly complained about when they were carelessly left at the bottom of the stairs. 'These damn things,' he would hiss. 'I'll put the axe through them if he leaves them lying around again.'

He was always either absent or grumpy and I started to think that it was better all round when Stu was working late as we could go about our business in peace.

As so often happens, all things come at once and Mam chose this time to have a bit of a health scare. She was down at her local shops getting the paper and the milk when something came over her. 'I felt a bit dizzy, Jen,' she told me later. 'But fortunately, I was able to sit down on a big stack of newspapers until I felt a bit better again.' She somehow made it home but there was then a series of runs to the doctor and tests to be done. As it turned out, she was simply suffering from a case of low blood pressure. A few tablets fixed it up but she needed a little tender loving care and moral support.

Molly picked up a gastro bug from child care, which she passed onto the boys, so we had to contend with hurling of the other sort and the washing machine was in constant commission cleaning sheets and bedclothes. We all know how difficult they are to get dry in Ireland! As well, Mr Hoare, Stuart's father, was getting worse with his Alzheimer's. Stu's Mum needed emotional support from someone and, as no one else was around, it had to be me. I felt sorry for her as, over the years of being married to an army officer she had almost forgotten how to make her own decisions, and now she had to think and reason for the two of them. It must have really been hard.

Throughout all this, Wendy was a great support, filling the gaps when I was supposed to be in two places at the one time. She was great with Stu's mum, dropping in on her when she was passing and sometimes taking her to appointments. She laughed it off, saying it was her 'social service' and that she was sponsoring a granny in the Emerald Isle rather than a child in Africa, but I knew she was doing it to take some pressure off me. Stu was working late most nights so Wendy and I often had the chance to have a cuppa and chat before she headed home at the end of the day.

I was so busy at that time that I hardly noticed that Stu was stewing, so to speak. He was preoccupied with work and didn't take the same interest as he usually did in the boys. He was also beginning to look his age. With all the takeaways he had been eating while working back at the office he had added a few inches to his waistline. He had let his daily run slip and I don't think he was attending the gym like he had done in the past. He was drinking more whiskey and seemed to have lost interest in most things. He wasn't sleeping well and was generally an all round Mr Grumps. When he was at home we were all tiptoeing around him so as to avoid confrontation.

Like a bursting boil, it all came to a head on the weekend of the much anticipated hurling tournament. I just naturally assumed that Stu would come with us as he always had in the past. Even though Junior wasn't now playing, he was a part of the team and we were all coloured up in the two-blue strip with streamers and balloons to keep Richie and Molly amused and were ready to go.

'I just haven't got the time,' announced Stu thirty minutes before we were due to leave. 'I have far too much on my plate at the moment. In any case, Junior isn't in the team and I have no intention of sitting there for two days watching other kids run around the pitch.'

This was the worst possible thing he could say as far as Junior was concerned. The poor lad firmly believed he was an essential part of the team and even though he wouldn't be out there with his stick he would be in the coach's box keeping the stats - and that was important. By saying what he said, Stuart had taken the ground from under his good leg.

I just couldn't understand him. Internally, I was as angry as the devil himself! So, the rest of us got in the car, went to the tournament and had a great time cheering the squad on, eating the snacks and sandwiches I had packed and playing with the other children. The team did well but not enough to win. They did, however, have an excellent table of statistics.

On the Sunday night, once the children had gone up to bed, I took a deep breath, marched into Stu's study and made my stand. I figured that even if he did boil over and perhaps even attack me, then it would be worth it. This had to be said.

'Stuart,' I said straight off, 'to my mind, how you have treated Junior in this situation is totally unforgiveable. He was so keen to do well, to prove to his father that he had a talent and that he was really good at something. You were the first he wanted to tell when he got picked in the team, but you weren't around, as usual. Then, when he got hurt and couldn't play, you just dumped him. You showed you couldn't care less about him because now he was holding a clipboard instead of a hurley, and that hurt. That really hurt him.'

I was rather surprised with myself as to how easy it had all come out, in one breathless sentence. But I was even more surprised at Stuart's response. As I stood there, rock-solid with my arms tensed down by my sides, ready to take him on, Stuart looked up at me and burst out crying! He began shaking as uncontrollable sobs wracked his whole body. It was all pretty surreal. Not for the life of me would I have ever imagined Stuart, my husband, who was always in control of everything in his universe, breaking down and crying like a baby.

It was not pretty seeing a grown man bawl like that, but I held myself high and told him to, 'Pull yourself together, for God's sake.' But there was more to it than Junior's situation and I soon discovered that he'd hardly been listening to me at all, for when he finally started to speak, it came out that he was crying over money.

Good God. He wasn't crying over having let Junior down by not being at his tournament. That was regrettable.

He wasn't crying for his father who had been diagnosed with Alzheimer's disease or his poor mother who was handling a very difficult situation as her husband retreated into a childlike state. That was sad.

He wasn't crying about the reports then being published about the victims of child abuse who had had their lives ruined through sexual and physical abuse by people and institutions they trusted and who were supposed to be looking after them. That was unforgivable.

He wasn't crying about letting me down by not being there to help me through when the going got tough. That was typical.

He was crying about money, for God's sake.

Here we were sitting in a beautiful house in one of the best suburbs of the city, with three lovely children, not wanting for anything, and he was crying over money. Now I'd heard everything.

He babbled a sorry tale of how the financial markets had collapsed and how his business and his clients were suffering and how everyone was upset. I listened but was not really impressed. I didn't see how this affected us.

'Well, have you lost your business then?' I asked.

'No,' he answered, 'it's this project at Tallaght that we had such high hopes for. It's come to a halt.'

'Get a grip on yourself,' I advised, 'the sun will come up tomorrow and it will all be sorted out in the end. No one has died, you still have your company, things will be fine. Get over it and pull yourself together.'

He stared at me for a while, got up, shuffled over to the sideboard, poured himself a whiskey, sank it in one swallow, and composed himself. And I thought that was that. But not so!

'Because of all this, we will *all* have to tighten our belts a bit,' he pronounced, his voice suddenly firm again. 'I'm going to reduce the household spending budget until we come through it, if that is okay with you.' It wasn't okay with me and I let him know it. I figured I had already had one go at him and survived unscathed, so why not keep it up? 'Why should the kids and I suffer because you're so greedy and want to have the biggest nest egg in the cemetery when you die?'

This was taking things too far. He marched right up to me and hissed in my face. 'We all have to suffer, get it?'

I could see the flames simmering and knew it was time to retreat. So, I gave up and I relented – and took a 30% cut in the housekeeping budget.

But when I went shopping in the following weeks I made sure that the kiddies' things were purchased before I bought the soft toilet paper Stuart preferred, the chocolate teddy bear biscuits he liked to eat with his coffee, the sweet and sour jubes he chewed on when he was watching his sport, and the French blue vein cheese and nibbles he liked with his whiskey before dinner. I substituted cheap razors for his expensive ones and generic deodorant for his preferred designer brand. Many of the other things that he liked so much somehow did not find their way into the trolley. There is more than one way to skin a cat!

In all of this, I reckon it was the crying thing that had spooked me. He had burst into tears because he had lost money - money, I might add, that he had been stashing away for years, extra money that made no difference to the family or his business and which he had plunged into a development. For the life of me, I could not justify a grown man crying over losing a bit of spare cash when he had a good job, nice home, healthy family and status in his community. I realised that night that we certainly were from two different planets and the gulf between us was enormous, and widening.

I looked at him with disgust. There he was, sitting with his Dutch courage in his hand, eyes red and swollen from crying and his credibility lying on the floor. I walked over it and out of the room.

I angrily turned on the computer, something that I hadn't done for more than a month, checked my many emails, most of which were alerts from Facebook stating that this person or the other had written on my wall. There are two types of notification - one that is on your wall for all and sundry to see and one that is private and reserved for more personal notifications. There was a private message in the box. I clicked on it and saw it was from Tommy. I opened it without hesitation.

Chapter 21

Dear Jobby,

*Please don't dismiss me like that, I just want to talk.
I'm just so delighted to have made contact again as I have
thought of you almost every day since you went away and
left me.*

*God how I loved you! I loved your Irishness - all of it
- your laughter, the accent, the red hair and green eyes, the
little sayings and superstitions, your ability to party even
though you didn't drink, your family ties, the way you
didn't like people to get above themselves, the way you
cared for your friends, your generosity. We had such fun
didn't we? All the things we did and the people we played
with. Do you remember the Greenpeace trip to the Pacific?*

*What about the share house in Blossom Street? I
loved having you there with me, skipping along by my
side, steadying me down when I went too far, making me
laugh with your matter of fact humour, dancing all night
like there was no tomorrow, doing the dishes when there
were no clean plates, making sure we were fed, putting
drunks to bed! My friends loved having you there. You
and Rhani gave that house its soul and when you left it
was just a cold dank place. How I missed you!*

*You were such a revelation to me, so different to what
I was, and so conscientious!! You even finished your
degree.*

*That time I met your family I was so envious of the
happy way you all took the Mickey out of each other and
had so much fun together with your Irish wit and devil*

139

may care attitudes. I really envied you then and really wanted to be part of it, but it also scared the hell out of me.

You didn't take your bike back to Ireland with you. I brought it back to London with me and kept it in my bedroom for years hoping you would come back for it. Eventually I gave up hope and took it down to a charity shop a few years ago.

Do you still like to dance the night away with anyone and everyone? Is your mantra still, 'Party hard tonight because tomorrow we might all be dead?'

Do you still ooze with individual style and that zany attitude? I am sure you do because you were always so true to yourself, Jobs.

Do you still wear all those fabulous, quirky clothes? The ones that made you the envy of all the girls on the campus?

And when you have misplaced something, I suppose you still ask Saint Anthony to 'come around, something's lost and can't be found.' Sometimes I use that myself and it works!

I can't imagine you changing, please tell me you haven't. I am waiting by the computer to hear your reply.
Love always,
Tom.

Imagine remembering all of those things! I hadn't thought about anything like that for years. At least, not the good times. If I ever thought about those days at all, I always dwelled on the final twelve months, the dark times.

Now I remembered that time on the sailing ship in the Pacific when our love was so tender and young, how music dominated our every waking hour - the music we listened to and the music we made - the laughter that was ours simply because we were young, together and alive, all the people that revolved around the sweet nucleus that was us, the familiar streets of Cambridge, quiet and still in the early morning dew as I rode my bike back from Blossom Street to my college after a night on the town with the lads. Life was simple then and yes, we did have fun because the world was ours.

'Well, there's a turn up for the books,' I thought, 'Tommy telling me that he hoped I hadn't changed!' It occurred to me that Stuart had spent the past fifteen years trying to change me because he didn't totally approve of the raw material that was Jennifer Mary O'Brien. And he had all but succeeded!

I had changed, you know. I was so far from that girl that Tommy described that it just wasn't funny. I couldn't remember the last time that I'd had a good old belly laugh. Occasionally, with the Mother's Group I let loose, but now that the children were all off to pre-school, we no longer met like we used to. Wendy continued to make me smile but she didn't make me laugh out loud anymore. She was a darling and I knew she was there for me but she was reckless rather than humorous. Mam had always made me laugh because she had a bit of the devil in her and had this happy knack of cutting through the bullshit to tell something exactly the way it was in a wicked but harmless way. But I didn't see her as often as I had in the past because on weekdays I was busy with the kiddies and at weekends Stu liked me and the children to be home with him.

He made it quite clear that he found the O'Brien family hard to take, particularly my mother, who he said pampered me and could never see anything wrong with anything I did. He positively disliked my Kerry connections to the point where we hardly saw them anymore. 'They're all mad,' he would complain. 'Those bog dweller relations of yours all see me as fair game because I am a Protestant. They hold me personally responsible for all the troubles in the north and all the political fallout from Fianna Fáil. It amuses them to get me all worked up and hot under the collar.'

I really only laughed when I was alone with the kiddies - they made me laugh with their funny little ways and the innocent things they said.

My God, I thought, I had become an old curmudgeon, serious, straight, predictable and worthy. A clone of Stuart, right down to chanting his mantras!

Having considered all of this, I thanked Mary, the Blessed Mother of God, for my Buddhist faith. Without it I would have lost myself completely. Over the years it had expanded and grown, and my spirituality was a great comfort to me. On reflection it was really nice after all this time to be told by Tommy that I was not the bad person I thought I was but in fact I was still a very good person, just the way God made me. And that is why I wrote back.

Dear Tommy (Or should I say Tom now that you are all grown up?)

Where has the time gone? Was it my old Irish mate, Bernard Shaw, who said, 'Youth is wasted on the young?' He was right, we didn't appreciate it at the time, did we? We just lived it like there were no tomorrows and it was fun.

Tell me about your 'tomorrows.' Please answer the questions as set out below. Marks will be attributed according to criteria already set by examiners. Do be honest as checks will be made.

1. *Have you a wife?*
2. *Have you children?*
3. *Do you still play the drums?*
4. *Do you still see anyone from those old times?*
5. *Have you given up the weed?*
6. *Does your Dad still keep you in money?*
7. *What have you been up to since I walked out the door?*
8. *What have you learned from life?*
9. *Would you do it all again?*

There you go - just a few queries to bridge the twenty or so years since we last met. Tell me all.

On the other hand, me? Why, even I didn't recognise the girl you spoke about from times gone by. Not much of her left at all.

Profile of Jobby twenty years on:

Housewife of Dalkey ... Married to Stuart Hoare ... Three beautiful children who fill her days ... Practicing Buddhist in the Celtic Tradition ... Non-drinker ... Non-smoker ... Vegetarian ... Loves a good chat ... Boring.

That's it, there is no more. Jobby O'Brien is now Mrs Jennifer Hoare. That's who I've become.

Looking forward to hearing your reply.
Take care,
Jennifer.

I sent it off and went back to my other notifications and emails. At that point I wasn't smitten. I really thought that Tom and I could communicate in an adult way and perhaps build a friendship where there had once been a tragic love affair. Perhaps with all problems of the heart out of the way we could pick up where we were before in a civilised and non-compromising manner and we could chat about popular culture and music and other things that made the world go round. It needn't be complicated and it could be casual. It wasn't long before the reply came.

Dear Jobby (or Jennifer as you now call yourself)

You can't imagine how good it was to hear your news. I see you haven't lost your sense of humour and ability to laugh at yourself. I always envied you that; the fact that you never took yourself too seriously.

Now me, I did. In those days it was all about me; I had my plans and they were pretty much set in concrete. In fact I can't remember you ever mentioning goals and aspirations that you might have had. Did I ever ask you that? Please tell me we discussed it because sometimes I cringe when I look back and realise how egocentric I was then. Was it just me, or are all young men the same? Just to dispute your last point, you could NEVER be boring!

In answer to your questions:

1. *Have I a wife? No.*
2. *Have I children? No.*
3. *Do I still play the drums? Yes.*
4. *Do I still see anyone from the old times? Sometimes I catch up with Jacko and Mitch as they live here in London, but on the other side of the city. They both have families and are pretty tied up with work and home so it's not often. Miriam and Alex ended up getting married and they live in the countryside near Ripley in Surrey. John and Faye got married and then divorced. Arthur is a big shot at Westminster, some sort of department under-secretary. Phillip died of a drug overdose not long after you left. That sort of broke the house up as we were all horrified and shocked. With you gone, that happening, and a job offer that required me to shift, there was nothing left in Cambridge for me so I moved here to Barking Road in Canning Town in East London. It's handy to everything without being posh and I like it, the bus runs by the door and the train is down the road so I get by without a car which is good for the environment. I never did finish that Degree. Fill me in, did I ever go to lectures?*
5. *Have I given up the weed? Almost, but not entirely.*
6. *Does my Dad still keep me in money? No. After I dropped out, he gave me the classic father/son dressing down, handed me a wad of cash as a deposit on this little mid-terrace, told me I'd have to find a way of repaying the mortgage myself and*

said I was on my own from then on. He should have done that years before, because I did what he told me to do and haven't asked him for money ever since!

7. *What have I been up to since you walked out the door? I don't really remember much about the lead up to when you went. I just have this deep-down uneasy feeling that I was a real jerk, so if I did or said anything to hurt you, Jobby, I apologise. In my defence, your honour, it must be said that it all happened just when me and the guys were starting to really get somewhere with the band and it was all new and exciting - a real adrenalin rush, an amazing lifestyle. Money, drugs, sex, rock 'n' roll. All that and more! The people we met were mind blowing. I was hardly ever home and when I was, I was sleeping. But we never really capitalised on the Stones tour. We played plenty of gigs and got a bit of a fan base going, but the two singles we made never charted, the tracks we recorded for an album are sitting on a shelf somewhere and our recording contract got ripped up. We all went our separate ways and my ego was very badly dented, I can tell you. Luckily, the label said that they didn't want to lose someone with my talent and suggested that if I was prepared to relocate to London, they would keep me on as a studio drummer. After a bit of procrastination and soul-searching, that is what I did. It's supposed to be nine to five, but believe me it's all hours. However, I don't mind because this is where I want to be.*

I'm still with the same studio but I also freelance for other artists and bands.

8. What have I learned from life? You quote your Irishman, George Bernard Shaw, so I shall quote our English Bard, William Shakespeare. 'Men shut their doors against a setting sun.' That's what I did when you left, Jobby, and I don't think the sun has ever risen for me again.

9. Would I do it all again? Yes, Yes, Yes, Jobby, I'd do it all again but, given half a chance, I would do it so very differently.

YOH! Tom

PS. Your turn, don't worry about questions. Just talk to me.

I stared at the answers, then read them quickly again to make sure I hadn't missed something. That was so typical of the jerk! Not one word about what happened to me and his baby. I felt so vindicated in leaving him and should have left it there and then. But I wanted the last say.

Tom,

I can't believe what you have just told me! You say you don't remember much about the lead up to my leaving England. That makes me so angry. I do! It was horrible and it has affected the rest of my life. I loathed myself for years over it and still do. I thought I'd forgiven you, but now as well as hating myself I hate you because you can skim so lightly over the whole episode. You know what I'm talking about!

Jennifer.

As far as I was concerned that was the end of it. I hadn't needed him for the last twenty years and I was silly to be opening up old wounds. I left it there, but Tom was not going to do give up so easily.

Dear Jobby,

Please don't be like that. I have absolutely no comeback. What can I say? I was despicable and I treated you badly. We are both Buddhists and we both know that life is all about embracing change and using it to make ourselves better people. I am doing that. And in order to deal with what has gone before, I need you to forgive me so that I can move on. I know that that is not a small ask so I humbly implore you to set me free from my past. The universe has punished me - I have no partner to share my life with, I have no children to make me immortal by carrying my genes forward, I have no family I can go home to. I just have myself and my regrets, the biggest one of which is what I did to you when you needed me to hold and comfort you. We could have got through that time together but I now know that because I didn't embrace the change and go with it, I lost you. Please forgive me, precious Jobby.

I have loved you always, Tom.

What could I do? I didn't want to be the one who stood in the way of Tom's journey to self-realisation. The past was the past and I know that once we become victims to the past we cease to move forward. I had to reach out to him, offer my forgiveness and allow him to move on. After all, I had moved on myself. So I wrote back.

OK Tom, I forgive you. We will leave the past where it should be, learn from it and move on. I am happily married with three young children and my life has changed. We can be friends without fighting. We spent the best years of our lives together so let's put all the horrible things to one side and go forward from there. I felt so sad and sorry about Phillip even though that was a long time ago. He was always a bit more adventurous with drugs than the rest of us. What happened?
Jennifer.

That's how it began again. He wrote back about how Phillip had died from the effects of a particularly pure dose of heroin, and from there the communication between us began to gradually fill and colour the bits of our being. We talked about the past and about our lives at present, but never broached the subject of the future because we both conceded that there was no future for us. Tom was genuinely interested in me, the kiddies, my family, our common faith and my life in general. It was grand to have a sympathetic soul who listened with an empathetic ear.

Almost before I knew it I was addicted. I couldn't get enough. I awoke every morning planning how I would get through the chores so that I could log in to the computer and hear what Tom had to say. I never went to bed at night without first checking my messages, just in case he had written.

The communications varied between short succinct words that illustrated a thought or painted a picture to long diatribes about what we were doing, what we thought and, over time expanded to what we planned for the future. If Tom was online and available to chat, I would sit at the keyboard until the early hours.

I became possessive of the family computer. Every time I had a minute I would log on, which only raised a different tension in the house. The kiddies liked to use it for their homework and games and usually either one or other of the boys was on it from the time they came in from school until their bedtime. Like me, Junior had discovered a social networking site and he was online chatting with his schoolmates at every opportunity. When I asked could I possibly have the computer for ten minutes he'd say, 'But Mam, I'm in a three way conversation with Sean and Eoin, can't you wait a bit?' With the broken leg and all he was at a bit of a disadvantage, so I always gave in and let him have his fill of it, but not without a show of spirit. 'But you just saw them half an hour ago at school. You've been with them all day. What more can you possibly have to talk about?' And so it would go on.

Not that I think that Stu noticed our war of the airwaves. He was always vague and distracted, spending a lot of time at work and in his study. He seemed to have lost all interest in his domestic fiefdom. It was ages since he had come in from work, run his finger along the mantelpiece, looked in disdain at the dust it had collected and asked, 'What have you been doing all day?' He didn't seem to care any more.

Which was good, because I had cut corners on the housework, not because I meant to but because I was always running behind time due to having spent hours on the computer between school drop-off and pick-up time. Meals were becoming a bit hit and miss as well. I went from vetting every morsel that went into my children's mouths to not really caring much about what they ate as long as they weren't hungry. 'What's for dinner, Mam?' they would call out as outside the clouds darkened indicating that the sun had ceased trying to shine through for the day. 'How about chicken nuggets and chips/fish fingers and chips/eggs on toast/sausage rolls and ketchup/store-bought lasagne/baked beans on toast?' I'd reply, leaving the computer and coming into the kitchen. Sometimes we just drove down to the chipper and the kiddies could choose their own poison.

Stuart and I existed on a diet of Marks & Spencer or Tesco cook-at-home meals, the ones where you buy a main course, a side dish and a dessert for two, plus a bottle of wine, for eleven Euro fifty cents. Not that Stu seemed to notice; he still thought it was home cooked stuff. I had changed from a person who used to grow her own vegetables and herbs, bought organic produce, cooked lots of fresh fish and watched every portion of food my family consumed, into one who now filled them up on junk. My mantra had always been, 'You become what you eat,' and I had been determined that my children would grow up healthy and strong. But now, I just didn't have the time or energy to be fussed any more.

Wendy noticed and brought it up with me as we were walking the Cruagh Wood Path, a track that winds uphill through forest area above Dublin. We took the new, dry, mountain path that was still under construction and which led up through the forest and onto the top of the mountain so that Dublin lay spread-eagled below, the twin power station smokestacks that guarded the harbour being the most dominant feature of the otherwise flat land-scape. To take a breather we sat amongst the heather on a white, large flat stone, thinking, contemplating, taking in the sweet mountain air.

'Jen, I know it's none of my business, but...'

'Oh, here we go,' I thought, but instead replied, 'Oh yeah, what's none of your business, then?'

'Well, this is just how I see it and please tell me if you think I'm out of order. I love your kids and I hate to see you neglecting them the way you have been lately. Something is going on. Is there something wrong, something that I can help with? Are you not feeling well, have you got something you want to share? You know I am your friend and I will do whatever you want me to do.'

My hackles immediately went up and I was on my high horse. 'What do you mean neglecting my children? I have never neglected them. I am there for them day and night. How can you say that?'

'Calm down, Jen, just step back and have a look at yourself. Don't tell me that you haven't changed in these last few months, because you have. You seem to be living in your own little world. Your family and I knock on the door and you won't let us in. You seem to be always distracted, just look at the gunk you feed the children these days. It's just not like you. You used to be so fussy about what you all ate. Why have you changed, what has happened?'

I knew she was right but it really annoyed me that she was spelling it out like this. Fancy having a go at what food I served my family; now that was cheeky. She was quite right. It was really none of her business and I told her so!

Wendy wasn't one to go into her shell so she came out fighting, listing for me the occasions she knew of lately where I had either neglected the children's needs or been distracted and cross with them. I must admit I was a bit mortified because I thought that I had everything under control and that nobody could possibly know that I had become obsessed with the computer. If she had picked up on it, then maybe Stuart may have noticed as well.

Eventually, after the lecture, I took her into my confidence and told her that Tom and I were now talking on Facebook. 'Well, well, well,' she said, 'who would have ever guessed?' From being my critic, she became my friend again and we discussed first love and how it can be so bittersweet and innocent and we wondered whether anybody quite forgets that first lover. Do we not all have a little pocket at the bottom of our heart where a precious memory is encased in a delicate organza envelope and locked away only to be brought out and examined in the most private of moments? We had a bit of fun with it, laughing about the awkwardness of our youth when our sexuality was first awakened thus putting a red marker between what had been and what was to come.

That day Wendy became my fellow conspirator. Not that we had anything to conspire about because at this time it was all pretty innocent. I was merely dabbling with danger but hadn't jumped headlong into it yet.

'Take it easy, Jen,' she warned, 'don't start living permanently in cyberspace. Keep your head firmly on your shoulders and keep yourself grounded. You're the only one of my friends who has it all, so don't throw the lot away on a whim.'

I took it on board and for a few days at least I consciously limited my time on the computer and made a bigger effort to be there for the kiddies. But I wanted more.

Being a very private person, Stu hadn't said anything more to me about the Tallaght project, but I think he was finding life difficult at the golf club as some of the other members had put money into it on his recommendation. They had all loved him when he was helping them make money but now that they faced the prospect of losing it, I think they were turning on him and ostracising him, making him a scapegoat for their greed.

Lately, on a Saturday, he had begun taking Junior to golf with him, ostensibly for him to caddy and learn the game and its etiquette. But in retrospect, I think he started doing that because he felt awkward and alone amongst his fellow sharks. Edna, one of the golf club wives, had a go at me one day when I was shopping at Dunnes. Cheek of her! I was packing the groceries in the boot of the car and she came up and stood in front of me and said, 'Hello Jennifer, I see from the new Audi you're driving that your dirty, low-down, thieving husband obviously didn't take his own advice and invest his money out there at Tallaght like he advised the rest of us to do. He has left us with nothing!'

I stopped what I was doing and straightened myself up and said, 'Well, I'm sorry to hear that, Edna, but he had money in it, don't you worry. And after all, your husband is a banker! So who got us all into this mess in the first place? If I could get my hands on him, he and his banker mates would be singing in high C, and most of Ireland would be supporting me. So, tell your dirty, low-down, thieving husband that!' I slammed down the boot, turned on my heel and returned the trolley to its cage.

By the time I got back Edna had screeched out of the car park leaving a good bit of rubber from the shiny wheels of her SAAB convertible behind. I felt good about the exchange but when I related the story to Stu that evening he wasn't too impressed and it seemed to push him further into the mire.

'I wish you wouldn't fly off on a tangent like that Jennifer,' he said 'it doesn't make things any the easier for me.'

'I was simply defending your honour,' I shot back. 'Besides, it made me feel good to tell that two-faced snob exactly what I thought of her and her wanker husband.'

'Have it how you like,' he replied despondently and poured another whiskey.

Increasingly, I was becoming frustrated about not being able to access the home computer when I wanted to, so I thought that now he was feeling so defenceless it was a good time to broach the subject to see if I could persuade him to buy me a laptop for my birthday. He didn't exactly embrace the idea but I rationalised with him and told him that the children were needing the computer for homework and sometimes the two of them wanted it at once, so I felt that Richie was missing out a bit and that his school work was being compromised. Also I pointed out that soon I would be looking for a job and I would resume my career in IT so it was important that I have something portable I could use professionally.

That seemed to strike a chord. He really liked the idea of me earning some money to help with the schooling and household expenses. Give him his due, he must have listened and taken it all in, because on my birthday he brought home a good second hand laptop for me and also one for Junior. They had a few in excess at work because they had had to put off salesmen due to the recession. There was no looking back then!

Chapter 22

I now had my own computer and because it was a laptop and had wireless I could take it anywhere and communicate with Tom at any time. I was still going about my everyday business but, I have to admit, that now I could be online at any time of the day or night, the Tom thing was becoming an obsession.

While I was waiting in the car for the children I would have it going; after school drop-off, I would take it into the library and spend two hours online chatting away; on a fine night after dinner, I would call out to Stu and the kiddies that I was going for a walk, pick up the laptop and spend an hour in the park writing and talking. If I missed a day I would pine. It had become an addiction. Tom and I talked about it because he said he was behaving the same way. All the time I was online with him I had this stirred up feeling in my being, an adrenalin charge almost, knowing that I was overstepping the mark but daring anyone to stop me.

Wendy saw what was happening and warned me, 'Girl, you are getting in over your head. I hope you know where you are going with this?'

To which I replied, 'We are going nowhere, nothing has happened. We haven't even met up; it's all harmless fun on the computer.'

'Well, just be warned. In my book what you are heading toward is called cybersex, so please recognise it for what it is and armed with that information, deal with it as you will. Just because you are on the net, that doesn't mean you are not being unfaithful to Stuart. God Almighty, Jen, have a good look at what you have and don't throw it all away.' Imagine Wendy telling me to be careful! She who had acted on impulse all her life and had often messed things up big time.

'What Tom and I are doing is just chatting and talking. We are on the same wave length and he understands me, whereas Stuart doesn't. Besides, Wendy, you and I both know that Stu is not the most exciting conversationalist in the world. His pet topics are his golf game, the economy and why gays should not be allowed to marry, or do anything for that matter. Tom talks about things that interest me and he listens to what I say. There can't be anything wrong with that!'

I should have been shocked at Wendy's summation that I was on the edge of partaking in cybersex but instead I was excited. It sounded intriguing.

I did a Google search and brought up 'cybersex' on the screen. Eventually I found a site that said cybersex was an intimate sexual action that occurs when a person is in communication with another on the internet. I certainly wasn't getting my rocks off while online, although I must admit I did become excited and energised when I spoke to Tom, and the anticipation was a bit like that of a young girl when she is about to go on a date with a boy that she likes a lot.

I also read that unspoken difficulties or lack of sexual satisfaction in a relationship could lead to cybersex; that it could become addictive; that it is cheating if it goes too far. I discovered that on the internet you could conduct a courtship, send virtual flowers, plant a cyberkiss, commit to each other in an electronic wedding witnessed by an e-family and take your honeymoon in cyberspace. I gathered cybersex was like phone sex, where you connect with another person even if you can't feel or see them. It also warned there was always the possibility of moving onto the real thing.

I shrugged at that last statement, because I could not foretell any circumstance whereby Tom and I would ever meet up in the foreseeable future. He was in London, I was in Dublin, I had three children to care for and a husband who watched my every move. What was between us would stay on the internet.

I disregarded what Wendy had to say because I rationalised she was jealous that now I was online to Tom so often I was not as readily available to her as I used to be. Our friendship, although still warm, was not as intense as it had been. No doubt Stu was pleased about that.

Chapter 23

Was there a specific moment when our innocent internet chats began to get raunchy? Probably not. Suffice to say that every now and then Tom would say something that indicated that he knew me in the Biblical sense. I didn't take much notice at first. But little by little he reminded me of our passionate moments together, the things I liked, the things I disliked and the known triggers that turned me on. He said he had thought about me and fantasized about me every day since he had moved to London.

This was very complimentary to me and it sort of made up for the previous pain that Tom had caused. It was good to know that I had not just been a piece of flotsam washed up on the shores of his life, that I was a living being that was cherished in his memory. 'I have had other love affairs but they were shallow and unfulfilling,' he said, 'I have never loved anyone else like I loved you and I still do.'

I began to realise that Tom knew me more intimately than any other person and that he was still in love with me. He had been in a sad time warp, and in his mind, our love affair had grown and developed over the years. He sent me the lyrics for my favourite song of our time together, *Slow Hand*, the one by the Pointer Sisters about the lover with 'the easy touch' who won't come and go 'in a heated rush.'

He reminded me of how I would put that song on the record player at the old Blossom Street share house and dance before him, inviting him to join me in the tango of love. We would slowly circle each other, exploring, searching, moving in close embrace, sometimes touching but never fully connecting, our rhythmic movements becoming stronger and stronger with musicality and playfulness, until the final chords resulted in a rainbow of exploding bubbles and fireworks. When I read the lyrics again, it was as if I was transported back there.

Tom knew things about me that only a lover could know. 'Did your left nipple stop being inverted when you had children, like that doctor told you it would? Which of your three children can curl their tongue like you can? Have you still got that cute arse with the star-shaped raspberry mark on the left cheek that used to send me crazy? Are your pubes still blonde or did they darken with age? Can you still do that thing with your shoulder blades?'

Perhaps the questions were a bit personal, but considering what we had shared in the past I took them as conversational and took no offence. I liked them because they implied the raw intimacy that we had once shared, an intimacy that Stu and I had never truly possessed.

We did a lot of catching up. We explored all aspects of each other's lives and our ways of think-ing, so I can truthfully say it wasn't all sex at first. I simply wanted to know all about him. His music had kept him all these years, sporadically, sometimes in splendour and at other times not so elegantly. He'd paid for his house and he had enough to live on. Every now and then something would come along that would provide enough cash to keep him going for twelve to eighteen months and he would rejoice. His drumming had allowed him to travel extensively so he had seen the world, most of it from hotel rooms and entertainment venues, but nevertheless he had experienced what many people could only dream about.

His mother lived by herself now, the diminution of her sexuality finally freeing her from control by the opposite sex. She was happy and, at last, she was exclusively his. His step-sisters, the twins, had grown up to be surprisingly nice people and he saw them irregularly but often. They loved that he was able to get tickets to the best concerts and he liked to do this for them. His father and stepmother? He did not see them at all. He never really forgave them for making him redundant in his own family.

It unfolded that he had had several long-term relationships that had all broken up at about the five year mark or on the first mention of the 'm' word. Marriage was a concept that Tom did not want to know anything about. We speculated as to whether this was because of his parents' break-up, which had reduced him to always being on the outside looking in. Had this caused him to lose trust in the institution? Or was it that our own love had been so sweet that nothing that came after it could quite measure up? Tom declared that the latter was the case; that it was me that he had always wanted. 'Believe me,

Jobs,' he wrote, 'you are the one I have always been waiting for.'

Little by little our feelings became exposed and talk of the past escalated into our present circumstances. In the middle of a conversation, Tom would say something like, 'You do it to me every time, little green-eyed doll. I have become so hard just talking to you that I am going to have to unzip my jeans before I do them or myself damage.' Or, 'I had to wash the bed linen again this morning and it is your fault. I dreamt that you were in bed with me and I exploded all over the clean sheets.'

Next thing I knew, he was asking me to take my knickers off. I surprised myself by doing just that and bizarre as it may sound, I found it turned me on. That was just the beginning. Things were starting to get out of control.

After that, whenever I was on the net to Tom I made sure that I was wearing no knickers and I always told him this. That would start us going. Small talk would lead to innuendo, escalating our conversation with titillating and suggestive remarks until we reached a crescendo where we both relieved our sexual frustrations.

This was cybersex and we were enjoying it. Soon we were performing it on a regular basis. I told Wendy this and, after she had finished laughing, she said I was doing no harm to anybody except myself and therefore not to get my knickers in a twist, so to speak. 'But wouldn't it be better to have a real affair?' she suggested. 'Come with me to a club,' she begged. 'It seems that you want to get laid, so let's do it in the real world. If you really want to know what I think, I'll tell you. This cybersex business will get you nowhere. All it will do is screw with your head.' I wasn't about to be convinced.

Hi. It's your redheaded siren and I've got no knickers on.

Are you sure you have no knickers on?

They're lying on the floor at my feet. I can feel the air blowing onto my thighs and into my vagina. What are you thinking?

I'm thinking of you and of how much I want to take all my clothes off and lie with you, taking our time and just enjoying being together, touching, stroking, kissing.

That's what I want too. I want to nibble your lips and then slowly, slowly, s l o w l y move down to your nipples past that little hairy line that goes down to your manhood, smelling your smell, touching you ever so lightly, stroking your manhood, hearing your heart beating.

Your skin is so white against my brown body, you are so soft, so lovely, so beautiful. So soft and I am so hard. So lovely and I am so hard. So beautiful and I am so hard. Hard, hard, hard. Take my penis in your hands, lick it like a chocolate ice cream, up and down, up and down.

I'm doing that. Don't breathe, be still, don't move, taking it slowly, slowly, s l o w l y. I have your penis and I am licking, my tongue is lapping, licking, lipping. This ice cream is good. It tastes delicious, I want more, I am slurping it up, slurping it, slurping it, S L U R P! I want more. I can't suck it hard enough. I love chocolate ice cream.

I'll have to stand up. I can't sit down with this erection. You do it to me every time. Have as much ice cream as you want. It's a bottomless cone. Suck as much as you want. Take more.

Don't stand up, don't move. Stay still, stay perfectly still. I forbid you to move. I forbid you to do anything except breathe. Slowly. I am eating ice cream. I can't get enough. I want more. Please wait while I have more. Stay perfectly still and let me eat and suck and lick the ice cream. I have the cone in both hands and I am sucking all the ice cream you can give me. My tongue is reaching in. I want that piece way down the bottom. Wait. Stay still. My vagina is fluffy, rich and creamy just like the ice cream. I am excited.

I want you so badly Jobs. I can't hold out much more. Tell me when you are wet and ready for me. Tell me when.

My whole body is ready. My legs are wide apart, my vagina is dancing, my nipples are standing, standing and saluting. My mouth is on your penis.

Where's your bra?

It's lying on the floor with my knickers and I haven't put my top back on. I'm naked. I want you.

Your nipples are so big. Let me suck them. Ah, strawberry flavour. Can I please suck and lick your tits one at a time. I love this strawberry ice cream. Let me suck and lick, suck and lick.

Don't stop. Take it slowly. Slowly with your tongue, slowly with your hands, slowly, slowly. Let me do the same with your penis, suck and lick, suck and lick, slowly, slowly.

Don't stop. Let me rub my penis against your breast.

Please come inside me. I want you inside me. Come inside where it's soft and warm.

I'm gently coming inside you, so slowly, so slow.

I can wait. Tell me when you are ready to explode and we will do it together.

Yes.

Now, Tom, now.

Yes. Yes, yes, yes.

Tom?

That was good, Jobs, better than good. Beautiful, out of this world. Thank you my lovely girl.

I suppose you could say it was weird because it was all in the mind. None of it was real and that is why I didn't feel guilty. I wasn't doing anything except imagine.

The Irish Catholic schoolgirl in me had me justifying myself by thinking, 'Well, I'm not doing any harm and at least, this way I won't get pregnant.' In any case, I asked myself, 'How come Stuart cannot bring me to a climax and yet Tom can by just talking me through it?' I rationalised that I was just masturbating. I was a healthy woman who wasn't attaining sexual satisfaction within her marriage so I had taken it on myself to do something about it. I didn't really want to believe that I was cheating on Stuart because, to me, it was all words and no action. 'It must be good for my mental health,' I said to myself.

Nevertheless, I was really surprised at the depth of the sexual feeling Tom was able to awaken in me. He could take me to that place in the Pacific with the sails flapping in the breeze when the world belonged to the two of us, where the waves lapped gently against the ship as we lay on the bunk excitedly exploring each other's bodies, whispering to each other lest we wake the other sleeping crew.

I was now a woman in her forties who had resigned herself to an almost celibate life. I hadn't reached a climax since before the children came along, so this cybersex stuff made me feel pretty wonderful. I knew that we were heading down a dangerous road but I loved the adrenalin rush. It made me feel alive.

Don't ask me where Stu was when all of this was going on. Because I don't know! I wasn't paying attention. I do know he was grumpy most of the time and had no patience with me at all. Things that I had always done and which he had found strangely endearing, he now could not tolerate. He hated my freewheeling attitude to discipline with the children, the fact that I increasingly managed to leave a trail of untidiness behind me wherever I went and the way I put my spirituality ahead of the many things he deemed important. Sometimes I didn't even have a shirt ironed for him!

I knew I had taken my eye off the ball as far as the children were concerned. I just wasn't as attentive or in tune with their needs as much as I had been. One of the mums at school had a go at me, claiming that Richie was bullying her son. I was tired from being up late the night before and my coping skills were low. In any case, her son was a bit of a pansy so I let her have it, drawing on some of the things Stu would say to me about mollycoddling boys. 'If you're not careful, he will grow up to be homosexual,' I said to her. She was more than a bit upset, telling me, 'I brought this matter up with you, Jenny, because I thought that you should know that Richie is not a nice boy of late. It just isn't like him. I only told you because, as his mother, you might be able to find out if something happening in his life is making him angry. I am fond of Rich and I thought that I was doing the right thing by alerting you to this. But from the way you are reacting it is obvious to me that you don't want to know about it. So just to let you know that I will be keeping Dominic away from Rich until his attitude changes. Sorry, but that's all I can do.'

Apparently she told her husband, who had a word to Stu. 'Why do you never think before you speak, Jennifer? You always jump in, boots and all,' he growled at me later. 'Your tongue will get you into more trouble than enough. Why couldn't you stop long enough to think that her husband is a surgeon and the match day co-ordinator at the golf club? I have to deal with him and you don't make it easy. You're becoming a bitch, so curb your tongue, woman.'

Family life went on; Junior's broken leg mended and he was back to his sport again; Richie showed promise on the piano and had begun to go in eisteddfod competitions; and Molly just hung out with me when she wasn't at pre-school. Stuart became more demanding and sadly I cared less and less what he thought. I'd always been up for a good argument and I had decided that I was not going to bow to his every instruction any more. He would just have to learn to cope, even if he didn't find it easy.

I continued to go on my meditation walks with Wendy and Karena and some of those things we discussed and some we didn't. Karena was not in the slightest interested in the physical side of my life. To her it was irrelevant to our spiritual liaison and although she would allow me some words about what Tom and I were up to, she would always cut me short by saying something like, 'Please, this is between you, your husband and this man, do not involve me.'

Wendy, on the other hand, despite her concerns about the danger, was all ears and wanted to know the ins and outs of everything. She was also there for me when needed and picked up the kiddies and minded them or took them places if I was otherwise engaged. I think she was secretly pleased that it was me who was getting herself into a pickle for a change and not her as usual. But to give her credit, she did warn me about becoming addicted to cybersex, continually counselling, 'If you're going to get your rocks off, Jen, do it in the real world, it's much more fun.'

I knew Wendy was right and that I was starting to lose touch with reality. My life had begun to revolve around my virtual existence. Even when I was not on the computer I was thinking and anticipating what Tom and I would do when we next connected. Once I sat down to that keyboard I lost all sense of time. One day I even forgot to pick up Molly and Stu was called at the office. He was not happy at all about that but I pretended that I had had a migraine and had been home asleep in a darkened room.

Dinner was rarely on time, the chores weren't getting done and I hardly saw friends or family any more. I became very sneaky about my computer use and lied about when and for how long I was using it. I realised that it was all getting very weird and something had to be done to stop it or at least back off a bit, but I didn't want to lose Tom now that I had rediscovered him.

I voiced these concerns to Tom and after some discussion we decided that we should put the cybersex to bed, so to speak, and to meet up to determine for once and for all what we really thought about each other. 'For the sanity of both of us, we need to take this relationship to a more rational state,' I said. 'This will sort it out one way or the other.'

We realised that getting together would be difficult as we were living in two different countries. We also agreed that it was probably better to meet in London than in Dublin, still a very small town by comparison where everyone knew everyone else's business. As luck would have it, the fares on Ryanair were getting cheaper by the minute and so as a cover, we devised a Buddhist Yoga weekend.

'Stuart won't be suspicious of that,' I told Tom. 'I've been on these before and, although he doesn't like it, he usually relents after he's given me one of his sermons about the inherent weakness of a Godless philosophy.'

In any case, I was going and that was that.

I set the stage by going out of my way to be nice to Stu and making a concerted effort to get things right at home so as not to arouse suspicion. I mentioned that there was a weekend coming up at Stonehenge to celebrate the Summer Solstice and that my Buddhist group was making the pilgrimage. I put it to him that I felt I needed the time out because I had been getting a lot of migraines and that a solid dose of spirituality would do me the world of good. 'I know I haven't been easy to live with, darling, but this should clear the air,' I said.

With a flourish, I marked it on the house calendar - June 21, a Saturday - confirming with Stu that if I could go ahead I would arrange for the kiddies to be cared for. He was miffed and a little hurt when it dawned on him that that I would choose to go away on our wedding anniversary. I pointed out that I couldn't change the Summer Solstice and that instead we would celebrate on the Thursday before. He was not happy but after a fair bit of cajoling he finally said 'yes'. When I told him that Wendy had agreed to care for the children in our home, he quickly volunteered to do the job himself.

'I'll be fine,' he said. 'Just leave it to me.'

Just as I suspected, he didn't want to have to put up with Wendy all weekend!

Chapter 24

You can't imagine how excited and on edge I was about the forthcoming tryst. But before I could set out to see Tommy again for the first time in twenty years, there was one important thing I had to do. Tell my mother the whole story.

So when I asked her to care for Molly while I was away, as I felt the boys would be enough for Stu to handle and I didn't want him to be stressed any more than he already was, I told Mam everything. I told her about my early love affair, the abortion, my despair afterwards and our soulless marriage. Of course, she was shocked.

'And why could you not have taken me into your confidence and told me these things at the time?' she asked. 'For the love of God I am your Mam, I had a right to know when my only daughter was suffering. And an abortion! You know what I think about that. That's murder. Sure, I would have brought up the dear little mite myself if I had known. I knew that things weren't right when you first came home but you never told me. How could you leave me out in the cold like that - and me, your own mother?'

'Mam, how could I have told you? I could never have come home to Ireland pregnant. You and Da would have disowned me. I had no choice. You would have been so ashamed to face up to the neighbours and the priest. You know that you would have been so disappointed with me; you would have thought I had committed a mortal sin and that I would go to straight to Hell; you would never have understood.'

Mum was hurt that I had not trusted in her, but deep down she knew that what I said was right. In those days she and Da were so fiercely Catholic that they would have chosen the Pope over their own daughter. That was just the way it was then in Ireland. 'And now you want me to help you to deceive Stuart. You want me to stand by and watch you break up my grandchildren's home. You want to dredge up the past with no thought for the future and you want me to help. Mark my words, it's a dangerous thing you are doing, Jennifer.'

Mam did her best to make me see reason and cancel the trip but I was determined and somehow talked her round. I got her on my side by revealing that Stu and I had been living a parallel existence for years. 'We're not really a husband and wife anymore, Mam,' I said. I stressed that I needed to meet with Tom for my own mental health so that I could reach closure on the past. I did not add that I needed to test this new relationship with Tom to see where it was taking us.

'Ma, I need to forgive him,' I said.

She remembered how broken hearted I had been when I had first returned to Ireland. Although it didn't exactly please her, she saw my anguish and my delicate mental state.

'I understand now. I understand a lot of things now,' she said. 'I'm sorry I wasn't there for you, Jen. I really am, but you know that was how your father and I were and how we thought in those days. It's the grandchildren who have taught me a lot of things, they have made me rethink some of my ideas. I'll help you but I'm not agreeing with you. So, what do you want me to do?'

Reluctantly, she agreed to take Molly for the three days. Of course, this was excellent cover for me as Stu would never dream that Mam would conspire with me on something so sinful.

The big day came and I was like one of those rubber beds that self inflate once they are released from their bag. I was excited and rearing to go but had to keep a lid on it so that Stu wouldn't suspect.

Wendy came by to pick me up to take me to the airport and Stu just naturally assumed that she was making the journey to London with me which, of course, she wasn't. The boys were ready to go to their hurling, so with a few last instructions about casseroles in the oven and clean clothes drying in the boiler cupboard, I gave kisses all around and I was off and out of there. I had done it. I had flown free. Wendy and I sang all the way to the airport and I didn't even feel guilty.

The other end is all a blur. I flew into Stansted and was planning to take the train to London as Tom didn't have a car, so it made sense to meet him at Liverpool Street. But as I walked off the plane with just my hand luggage, there he was, outside the landing gate waiting amongst a throng of people; I would have known him anywhere. Slight build, tanned skin, beautiful Eurasian features and a smile that lit up his black eyes. That was my Tom and the years had been good to him. He caught me unawares as I wasn't expecting him to be at the airport.

Time peeled back, we rushed into each other's arms as if we belonged exactly there. I could feel his heart beating against his brown velveteen sports jacket and although he wasn't a tall man, my head fitted perfectly in the comfy groove between his shoulders and the arm that was encircling me. In the intervening years he had filled out a little, growing from a boy to a man, solid and comfortable. I rested there and stayed, taking in his smell, his feel, his aura. I was at peace. I was home.

Eventually one of us stirred and we withdrew ourselves from our reverie, stood back and just looked at each other. The amazing thing was that it just felt so natural. Now that we were physically together, there was no sexual tension. We didn't want to race each other off to bed there and then. We both knew that would come when we were alone. For the moment we were happy just to be, to relish each precious moment, to be each in the other's company.

We decided against the train and instead hailed a cab. The driver was one of those talkative chaps who had an opinion on everything - the traffic which was getting worse by the day, the economy which was going quickly down the gurgler, the politicians who had their sticky fingers in everyone's pockets claiming expenses that would keep an average family for two years, the war in Afghanistan that was going from nowhere to hell, the marriage breakup between Peter Andre and Katie Price. We didn't care. We sat in the back with our fingers firmly intertwined, making appropriate 'mmmm' noises and letting him expound away on his pet topics. I put my head on Tom's shoulder and let it all whiz by me.

Once we arrived at Barking Road, Tom paid the fare, adding a good tip, picked up my bag and rattled his keys as he opened the front door. He put the bag in the hall and pulled me inside, taking me in an embrace and holding me like he never ever wanted to let go. I relaxed and stayed still taking in his essence and knowing that this felt so pure and right. I put all thought of anything else out of my mind except this moment, Tom and me.

There was no going back now.

Tom led me to the bedroom where we undressed, one piece of clothing at a time, and after each reveal we resumed our embrace until we could move on and discover more. Eventually, clothes divested, each stood naked before the other, no pretensions, looking at each other and slowly moving forward into an embrace, my fair white skin touching and melding with his brown wiry torso, his penis coming out to greet me and pushing its way to where it needed to be. Once again, we danced the dance of love, moving together, mesmerised, unified. When we could take it no more he moved inside me and paused, relishing our closeness, at one in our stillness. Silence, then a rush of blood! The slow waltz metamorphosised into the sensual beating of African drums, ever increasing in depth and tempo. Louder, stronger, louder, stronger - and then release.

Our love making was passionate but gentle, desperate but unhurried, sensuous and tender. More than twenty years had passed since we had loved together but it was almost as if only we possessed the guide map to each other's bodies; we were so right for each other, fitting gloriously together and moving each other like finely tuned gears on a luxury motor car. No other person ever had or ever could make me feel like Tom did. We were one.

That weekend we didn't move outside of Tom's house, which was very much a bachelor's pad. It had all the home comforts without any grand design, the furniture was just where it happened to be and there was absolutely no attempt to match anything. No Feng Shui here! A set of expensive drums was in one corner, the same corner as a small drinks fridge, in fact. There was a large black leather couch and a red arm chair in front of a big television, a coffee table and a few odd chairs, lots of electrical equipment of one kind or another, an 80s kitchen that was clean without being spotless, a fridge which had more drinks in it than food, a dining room with a table covered in books and paperwork, and a couple of bedrooms.

Tom told me he had bought new sheets for his bed as the ones he had been using were threadbare. So different from my own stylish house, but it felt absolutely right. We talked, we ate, we made love, we talked some more. It was all about us. We were alone in our world, together at last.

The weekend passed all too quickly and I found myself a reluctant traveller, on the aeroplane and back to family and reality. The horse had bolted.

Chapter 25

'I have been thinking about us for a long time now,' Tom had said as I was about to leave for Dublin, 'I have something in the pipeline which I have been working on, so don't worry, it won't be long before we are together again. I will organise it and let you know.'

'What about Stuart?' I worried, 'what should I tell him? I know I want to be with you, but I don't want to lose my children. If I don't handle him right he will turn on me and he won't let me near the kiddies. What am I going to do?'

We had stirred a hornet's nest and I knew it.

'Leave it with me. We'll carry on like we have been and we won't say a word just yet. I know things have changed now and there's no going back. We'll work it out together but don't rush into things. Trust me. I won't let you down.'

He told me that he had all but secured a drumming gig in Dublin at the RTE studios where they were producing a new quiz show called something like *Who, What, When?*, a show of music memorabilia where the studio band played riffs of pop numbers of the day and of days gone by and which the contestants had to try and recognise and then buzz in first. It was to be filming three days a week, Tuesday, Wednesday, Thursday, once a month for the next six months and, if it took off, another six months after that. Tom would be in Dublin for four days every month. He was awaiting confirmation.

I think that is the only reason I could return to Dublin that day; I knew I would see him soon.

Stu and the boys met me at the airport. They had enjoyed the weekend but they were pleased to see me. When we picked up Molly from Mam's on the way through, I promised her discreetly that I would fill her in when next I saw her, thanked her and Da and didn't dally. Things were a bit strained between Stu and me, but the kiddies had so many things to tell me that I think it passed unnoticed. I said the weekend was good but tiring and I went early to bed, not long after I had settled the children down. I lay in my bed, reliving and savouring the weekend in my mind and dreaming of Tom, just as I would do every night from then until he came to town.

I took up my life where I had left off, and even though I knew things would never be the same, it really surprised me how easy it was to carry out an affair. Of course I had to be a good liar, but I had pretty much mastered that; I needed a compliant co-conspirator and surprisingly, my Mam was reluctantly filling that role. The day after my return we spent two hours having a good heart to heart in the kitchen at her place. Mam told me that she thought I was self absorbed and that I should put Stuart and the children first and stop this affair while it was still in its embryonic stages. She found it hard to fathom why I would put all Stu and I had built up in jeopardy for a man who had treated me so badly in the past and she questioned my wisdom and integrity in wanting to pursue this affair.

'The fact is, Mam,' I said, 'that now I have rediscovered Tom I cannot live without him. If I stay with Stuart my life will be a lie and that is not fair to him, me or the children. The universe has offered me a second chance and I don't want to go to my grave knowing that I threw it back at her. Life is about change and I have changed. I want to be with Tom.'

'And what about the children?' said Mam, wringing the tea towel she had in her hands. 'You know that Stuart will never part with the children. Where do the children come in all of this, Jennifer?'

I knew I was in strife because she never called me anything but 'Jen' or 'Lovie' unless she was annoyed with me and then it was 'Jennifer' with a long roll of the tongue on the 'er'. She was not a happy mammy.

'Don't think I haven't thought about the kiddies, Mam, because I have. I have done nothing but think about them and I know they will be better off in a house where there is no acrimony. You don't know what it is like at home now. It's not been a happy place for a long time. I'm miserable, the children tiptoe around in case they irk Stuart and he blows his fuse at them and I just try to keep out of his way. The boys were happier at home by themselves with Stu while I was in London because there was no tension in the house. Junior told me that. He said, "Mam, Da was really good fun when you were away, we got the hurleys out and had a five a side game with the other boys in the park and we came home, got take-away and played Monopoly that went on just about all night. Then the next day we went through the castle and saw some of the new things they've got there now. And we went over to Gran's place and had one of her delicious roasts. Grandpa was funny, he kept forgetting our names."

'So, you see, when I'm not there Stuart is more relaxed and the boys have a good time with him. They don't seem to need me so much now. But I won't do anything until I know they will be okay. Promise!'

At that point Da, who had been sitting reading the paper at the table and apparently not listening, entered the debate. He put the paper down, took his reading glasses from his nose and laid them carefully on the table, stood up, shook his index finger at me and warned, 'Jennifer, if you do this thing and throw your marriage vows out the window, then you are not welcome in my house. That is not how we brought you up. You have three children and a husband to consider. It's not just about you anymore, so don't you go doing anything that will destroy your family. I mean it. Look at Paddy. He went off on a whim with his secretary and look what's happened! The house had to be sold, Kathy has gone home to Tipperary and taken the children out of their schools and away from their friends and we don't see them any more and neither does Paddy. And the secretary woke up one morning, took a look at Paddy after a night on the lash and decided that he was too old for her and took off to backpack in Australia. So he's left looking at the bottom of his glass of stout in an empty apartment and the children are running around with spud farmers. Don't do it Jennifer.' He sat down and thumped the table to emphasise the words, 'What God has put together, let no man put asunder.'

'Da, you can't mean that. I'm a grown woman and I make my own decisions. I love Tom, I don't love Stuart. I have to follow my heart and even though I would like your blessing, I don't need it.'

'Be that as it may, Jennifer, but in the name of the Good Lord, I mean what I say. We never brought you up to be an adulteress. Stuart is your husband and the father of your children. You take yourself off home and work it out with him. You have no right to break up the children's home. I will have no part in any of this.'

I burst into tears. Da had never laid down the law with me in his life. Surely he couldn't mean what he was saying? He was turning on me. I got up and left the kitchen, not looking back. I didn't need their approval. I was a grown woman, for God's sake, and even though I would have liked them to understand and be on my side, I could do what I wanted. Still, it made me sad as I had never before had a falling out with Mam and Da.

Wendy proved to be surprisingly moral about the whole situation, which didn't really sit well as she was the lady who'd had as many affairs and one night stands as she'd had menstrual periods. I suggested that and she indignantly replied, 'This is not about me, Jen, it is about you and your family. Sure, I know that Stuart is not the most exciting

184

person in the world, but he is solid and he is faithful and he is reliable. They are three impressive characteristics these days in any man. I love your family, Jen, and I don't want them to be unhappy because you make a bad decision. Please, just take a step back and look at what you have here. Do this thing if you must but make sure it is love and not lust that you have with this Tom fellow.'

Nevertheless, Wendy was my friend and she was on my side. She said she would support me in what ever I decided to do, knowing that I was determined to follow my heart.

Before Tom's first visit to Dublin on the third week of that month I was beside myself with excitement and anticipation. We agreed to meet in his hotel room as soon as I had seen the children off for the day. He had to be in the studio at 3.00 pm so that fitted in well with my timetable. In the lead up I did all those things that a girl does to make herself pretty for her lover; I shaved under my arms, waxed my legs, my landing strip and my eyebrows, put on my sexiest underwear, pondered over the outfit I would wear, applied my favourite perfume and washed and blow dried my hair.

On the drive into town, my stomach was churning with anticipation. Room 212. I knocked on the door and there he stood in his boxer shorts. We fell into each other's arms and stayed that way until it was time to go our separate ways, me to pick up the children and him to do his television show. At 11.30 am I took my phone call from Stuart as usual. For three days between the hours of 9.30 am and 2.30

pm that hotel room was our world. That was the only place I wanted to be. Of course I was distracted at home - but because Tom was tied up with his work I wasn't on the internet in the evening and so I kept up with my domestic duties, planning ahead and getting everything done. With the first month of our affair gone, I knew that I had to be with Tom and I waited impatiently until he would come again. I had to start thinking and planning for what lay ahead.

I hadn't seen or heard from Mam and Da since the day in the kitchen when I had rushed out in tears. Surprisingly I hadn't really missed them as I had been looking forward to Tom's visit and so two weeks had passed when I got a call from my lovely mother.

'Jen,' she said, 'I don't want us to be enemies over an affair of the heart. Let's forget that we ever spoke about it because I really don't need to know. Let's just go on as we were. Now if you want me to mind the children, or to come over to the house, just ask me like you used to do, but I don't want to know any reason. I'll just come and look after the children and that will be that. And you needn't bring your father into this. He has his ideas and we'll just leave it at that. He doesn't need to be bothered. Just ask me if you need anything or if you want to talk. But not in front of your Da, now mind! I'm doing this because I want you to be happy. I don't approve of it, mind, but I wasn't there for you when you were younger and I feel very bad about that. I'm trying to make it up to you and I am praying to the Blessed Virgin that you chose Stu and your family. The way I see it,

Jenny sweetness, it's an infatuation; if you get the sex side of things out of the way you will see reason and find that it's just lust. That's all I'll say, but you have to sort this out. Don't forget now that I am praying to St Theresa of the Little Flower, the Patron Saint of Purity for you. She won't let me down.'

In that way, Mam became my fellow conspirator.

The boys were at the age when they were becoming more independent each day and making their own way to and from school. Each had his own house key plus a mobile phone for emergencies and communication with home. They let themselves in after school and were quite happy to be at home by themselves. On subsequent months Mam filled in for me as far as Molly was concerned, so on days when I saw Tom, she picked her up and looked after her until I could get back from the city. I never mentioned where I was going, just saying that I was going into Dublin. Mam and Da loved having the little one around, so Mam didn't complain and Da was so tired from the childminding duties when I picked her up that he asked no questions. It became a pattern that on the third week of every month Tom and I squeezed our love affair in between children, drumming commitments and Stu's daily phone calls.

You learn to be a good liar when you are carrying out an illicit relationship. The first time my mobile rang when we were in the full flight of passion, Tom said to ignore it. I couldn't do that as I knew who it was and to not answer would have instantly drawn suspicion, so I answered it and carried on a polite conversation with Stu as if I was working in the garden. Tom was incredulous when I told him that Stu phoned four times a day. 'That man is a total control freak,' he said, 'it's a wonder he doesn't give you a time sheet to fill in.'

We mostly met at the hotel but on a couple of occasions Tom came to the house. The first time he came home with me was because he insisted on seeing where I had lived for the previous two decades. We intended just to take a quick trip there, have a cup of coffee and a look around the place, and then go back to the hotel. But we very nearly came undone. Stu unexpectedly came home to pick up some papers and Tom had to disappear pronto out the back and hide behind the garden shed.

Fortunately we had innocently been eating lunch when we heard Stu's car pull up. It had a diesel engine with a distinct, recognisable sound that resonated against the garage walls. The family always knew when he was arriving home. As luck would have it, he stopped for a couple of minutes to chat to the postman who happened to be at the top of the driveway and so I had time to hastily gather up the dishes from the table and begin washing up.

'Have you had people here?' asked Stu when he saw me at the sink.

'Just Mam! She dropped by and has taken Molly down to see the seals. I got caught up in the garden, so I'm a bit behind schedule. Do you want me to make you a sandwich?' Luckily, he didn't as he was meeting somebody for lunch and he needed the documents, so he threw a kiss my way and made a hasty exit.

Tom came in from the cold as soon as the car purred off down the street. The adrenalin was pumping so hard in our bodies that we made hard, passionate love there and then on the family room couch. The blinds weren't drawn but I didn't think any of the neighbours could see in. We were getting careless.

Another time, Junior was at home with the 'flu. I telephoned Tom and said that I couldn't come in as my child was sick but he insisted that he come to me, so what could I do? I knew it was risky but our end of the house was away from the children's bedrooms, so I settled my sick boy with the television and a laptop, made sure he had plenty of water and was comfortable and locked our bedroom door with me and Tom inside.

Afterwards, Junior came into the kitchen as we were drinking tea together but I normalised the situation by introducing him to Tom. They had a chat about pop music and the new bands in Ireland and the UK and Junior tried to explain the game of hurling to him. They got along famously and although I didn't like having Tom at home on my turf, I think that we were both so natural about it that Junior went back to bed and forgot the whole episode. At least, I hoped that he would.

Chapter 26

I was committed. There was definitely no turning around now. I knew the time was drawing near to confront Stu and to face the consequences. I was getting pressure from Tom as well.

'We have wasted too many years already,' Tom pleaded. 'Let's not lose any more of our time together. Come and live with me in London.'

'But, how are we going to get by?' I said. 'The money you get from your drumming is only just enough for you.'

'You've been married for nearly twenty years and brought up Stu's three children, so he will have to pay up. You'll get half of everything. We can buy something bigger with plenty of room for the kids to come and visit. Please, let's move on and do what we have to do now.'

If only it was as easy as that! Not long after, however, my hand was forced when the shite really hit the fan. Stu, who all along had appeared as if he was completely unaware of all that was happening around him, put two and two together and worked out that I was spending far too much time on the computer.

Apparently he had done some research and had got the boys to describe some of the features of their social sites and, armed with this information, had pried into my page. He had somehow worked out that my Facebook password was 'Molly', and voila!

He spotted Tom's picture in my short list of friends and immediately assumed I was having an affair with him. To me, the fact that I was, was irrelevant. What concerned me was that Stuart would jump to such a conclusion when I had been faithful to him all those years and had never put a foot wrong. This to me was proof that there was no longer any trust left in our relationship.

How he picked it was Tom that was the culprit was also a mystery, as I could not remember ever having told him anything about my university love life and there were other men in our Buddhist group whose pictures were amongst my friends. It just didn't add up. Perhaps it was just a lucky guess.

One evening he stalked into the study where I was talking on Facebook, not, as it happened, to Tom but to Karena, who was helping me reach nirvana, and went ballistic. Completely out of his head! He slammed the lid of the computer down catching my thumb, bruising it badly, and grabbed me by the hair, pulling my head right back until it almost rested on my shoulder blades. My face was looking up into his as he steamed over me, frothing at the mouth. He had me so tightly held that I had to push myself down into the chair. He twisted his grip, removing whole chunks of hair from my head.

'You slut!' he hissed, 'tell me about that feck-arsed Tom. You feckin' dirty, slut, tell me about that half Asian, half English, short arsed, drumming, drug infested bastard that is after you for my money. Tell me!!!'

It crossed my mind to deny it as he could have been just guessing and was waiting for my reaction. I struggled in my seat, but he kept his grip on my hair.

'He's just a university friend, one of Rhani's mates. I've known him for years so leave me alone. You will make me hate you if you continue to act like this.'

'Hate me if you like but I know about you and that half caste,' he carefully enunciated in a soft menacing voice at the same time giving me a karate type punch to my ribs for good measure. The one that comes in low and hard with hardly any back-swing. It packed a lot of energy and I crumpled. It hurt like it was splitting me in two but I tried not to give him the satisfaction of seeing me cry out in pain. I couldn't anyway. It hurt too much and I was winded.

'I know about London when you had your old mother and me looking after the children while you had a break. You made fools out of us. Fools! You bitch, how you could do that?' He pushed me across the room so that I hit the wall.

Bending over in agony, I sobbed, 'All right, okay, I will tell you. I love Tom. I don't love you. You disgust me! You have no control over me any more, I love Tom and Tom loves me, so piss off.'

He grabbed the computer from the desk and threw it out the open window and onto the driveway underneath, smashing it so that bits flew off in all directions. He turned and stormed out muttering something like, 'Tom, Tom, the feckin' piper's son …'

This row caused the kiddies to unplug their personas from the television in the family room where they had been glued to *The Simpsons* and come to the bottom of the stairs. Stu pressed past them, out the door, into the car and disappeared up the street in a spin of tyres. Richie and Junior looked in bewilderment up the stairs, 'Are you OK, Ma?' Junior called. They stood there for a few minutes, concerned but unsure of what to do, before returning to their show.

'Are you and Daddy angry at one another?' asked Molly in a tiny voice at my side. 'Please don't cry Mummy.'

Angry! I was more than angry. I could hardly straighten myself up where he had punched me and every time I breathed I struggled to catch my breath. I was now determined that this thing would reach resolution and that there was no way that I would stay with that man. I was not in love with Stuart and now I had no respect for him; I loathed the man. I was in love with Tom and to be true to myself, I had to leave this relationship. I was resolved!

Pulling myself together as best I could, I packed a bag for Molly and as I passed the family room I informed the boys that we were going to Nanny's house and I would be back tomorrow. They were fixated on the antics of Homer and Bart and although they looked up and grunted, they didn't seem too concerned.

Mam and Da were horrified when I turned up at their place with Molly in tow, me in tears and hardly able to move without crying out in pain, my thumb all swollen and bruised and with lumps of my red hair missing. Mam put Molly down to bed while I telephoned Tom. After that, my parents and I talked well into the night. Fortunately, they already knew a lot of the sorry saga but realised now the situation had escalated to a violent one and something needed to be done.

Next morning Da spoke separately to Stuart on the phone in order to assess the situation and to gain a perspective. Stuart was remorseful and explained that he had been pushed and felt within his rights to rough me up a bit. I was his wife and I had been having an affair. It was to stop. Da agreed with him and promised that he would do his best to talk sense into me. I felt betrayed.

Da also phoned Tom and told him that he was supporting Stuart and the marriage and that he would appreciate it if he didn't come over making trouble for innocent families. Apparently Tom told Da that he would go to the world's end and back for me, that he would come to Ireland on the next plane and collect me and take me home with him, that we belonged together and that I was not to go back to that violent house with Stuart.

Da told Tom to stay where he was and not to come over here causing more trouble than he already had, just feck off and stay away. Tom had only met Da once in his life and so he wasn't going to be taking orders from him and he told him so.

While this was all happening, Mam came with me to the doctor's surgery to have my injuries documented. As it turned out, it was no wonder that

I was in so much pain, the bastard had broken two ribs. 'Do nothing, you must wait for them to heal themselves,' was the doctor's advice. He strapped my swollen thumb and gave me painkillers for my ribs.

When we got home, Da had made his calls and had been doing a bit of thinking. 'Stuart needs to be confronted about his behaviour in person,' he suggested, 'and you, Jennifer, should not be doing that alone. You never know what he might do to you after how he behaved yesterday, so I think it best that me and your mother come with you to speak to Stu and lay down the law with him a bit. He needs to be told in no uncertain terms that his behaviour is just not acceptable.'

I thought about that and agreed, but I didn't want to have my parents any more involved in my troubles than they already were. Besides, I knew that deep down Da was on Stuart's side, so I refused his offer of help.

That afternoon I returned home and when Stu came in from work I was there waiting for him. He went to water, just like that night he crumpled over the prospect of losing money on the property development. He cried and he stammered and he apologised for hitting me and he said he didn't know what had come over him and that I had taunted him and that he was sorry. It wouldn't happen again but I must please stop this nonsense with this 'Asian drug dealer' with whom I was making a fool of myself.

Once he thought he had gained my sympathy, the tears stopped and the nasty Stuart appeared.

'You are to stay here with me,' he said, his voice firming up. 'It is your place to be here with me and the children. You are my wife and their mother.'

Then he started to get into full stride. 'And besides, there is no way on earth that I will give you a feckin' divorce, so don't ask for one. If you think that that I am going to sell up and give half of everything I own to you and that feckin' little prick, you can think again. It will not happen.'

'And,' he added, shaking his fist at me, 'the children are my children and there is no way they are going to live with you and that low life in a London squat. Don't push me Jennifer, because if you leave, I swear to God that you will never see the three of them again. Believe me, you will be sorry that you had ever been born.'

With this menace, he stood up to leave the room. I never said a word but if looks could kill, then dear darling Stu would have been lying at my feet, dead.

'Sure as hell,' I thought to myself, 'you're right about one thing, you won't be belting me again. You won't have the opportunity, you coward.'

With Stuart's threats of retribution resounding in my ears, I went into the kitchen and began to prepare dinner, reflecting on everything as I worked. One good thing was that he was losing his control over me; I didn't care what he thought any more. If I had previously any doubts about breaking up the family, then his words had now made me even more firm in my resolve to escape.

But I knew that I had to have a plan; I would play the waiting game and when things were in place, I would leave.

Chapter 27

Of course, it did happen again; abusers don't suddenly stop abusing. He never actually hit me as hard any more because I didn't give him the chance. But he adopted a way of menacing me when he talked to me, of humiliating me when he checked up on my every action, of questioning me and making it clear that I was not to say anything negative about our situation to his boys. Things were not happy at all around the home, for me or for the children. Stuart and I were living in the same house but sleeping in different bedrooms. We were separate in every way except that we were under the same roof. Yet he tightened the shackles that bound me to him and the home by wanting to know where I was and what I was doing at every minute of the day.

I did not know whether he knew about the three days a month that Tom and I were spending together, but I was past caring. I just knew that if I had not had those moments together to look forward to, I would have committed suicide. Tom kept me going.

I was biding my time, putting my plans in place methodically and slowly before I made my move. Tom wanted me to do it right there and then. 'Leave him now, Jen,' he would plead, 'don't wait.' He believed Stuart was dangerous and capable of anything, that I was better to get out while the going was good. He had seen it before when one of his band mates had thrown burning oil over a lover who dared to exit the love nest without his permission. 'That man is a walking time bomb,' Tom said. 'He thinks he owns you and will stop at nothing to keep you with him. We've wasted too much time already, get out before it's too late.'

How I wish I had listened to Tom. Things may have ended differently. Perhaps I should have got out straight away, but deep down I knew that if I simply moved to another location within Dublin then Stuart would have soon found out where I lived, came after me, taken me home and made my life even worse. I needed a plan that was foolproof. I especially wanted to be sure that the children were going to be okay, and to do this I had to wait until Stuart accepted the fact that he and I were never going to be a couple again, that it was over and that nothing he could do or say would change that.

I had done a lot of thinking about my situation and that of my precious children. I recognised that both Stuart and I loved them and they loved us. They did not belong exclusively to either one of us and it was our duty as parents to do what was best for them in a traumatic situation. I considered minimal damage would be done to them if most things remained constant in their lives.

I reasoned that the boys were now adolescents and needed a solid male role model. They were growing up rapidly. Junior was fourteen and Richie was twelve and both were both happily ensconced in an excellent secondary school, Junior in many sporting teams and Richie doing well with music and drama. It would be unjust and disadvantageous to disrupt their lives by taking them with me to London where their lifestyle and life choices would suffer considerably.

At that age a boy needs his father more than he needs his mother. I knew this because I had read the book *Raising Boys* by Steve Biddulph and I had attended the parents' forum at the school on that topic. I was willing to sacrifice my time with them so that they would grow into good men. They would understand that when they were older and loving someone themselves.

Besides, I wasn't sure how Tom could accommodate me and Molly plus the two boys in his small terrace. The way I saw it, the boys could stay in Dublin, living in the same house, in the same suburb with the same friends going to the same school and with their father as their guide and mentor. Stuart had always said that the boys were his and that I mollycoddled them too much. He adored 'his boys' and loved being with them.

Difficult as it might be, I determined that they would do best if they stayed on with him, allowing them to continue their studies and to remain in the peer groups they had belonged to since they were babies. 'There's plenty of family to look out for them and they can visit us every school holiday,' I said to Tom. That way I wasn't taking absolutely everything away from Stu. I was only taking myself.

With Molly, things were different. She was a girl and Stuart had no real interest in her. As well, she was too young to be separated from her mother. She would come with me. I had always secretly thought that Stu had never bonded with her like he had done with the boys. He always brushed this query aside when I brought it up with him, saying that babies generally weren't his thing and that he would be better with her when she was older. Stuart wouldn't really mind her going with me as he had always asserted that she was 'my' child.

All the time I was thinking and planning, the situation was becoming more unpleasant at home, something that the children could not have failed to notice. Stu and I barely said a civil word to each other when we were alone. If there were other people around, we put on a good act. After all, Mr and Mrs Hoare had to keep up appearances!

Then something happened that brought everything into focus. Stu went snooping around in my bedroom and found a packet of contraceptive pills on the dressing table. He confronted me, accusing me of being unfaithful. 'It's for my period,' I said, hoping that the mention of something as female and personal as that would unsettle him. 'It helps ease my heavy menstrual bleeding.' As I suspected, it set him back momentarily. He glared at me, threw the packet back on the dresser and silently pushed past me. I felt a small sensation of relief. But it hadn't unsettled him quite enough. Once he was behind me, I could hear him turn around. 'Liar!' he snarled before karate chopping me across the back of the neck. As he stormed out, I clutched the dresser with both hands to steady myself and hold back the tears. And as the blood started dripping from my nose on to the beige carpet, I knew then that the moment for procrastinating any further had passed. It was time to leave.

Saturday dawned, one of those warm, balmy autumn days Ireland sometimes produces. A day that persuades everyone that summer has come at last and winter will now be leaving us alone. It can be the nicest time of the year on our little island. The leaves from the trees were gently swirling around in the puffs of breeze and the sun was shining. Stu was making the most of the good weather by leaving early for golf, taking the boys with him. Now was my chance.

Knowing it would take him most of the day to play eighteen holes, I had time to garner my troops and put my plan in place. I had spoken to Tom online the night before and he was catching an early flight to be by my side when I would confront Stuart and tell him that I was leaving him forever to go to London to start a new life.

I had booked my tickets to London, too, one for me and one for Molly. As it was a last minute purchase, they were expensive but I didn't care what the credit card statement would say. By the time Stu examined it, I would be well away from him.

I picked up the phone and rang my brother Kevin and told him of my plans.

'Can you come by this afternoon, please, Kevin, and provide some moral support for me?' I asked.

'And physical, too?' came the stern reply.

'Only if you have to, but I hope it won't come to that. He'll be shocked, probably more at the fact that

I have got the strength to do something like this, but I think he will come around.'

Kevin already knew something about my situation as his wife Amy and I were close and I had spoken to her, but he was a little surprised that it had come to this. Being my protector brother, he put his plans for the day aside to help me. 'Anything for you, Jen,' he said. 'If it will make your life happy, I'm only glad to be there for you.'

I also enlisted Wendy to provide some moral support, mainly because I knew that she would be there for the boys if they were upset and needed consoling.

After the earlier incident when Stuart had smashed my ribs, I had spoken to Moira, his mother, and had told her what was going on. She and I respected each other and although I knew she would not be happy about the situation I also intuitively knew that she would do what was best for the grandchildren. She had been horrified when I had told her about my injuries, breaking down and crying. 'I put up with that sort of thing all my married life,' she had sobbed, 'I accepted it because the Army told me that it was shell shock. He always said it wouldn't happen again and it always did. I have tiptoed around Stuart's father all my life. I was petrified of him. If it happens again, don't stay, go! Do what I should have done years ago.'

That is why I telephoned Moira and asked her to come over, to be there for Stuart as I was sure he would need her support and I believed that he would behave better if she was in the room. She agreed, begging me to leave the boys behind as they were so settled at school and Stuart would be devastated if they were taken away from him. 'I'll help Stu to take care of them,' she pleaded. I told her that I had already reached that decision and I would be very grateful of any help she could give. Although it broke my heart, I knew that Mam and Moira, like the wonderful Irish women they both were, would support Stuart in caring for the boys.

I then telephoned Mam to tell her of my intentions. 'Can I be there, Lovie?' she asked. 'We don't want violence like the last time. I want Stuart to know that he is not to lay a hand on you, but that I will be there to help and support him with the boys, God bless them. I am so going to miss my little Molly, but of course she must be with you, she's too young to stay. I won't say a word about it to your father until after it is all done. You know what he thinks and he won't change his mind. Best he be kept in the dark and not know anything about it.'

No one was entirely happy about the situation. But they all knew that the time had come and it had to be done.

Chapter 28

At about 3.30 pm everyone assembled in my lounge room - Tom, Mam, Moira, Kevin, Wendy, me and Molly - and over tea and cakes we talked about what was happening now, the plans I had made and how I hoped things would pan out in the future. Tom and I were excited but tentative, thrilled but anxious, knowing that what was about to happen was not going to be pleasant but recognising that it had to be done before we could be free. He had got a cab from the airport and once he was there by my side my nerves settled a little and I knew that what we were doing was right. I outlined to the assembled crowd the what, when and how of the situation, so that we all appreciated where we stood. They all sat tentatively waiting and the mood was sombre.

Then, the moment came - Stuart returned from golf with the boys. He was a bit taken aback when he arrived home to a tea drinking crowd in his front lounge, but his mother immediately side-lined him and suggested that he go to the study with her. 'We need to talk, Stuart,' I heard her say. Apparently she spoke to him very calmly, outlining to him what was happening and why and how it had come to this situation. He seemed to listen and to take it all in. She reported later that it had been a very emotional scene with Stuart stoically taking in her words while doing his best not to break down.

While Moira was explaining the situation to Stu, I took the two boys aside and gently spoke to them, outlining my plan, trying to make them understand and promising that as soon as I was settled I would have them over for a holiday and that I would come to see them often. Amazingly, they seemed to take it in their stride, both agreeing that they didn't want to change schools nor live in London. I assured them that their two grandmothers would make sure they ate well and that Aunty Wendy had volunteered to be their taxi service when their father was unavailable. I told them that I loved them very much and that this arrangement was very hard for me but that I wanted as few things as possible to change for them. 'Junior, Rich, it is all for the best,' I said soothingly. 'Mummy and Daddy both still love you.' Richie, a little perplexed, clung to me sobbing, saying he would miss me and Molly and asked, 'Do you really have to go?' Junior, in the mould of his father, stared silently into the distance and did not seem to worry. It was all very upsetting.

Stu and his mother eventually emerged from the study and came into the front lounge. That was when he noticed Tom. The angry Stu quickly surfaced. 'What are you doing in my house, you feckin' family wrecker?' he snarled at him. 'Get out! Get out and never come near me again.'

Tom went to say something but I squeezed his hand and he remained silent. This did not deter Stuart, who kept up his rant.

'And you can take my wife with you, you bastard. Take her and good luck to you. But don't think you're getting any of my money or anything that belongs to me. Take the bitch and I hope you both rot in hell.'

He took a deep breath and was about to launch into some more, when Moira cut him off and told him to mind his language. 'Stuart,' she said, 'there are children in the room listening to every word. This is no time for recriminations.'

Already upset because of the boys, I tearfully told Stu that I didn't want things to be like that. 'But I have to take my chance at happiness,' I said. In my defence I tried to explain to him how fair I thought I'd been in allowing the boys to stay with him. Stuart was controlled and deliberate in his reply. 'The boys deserve a mother *and* a father. You had that. I had that. You are depriving them of that by running off with this low life and wrecking their lives. You're a selfish conceited bitch who thinks the whole world revolves around you.'

Then, almost as an afterthought, he turned to the subject of our daughter. 'What about Molly being separated from her brothers, eh?' he snarled. 'Don't you think she needs a father? What about that? She's entitled to be with her family and her family is you, me and the boys. She should be here, with me and her brothers. You do this, Jennifer, and you will be sorry. You do this and I will take you to the cleaners. I will make sure that you have nothing that is mine, nothing!'

I thought he was talking about the house and his money so I replied that I wasn't asking for anything that didn't belong to me, but that I was entitled to half of everything that we had built up together since we married. Stuart declared again that I would get nothing from him, to which I replied that we would allow the courts to work that out. In hindsight, I now realise he was talking about more than just his money.

'My mind is made up so it is useless scraping over old ground,' I said.

It was a very tense situation, but Tom was by my side and so I was strong enough to face Stuart and put my case. The members of our families sat primly on the sofas, eyes down, hands clasped, embarrassed and entrapped in the uncomfortable situation as the exchange took place. Then suddenly, Wendy excused herself and got up to leave, saying that it was not her place to be there, to which Stu scathingly agreed. After she had gone, I looked at my watch. 'Heavens, we must go, too,' I said. 'We have a plane to catch.'

I moved towards the door where our bags were packed and made ready to leave; the others all stood up, grateful that it was over and that we hadn't come to blows. Stu seemed to calm down. He pulled himself together and made one final speech with conviction. He agreed that he would be able to care for the lads with the help of the two grandmothers and that Molly should go with me and that it was all very regrettable and no one was sorrier than he was that it had come to this. His shoulders visibly sagged and he went to the sideboard and poured himself a whiskey, offering one to Kevin who declined since he was driving. It seemed to me that we had got through the worst and now all was settled.

I cuddled the boys who stood stoically upright, shoulder to shoulder, biting back the tears as their father had taught them that men should do. So young and innocent, so vulnerable and fragile, so raw and tender! I reassured them that I loved them and that I would call them that night and every night. Molly, Tom and I went outside, followed by everyone else, and packed the bags into Kevin's brand new SUV.

We were about to take our leave when Stuart surprised us all by coming out and suggesting that he and the boys accompany us to the airport to say goodbye to Molly and me. He said he'd like a ride in Kevin's spanking new car as, being a self-confessed 'petrol-head', he'd like to see how it performed. 'Besides,' he added, 'I won't be seeing Molly for a while and so I just want to make the most of this time with her. I'll be happy to sit in the back seat with her.'

That meant that we would have to take two cars, with Tom driving our Audi and taking the boys with him. Stu and the boys would then have a car in which to return from the airport, thus saving Kevin a round trip, as he lived on the north side.

While it all sounded reasonable to everyone else, it seemed to me that this was just another of Stuart's clever ploys to control me one last time and to further delay me from being with Tom. He was separating us by plonking himself firmly in the back of the car in which I was travelling and putting Tom in another car altogether.

I knew what he was doing and I was annoyed, but I had no more fight left in me. I rationalised that in two hours Stu would be out of my life and Tom and I would be together forever. We were already running late as we had taken more time than we had estimated and could not afford to quibble. Although it was the very last thing I wanted, I acquiesced because Stuart was now being civilised and he did have a point about not seeing Molly for a long time. I nodded my agreement to Tom who took the keys and got into the driver's seat of the Audi with the boys in the back, ready to follow us.

Kevin, Molly, Stuart and I prepared to get in the new car - me in the front with Kevin, father and daughter in the back. It was awful saying goodbye to everyone but exciting as well, because my new life was just beginning. I bade a tearful farewell to the oldies, pulled myself together and opened the front door to Kevin's sparkling SUV, climbed inside and sat down.

If I had been able to see into the future I would never have got into that car.

Stuart took his place next to Molly in the back and when I turned around he was holding her hand and playing 'Can you keep a secret?' I smiled to myself, thinking that at long last he, like me, knew that we had come to the end of our journey as a couple. He was accepting it like the gentleman he was. I suddenly felt a pang of tenderness towards him. Perhaps he wasn't so bad, after all. I smiled and said, 'Thank you, Stuart, for making this easy for everyone. I appreciate it.' He gave the slightest half smile and grunted an affirmation. But the nasty Stu quickly returned, saying, 'You must feel happy about all this, bitch. You've screwed me good and proper and I'm telling you that you and that fancy man of yours will not get one penny out of me. I'd rather give it all to the feckin' cat's home.'

I flew back at him, 'Money! I don't want your money. That's all you ever think about. Everything in your world is measured by money. And now you've made us late, mucking us around, wanting to bring two cars. We'll miss the plane because of you and you'll be pleased about that, won't you? But I'm telling you, I've made up my mind and I'm going, I'm leaving. It's over, Stuart. O, V, E, R! Over!'

Kevin opened the door car and slid into the driver's seat. 'Shut up Jen, that's enough,' he said. 'I'm not taking anyone anywhere if you're going to fight all the way, so calm down.'

'I am calm,' I declared through gritted teeth. And so with Molly looking tired in the back, we pulled out of the drive and headed to the airport and my new life.

Don't ask me to retrace our journey that day as I had no idea where we were going and I was as uptight as a hot-air balloon. It was a nightmare. There had been a big game at Croke Park and two other major events in or near the city and with all the changes in arrangements and the reorganising of cars and drivers, by the time we set out the traffic was crazy. The radio reported big tailbacks onto the M50. Being in Ireland where the clouds are always full of water hovering overhead waiting to unload, it wasn't long before it began to pour with rain. I was more than a little edgy lest we miss our flight.

Tom was following us as Kevin set out on a route that in his mind would bypass all the reported traffic snarls and get us there on time. He travelled the city as part of his job as a builder's product salesman and assured me that he had it all under control as he did a right hand turn here, a left there and God knows what else in the other place. After what seemed an eternity, we were almost there, but on the wrong side of the motorway. There was just one flyover to freedom but as we turned the corner, went up the ramp and levelled out, our line of traffic came to a standstill. The motorway lay directly below us, with vehicle after vehicle noisily whizzing in opposite directions in continuous motion.

Two cars in front of us, a motor cyclist had been knocked off his bike on the slippery surface and although he was not dead he was certainly not looking in good shape as he lay screaming in the middle of the road, blocking the traffic.

We were stationary, stuck on the flyover, the cars underneath us thundering both ways, with Tom in the Audi behind looking confused and anxious. I could see the airport in the distance, but could we make it on time? I looked at my watch. I doubted it.

It was all too much. I completely lost it. It certainly seemed to me that this was all Stuart's fault and I told him so. 'If you had not insisted on coming with us we would have been through here ten minutes earlier,' I yelled. 'We would have been over there, at the airport, checking in,' I added, angrily pointing at the control tower in the distance.

This was classic Stuart; the nasty, controlling, devious Stuart that I knew so well. He'd delayed us and he'd done it deliberately. It's just the sort of thing he would do to assert his hold over me - make me late so we'd miss the plane. 'I hope you're happy now, Stu,' I hissed, not looking at him but staring straight ahead. 'You made us late, you did it on purpose. You knew what you were doing, it's so typical ...'

There was a sudden rush of cold air onto the back of my neck as I heard a rear door open. Stopping mid sentence, I turned to see Stuart, with little drowsy Molly in his arms, stepping out of the car and alighting onto the flyover. The traffic on the motorway zoomed relentlessly by underneath. What was he doing? Where was he taking her? I tried to scream at him but no sound would come. I tried again - nothing. I fumbled at the switches of the new car but couldn't make them do what I wanted. How do I get the window down? Where is the door knob? I had to get out of there and stop what was happening. Again I screamed but no sound would come. Kevin was oblivious, watching the driver of the car in front tending to the injured motor cyclist. His blood was mixing with the rain drops and spilling into the gutter.

In the cocoon of the car, my world was in pandemonium. Over the roar of the traffic, the sound of beating drums and fluttering bat-wings began pounding in my ears. I knew something horrible was about to happen but I was powerless to stop it. I screamed again; an ear-shattering, desperate sound that gathered all the previous screams from the back of my throat and released them together so that they resonated above the chaos that was about us. 'Stuart!!'

We were no longer on our way to the airport, but on our way to Hell on a one-way, non-refundable ticket.

His Story

Chapter 1

The truth be known, the first time Jennifer and I ever actually touched, I recoiled from her. Considering how things panned out, that action now reeks of the most overwhelming irony. If I had left it at that, followed my usual instincts and moved quietly into the background, our hearts and our souls would never have become so intrinsically intertwined as they did. Rather than a tiny, incidental brush of our hands leading to romance, marriage and children, we would have gone our separate ways, continuing our grinding parallel ride down the gloomy fast track to loneliness. Our lives would have been less productive, less colourful, less meaningful, certainly less complicated and undoubtedly far less tragic. I would never have found myself standing on that motorway flyover with my sleepy little daughter in my arms, the roar of traffic thundering in my ears and a catastrophic surge of blind anger and white-hot fury coursing through my veins.

However, let's be clear. On that first meeting, I did not pull back from Jennifer out of revulsion or fear. Not at all. It was purely out of politeness.

We both had turned and reached for the last sandwich on a plate in the middle of a long serving table. As the occasion was a cup of tea after a very sombre funeral, our reactions were both straight out of the book of good manners, trying to do the right thing. I pulled my hand away and whispered, 'I'm terribly sorry.' She quietly replied, 'No, no, it's all yours, take it.'

That's not the smartest thing to say to someone who had grown up as an only child. I knew my place in the food chain. At the front of the shortest of all possible queues! But I was also brought up to be polite and courteous. And when I looked down and focused on those pretty features surrounded by a beautiful aura of auburn hair, I was intrigued. Instead, I picked up the plate, gave a little bow, and presented it to her as if she was the lady of the manor. 'I am your humble servant, M'am,' I said. I don't usually do quirky things like that. I'm an insurance salesman.

As I peeked up from my subservient position, I could see that although she was reaching for the food, she was peering at me with the most delightful look on her face. Sure, we were at a funeral and the atmosphere was thick with melancholy, but the sparkle in her green eyes re-energized my spirits.

We might have just buried one of my mother's cousin's boys – only 14, he had been knocked over by a motorcyclist wired on coke trying to out-run the Garda in Limerick – but I was beguiled by the cheery laughter in her voice.

We had just been overwhelmed by the tear-stained singing of the young boy's classmates, doing that U2 song about trying to find something they were looking for, but here before me was the most engaging smile, emphasised by brilliant cherry-coloured lipstick. I just had to keep the conversation going. But what to say?

'Poppy,' I blurted. She looked confused. 'Your lipstick. Poppy King, isn't it? She's Australian and the colours are like the country, big and bold.'

She looked down and began pulling her coat tightly across her body. It was red like her lipstick and even I knew that it was very fashionable. I figured she was cold and so I began looking around somewhat helplessly for the controls to the room heating. Then it dawned on me that it was not the cold she was worrying about, rather my mention of the lipstick. It had made her re-consider her outfit. She hastily explained that she had been on her way to work when she had heard about the funeral. 'I guess I should be wearing something more appropriate,' she added, trying to cover the short skirt underneath.

'You're not out of place at all,' I said hesitantly. 'You look … beautiful …'

And that's how it all began. After I had unaccountably uttered those words – in all of my thirty-eight years I had never been so forward with anyone – I felt that if the poor dead boy's grave had opened up before me right there and then, I would have jumped in. But that was the characteristic I was to constantly discover and re-discover about Jennifer. She never got fazed by things like that. She would just tilt her head and smile again, and if the previous smile had been fetching, the next one would be breathtaking. The white, even teeth dazzling through the bright lipstick. She simply leant forward, took my silver-grey mourning tie in both hands, gently pushed the knot up to the top button of my white shirt, patted it down and said, 'You look pretty swish yourself.'

'Blimey,' I replied.

She giggled loudly. 'I haven't heard blimey for years,' she said. 'That's English, isn't it? Cor blimey and all that?'

I explained how I had inherited the expression from my father. How he had been born in Ireland, but went over to England with his migrating family in the 1920s when he was a boy and eventually served in the British Army, picking up a lot of their sayings.

I knew from what Dad had told me and from my history lessons at school that at one stage there were more Irishmen serving in the British Army than Englishmen. But seeing as we were standing in a room in Dublin, the capital of the Republic of Ireland, a country that had not entirely enjoyed its eight hundred years of British rule, this could have elicited any response. Not the least of which might well have been a lecture replete with deep-seated hatred of the English. 'My Mam is also Irish,' I added hastily.

Instead, this pretty young woman standing before me laughed and said that I was quite a combination. 'Irish scattiness sharpened by all-conquering English discipline,' she said. 'So, at the end of the day, which one has come to the fore?'

'I let other people judge that,' I said. 'I just keep my head down, try my hardest and hope for the best outcome. What about you?'

Her eyes looked to the heavens. 'Wow, have we got time?' She laughed. 'The classic Catholic upbringing to start with. With a name like Jennifer Mary O'Brien, what would you expect? But now I'm Buddhist.'

It was my turn to be put off balance. I didn't know much about Buddhism other than what I had seen in the media. Monks praying in orange robes, long-running but unsuccessful resistance to China controlling Tibet, the Dalai Lama turning up to conferences on humility in a Mercedes. But I had obviously steered things towards her favourite topic. She made the declaration with such a happy lilt in her voice that a group of mourners near us stopped their conversation and turned to see who on earth could be finding something funny about a funeral.

I asked her about how she got involved in Buddhism and the answer, quite frankly, was a bit rambling. Something about how she had studied at Cambridge University, which I found most impressive, even a bit daunting, and how she had met a few people there who had something to do with people in Thailand, a very committed Buddhist country, and how she started to appreciate the philosophy and then travel around a bit and meet other people and now she was practicing it. So I asked her how Buddhists worshipped God, and she replied cheerily, 'Oh, we don't necessarily believe in God.'

'You don't believe in God?' I replied loudly. The whole room came to a halt and an elderly man in a blue-serge double-breasted suit with long swept-back silver hair broke away from his group and marched deliberately towards us. He stepped up to me so closely that I could see the tiny pink whiskey veins hatching out of his red bulbous nose. He hissed at us to be quiet. 'The religious beliefs, fanciful or otherwise, of you and your lady friend here are of no interest to anyone, especially at a terrible time like this,' he said.

He nodded at me as if to emphasise his point, turned and looked at Jennifer angrily, then wheeled around abruptly and walked away. I could hear the next giggle welling in her throat, so I lightly took her by the arm and hurried her away from the table towards a quiet corner. I looked down and, to my horror, realised that I was touching her – bustling her along, in fact. To my great joy, she was not resisting. Indeed, here she was, quite happy to come with me, her high heels click-clacking on the polished boards. A surge like an electrical charge went through my body. This had not happened to me for years.

We found a spot by a sickly-looking rubber-plant near a window overlooking the grey, wet, Dublin street below. She looked up at me, giggled once more, then continued unperturbed, saying that she had grown up Catholic and therefore could understand my response.

'But as a Buddhist, God is not an issue for me,' she said.

'I wouldn't want my mother to hear that,' I replied, looking anxiously back towards the room. 'She thinks God plays a significant role in the Church of Ireland. Quite a substantial one, in fact …'

'Hmm, Church of Ireland!' she said, jumping on the reference to my Protestant upbringing. 'Well, I suppose we're both something of the rebel then.'

She smiled and leaned in close to me. The musky aroma of her perfume – Lulu, I reckoned, based on my experiences with doctor's surgery magazine scratch-and-scent advertisements – was absolutely intoxicating. 'Me, perhaps, a little more than you,' she cheekily added. 'But I'm sure down the track that that won't matter.'

I smiled weakly and put my hand on the window sill to steady myself.

'Blimey,' I whispered, staring straight into her green eyes. 'Blimey.'

Chapter 2

It has taken me a very, very long time to appreciate an intriguing fact of life: not everyone is fascinated by the world of insurance.

Why, some people even think it is a bit dreary. That astounds me. I think insurance is a beautiful thing. That's because it is a matter of selling an intangible, a notion, a possibility. And not a lot of people can do that. It requires a level of patience and a touch of guile that not everyone has in them. Over the years, I have observed many of my associates struggling with that challenge. They would join our brokerage with a great track record for selling tangible, touchable products like cars or houses or lawn-mowers but were unable to reproduce that same level of sales success. That's because insurance is based on the possibility of something terrible happening. And I was very good at outlining what the 'something' might be to potential clients.

'Sir,' I would say, 'if something goes wrong, we step in and clean up the mess, pay your bills, get you back on your feet and return things to where they were before. You may even be better off.'

'Sir,' I would add, 'the decision is up to you. I know you're an intelligent, honest, reliable man, who does a good job looking after himself and his family. You never do anything to put yourself at risk. But, what if? You know, what if ..?'

'Sir,' I would continue, ramping things up, 'I don't need to tell you, it's a fast-moving world out there. Anything can happen. Things get out of control. You could get hurt. People are so unpredictable these days, on the drug and all that. Not that I'm saying something like that will happen to you, but you never know. Better to be on the safe side and sleep well at night. That is the question you have to ask yourself: can you sleep well at night?'

Then I would ask him three questions.

'Can you sleep well, knowing that your car is not locked up in a garage, but sitting out in the street, providing some angry young punk, whose mother never breast-fed him and whose father was always at the betting shop, with the perfect opportunity to steal it or smash its windows or torch it for the hell of it?'

'Can you lie back, knowing that you might get laid off one day and the mortgage will still have to be paid? Things are getting very, very tough you know, and those banks, they hold the money, they play with the money, they do what they like with the money, but they never give the ordinary man any of the money.'

'And can you nod off, knowing that although you're healthy now, you will get older and your physical wellbeing will, naturally enough, begin to deteriorate? We all know the statistics; that the husband usually dies before the wife. Wouldn't it be good to know that she'll be financially secure after you've gone? I'm not trying to be morbid here, but you know what I mean, having that warm feeling deep down that you've done the right thing by her.'

That was the game and that's how it went and that's why I liked it. Talking to people about the unthinkable, the unlikeable, the unpredictable – nevertheless, things that we all knew could actually happen – and helping them create a reserve force that they could call on if need be. It was all in the insurer's handbook.

Another reason I liked insurance was that I had endured two other serious 'careers' before I fell in love with the game, both of which were desk-bound, and both soul-destroying. One was spent in the civil service shuffling papers and the other was wasted trying to make sense of patient registrations at a hospital. The first seemed to have no point in it at all while the second involved people constantly whingeing. I hate whingers. So from the moment I joined a small insurance agency and very quickly began successfully selling policies door-to-door, I knew it was for me. Within twelve months I was their top salesman; by the end of three years, I was deputy manager; two years after that I was sitting on the board. Recognising the advantages of running my own business, I persuaded Derek Smythe, another successful operator in the building, to go halves in buying the place out. The owner, Frank Cunningham, the last of the insurer gentlemen, had lost his enthusiasm after his wife had died of a terrible cancer and was only too glad to hand it over to young blood at a modest price.

Above all, I liked selling insurance because people trusted me. They saw me as straight, honest, reliable. The type of person that wouldn't scare the horses or start the dogs barking or do anything crazy and act out of character. I was always polite, I took a great interest in their personal lives and I knew when to drop a line into the conversation with a little dash of humour. I also presented very well. I always wore quality charcoal or blue pin-stripe suits, freshly-pressed white shirts and sombre but expensive ties. I had my hair, which had prematurely turned from a mousey brown to a distinguished grey, trimmed regularly. I wore the latest spectacle frames and made sure that my shoes were polished to a mirror finish every morning.

My father's military approach, that you should give off an impressive, commanding image at all times, was well ingrained in me. 'You have to look sharp as a tack,' he would say, circling me as if inspecting a parade, 'whether you're in uniform or wearing mufti.'

I became acknowledged for my presentation and professionalism and got to deal with a lot of people from a broad spectrum of life. Employees, employers, businessmen, businesswomen, housewives, young men and women climbing the executive ladder, even the occasional celebrity. The yuppies were the toughest to crack. They made a lot of money rapidly and spent it just as quickly, mainly on preening, enhancing and amusing themselves with not much thought for the future. They were convinced they were indestructible. Deep down, I will admit, I didn't like their attitude. It took a lot of time and effort, surreptitiously of course, to convince them that their future, so cocky and self-assured as it was then, would need protecting.

Sometimes I also came across artistic, hedonistic characters that made money in large episodic chunks but couldn't control it. They wrote or painted or made music or just 'were'. Things happened to them, good things, and they would laugh and celebrate and people would throw themselves at them. Then bad things would happen to them, and the hangers-on would disappear and I would be left to console these so-called superstars in their helplessness and sort out a plan to get them back on track until the next pile of cash inexplicably surfaced through some flukey project coming off or magically appeared out of the wallet of a star-struck celebrity-seeking benefactor. They were an insurer's and financial planner's nightmare.

Selling insurance therefore required patience, diligence, the ability to remain calm while a potential client pondered the plan so carefully presented. I never got angry or frustrated. Certainly not with customers, anyway. That was my hallmark. People would always comment on my calm, relaxed approach. I guess I was good at burying the frustration deep within me. I bottled it all up but always remained tranquil on the surface, even with something as tricky as marine insurance, when cargo was damaged or stolen or, as happened once, the actual ship disappeared off the face of the earth.

My usually unflappable father would get excited about my job when something like that happened. 'When you say the ship disappeared, do you mean sunk? Or pirates? Or aliens? Or what?' he would ask, twitching his moustache. As an old army man, this was the only aspect of my otherwise apparently humdrum career that fascinated him. There could be an enemy involved and he loved a good enemy. That was because from the broader perspective my job, my approach, my very existence had been a complete disappointment to him.

Sure, I had inherited his apparent coolness under pressure – 'a vital part of any good soldier's make-up,' he would tell me – but none of his swagger, will-to-win or bloodlust. I was like Mum. Patient, reserved, staying under the radar. Holding things in, bottling them up. That's how she had handled life while Da's career dragged them from posting to posting, from army camp to army camp, from the same dreary sergeant's quarters to yet another scantily furnished home. I remember a stretch when we occupied half a dozen different places in nine years.

The fact that I was their only child simply added to Dad's aggravation. He had fired the one shot he had in his locker and as far as he was concerned, it had fizzed. I had not become an officer. Hadn't even tried to get into the army. He had seen that as the way for me to make up for his own work-a-day role. After my schooling, he was convinced that I would go to university, get a degree and become a leader of men, directing their every action with cool military precision from the safety of the bunker behind the lines and then heading off to the officers' mess for a brandy with the chaps.

Shifting from school to school did not help my self-esteem much, so on one occasion they tried to break the circuit by enrolling me in a boarding college. In many ways, I liked the place. There was a discipline and a surety about it. You knew what was going to happen and when. There were rituals to be followed and games to be played. The teaching was excellent, albeit brutal at times, and I excelled particularly in the maths and commerce subjects. But apart from developing a friendship with a genial lad named Olaf Hendrikson from Sweden, whose father had been transferred to England on business, it was a very isolating experience for the son of a sergeant amongst the offspring of the officers and the well-to-do.

I very quickly ran into the thick brick wall known as the English class system and rapidly learned that name, pedigree and dynasty bore fruit, not necessarily brains, talent and dedication. In the showers, on the playing fields, at the back of the class, I was bullied by over-bearing chinless wonders with hyphenated names. They lampooned me for having a father who was a mere workaday soldier and not an officer and gentleman. They teased me for my so-called lack of class and my mongrel heritage of being born in England but of Irish parents. So, they pushed my head down the toilet bowl and flushed it. They coated my genitals with boot polish. They cut a single sleeve off three of my shirts.

And, of course, they loved my surname of Hoare. In my opinion, Hoare is not such a bad name. It comes from the Old English 'hoar', meaning white or frosty or grey, and amongst the Hoare lineage is a former British Foreign Secretary and an internation-ally successful computer whiz.

But my tormentors went for the obvious. They couldn't believe their luck that some poor sod had come onto their radar with a surname that matched perfectly with 'whore'. I was therefore the ideal target for adolescent taunts about prostitution. 'Hoare, you fucker, you do it for money,' they would say. Or, 'How many did you sleep with last night, Hoare?' And a chant that they just loved to get going: 'Hoare, the whore, he's got no class. Hoare, the whore, he takes it up the arse.' Looking around the cold, grey-stone dormitories of the English boarding college, ruled by predatory masters, I thought that that was hardly an original attack. Mercifully, I was at least saved from that indignity because – as it dawned on me years later – I innocently undermined any attempts by teachers to inculcate dangerous friendships through my characteristic aloofness. In my own quiet way, I simply hung on, survived and bottled it all up.

The key was to never respond to the gang's bullying taunts. I absorbed their punishment, stored it away and let it simmer.

Then, just when I was starting to make some headway – my stocky build earning me a place in the rugby squad and a modest talent for music securing me the role of piano accompanist for the choir – it happened. One of the thugs pushed me too far. But he made the grave mistake, perhaps being too cocky, of being by himself this time and not backed up by the rest of the group. 'So, if your father is a Hoare, is your mother a whore, too?' he sneered. This mention of my mother in that context was too much. I snapped. The simmering anger, subdued for nearly two years, burst to the surface in an uncontrollable rage. I flew at him and, even though he was several centimetres taller and a few kilos heavier than me, I caught him flush on the jaw with a wild, round-house, bar-room brawl swing.

As he dazedly toppled to the ground, shocked and momentarily disoriented, I jumped on him, pinning him down with my knees on his shoulders, and started flailing into him with lefts and rights. I could feel the stinging pain in my knuckles and hear the sound of ripping flesh as I smashed my fists into the side of his head, onto the bridge of his nose, down the side of his jaw, and around his eyes. Months and months of bottled up anger was let free in one breathtaking, vicious assault. It was like another person had taken over.

For once in my life, I felt enormous power and control as I belted into him, his pleas for me to stop drowned out by the shouts of a group of kids who had gathered around, many of whom were thrilled to see this thug finally cop the punishment he deserved.

Their noise eventually attracted the attention of one of the masters and I was pulled off, giving him one final salute, a kick in the balls, as they dragged me away. My tormentor was battered and bruised, shaken and humiliated, his face and shirt covered in blood, his left eye closing, as they hurried him off to the infirmary. It was my one great triumph in the school yard but it was also my downfall.

In the inquisition that followed, class distinction and aristocratic pressure won out. I was expelled, while my tormentor and his cronies survived and went in search of another innocent target. I heard later that they found him in the son of an aspirational lorry-driver named Whitcombe. It turned out I was considerably luckier than him. After two terms of relentless torment, he went into the groundsman's shed at the bottom of the playing fields, swallowed half a bottle of weed-killer and found blessed relief through a most horrible death.

My mother insisted that we never speak about this extraordinary blow-up again, although my father was secretly pleased that I had shown such gumption. I was left to ponder whether such an outburst of violence would ever happen again and, if so, what sort of circumstances would be needed to trigger it. The incident was quietly written out of the family history and I was soon back to the same old education treadmill, tramping from school to school and finally getting my A levels. It was years before I got any tertiary qualifications, having to go through night school when we moved back to Ireland. My entry-level diplomas in finance and business came from slogging away at work during the day and sitting through endless classes in the evenings.

In some ways, it was a pity the boarding school opportunity collapsed, because my parents had tried so hard to ensure that I would not be a poorly-educated, poorly-paid hireling like Dad was, exposed in the field, shouting at indolent foot-sloggers and keeping them in line. He had done that in North

Africa, Greece and Burma during the war, before finishing up in India, where he and Mum had hung on after independence for as long as they could before my impending arrival forced them to return.

I don't think that it ever helped his demeanour that they had finally settled in Ireland, Mum's place of birth, rather than England, where he was brought up and for whom he had so faithfully served, even though he, too, was Irish born. When he finally retired on his diminutive army pension, he would stride around the tiny flat on the outskirts of Dublin, peering out the window, waiting for the enemy to appear. No one came. No enemies. No friends, either. Pulling on the uniform of the nation that had once occupied the country was a reasonable means to an end for some Irish but unforgivable as far as many others were concerned. He cut a lonely figure huddled over his whiskey in the pub at the end of the street.

Sometimes, in moments of melancholic reflection, he spoke about his experiences in the war. The circumstances had to be right; a wandering mind, a few too many drinks and a sound or smell.

It was the tale of the German soldier that he had bayoneted in a little village they were fighting over in the battle of Crete that would bring the tears to his eyes. 'Only a boy,' he would say. 'I surprised him from behind and he turned, yanking his revolver out of his holster, aiming straight at me and pulling the trigger. But it jammed. The gods of war move in strange ways. He threw the pistol at me and turned to run, tripping on the rough stone. As he lay sprawled on the ground, I plunged the bayonet into him. Once, twice, three times. Had to save my ammunition.'

Then he would stop and vacantly stare into the distance and the tears would roll down his face. 'I was doing my job but he was only a boy,' he would mutter, shaking his head. 'He was only a boy. And so was I ...'

Mum and I always knew it was senseless to try and comfort him. She would busy herself around him, silently plumping the cushions on the sofa and dusting the mantelpiece while I would look around the room quietly, waiting for him to bring himself back into the present.

There was not a lot about that in the insurer's handbook.

Chapter 3

As an only child, I grew up a lonely child. Until I met Jennifer, making female friends had proved to be an extremely difficult process for me.

I would make tentative, awkward steps to draw a girl into friendship but I never had the confidence or the wherewithal to, for want of a better phrase, go in for the kill. It used to frustrate me to see flashy fellows at work with half a brain chatting up girls and getting them to smile, then giggle, then agree to go out with them, all in a matter of minutes. How did they do that? When I tried the same approach, I would run up against a brick wall.

At work or with a group down the pub at the end of the week, my conversation aimed at asking someone out was always a set piece that I had pre-prepared in my ordered mind, carefully rehearsed with a clear target at the end. But if the girl deviated from the script, I would lose the plot quickly and withdraw in disarray, a tongue-tied, nervous wreck. There is no more frightening experience for a young man than facing up to a group of girls standing in a tight little tribe, no greater challenge than trying to ask one of them out, and no more embarrassing sensation when it all goes pear-shaped and he turns and walks away, the sound of only slightly smoth-ered, hand-over-the-mouth snorting ringing in his burning ears.

Such was my fragile, nervous state, my first ever serious girlfriend, a young woman named Patricia, used to psychoanalyse me. She would plumb the depths of Freud when we got into discussion about the importance of 'self' as our spluttering romance blossomed in chaotic fashion. 'There's an entire seminar on the development of single-cell existence in you,' she would exclaim.

I had been attracted to Patricia because she looked like my mother. Short, brunette with deep brown eyes and an enigmatic smile. But I soon learned I was going out with my father. Under the benign camouflage lurked not just a sergeant, rather a camp commandant. She was incredibly decisive, insistent and powerful. Few people could get a lazy restaurant waiter hopping like Patricia could, or castigate a Garda and get the speeding ticket torn up, or belittle someone who had carelessly thrown an empty beer bottle onto the footpath. And in her role as a publicist or marketer or event manager – whatever it was, I could never quite get a grip on it – I think she took me on as a challenge. It was the *Pygmalion* scenario, albeit in reverse; her Henry Higgins to my Eliza Doolittle. And it was perhaps not so much my accent that she wanted to change, rather that I would actually speak up in the first place.

In those early days, the only people I spoke to with any confidence were my mother, my male work-mates and myself – the latter when no one else was looking, I might point out. In social situations, when faced with discussion with other people, I tended to reply with polite but nevertheless mono-syllabic responses of the 'yes' and 'absolutely' variety. 'He's a nice young man,' they would whisper to each other, not quite out of earshot, 'but he's very quiet.'

Patricia did have some success in getting me to speak up. The first time she undressed before me, I uttered 'Good heavens', and at the apex of us making love, I exclaimed 'Blimey'. Seeing as I had just made love to a real live person for the first time, seven weeks and five days after my twenty-third birthday, I felt that something strong was needed. So, 'Blimey' it was.

Patricia was not so impressed. I never saw her again.

Thus wounded, it took me another two years to establish a relationship. And this time, with Tanya, things moved quite a bit down the track. She was blonde, she was blue-eyed, she was beautiful. As well, Tanya was less predatory than Patricia, something I relished after such a long period of regaining my confidence to approach a girl again. In fact, if anything, the roles were reversed. Whereas I had been the work in progress with Patricia, I found myself taking the lead in Project Tanya. If it was at all humanly possible, Tanya was less sure-footed than me. 'Golly', I thought, 'if my father was a sergeant, then her Dad must have been in the Marines. She's been ground totally into the dirt.'

She was like a deer stuck eternally before the headlights, the product of a broken marriage, a sporadic education and some deeply hidden secret that I never really unearthed. We sort of meandered into romance - we went to movies, ate at cheap Turkish restaurants and visited tiny art galleries off O'Connell Street exhibiting works by moody artists obsessed with death - and then we sort of meandered out of it again.

I started to notice the extraordinary number of bottles of pills in her handbag. They rattled like the Queen Mother's jewellery. She became vaguer and vaguer and her pretty looks began to harden. One day a phone conversation about meeting up to see a film – she wanted to see *Kramer vs. Kramer,* the big weepy of that year, while I was pushing for *The China Syndrome,* which had more of a political edge – slowly trailed off. My closing farewell, 'I'll talk to you later', was never fulfilled. I was mortified the next time I saw her. Or at least, the photo of her in the newspapers. Her face was puffed, there were dark circles around her lifeless eyes and her once shining blonde hair hung like limp, lank string. How she got the energy much less the wherewithal to try and rob a Post Office I will never know. The judge was similarly bemused, particularly as her weapon of befuddled choice was a blunt table knife. He mercifully ordered a suspended sentence, detoxification and clinical care rather than a stint in gaol.

Dad just ticked this experience off as yet another failure on my part while Mum wrung her hands, praying and hoping that the right girl would turn up one day. After the searing experiences of Patricia and Tanya, it was a long, long time before I ventured into the world of romance again, and I vowed that if I did, I would play things very cautiously.

Chapter 4

With a woman like Jennifer, things were totally different. Maybe it was because we were both mature adults. Perhaps it was because we met in such a strange and unlikely setting. Either way, our relationship got off to a good start. At the funeral, my interaction with her was spontaneous. There had been no time for preparation. Instead of scripted words, I had to think on my feet and for once the natural me just shone through. At least I think it did, and I hope that that was what attracted her.

Afterwards we slipped away to a dark little bar just down the street. I had a South African chardonnay while she pointed out that alcohol was not really her scene and ordered a lime, soda and ice which came in a tall, thin glass. 'Wow,' I thought, 'she is naturally vivacious, doesn't need any artificial stimulant.' We told each other about ourselves and laughed and philosophised and I had a second glass of wine.

I will never forget that hour or so at the bar. It was one of the most thrilling times of my life, a most absorbing memory being that when she put her glass down, she left a huge cherry-red lipstick mark in the perfect shape of her lips on its rim. As we left, the careful insurance man in me was briefly abandoned. I was so taken by the glass, I stole it. While she was organising her coat and - I fervently hoped - no one else was watching, I slipped it into my overcoat pocket. When I got home that night, I sat the glass on the coffee table, flopped into a chair and just sat there, smiling and happily staring at the outline of her lips.

I couldn't believe my luck. So much so, that a couple of days later, without feeling the usual sense of forboding and dread, I phoned her and asked her if she would like to meet up for a drink, and she said yes. After a coffee in a city café, we went for a stroll through the beautiful grounds of Trinity College and as we walked past the library where people were still queuing up to see the Book of Kells, I was almost floating on air.

Things moved rapidly, and one night after a marvellous dinner – not at a cheap restaurant as with my previous romances, but at Thornton's, the upmarket fish place, then in Portobello Road – she peered up at me as we said goodnight and gave me a look that melted my soul. It was a look that I had never seen in a woman before, other than in the movies. Her eyes were soft and glistening, yet focused right on me. She dropped her head slightly in a delicate movement, her chin dipping down toward her breast. Then she peeked up at me, appealing, beguiling. After a few seconds, she stood up on her tippy-toes and gently kissed me, stepped back and looked at me again. Not a word was spoken. There did not need to be. Typically, I had remained a little reserved up until then. I wanted to be sure of one point; was this for real? But that moment, that look, that kiss convinced me that it was. About a month later, after a meal, a night at the theatre and a double whiskey for me, we ended up in bed. 'Blimey,' I said, as we came to a crashing climax. 'Blimey.'

I was in love. Absolute, genuine, for-certain love. I had found someone who actually seemed to appreciate me for being me. And I wanted her body, mind and soul for me and no one else.

The beauty of it was that there was no giggling behind hands this time, or nasty commands and vitriolic comments, or airy-fairy notions going nowhere. She was beautiful, she was quirky, she was delightful and she was mine. 'Hoare,' I said to myself in the mirror one morning, 'you lucky, lucky man, you! At the tender age of thirty-eight, you have pulled off a miracle! She is absolutely gorgeous. What have you done to deserve this?'

I wanted to go and shout out loudly in the street that I was indeed a fortunate man. I wanted to trawl through the old boys' contact list from my boarding college days and phone up the thugs that had made my life so miserable and say to them, 'So, who's laughing now, you bastards?' I wanted to take her around and show her off to the money makers in the upmarket restaurants of Dublin 4; to the students and grafters in the noisy back streets of Temple Bar; to the busy shoppers in bustling Grafton Street. Instead, I took her to a judo match in Cork.

It was just that I was getting involved in the martial arts at the time. To my few friends and associates, taking up judo seemed an odd choice for a quite, unassuming insurance salesman in his late thirties spooked by the war experiences of his father.

But it was the discipline and philosophy of it that appealed to the insurance man in me. Like insurance, you go through a lot of training and preparation in judo; like insurance, you are fully prepared to step in and take action when something goes wrong; and like insurance, you hope that it won't. Besides, I figured it would help keep me fit. So when I saw the advertisement in the local paper, I made the phone call to the little club in the Liffey Valley and booked my first lesson.

A small bonus was that even Dad liked me for taking it on, in his typically oblique sort of way. While he viewed it as a ridiculous Japanese concept – 'Silly little Asian buggers running around in their pyjamas going chop-socky' – he concluded that at least it had a bit of aggression in it, which appealed to his military upbringing. 'Now you can stand up to anyone who's having a go at you,' he said enthusiastically, 'rather than letting them walk all over you.'

Jennifer became similarly intrigued with the concept of me going into combat. 'Do you get a thrill when you belt your opponent?' she asked cheekily. I tried to explain that it was not really about 'belting' people. It was more a philosophy, a cultural thing, a way of going about your life. 'You're a Buddhist, you should understand,' I said.

'Buddhism does not include any form of violence or physical attack,' she replied, with a firm level of conviction. 'Even the monks in Tibet pursue non-violent protest against the Chinese takeover of their country.'

I explained how judo was more about defence, about disabling the other person. Grappling with them, deflecting their attack and bringing the exchange to a rapid end. 'You don't sink a steel-capped boot in him like some Limerick thug,' I said. 'Judo means "the gentle way".'

She giggled, squeezed the biceps in my left arm with one hand while putting the other to my forehead. 'I get it. The thinking man's fighter,' she said. 'Isaac Newton meets John Rambo.' That was the disarming thing about Jennifer. The chirpy laugh and the rapid summary of the situation that left you disarmed.

After a just a few lessons, my coach, an ancient stalwart of the game named Len, reputed to have represented Ireland at the Tokyo Olympics, concluded that I was ready for competition and entered me in a big Bank Holiday weekend event in Cork. I said to Jennifer it would be wonderful if she could come along. She frowned as she watched me pack my judogi, the traditional white uniform. 'Isn't it a bit early to be testing yourself against others?' she asked. 'You've only been doing it a few months.'

I said that I figured that I had to start somewhere and was heartened by the fact that I, along with my classmates, had been graded for the competition and therefore would be up against someone of similar skill.

'It's not the level of skill I'm worried about,' she said. 'Have you seen how big they are down there in Cork? Those Munster fellows that play rugby? My brothers have been up against some of them and they're gigantic!'

Two days later I found out what she meant. When I walked to the centre of the mat to bow to my first opponent, I nearly wet my judogi. Opposite me was a Belgian Blue bull cleverly disguised as man. His barrel chest split his uniform to the navel, the yellow sash – signifying that, like me, he was at one of the lower grades – barely lashing it to his waist. Hairy muscled forearms the size of legs of lamb peeked out from the loose sleeves, at the end of which were gnarled, work-scarred hands with fingers that resembled jumbo bratwurst. When we went back to the edge of the mat to start the bout, he squatted on his massive thighs, grinning through his bushy beard as if he was going to actually enjoy killing me. At a rough estimate, I figured he weighed 120 kilograms, about half my size again. This was not going to be fun.

From the start, the big fellow rushed headlong at me and I called on God to forgive me for all my transgressions. Don't know if that is in the insurer's handbook, but my mother would have liked the concept. He grabbed me, threw me to the ground and got me in a joint lock. I don't think I have ever tapped the mat as quickly to show submission as at that moment.

He got off me, stepped back and smiled. As the referee pulled me up and gently headed me in the general direction of my very patient teacher, I vowed that this would be my last fight. But no. 'Good lad, great learning experience,' said Len, patting me on the back. 'Next bout in forty minutes. See if you can be a little more, ah, aware, next time.'

If it was possible, my second fight was finished in even quicker time and was more embarrassing. In this bout, my opponent was not at all bulky but instead tall, slim and elegant. He was also extremely calm, well balanced and very talented. He stared at me coolly as I mentally went over my game plan. 'Whatever you do,' Len had warned me, 'don't go to his left and let him get you on his hip.' The bout started, I moved toward him, went straight to his left and let him get me on his hip …

Why is it, like a moth to a flame, that the thing we so determinedly promise ourselves we will never do, we then go and do?

He flashed a grin as I hurried obediently into his trap, flicked me over and landed me on the floor in an un-winnable position. The referee declared it all over, after just one deft move, to the sniggers and polite clapping of the audience.

By my third and final match the crowd had almost doubled, enhanced by whispers to go and see 'this eedjit from Dublin who doesn't last more than two feckin' seconds.' In the west, they love sticking it to the city slickers, whether it's judo, football, hurling or drinking pints.

One look at my final opponent and I figured two seconds was an optimistic prediction. If my first challenger had been big, then this man was massive. The stadium shook as he climbed onto the mat and the crowd went wild, baying for blood. Rather than exhibiting typical judo humility, he waved his arms

and whipped everyone into a frenzy, like Moham-
med Ali before a fight.

As he lumbered straight at me, I did the only
thing a wise man would do. I jumped to one side and
got out of his way. He kept going in a straight line
and shot past me, trying to stop himself at the edge
of the mat before crashing into the spectators.

He turned, the look in his eye even angrier, and
rushed straight at me, this time catching me front on.
I expected him to turn to one side and put me down.
But he didn't. And obviously couldn't. He kept
coming at me, pushing me out of bounds, causing the
judge to pull us apart and start again. I thought, 'This
is sumo, not judo! He's only able to come in a straight
line.'

Jennifer was on the money when she mentioned
Isaac Newton. What did he say? For every action,
there is an equal and opposite reaction?

As my enraged opponent charged at me, I stood
deliberately and provocatively still. He crashed into
me again, not deviating from his line. Perfect, sir,
welcome to the world of the mild mannered insurance representative. Grabbing the lapels of his
judogi, I let myself fall backwards, stuck my feet
forcefully into his stomach, yanked as hard as I could
and kicked as high as possible. The force of his
motion kept him hurtling over my head. In a
beautiful display, he completed an exquisite somer-
sault in the air and landed flat on his back. I could
hear the groans as he thudded onto the mat. The
crowd went wild, the referee giving me a wink as he
helped me get up. 'Not exactly text book,' he

whispered as he declared me the winner, 'but effective.'

Len shook his head in disbelief. My opponent's handlers carried him off as he writhed in pain and clutched at his shoulder, which proved to be dislocated. 'God,' I thought, 'wasn't that great? That'll show them not to mess with Stuart.' Jennifer rushed to meet me. 'Clever boy,' she said. 'Newton's Third Law, with a bit of Sylvester Stallone thrown in.'

That night, as we ate our special treat of haddock and chips at Fishy Fishy in the beautiful port of Kinsale, acknowledged by just about every guide book as the best seafood restaurant in all of Ireland, every muscle and joint in my body was racked with pain. So, if my endeavours in the third bout were courageous, then I thought my efforts in getting down on one knee and proposing were simply heroic.

Yes, I asked Jennifer to marry me. It had only been a matter of a few months, but I was in love and the careful insurance man in me told me that it was the right thing, a sure thing, the proper thing. Out of the blue, I just asked her there and then. I wanted her for myself.

By now we had driven up to the old fort overlooking Kinsale's spectacular bay after a few drinks at The Spaniard Hotel where they played the fiddle and sang songs about the infamous 1601 siege of the town which had fully stamped English control on Ireland. The wind coming up from the sea rustled her beautiful auburn hair and she looked down at me kneeling on the cliff-top grass.

'Stuart Hoare, you wild thing, you crazy, crazy man, do you mean it?'

'I wouldn't have it any other way,' I said solemnly.

'Good,' she said. 'So, where's the ring, then?' And she burst into a joyous peal of laughter that only made me more happy and confident in my decision.

In my haste, and this shows the effect she had imparted on the otherwise controlled purveyor of financial services, there was one thing significant missing. The ring. But I did have a few spare loops on my key-ring, one of which I spiralled off and solemnly slid on her finger, making her laugh even more. We resolved the issue the next morning, finding a quaint little silversmith's shop in town. The ring we bought was exquisite; an original design, hand-made by a craftsman, who if I remember correctly, was Welsh. With a large diamond surrounded by four smaller ones in an asymmetrical shape, it not only captured the beautiful feel of Kinsale but it also encapsulated our love.

I might have been wracked with pain from my bouts with Cork's finest and biggest, I might have won only one match out of three, but right at that point, I was the victor. The happiest man on earth.

Chapter 5

The most enduring memory I have of our wedding is the disbelieving looks on the faces of my family as we assembled for the proceedings. Coming from the deeply conservative Protestant ethic of the Church of Ireland, they were somewhat under-prepared for a Celtic Buddhist ceremony under the full moon of the summer equinox in a Roscommon forest by the banks of the Shannon.

But that is what Jennifer wanted, and I wanted her so much, so who was I to argue?

My mother's usually cosy smile straightened into thin lips as we embarked on the gentle walk from the restored 18th century mansion through the manicured gardens into the woods. Dad – who up until then had been so supportive of what was happening between me and Jennifer because I think in some strange way she reminded him of his mother – muttered dark predictions that any marriage based on 'this Merlin the Magician madness' was doomed.

Fortunately, there were only half a dozen family members on my side to get concerned. Historically, our lineage had not been enthusiastic breeders. When we had been preparing the invitation list, I had suggested that anyone on even the remotest edges of our circle, as long as they could get a decent haircut and present in a suitable outfit, be press-ganged into attendance. That ended up being Mum and Dad, Mum's cousin and her husband, both still very bruised from the death of their son, plus their daughter Mary. Our party was rounded out by my business partner, Derek, and my good friend and trusted insurance valuer and consultant, Buchanan, plus a handful of other friends and assorted acquaintances, including Olaf Hendrikson, one of my very few valued mates from my boarding college days.

Olaf, a smart, very loquacious sort of fellow and loved by all, had kept in contact with most of our former classmates. So I felt good having him there, knowing that he would pass the word around the old boys' fraternity, even to those thugs who had given me a hard time, that 'Hoare the Whore' had made something of himself, including marrying this most astonishing, beautiful, vibrant woman.

My group contrasted with Jennifer's colourful, noisy tribe, and I use that word in the nicest possible way, who gathered in their dozens, even though she had said it would be a 'small and exclusive' gathering. Typically, they all turned up whether they had sent back an RSVP or not, and many went with the flow when they spotted the suggestion of 'appropriate dress' on the invitation.

Whereas my guests were suitably but sombrely dressed in outfits that were clean, neat and could have just as easily been serviceable at a funeral, Jennifer's mob was a fascinating, rolling cartwheel of colour and flair. Even the most mature turned up in robes and saris reflecting the Buddhist ethic or in tunics, tops and leggings in keeping with the Celtic theme. There were layers and layers of thin white cotton billowing in the slight evening breeze, yards of saffron robes, headbands holding together even the most greying of thatches, thick-strapped leather sandals and baggy trousers held up by multi-coloured scarves. They moved amid a constant rattle and chime of bangles, bracelets and necklaces. If the Dalai Lama himself had have pulled up in the Benz to join the throng, no one would have been remotely surprised.

Memories of his Indian times came flooding back for Dad when he spotted the page boy dressed in a green outfit of trousers, waist-coat and turban. Several of Jennifer's little nieces floated around excitedly in green dresses with angel wings attached to their backs. As we headed down the path, the crowd seemed to grow bigger and noisier, our way being made clear by attendants carrying torches that crackled in the balmy summer air. We reached a clearing by the banks of the river and gathered in a circle under the mystical, bright light of the full moon. 'I've been reading that this is where they keep reporting all those UFO sightings,' Mum whispered to Dad.

What happened after that is a bit of a blur. Celtic Buddhism is a strain of the philosophy that was begun by an American guru in the 1970s, the view being the Celtic concepts of mythology and sorcery run more or less parallel with Buddhist contempla-tion of the meaning of life, both seeking infinite wisdom. As a result of this quirky combination, in that beautiful clearing under the sparkling moonlight, we exchanged vows before a priestly figure named Davina adorned in silver and purple robes. Quite frankly, I would have married Jennifer in the back bar of Dan Foley's pub in Youghal if she had wanted to.

Everything was done in the original language of the Celts. I had rehearsed assiduously in the weeks beforehand to remember my lines and get them right. The energy from the crowd was palpable. When I looked like I was going to stumble on any of the words, their positive life-force lifted me over the line.

So after Davina declared that we, Stuart Richard Hoare and Jennifer Mary O'Brien, were now man and wife, I turned to kiss my new bride and felt a sensation of utter relief combined with pure joy. She had chosen a simple outfit, the lightest of light green, sleeveless, slightly billowing and tied at the waist, and on that night, under the full moon of June 23, 1991, as the summer solstice was about to herald a beautiful new beginning, my Jennifer looked a goddess. Her glorious red hair, rolling down to her shoulders in carefully-prepared ringlets, picked up a silver-tinged aura from both the moonlight and from her jewellery – long, dangling ear-rings which featured the traditional yin and yang Buddhist motif and a broad silver bangle on her left wrist etched with ancient Celtic symbols. Her green eyes sparkled and in keeping with the simple tradition, she wore little make-up and none of her favourite Poppy King lipstick. This, to me, only served to highlight her natural beauty. I was smitten. I wanted her to stay that way forever.

As we all walked back for the reception, sited in a cobbled courtyard amid a circle of flares, even my family began to unwind. Mum concluded that, odd as the ceremony had been and far removed from the concepts of the Church of Ireland, it still had a nice feel about it. She was made to feel even more relieved when she was informed that underneath the purple and silver outfit, Davina was actually a legally registered marriage celebrant and not a daughter of Satan. Everything was legitimate or, as Dad put it, using an old army expression he had picked up in India, 'tickety-boo.'

Whatever it was, Mum figured it was grand because I was now legally married and had a partner for life, something she had yearned for across the years. Seeing as I was now nearly forty, she was a very happy mother. Her smile got broader and broader throughout the night because she was finally fulfilling one of her major wishes. I know my social awkwardness and occasional forays into disastrous romances had pained her greatly and there were times when she thought that marriage for me would never come to pass. She never said it directly to me over the years, but I knew that in her heart that this was really all she wanted. Her references had always been well-meaning but transparently unsubtle, such as, 'There's a new family that has joined the church congregation. They seem very nice, especially their daughter.' Or, 'A good woman does wonders for a man.' And now, that good woman had appeared.

To make things absolutely perfect, Dad also discovered that the celebrations would accommodate all Celtic traditions including the drink. Once a single malt whiskey was thrust in his hand by a waiter dressed as a tribal chieftain, all concern about the bizarre nature of the ceremony was gone. When the Irish fiddle, squeezebox and bodhran were cranked up by the band and we danced by the light of the moon and the flickering flames of the flares for hours on end, Dad sat on a chair at the edge of the circle with a smile that got broader and broader throughout the evening as the music got faster and the staff plied him with more grog. And even if there was only a handful of guests from our side, my trusty valuer Buchanan in his inimitable style made up for our lack of numbers with a vintage performance on the dance-floor. Proving to everyone that not all insurance salesmen are stolid, dreary types, he reeled, rolled, and rocked with his wife, with my new wife, with my mother, with Jennifer's mother, with anyone who wanted to strut their stuff.

At one stage he whispered in the band leader's ear, gathered all the little ones in their pretty dresses and outfits and started a conga line to the music, which eventually collected most of the adults and we weaved our way in and around the tables and trees and flares amid raucous laughter and singing. At the end, Buchanan climbed on a table with a pint, held it aloft and declared a toast. 'To Stuart and Jennifer,' he shouted, 'starting much bloody later than the rest of us, but may they have a wonderful life together.' The responding roar echoed through the forest and across the grasslands.

We had booked out the entire recently-refurbished mansion for the whole wedding party to stay, so no one had to rush off, rather they could sleep in the newly renovated servants' quarters. As we were miles away from anywhere, the music blasted into the early hours and when Jennifer and I finally collapsed on the bed in the bridal suite, formerly the bedroom of the master of the house, we were spent. We flopped on the four-poster, sank into the lush mattress, embraced, kissed … and slept. My last recollection is of rolling over and seeing a painting on the wall opposite. It was of a little girl, aged about five, with reddish hair and beautiful green but quite sad eyes, her face tinged with a state of melancholy, as if she was lost. It was unsigned and had no caption or indicator who she was, so presumably it was a print that the new owners of the house had bought as part of a job lot to decorate the place. Perhaps it was a reaction to such a long day, or the many champagnes, wines and whiskies that I had drunk, but the little girl's sad eyes seared into me, in an almost scary, foreboding manner.

In the morning, I awoke and those eyes were still staring at me, forming a powerful image that was later to come back and haunt me. I turned away and said nothing to Jennifer, as we packed and headed off to Dublin for a night in a hotel, where at last we made genuine love – real, enjoyable, man-and-wife-for-the-first-time 'Blimey' love – and then set off for our honeymoon.

Going to Bermuda was not only my idea, but my little secret, revealed only at the very end. For weeks before, Jennifer had tried to tease the location out of me. She attempted to seduce it from me one night with a bottle of chilled Portuguese rose and my favourite hot curry, but I would not bend, only reluctantly admitting under intense pressure and much tickling that our mystery destination was 'beside the seaside,' was 'terribly English' and started with 'B'.

'The bastard's taking me to Bognor Regis,' I overhead her laughingly say to a friend on the phone one night, which caused me considerable amusement and only added to her curiosity.

The best part was that not only had I secured an excellent flights-and-accommodation package but I had sealed two big insurance deals in the weeks leading up to the wedding and with the handsome royalties was able to upgrade us to a bigger apartment in Nassau, overlooking the beach. The Carribean weather was perfect, the food was brilliant and the water-sports were fantastic.

Jennifer even agreed that my hint that the place was 'terribly English' had some merit, even though the island chain had gained independence from Britain in the 1970s. They still spoke English, called themselves The Commonwealth of Bermuda and played 'God Save The Queen' at official functions.

But, oddly enough, she didn't concede much else. Or contribute that much, either, preferring to stay in the apartment most times while I headed for the beach. She was listless for most of the seven days. No doubt from the pressure and stress of it all, I figured, which was a real pity.

I plunged under the sparkling waves, my pink flesh surfacing wet and salty, and I could not have felt happier. We had been married by the light of the moon and now we were going to enjoy our time in the sun.

Chapter 6

Jennifer's family was the absolute opposite of mine, not only in number but attitude. While on my side there was me, Mum, Dad, and a handful of occasionally seen relatives, Jennifer not only had her parents but four older brothers and a seemingly endless host of aunts, uncles, cousins, nieces and nephews stretching across several generations. If my family was a planet with a couple of moons, then her lot was the entire Milky Way, an extraordinary collection of heavenly bodies whirling, gyrating and streaking across the sky, stretching to infinity and beyond.

You couldn't fault their graciousness and well-meaning. Whenever we gathered, the women constantly fluttered around me, filling me with endless cream cakes, jam scones and hot cups of tea. They would pump me for information about my family and praise me to the high heavens for being the knight in shining armour who had ridden into Jennifer's life on his valiant steed at such a crucial moment, thus saving her from spending the rest of her life languishing on the shelf, which to them seemed to be a fate worse than death. In between, they talked ceaselessly about babies, children, food, recipes, schools, mothers groups and their well-meaning, boisterous but quite often ineffective husbands.

The raucous babble as they gathered in groups at family functions was matched by the waving, nodding and gesticulating as each endeavoured to get their word in. Somehow, six conversations could be conducted at once between five people and no one would miss a beat. Coming from my discreet little clan, they were an eye-opener to me; beautiful women, mothers, grandmothers and mothers-to-be, with a wonderful humanity and insight into the human existence. I don't think they appreciated just how savvy they were. Or if they did, they did not have time to stop and evaluate it. Caring, generous, concerned, joyous, enthusiastic, they took me in, made me one of the family and fed me up.

With the men, it was a bit different. Jennifer was the only girl in the family and despite their outward friendliness and enthusiasm, her father, Seamus, and four brothers – Patrick, Daniel, Brendan and Kevin – still gave off the air that no one was ever going to be good enough for their much-loved princess. Kevin in particular was the one to be wary of. He was next in age up the line from Jennifer and saw it as his duty to protect his little sister at all times. Just in what way he saw that role, whether it be morally, spiritually or physically, was not clear, least of all to him. But if he felt he detected something or somebody looming on the horizon that would cause her grief, then he would march out, jaw set, eyes narrowed and guns at the ready to see the miscreant off.

The five of them, Jennifer's father included, were all big chaps, gregarious, with florid cheeks and a ready joke, a wink and a laugh. They constantly slapped me on the back, poured pints down my throat whether I wanted them or not and worked diligently at trying to deconstruct my Protestantism and re-create me in the Catholic mould. They endlessly took the mickey out of me because of my strait-laced approach, reactive thinking and cautious contributions at family get-togethers. I suppose I did not help matters with my predilection for writing letters to the more serious newspapers, publicly outlining my opinion on current events, proffering a view that I will readily admit was rather conservative, and which Jennifer regularly described as 'fuddy-duddy.' I was astonished that the boys read anything other than *The Sunday World*, but sure enough, after one of my considered opinions would be published in say, *The Independent* or *The Irish Times*, on the lack of discipline in modern schools or the dissolution of social etiquette or some similar topic, they would be on to it like a shot. 'So, we are all disappearing down the sewer of moral turpitude, are we, Stu?' they would say. Or, 'By God, Stu, you are right, society has reduced itself to the level of the chimpanzee.'

Sometimes, they would call me 'Bertie,' which at first I thought was a friendly jest at my admiration for Bertie Ahern, the Prime Minister who I considered was leading the country out of ingrained poverty into glorious prosperity. Then one day I discovered they meant it as a short form of 'Bertrand,' as in Bertrand Russell, the philosopher. 'No doubt about it, Bertie,' they would say, 'you're the thinking man's thinker.'

I copped all this with an array of silent smiles, false laughter and the occasional riposte, but knew that no matter how hard I tried, I would never be fully part of the O'Brien clan. As I was coming out of the upstairs bathroom of the family home one day I heard Patrick, standing at the foot of the stairs, say to his father, 'He's a nice poor bugger, but he's a bit of feckin' goody two-shoes, isn't he?'

Another time, when I was retrieving a plate of food and a bottle of wine from the back of the car as we arrived for a family lunch, I spotted Seamus out of the corner of my eye standing on the broad patio of their beautiful Blackrock home, giving me the slightly bemused look of a man who was pleased that at last his daughter had settled down, but not entirely convinced that her choice had been the right one. Seamus was originally a Kerry man, a true son of 'The Kingdom', as they call it down that way. It's a completely different world, exemplified by their love of GAA football and their sheer delight every time the green-and-golds trample the fancy-nancy blue boys from Dublin on their way to yet another All Ireland title. Your Kerry man is a robust, hail-fellow-well-met type full of good cheer and self-belief. I always got the impression that every time he saw me in those early days Seamus mentally ticked off all the major and minor points of Jennifer's previous boyfriends and partners and then sadly came to the conclusion that whatever colour and sass and energy and originality that they had brought to the table, it had all been put into one big pot and boiled down to me, a well-meaning Protestant insurance salesman.

Meanwhile, the brothers, while friendly, could be quite over-bearing, particularly after a few drinks. At first they treated me like some sort of manipulative fiend who had stolen their little princess away from them, until I plumped up the courage one night to remind them that she was no longer sixteen with her hair in bangs. 'She's a mature woman, in her thirties, capable of making her own decisions,' I said.

This set them back for a while, particularly the ever-vigilant Kevin, but they never entirely went away, their thinly-veiled jokes about my religion, being so old when I got married and the humdrum of the insurance business remaining always close to the bone. I never really had a balanced, two-way conversation with any of them. Rather, they would hector me into submission, their style of social intercourse based on making a broad, outrageous statement extolling their view on any given topic and ending with an overbearing, 'Are you not agreein' with me now, Stu?' Or, 'I'm telling you, Stu, that's the way it is.'

These statements, generally about how the rest of the world did not live up to their lofty standards, were so breathtaking in their simple-minded, audacious self-belief that finding a quick-fire answer on the spur of the moment was almost impossible. I was always left to mumble a pathetic, 'Yes, probably.' Later, in the quietness of the bathroom, standing before the mirror, I used to curse myself for not having the wherewithal to come up with a snappy reply that would have stopped them in their tracks or at least made them think. Something akin to the content of one of my well constructed Letters To The Editor, but produced there and then, on the spot. Then one day it dawned on me that it would not have mattered what I said because they never listened and they certainly didn't think.

The best thing was to play along with their little game. So I outwardly expressed suitable shock, concern and revulsion when the oldest son, Patrick, was caught having an affair with his marketing manager.

Slinging his clubs into the boot of the car, he had told his wife Kathy that he was off to a weekend business convention in Galway, which would include a round or two of golf. In fact, it was a conference for two, invitation only, and golf was most certainly not on the agenda. He got tripped up when he returned on the Sunday night and Kathy asked him how the golf went, particularly the new putter she had bought him for his birthday only a couple of weeks before. 'Great,' he had replied, 'it worked beautifully. I was rolling them in from a long way out.'

'You certainly were,' she said, producing the putter from the pantry. 'All the feckin' way from here.'

She had taken it out of his bag before he'd left, and as the clubs had stayed in the back of the car all weekend, he had not noticed. His betrayal of his wife and five kids brought his real character to light and after that, while he tried to clean up the mess by perversely seeking a Papal annulment of the marriage, Patrick and his brothers left me pretty much alone.

I can tell you now, when Patrick's world came crashing down, I tut-tutted along with the best of them, and said how terrible it was for the kids. But internally I harboured a great, unbounded shout-it-from-the-roof-tops feeling of unadulterated joy. 'Ha, ha, ha,' I thought, 'Paddy, you smart-arse son of a Kerry man, you got sprung.'

The annulment thing really got to me. How could it be seriously judged that even though five children had been born, the marriage did not exist in the first place?

For me, a marriage should last forever, no matter what. I was determined ours would.

After all, Jennifer was mine; we were a beautiful unit, the complete package.

Chapter 7

One of the greatest shocks for a newly married man, especially one who has lived the bachelor life until his thirties, is what suddenly happens to his possessions.

Throughout my childhood and adult years, I had never had to share anything with anyone. My toys and sweets and games had been all mine. My books and money and car had been all mine. Even my parents were all mine. I did not have to share them with anyone else either.

When I worked hard, saved my money and finally moved out from Mum and Dad's, the apartment I bought in Dublin was all mine. My name was on the title. Now, so very quickly, it had become 'ours.'

This nettled me a bit. Sure, Jennifer was bringing a property to the marriage. But it was a tiny little terrace in Harold's Cross, stuck right on a busy, grubby main thoroughfare, opposite a 24-hour convenience store that attracted some very unsavoury characters. It was lucky to be half the value of my place, a three bedroom condominium in the heart of Dublin. After a lot of research, I had carefully picked it out and got it at an excellent price because it was a quick-fire 'must-sell' following a messy divorce between the previous yuppie owners. Having saved diligently over the years, I was able to buy it with a substantial deposit and a modest loan.

It was almost new, bright and clean, with floor to ceiling windows, plush carpet and plenty of space. I may have fitted it out in typical bachelor style – Jennifer particularly hated the big-screen television slotted in front of the patio doors – but it suited me. It was my place.

The first time I heard Jennifer refer to it as 'our' place was in a conversation over chicken Kiev with two other couples, shortly after we had returned from Bermuda. You know those events, when you're invited to a home dinner party along with another couple you've never met before. Conversation bounces backwards and forwards as the two guest pairings try to work out where the others fit in on the social strata, what they do for a living and what their attitudes are. Heading the list of topics of conversation used to establish these criteria are generally education, the economy and real estate. So, when we got to the subject of property, Jennifer jumped in. 'We're wondering what to do with our place,' she said. 'We think it might be time to sell it and get a house.'

While I was still pondering her use of the word 'our', the husband of the couple we had never met before leapt straight onto this. As it turned out, he was in real estate – well, there you go, then – and had a very clear idea on what to do. 'Sell it, Jennifer,' he enthused. 'Now's the time. You'll get a great price.' And he leaned across to hand her his card, apologising for bringing business to the dinner table but with that smirky shark smile that is the hallmark of the confident realtor.

I got very annoyed with this. 'Hang on,' I thought to myself. 'Isn't this *my* place we are talking about here? Suddenly, it's *our* place! And furthermore, he's ignoring me and talking to Jennifer as if she is the owner and offering her all the advice about flogging it off.'

I was so consumed with this sudden power shift, I stabbed my fork into the chicken Kiev with such force that I squirted hot butter all over the plate and onto the table cloth. 'Bloody hell,' I thought to myself, 'what has Jennifer financially brought into this partnership? Not much in the way of property, that's for sure.' I was about to utter something, a remonstration of some sort, but I thought better of it. What was I going to say? 'Hey, buster, yes, you, the real estate feller, listen, my name's on the title and if you want it, you'll get it from my cold, dead hand?' Hmm. Might put a bit of a dampener on things. Better wait until we get home and talk it over then.

The others continued to prattle on about interest rates, the booming state of the market amid this new, burgeoning Irish economic surge, and the best way to sell the property. They did not take the slightest bit of notice of me as I cleaned up my mess with the neatly-ironed linen napkin. This gave me a little time to calm down and think things through more rationally.

'I guess this is how it will be from now on,' I figured. 'That's what a partnership is all about. And Jennifer is right, of course. We are married, and we now share things. Everything. Our lives, our love, our bodies, our goods, our property. I promised to share everything in the vows we made in the clearing next to the Shannon by the light of the full moon. Mine is hers, and hers is mine. I am hers. And, most importantly, she is mine ...'

I felt a bit more comforted as all this revolved through my mind, and so I took a sip of wine and began to eat the chicken with renewed enthusiasm.

After a minute or so, I was brought back to reality when, out of the corner of my eye, I caught a blinding flash of light. I looked up to see that it was the gleam coming from the pearly white teeth of the real estate shark. He was smiling with enthusiasm, asking me what price would he like me to set on the apartment if we put it on the market right now! A bit taken aback by his cheekiness, I wiped my mouth slowly with my napkin, placed it down carefully on the table in front of me to cover the butter splashes and clasped my hands in front of my face in the shape of a church steeple. I could sense Jennifer getting mightily agitated. I slowly finished swallowing the mouthful of chicken, cleared my throat and said, 'Well, I'm not one to rush into things, but speculatively, I think ninety thousand would be reasonable.' The shark smile grew wider.

'Stuart, the big game is only starting,' he enthused. 'I can get you another ten, twenty, thirty, fifty grand! No problems. You will be able to buy wherever you want. And pretty soon down the track you'll be able to sell the next one for three times its price if you want. People in the know tell me that the nineties are going to be the biggest boom decade this little country has ever seen.' He leant over and handed me a card. 'Thank you,' I said unruffled, putting it into my jacket pocket. 'I'll, ah, that is, *we* will have a little think about it, won't *we* Jen?' I could feel the daggers from Jennifer's stare piercing the side of my skull.

When we got home, we had our first ever confrontation, of sorts. 'I was just making the point that, in the first instance, this is my house, that's all,' I said calmly. Jennifer turned to go to the bedroom. 'Well, it was yours, and now it's ours,' she said sharply as she headed away from me. 'And soon,' she added, 'it will be sold and we will have a new place!'

This unsettled me. It was a side of her that I had never seen before, a side I did not like. I followed her into the bedroom and as I walked past her to go to the en suite, I lifted her chin and lightly slapped her face and said to her quietly but firmly, 'Just be careful what you say, darling,' and left it at that. She looked at me, put her hand to her cheek, and went very quiet. I had never been one to fire back at people, but this time I did. And it felt good. I felt I had scored a little victory.

As it turned out, shark's teeth was as good as his word. Rather than the more traditional style of a private sale, he took the apartment to auction against my better judgment, danced across the stage in front of the crowd like Mick Jagger, used my compliant father as a dummy bidder to up the ante – a bottle of Jameson's insured his inspired participation – and came up with an extra thirty-seven thousand five hundred. It was an astonishing result, giving us the opportunity to buy a home in, of all places, Dalkey. Bang, we were suddenly living harbour-side in Dublin's dress circle, in a location many people would have died for. Dalkey is a beautiful suburb, right on the water, south of the port of Dun Laoghaire, and I detected just a little tinge of surprise bordering on envy from friends when we told them where we had bought. 'Feckin' hell, Stu,' said Buchanan when I told him. 'You'll be working your arse off to pay for that.'

Of course, it was good old shark's teeth who not only found the Dalkey home for us, but who also sold Jennifer's little pad, thus providing him with a bonanza in commissions. As the three of us stood out on the front lawn with the smell of the Irish Sea in our nostrils, I reckon his smile could have been seen from Liverpool. He must have loved to see strangers like me wander into a mutual friend's place for a chicken Kiev.

But I will admit, despite my original misgivings about what was 'hers' and what was 'mine', Jennifer and the real estate whiz-kid had been right in their determinaton to get things under way quickly. The day we moved into the house was for me almost as exciting as the day of our wedding. Our new home had charm, space, light, warmth and a beautiful family feel about it. It had only two bedrooms but there was opportunity to expand, plus a large, well-equipped kitchen and a lounge room that could almost have accommodated my old apartment. Sorry, 'our' old apartment.

In retrospect, I guess it was good that that this small but significant discussion about selling my place had happened in front of other people. I often reflect what I might have said to Jennifer if she had first used the expression 'our place' to me without someone else in the room. Say, across the breakfast table on a Monday morning as we were both heading out to work. Would I have got upset and fired back: 'What do you mean our place?', leading us into a heated discussion and onto God knows where. The whole thing could have blown up there and then.

No, she was right, and things were going to be fine. I may have lost sole ownership of an apartment, but I had gained a whole new beautiful home and a delightful wife to manage it. Now, that was a real possession. Something to be proud of. And to never let go, under any circumstances.

Chapter 8

Then, we slipped into second gear. I don't mean that in a negative or derogatory sense. I sometimes think second gear is a beautiful place to be in, providing of course we are talking about an original, classic three-speed gear-box, and not one of those hi-tech six-level electronic systems they use these days. Second gear is more productive and pacey than first and has a touch of acceleration about it. A sense of going somewhere, with the additional element of a slight roaring sound to add to the excitement. But it is not as exhilarating as third, and therefore not as dangerous. In second, despite its limitations, you are able to get anywhere and achieve what you want without going over the top.

Cruising along in second gear at home meant I was travelling nicely at work. I would go off each morning, proud of myself and my beautiful wife and our wonderful house, and concentrate on the job at hand all day.

While I was a part-owner of the business, along with Derek, I saw my role as a vertical one, handling a wide range of tasks from managerial at the top right down to sales. That's just the way I am in life, really. I like to be involved in everything. Sure, I trusted my staff, but I wanted to ensure that they maintained the standards that I thought were appropriate. I kept up selling, so as not to get stale. I loved sales. A sale of a new policy was always a delight for me, the presentation of a new product to the staff was a joy, and examining our constantly growing turnover figures provided me with a feeling of immense satisfaction. Even outlining policies to potential clients who I knew from experience were not going to sign on was an engaging challenge. I loved to walk them through the detail of the benefits, the bonuses, the premiums, the payment options. The art was to try and keep my enthusiasm on an even keel. Not get too pushy and come across as a salesman but hold back – drop into second gear – and become their confidante, advisor and friend, outlining to them how, at the end of the day, this was going to be good for them. I truly believed it and wanted my clients to appreciate that, too.

Not only that, I could see big things happening in Ireland. The economy, as our shark's teeth real estate man had predicted, was beginning to really boom and I had in the back of my mind that Derek and I could move the business even further into financial services – advice, brokering, property investment, that sort of thing. I was in a happy place.

But then, not long after we had moved to Dalkey, Jennifer started talking about having a baby! This came as a big jolt, right out of the blue. It was all a bit too fast for me. I would have preferred to have waited a little longer and enjoyed our time as newlyweds, appreciating the world and our new home together like two young lovers rather than being catapulted into the disciplined domain of parenthood. I wanted to be able to take my beautiful

wife out and, I will admit, show her off to the world.
I will make no bones about it.

Consider what had happened so far. By my
early thirties, I looked like I was going to be a solitary
man forever, sitting in my sparsely furnished Dublin
flat all by myself, making two minute pasta, watching the *Late Late Show* and reading biographies about
Bill Gates, Bill Cullen and Alan Sugar. Then suddenly, I had this vivacious woman at my side, a
person that even the harshest critic would describe as
a great catch, lighting up any room she walked into.
Why shouldn't I want to show her off?

One of the great advantages was that Jennifer
was brilliant with all people at all levels. While I had
certain comunicative skills, particularly in a business
setting, I always found events such as parties a
challenge. Removed from my comfortable platform
of the sales spiel, I found myself either standing in a
corner with a warm drink or being the silent one
amongst the group as all the others told heroic tales
or comical stories. With Jennifer, it was different. She
captivated everyone around her, but all the while she
couldn't wait to get home so that we could make
love. No, wait, let me re-phrase that. So that we could
have sex.

Now, I was not the greatest lover, I will admit
that. I had not had a lot of experience, and I know
that my first few clumsy attempts in the early days of
our relationship were pretty rapid fire. I just couldn't
help myself, climaxing very quickly, and I appreciated Jennifer's patience and forebearance. But even I
knew that within a few short weeks of our wedding

we had left the realms of intimacy and had lurched into the world of mechanics. Spontaneity was replaced by a strict regime centred around the calendar. 'Hear that?' she would say, cupping her hand to her ear theatrically. 'That's the sound of my biological clock ticking.'

'Yes, darling, I hear it.'

'It's five minutes to midnight and they're playing the last waltz, Fred Astaire. You'd better get your dancing shoes on.'

I loved her and was proud of her, but I was not yet ready to share her with children. Nevertheless, pregnancy became our number one target. And that, in Jennifer's mind, could only be achieved by total adherence to her carefully plotted strategy. It was high pressure and intensely technical. Phrases such as 'predicting ovulation' and 'cervical mucous' and 'basal body temperature' became part of our daily lexicon. Trouble was, despite the highly-scheduled logistics and our combined physical efforts, the system had a hidden malfunction somewhere. No matter when, where or how often we rigidly stuck to the cycle, nothing would eventuate.

Jennifer would disappear into the en suite with the pregnancy tester and I would hear her ripping the cover off it and having a wee, followed by the slap of the toilet lid as she would sit down and wait for the result. Then, after what would seem to be an interminable time, she would come out. The first few times she was disappointed but not defeated. Then over the course of the next few months there came expressions of despondency, frustration, anger, and finally the phrase I was silently anticipating. 'You,' she shouted after many months, waving the negative result at me. 'It must be your fault! You're firing blanks, you big useless bollocks.'

Maybe I was. That thought had regularly crossed my mind. I was getting older and had never fathered a child. I was from a family that were not big breeders, our miniscule attendance at the wedding attesting to that. I was not what you would call a sexual dynamo, a rumpy-pumpy master of the good Rogering, a Barry White love god. Far from it. It could well be that the fault was mine.

There was only one way to find out.

Under her instructions, I obediently made an appointment with a men's health clinic in Sandyford, and dutifully turned up at the spartan, ultra-clean office. The nurse gave me a small bottle and directed me to a little cubicle, inside of which there was a chair, a table and the only other accoutrement, a pile of well-thumbed men's magazines, amongst which I discovered a copy of *Penthouse*. After scrutinising the picture spread of that edition's centre-fold, a slithery brunette named Krista, followed by some rather embarrassing one-handed action, I filled the bottle to the half way point, tidied myself up, and offered both it and the *Penthouse* back to the nurse. She took the bottle and applied a sticker to it. 'You can put the magazine back in the room,' she said icily.

A few days later the specialist, a cheery, Scots fellow with rosy cheeks and flourishing ginger sideboards, slapped me on the shoulder, leaned close and said, 'Laddie, ye've got enough wee wriggly fellers in that bottle to impregnate an entire Highland village.' Praise the Lord, the test had proved Jennifer wrong! I still had plenty left in the tank. I walked out of his office beaming, only to disappear unsmiling into the desperate world of IVF.

Look, it all sounds very well. 'We'll take an egg from you, Jennifer, and some sperm from you, Stuart, mix them in a Petri dish, say a few magic words while waving our hands over the top, put it all back inside and Bob's your uncle.' At least, that was how it seemed to be presented to me. But, my God, it was difficult. It was a painful experience for Jennifer, her body being pushed and probed and bullied into submission. 'Harvested' was one term they used, which made my blood boil. It sounded like my wife, my beautiful wife, was some sort of field or tree from which they were going to reap grain or fruit.

The physical agony was only matched by the emotional stress as each failure confirmed in Jennifer's mind that the minute hand on her famous clock was edging rapidly closer to midnight. The last waltz was almost over and I could feel the soles on my dancing pumps wearing perilously thin.

And then one day, miracle of miracles, things 'took' and suddenly our first little baby was on the way. I can't tell you how powerful was the sense of relief and joy that swept through us both. I was walking on water and, better still, the furrowed, angst-ridden look that had begun to blight Jennifer's pretty face disappeared. If she looked beautiful the night I married her, then she absolutely blossomed through that first pregnancy. Morning sickness, the emotional see-saw, concerns about the health of the baby, they certainly came and went, but she overrode them all with a mixture of happiness and determination. The sense of achievement drove her on, and I thought to myself, 'You know, this is what she really wants.' And when a little boy arrived on a cold Dublin morning all pink and squishy, with a slight bruise on his forehead but otherwise perfectly healthy, we just held him and thought, 'Haven't we done well?'

Funny thing is, the next two babies – another little boy and then, nearly eight years later, a daughter for Jennifer – came without any IVF help at all. Anything can happen when you relax. Especially if you drop back into second gear.

Chapter 9

I think I was a pretty good father. An absent one maybe, perhaps at crucial moments when I might have been of greater assistance at home, but overall still pretty good.

I didn't get much guidance from my family in the art of engaging with children. For my father, the ever mobile military man, the way of launching conversation with me as a child was to ask, 'Geared up and ready for battle, Stuart?' And in terms of being parents themselves, Jennifer's father and her four brothers weren't particularly good role models either, especially Patrick, who sabotaged his whole family unit for the sake of a bit of sex on the side.

So while the world was rapidly changing around me and the New Age Dad was becoming de rigueur, I tended to adopt the old-fashioned view that I was the father and the bread winner and Jennifer was the mother and the family manager. Well, from my reading, that technique had worked successfully for centuries, so why fix it when it was not broken? Sure, I pitched in and did things more than my Dad and those of his generation did. I was not an entirely silent, non-existent father.

I loved to play with the kids in the evening and made a point of being with them as much of the weekend as I could, depending on golf commitments or judo lessons. But after two other fruitless careers, I knew insurance was my game, my opportunity for success, and it was important to me that I concentrated hard on that and made the best of it in order to benefit everyone. I saw myself as the provider of the family, the tribal head, the hunter, the gatherer. And in that situation, what the chief says, goes.

So there I was, a bachelor in my late thirties, a three-time Dad in my fifties. I read books with the kids and played hide-and-seek around the garden and held their tiny hands as we strolled around the port at Dun Laoghaire. I loved taking them down to Bulloch Harbour, which was not far from us, just past the Martello Tower.

We would wait patiently on the edge of the slippery blue-stone pier for the appearance of a pair of seals that had taken up habitation around there. The kids were always thrilled when the two large, black, quizzically humorous faces would suddenly break the water with a rushing, whooshing sound. This maritime odd couple would then stare at us with a look along the lines of, 'So, what are you doing here, then?' It was very hard to obey the signs not to feed them, but it was worth it, because we got to know the scene and the people down there very well. One of the perks was being able to order a nice fresh lobster for dinner. I always loved this part because although Jennifer was vegetarian, she considered fresh fish, particularly lobster, as not being too far out of her strict regimen and the meal we would have that night would be delicious.

I know I was a solid, conservative type but generally speaking, particularly in the early days, I would let the kids tease and manipulate me and I would take it all in good stead and come back for more. Within reason, of course. I would kick the rugby ball with the boys and help them with their hurling and soccer. I showed them some of the finer points of judo, particularly for their own self-defence, with a view to them perhaps taking it up.

There was one time that Jennifer bought them a kite for Christmas and we had a great time putting it together and taking it to a local park on a windy day. After a few failed lift-offs and some serious nose-into-the-turf crashes, we finally got it off the ground and it flew beautifully like a bird until young Richard managed to loop it over some power wires and we went home empty-handed.

The boys and I also worked in the garden together, turning the sandy soil over and planting little rows of flowers such as nasturtiums and clusters of veggies, including potatoes and carrots. Some grew well, and a lot didn't, but none through lack of trying. I was very insistent that the boys helped me with this task. I saw it as a great model of what life was all about; that is, you get out what you put in. 'If you select the right seeds, plant them at the right time, cultivate them carefully and tend the plot, you will get a good result,' I would say to them. 'But if you do it in a slapdash way, you will get very little in return.'

There were great moments of celebration in the kitchen when the boys would proudly and trium-phantly bring in some of their fresh produce for Jennifer to cook for dinner. But if they were tardy and weeds started to spring up, I would make it clear to them that they were not being responsible and that I was unhappy with their performance. Jennifer used to complain sometimes that I was getting on their backs about this too much but I felt that she was entirely wrong on this matter.

'As you sow, so you shall reap,' I would say to her. 'It's in the good book.'

'Which good book is that, darling?' she said to me one day. 'The Bible? Or the insurer's handbook?'

Despite her taunts or criticism, no one could take any of those fatherly moments away from me. But if the situation came down to deciding between spending the time at the office working on something important rather than being at home, then I felt that for the good of the family work and career came first. We had a beautiful house in an exclusive address with three lovely children, and with us both agreeing that Jennifer would stay at home and run it, someone had to pay the bills. That was me. And I was proud to do it.

Fatherhood is a challenging task, an extremely tricky business, particularly developing an enduring relationship with each of your children as they come along. My approach, despite my Protestant background, was to adopt the Jesuit philosophy: 'Give me a child until he is seven, and I will give you the man.' That is, I would begin with a clean slate and shape him or her into my own self image in those first impressionable years.

Buchanan, whose children were older than ours, thought I was crazy. 'Jayzus, Stu,' he said, 'they come out of that womb stamped with their own personality. They're hard-wired. You're taking on a big challenge if you reckon you can re-configure the little feckers to suit you.'

Well, I was up for it and as it turned out our first born, Stuart Junior, was well-named because he was a replica of me. Friends, family and sometimes even perfect strangers pointed to the similarity wherever we went. 'You'll never be dead while that one is around,' they would say, a rather gruesome sort of praise I always thought. He not only had my blocky shape and the dark hair I once had, but a lot of my mannerisms as well. He was thoughtful, reserved and calculating. He never rushed into things, preferring to weigh up all the consequences first before deciding on a course of action, whether that was stacking a pile of building blocks together or learning to ride a bike. He was the delight of my life. We kicked the soccer ball, threw rugby passes to each other, played Transformers and wrestled on the grass.

Initially I thought he was going to be a bit shy like I was and Jennifer and I worked hard at trying to draw him out – me because I had been through all that before and knew how crushing it could be and Jennifer because, as she used to say, 'Shyness is not part of my family's make-up.'

He blossomed into an engaging child, bordering almost on cheeky. He took great joy in ordering his little brother around and teasing his little sister and speaking up with confidence amongst friends, family and school mates.

Our second boy, Richard, was a different kettle of fish. He was the thoughtful, poetic type, more contemplative and arty rather than physical. Sure, he played games with me and Junior but he would pack it in if things got a bit rough. He would hang around the kitchen a bit too much for my liking, listening in on every bit of gossip that passed between Jenny and her family and friends. He knew everything that was going on around the place. Jennifer said it was because he had her sense of spirituality and was showing something called his 'feminine side', which quite frankly worried the hell out of me. In my opinion, that sounded like the first step down the path to homosexuality and I certainly did not want that to happen to either of my boys. I worked particularly hard on him to toughen him up.

After intense discussion, we had named him after my father – and me, too, seeing as Richard is my second name. Jennifer was not too happy about this, as she wanted to honor her Dad. I never actually laid it on the line, but I think she knew that while I appreciated Seamus as my father-in-law and would never speak ill of him publicly, privately I considered him a rogue. A loveable rogue, but one you could never really trust, and trust to me is one of the most important foundations of life. He was a larger-than-life, flight-of-fancy man with a loud voice, a thumping slap on the back, a love of a drink and an innate ability to win or lose vast amounts of money on the turn of a card or a photo finish at the Leopardstown races. He had a beautiful home in Blackrock and there always seemed to be plenty of cash around, but the path he had followed to achieve such a comfortable existence had been pretty rocky.

In the years since he had left his beloved County Kerry as a young man to seek his fortune, he had worked in an abattoir, dug ditches and driven lorries. Then he realised he needed to get into business for himself. From that point on he had variously bought and sold property, been in the motor trade, wholesaled fish, ran a fleet of hot dog vans and imported laptops, despite being totally clueless about computers. He could read the shift in the market beautifully, successfully developing a string of bouncing castle franchisees, having realised early on that that particular amusement was becoming a very important part of every Irish First Communion home party. Recognizing Ireland was becoming an island of ageing, creaking knees struggling to get up after genuflecting, he flooded the health food market with dubious fish oil capsules imported from God knows where, making a packet before the authorities shut it down.

Setbacks like that never stifled him and he would bounce back with his characteristic grin. If there was a quid in it, Seamus Fitzgerald O'Brien was prepared to have a go at it, no matter what the risk. Likeable rogue that he was, I did not want my son to be named after someone like that. So I came up with a compromise.

'You can use Seamus for a name if we have a third boy,' I promised Jennifer.

Of course, there were no more boys. But there was a little girl born much later and so when I suggested that she be called Moira after my mother, Jennifer was shocked. 'You said that I could name the next one after Dad,' she said. I replied that that was true, but seeing as this was a girl and not a boy then that had changed things. 'If we follow the theme of having used my name first and then Dad's name,' I said, 'then it is logical to name this little one after Mum.'

Jennifer wanted to name the little girl Mary after her own mother. 'That just doesn't fit,' I said. 'It ruins the sequence.' There was a moody silence in the house for several days over this issue, one that we both felt very strongly about. Eventually, she came back with a new suggestion. 'All right, if you insist on your method, let's make it a version of Mary,' she said. 'Let's call her Molly.'

Molly! I really didn't like that name. It sounded old fashioned, bog Irish and a bit common. It reminded me of that folk song about Molly Malone, the 'tart with the cart', selling shellfish in the Dublin streets, a business that I did not consider all that attractive although Seamus would have been in it like a shot if he had thought there was money to be made. I didn't want my daughter linked with that sort of image. I tried to push for something else but realised that in her post-birth state this was upsetting Jennifer very much and the house was losing its calm, tranquil atmosphere that I insisted on. So after quietly doing some more research on names, I came downstairs one morning and grandly said, 'Okay, Molly it is.'

You could see the look of relief in Jennifer's eyes and within a matter of minutes the birth registration form had been filled out. 'Thank you, darling,' she said. 'I'm glad you could see my view.'

'Oh, I'm happy, too,' I said. 'You know how you said that Molly is a derivation of Mary? Well, so is Moira, Mum's name ...'

She set her jaw firmly and marched out of the room and on that day the lines were set without another word being spoken – the boys would be 'mine' and Molly would be 'hers'. In an unwritten contract, I could take the boys wherever I wanted to, shape them into whatever I liked, and plan their whole lives without Jennifer's interference. In turn, the little girl could be hers to, as I used to say, 'Molly-coddle as much as you like.' I thought the play on words was pretty clever.

Stuart Junior developed my acumen for figures and I was sure he would go into something along the same lines as I did. I often entertained the thought that after he had been to university he could join me at the business and work his way up and ultimately take it over when it was time for me to retire. As for Richard, I figured that if I worked hard enough with him I would soon de-tune some of his arty-farty influences and toughen him up to take on life's experiences like a real man.

And Molly? Well, I always felt that with her anything could happen. She was certainly her mother's daughter. The same red hair, green eyes and palest of skin, mixed with the same flighty approach to life.

We used to play a little game where I would pick her up and pretend to drop her, and then catch her just as it appeared she was going to hit the ground. Sometimes I would start the game with her high up around my shoulders. Other times I would hold her out flat in my arms, as if I was making an offering to the gods, and let her go. I got very good at releasing her and then catching her at the very, very last second, which only added to the thrill and the enjoyment. My judo training helped me a lot with my reflexes but so did the fact that she was such a tiny little thing, always small for her age. 'Catch-Molly game, Daddy?' she would say. And, 'Catch-Molly again,' when she begged for more. Jennifer would just look away. 'Someone's going to get hurt,' she would mutter. 'It will all end in tears.'

One day, I caught her at the very last second, the back of her head just touching the ground and she looked up at me and I froze. The melancholy image of the little girl with the sad green eyes in the painting on the wall of our wedding night suite in the Roscommon manor suddenly came back to me, unsettling me for days.

But our little game aside, I knew that Molly was Jennifer's girl, her precious jewel. They held confidences between themselves, laughed at each other's quaint jokes and could almost read each other's minds. This concerned me. I felt excluded from their close-knit little club. I wanted some influence over her, because I didn't want her to grow up to be as frivolous as Jennifer. I often think that the development of this cosy little relationship irritated me so much that other aspects of Jennifer's approach to life started to get under my skin.

The constant chatter with everyone around her, especially her extended family, started to really grate. When we were over at the Blackrock family home she and her mother and her aunties would talk for hours and then, just when I thought we were going to leave and I could go home, pour a drink and relax in front of the television, one of them would say something like, 'Oh, did you hear Aoifa, you know, Sean's wife, is going to have a baby?' And someone would say, 'No way, never!' And it would start all over again and we would be there for another twenty frustrating minutes.

'Who the hell is Aoifa?' I used to think to myself. 'And who gives a damn?'

But the big change between me and Jennifer was this: once Molly was born, pretty much all love-making, which had been a reasonable part of our lives, if only as a means to an end, went out the window. I found this so frustrating especially as I had been what I considered to be a noble and honourable participant in our 'trying-to-make-babies' period, including the rather unsavoury experience of masturbating over a pornographic magazine in a little cubicle, and now I had been hung out to dry. This annoyed me. Particularly in the context of Jennifer's Buddhist beliefs. Where was all the peace, love, harmony and ringing of bells now? Weren't Buddhists supposed to be sharing, caring types? Make love, not war? They certainly talked up all that airy-fairy nonsense about spirituality and the afterlife, but when it came to the practical exercising of that option, they were sadly lacking. To rub salt into the wound, she would be on the phone for hours spreading the gospel of love among her circle of like-minded friends, especially Wendy, her little pal from New Zealand, and Karena who was some sort of guru. I said to Jennifer one day, 'You talk about the notion of love, you promote the concept of love, but you don't actually make love. Certainly not with me.'

So I fell in love with someone else.

Chapter 10

Was it love? It was probably lust. Whatever it was, it came about when my business partner Derek had to pull out of an international insurance conference at the last minute. 'Something's come up, Stuart,' he said. 'I have to stay in Dublin. You go instead.'

Being Stuart the reliable workhorse, I replied that flattered as I was, I could do no such thing. 'I have a pile of work on my plate a mile high and three very good leads that I'm certain can be converted into sales,' I said. But Derek was insistent. 'Go on, lad. You deserve it. And it won't be all work out there. Buchanan's going, too, so the craic will be great. And they say Dubrovnik is beautiful.'

I had never been there before. Having three kids, Jennifer and I used to opt for the family holiday in the Mediterranean each year. Usually Spain, sometimes Portugal. Having travelled to all sorts of places in all sorts of ways, she was happy to spend her vacation in an apartment by a beach. Sometimes as an alternative we camped, hiking through the hills and enjoying the beautiful crags and dales of Ireland and Scotland.

But Dubrovnik? It was a whole world away. A lot of travel for who knows what? Nevertheless, Derek assured me that if the three potential sales did come good he would ensure I got a suitable whack out of them. So whether I liked it or not, I was off to Croatia.

Looking through the schedule with Jennifer before I flew out, I figured it was going to be a hectic experience. Seven days of seminars, speeches and workshops on the theme of 'Insurance, Through The Looking Glass.' Now, despite my devotion to the industry, and there were not too many who approached it with the level of enthusiasm that I did, even I conceded that with a title like that it was going to be pretty dull. But I, along with the four hundred and thirty-five others who gathered from around the world, had not counted on the presence of Federica.

Federica Baumgartner was the keynote speaker for the conference. She was Swiss, tall and slim, with perfect white skin and long dark hair which she kept tied up in a bun. Her blue eyes, showing a clarity and intelligence that was almost frightening, assessed you calmly through a most impressive set of designer glasses. Her trim, athletic figure, chiselled no doubt through many hours in the gym, was accentuated by beautifully cut business suits matched with crisp white shirts and discreet although obviously very expensive ear-rings.

And did she know her stuff! Not only had she studied business in her own country, she had topped it off with a Masters at Harvard and then had gone on to rise through the ranks of a Californian electronics firm to the position of vice-president. She had apparently cut a swathe as she went, dragging it out of potential bankruptcy and putting it back on top before the glass ceiling stymied her from getting the top job. By the time she came into our orbit she had spent the previous five years travelling the world as a consultant, resuscitating flagging companies and speaking at seminars like ours.

As well as the main address, her contract also required her to stay for the week, sitting in on workshops and offering individual advice. How lucky were we? She strode briskly around the hotel like a Swiss goddess who had come down from the snow-topped mountains to save us. Even if she was out of sight, you knew she was approaching because of the click-clack of the Prada heels on the floor, the surge of energy that whooshed into the room and the subtle but sensuous aroma of her perfume. 'It's Bulgari Black,' an American women delegate whispered to me once as she floated past. 'Bergamot, vanilla and sandalwood. Very hip.'

Initially, I felt that it wasn't so much her looks that got people in, but what she said. Her opening speech was exhilarating, a powerful rally cry that dragged us out of our lethargy and had us primed to run through brick walls. Her performances in the smaller study groups and workshops were simply amazing. She didn't hector us from the lectern but sat amongst us, pushing us for concepts and solutions, preferring chunks of crayon on white paper to thrash out things rather than asphyxiating death by PowerPoint.

She had terrific ideas to throw into the mix and get us started. If she came to your desk, she would grab a chair and sit beside you, hitting you at eye level, looking at your work, encouraging you to push forward. Her passion for achievement was over-whelming, the ideas she threw up liberating and the challenges she gave us a genuine buzz. I have never seen people in the insurance game so excited about their products, their potential and their future. And believe me, that is saying something.

Of course, a handful of the older, burnt-out types thought it was a load of bollocks while some of the younger brigade considered it an interesting but minor irritant before the lunch-time lager, having taken a liking to the local brew, Velebitsko. But most of us thought it was riveting. Especially me. That was because, while I understood and tolerated Jennifer's pre-occupation with Buddhism and her zeal for all things New Age, to me that was a lot of beads-and-incense mumbo-jumbo. Airy-fairy stuff about finding yourself, sitting in ashrams and getting in accord with the positive vibe. I accept that we were married by the light of the moon in a clearing next to a river during the summer solstice, and externally I gave the impression that I was supportive of the general philosophy, but quite frankly a lot of that stuff failed to grab me. Jennifer might have had a bit of success before we met with her little books about finding 'the inner you', and I regularly acknowledged her for it.

The point was, they were really a fine example of marketing genius, somehow persuading people to buy sixty pages of homilies, believing that they were going to change their lives for good forever. In the real world, in the one-on-one, down-to-earth, let's-sign-the-contract-now business world, that sort of touchy-feely nonsense gets you nowhere.

Federica, on the other hand, had a powerful, straight-forward, believable message. An inspiring message. A realistic message. Not setting loony goals but achievable targets, working towards them, getting them done, then moving on to the next ones.

The thing was, she made me realise that I was a well-meaning, moderately-successful type that was a bit too stodgy, and who was simply digging the trench longer and deeper. Now, here she was talking about getting out of the trench, criss-crossing the field, digging fresh holes, finding new opportunities, creating new concepts.

'Above all,' she said, 'be an individual, be selfish, don't be ashamed, do it for yourself first! Then your business and your family can share in the success that will naturally follow. The world is there for your taking. Grab what you want, use it up and when you are finished with it, spit it out.'

Very quickly I began falling in love with her presentation skills. Rather rapidly I began falling in love with her ideas. Pretty soon I found myself falling in love with her.

Of course, I told myself, it was only a fleeting thought, a moment of lunacy, something that would surely never materialise. And then it happened. After sitting in on a workshop where I stood up and contributed a few words about the importance of remaining loyal to your clients, Federica discreetly sidled up to me at the morning coffee break. 'Hmm,' she said, 'Stuart, I see you're still in second gear ...'

Well, this floored me. Second gear! This was my own personal philosophy, something I had pursued successfully most of my life, particularly during our marriage. But it was a description that I had never mentioned to anyone, ever! Not even Jennifer.

'Second gear? How did you ..?' That was all I could utter, stumbling for words as the coffee cup in my hand began to shake. Federica looked straight at me with her steel blue eyes. 'Oh, I've been watching you,' she said. 'Don't worry, Stuart Hoare, it's part of my role. To observe all around me, see who is doing what, and decide where I can encourage talent.'

'Um, you've read me like a book,' I blurted.

She looked around the room and then leaned close to me. For the first time she was not speaking in her power voice or causing heads to turn. She was softer, more personal, very private. 'I can see a more capable, more effective person trying to get out, Stuart,' she whispered. She waited calmly for a few seconds and then went on. 'You have certain skills and a genuine desire to achieve. You are a nice man. But hidden underneath I can see a stronger man, a more in-control man, a man who could produce even better results. A real Celtic Tiger! I can help that man emerge.'

She touched my arm. My cup shook some more. She leaned closer to me. The aroma of the Bulgari Black was enchanting. If I had never smelt the combination of bergamot, vanilla and sandalwood before, I was certainly getting a nose full of it now.

'You can do a lot more in top gear, Stuart,' she whispered. She touched me once more on the arm, smiled, turned and left.

What happened after that? Well, I think it is called something like cabin fever or seminar syndrome, or some such. A couple rapidly developing an emotional link within the exciting, surreal and temporary environment of a conference. Isolated from the humdrum of their jobs, removed from the tedium of domestic life and charged up by the freedom, the food and the drink, they let themselves go. They find someone they can relate to, a person they can discuss different ideas with, a neutral associate they can pour their heart out to. And while it begins on a professional level, then a friendly one, then an emotional one, it can rapidly lurch into a physical one.

I was beginning to think, 'Why not? Jennifer and I rarely make love anymore and when we do, it's pretty perfunctory.'

Before I knew it, into the third day, Federica with her power, precision and vision had intrigued me, engaged me and finally besotted me. It's impossible to describe how it can happen in such a short amount of time but it did. We began sitting next to each other at every possible opportunity, including all meals. I would attend all her seminars and at the end of each we would head off and have a drink. In the evenings, we would go out into the Old Town of Dubrovnik, marvelling at the people, the art, the buildings, the restaurants, the entertainers.

It wasn't long before I found myself in her room. We had had dinner, it was late, and now we were quaffing drinks from the mini-bar; cognac for her, whiskey for me. It was great to share a real drink with someone instead of the usual situation where I would be the only one having alcohol while Jennifer would be somehow getting enjoyment out of a glass of exotic fruit juices topped up with wheatgrass. I knew I was in dangerous territory but, what the heck, I couldn't help it, could I? Federica kicked off her shoes, tossed her glasses onto the sideboard and pulled the comb out of her long dark hair, letting it cascade down to her shoulders. Up until this point, she had been business beautiful, now she was simply stunning. She began to slowly open the top button of her crisp white shirt. I thought to myself, 'Stuart, it's now or never, top gear or nothing. Perhaps even over-drive.'

But the brandy was having an effect and she was becoming less focused and letting her normally impenetrable guard down. She continued to talk. And talk, and talk and talk. As she went on, it suddenly dawned on me that over our time together we had chatted only very occasionally about me, my family, my job and my marriage. While she had forecast that she was going to draw out the hidden, inner me, ninety five per cent of the time the conversation had been focused entirely on Federica. About her background, her education, her career, her time at the electronics firm, her achievements, her fights with the board, her resignation, the growth of her consultancy, her ups, her downs, her defeats, her successes. I think there was some mention of a husband in there, now long gone, but I can't be sure. 'Poor bastard,' I thought, 'he probably died of boredom.'

I stared into my whiskey as the voice droned on, suddenly reining myself back into the present just in time to hear her say, 'But for all my achievements, Stuart, I am lonely. Very, very lonely. If you know what I mean.'

I knew what this meant. You'd have to be daft not to. I was about to say, 'And I think I know why.' But I thought the better of it and just stared straight at her.

'What?' she said, surprised. For the first time since things had warmed up between us, I had not replied like a lapdog. 'Didn't you hear me?' she asked.

'Er, yes, yes,' I replied. 'You're lonely, and that's not good. Excuse me, I have to go to the toilet.'

She looked puzzled and a little miffed as I stood up and headed through the door to the spectacular glass and marble bathroom. I flipped up the lid and had a pee, trying to regroup my thoughts and work out what to do next. One voice in my head, smooth, controlled, seductive, began telling me to take direct action. 'Go on, Stuart,' it crooned, 'be a man, get into top gear! Go back in there and screw her brains out. She's begging for a good old-fashioned shag and you're the man to do it.' Then another voice, anxious, almost hysterical, began calling for a halt. 'Stuart!' it hissed, 'you're a married man! You can't be unfaithful, no matter how bad you think things are at home.'

As I stood at the sink washing my hands and staring into the mirror, with both voices fighting for victory across the battleground of my confused brain, the buzz on my mobile suddenly went off, indicating a message had come through. I dried my hands, pulled the phone out of my pocket and called it up.

The message loomed into view. It was a picture Jennifer had sent of the kids. The three of them were all in their pyjamas and dressing gowns, ready for bed. 'Goodnight, Daddy,' the caption read. 'We love you.'

I stared at the picture and message for a long time, then looked at myself in the mirror and swore. I was shocked at what I saw staring back at me. My days and nights carousing with Federica had extracted a heavy toll. My eyes were bloodshot, they had bags under them, and my skin was flushed. I looked like Patrick did after he had been sprung. Washed up and ready to roll down the road into deserved oblivion. 'God,' I thought, 'he lost everything. Am I going to do the same?'

I took one more look at the photo, read the caption again, closed the phone and put it back in my pocket. I sprinkled some water on my face, dried it, tidied my clothes, slicked my hair back with my hands and took a deep breath and mumbled the burning question to myself. 'So, what's it to be? Fuck, or flee?'

I opened the bathroom door. There she was, already lying in the bed, covered only by a sheet. In a direct change to her usual orderly way of doing things, her clothes, including her expensive white satin bra and knickers, were flung all over the floor. 'Come on, Stuart,' Federica cooed, crooking her finger at me, 'time to get into top gear.' Without taking her eyes off me, she threw back the sheet to reveal her trim, fit body. The startling whiteness of her skin highlighted the blackness of her long flowing locks and the pinkness of her nipples. My eyes darted down to see how her pubic hair would stand out against this dramatic background, but perhaps not surprisingly, it had been waxed and shaved down to the barest vertical tuft with typical Swiss precision. My God, she was beautiful. That first little voice that had spoken to me, the evil one, was certainly on the money. She was ready for it and I was the man to deliver.

As she lay there on her side, gesturing me to come over, I put my hand out towards her. And then I suddenly pulled it away and put it to my forehead. It was the other voice, the good voice, coming on strong in my brain. 'Don't, Stuart,' it was whispering. 'Don't do this! You'll lose your marriage, your family, your business …'

My head jolted backwards. That was the clincher. I looked at Federica, put both hands up, palms out, and whispered, 'No.'

'What?' she said, incredulous.

'No,' I said. 'No. I can't. You're beautiful, Federica, an amazing woman, and I think I'm in love with you, but …' My voice trailed off and I began to head for the door. She pounced off the bed to try and stop me, shouting, 'What? What are you doing? Stuart, I thought that we had something …?' She might have been fit, she might have been fast, she might have looked absolutely gorgeous rushing at me with her pert little breasts leading the charge, but the brandy had dulled her reflexes enough for me to grab the advantage. I got to the handle first, swung the door open and stepped quickly out into the corridor.

She followed me out and stood there, unashamedly naked, her voice ringing in my ears as I strode determinedly away, not looking back. 'You weak little man, Stuart,' she shouted. 'You will amount to nothing! Fucking nothing!' Her voice echoed down the corridor. Then the door slammed. I could hear other doors discreetly opening, wary guests investigating what the noise was all about, as I scurried down the hallway towards the elevator.

Next morning, I had breakfast in my room; I attended none of her sessions for the rest of the day; I avoided her at all costs for the remainder of the conference. Our paths crossed just once, during a coffee break, and she simply stared right through me, shrugged and said, 'Ha!'

On the final morning, as we assembled in reception to catch the bus for the airport, I noticed Buchanan walking past in his swimming gear, towel draped over his shoulder, heading for the pool. I stopped him. 'What on earth are you doing?' I said. 'Aren't you on the same flight home as me?'

He grinned widely. 'I'm staying on for a day or two,' he said.

I stepped back, confused. 'What about the family?'

'Family?' he said. 'Stuart, they don't understand me. Nuala's on my back all the time and the kids just play computer games. My only friends are the goldfish and the dog. I'm better off here.'

He glanced over my shoulder at someone obviously standing some distance behind me and his smile grew broader. I didn't need to turn around. I knew who it was. The smell of bergamot, vanilla and sandalwood floating through reception was undeniable.

'Stuart,' he whispered, grabbing my arm, but not taking his eyes off her. 'You know what? She really understands me! She can read me like a book.'

'Buchanan!'

'No, listen, Stuart. You know what she said to me the first time she came up to me?'

I looked at him in anticipation. His eyes glowed. 'She said to me, "Buchanan, you look like you're in second gear …"'

Chapter 11

Living in Dalkey was paradise for us all. It is a beautiful village with lovely old shops and restaurants, an ancient castle and a fine example of the Church of Ireland at its most powerful and best, St Patrick's.

I loved attending service there, especially the times when I got to play the organ. Throughout my run-around childhood I had stuck with my music lessons at whatever school I attended and eventually proved to be a reasonable singer and a competent, although not necessarily exceptional, piano player. When I was about thirteen, the vicar of a church near the army camp at Fort George in Scotland where Dad served for a while, took a liking to me and allowed me to develop my skills on the organ and it was something that I maintained from there.

Of course, having just joined the St Patrick's congregation when we moved into Dalkey, I could not expect to immediately take over the senior organ player's role. That was held firmly by a Mrs Tunbridge, more or less a position for life. She had sat on that seat pumping out *How Great Thou Art* and other much-loved fare for fifty-one years and was not going to surrender it lightly. But I gradually worked my way into the post of assistant, filling in on the rare occasions when illness or family issues prevented her from playing, an opportunity that stood me in good stead when I successfully stood for election to the congregational committee.

I was proud of us as a growing family when we went to church every Sunday. It was a big decision for Jennifer to attend a Protestant church, but she was prepared to put aside the powerful influences of her Catholic heritage and her Buddhist beliefs for one hour a week and I really appreciated that. If I was playing the organ, it was wonderful to be able to look around and see my children all neatly dressed, sitting in a row obediently next to their beautiful mother. Such was my input, I was eventually elected to the parish committee, opening up a whole new world for me in terms of contacts and lending my support in shaping the future of the church and its community.

The hallmark of Dalkey is that it is on the seaside, with hills and cliff faces overlooking the water, the DART railway line jammed on its edge and winding roads leading south to Wexford. While Jennifer and I were walking along the shore one day, I had one of those epiphany moments that altered my life. There was a strong, flukey breeze blowing offshore and a sizable yacht was tacking its way out to sea with three people on board. Suddenly the boat started to yaw violently and looked like it was going to tip. Then the spinnaker at the front broke free and began flapping crazily in the breeze, making the boat lurch from side to side at a dangerous angle. I thought it was going to turn over. The boat was out of control and the man at the helm was in a state of panic desperately flinging the wheel one way then the other.

Then something pretty special happened. A fourth man suddenly appeared from below decks. He pushed the other man away from the wheel and grabbed it and began barking instructions. The man now freed up from his helm duties rushed forward to the bow of the boat to grab the flapping sail. Under instructions, the other two began to drop the spinnaker and trim the main-sail. Rather than flinging the wheel, the captain subtly turned it this way and that and within less than half a minute the boat was back on an even keel sailing beautifully once more. It was a marvellous performance by the skipper and I decided at that moment that I should apply the same principles to my family so that it could ride out any rough weather and quickly resolve any issues thrown at it.

The episode in Dubrovnik where I had drawn back from the dangerous abyss of adultery with Federica had confirmed my faith in myself, my belief in our marriage, and my determination to work even harder on it. Seeing this sailing episode now clarified everything further for me. I decided then and there we should look at things this way: we were all in one boat and therefore there should be only one captain. A person keeping things on an even keel no matter what challenges were thrown up. A sole tactician ensuring that the course we charted was clear to everyone. A supreme ship's master making sure we were all working smoothly as a crew and doing our appointed jobs to reach our destination. And that person should be me.

As far as I was concerned, I was logically that man. After all, that is how I had run my life up until that point and the technique had been successful, so why change now? On the other hand, Jennifer's life had been variable, episodic, bordering on the chaotic at times. From what I could see, her successes had been more the result of good luck than good management.

So, being a financial man as well, I felt it was essential that I kept an eye on every cent that went in and out of the house. Knowing from experience with clients how easy it was to slide into a financial catastrophe, I did not want to risk money being spent frivolously and unnecessarily. I worked out that the simplest way was to give Jennifer an exact amount for housekeeping each week and get her to show me the receipts after she had shopped each Friday so I could see where it had all gone. By keeping the paperwork, she could then justify any request for an increase in her allowance as prices went up, although I always tried to keep any improvement as close to the accepted inflation rate as possible.

Quite frankly I did not believe I could trust Jennifer with money. I valued every cent. But in her typical Catholic style, if she ever had any money left over she let it quickly slip through her hands. It took me a long time to realise that some of it was being handed straight on to her brother Kevin to help him finance his gambling habit at the race tracks.

I was furious when I discovered this, especially as he had taken it upon himself to be her protector, thus putting him in constant friction with me. He still seemed to think that it was his job to look after her, even though Jennifer and I had long been married. I demanded that she stop wasting money on this 'loser' as I once described him. 'Have you ever heard of a successful gambler?' I asked. 'No,' I continued, answering for her. 'These fellows, they shake every one down, often embezzling money from their own firms, yet they still can't get in front! It astounds me that they spend thousands and thousands down at the betting shop, and they can never tip a winner. Then they keep trying to recover those losses and only lose more. Are they stupid, or what?'

I knew I was on rocky ground criticising Kevin because not only was he closest to Jennifer in age but he had also married her best friend Amy and so the bond was doubly strong. I think he and Amy had been forced into getting married not long after they had left school because she got pregnant. That was pretty typical of a big sprawling Catholic family; they can never control their passion and they eventually pay the price. So discussing Kevin was an area I felt I generally should leave alone unless it directly affected me. And in this case, it did.

Another thing that irked me was that a lot of the money I allotted Jennifer went on frivolous things like clothes. And what really made me angry was the number of times she would go out and buy a dress for herself and which, from what I observed, she would wear just once. Or a pair of shoes that rarely saw the light of day from amongst the dozens of others in the bottom of the closet. I don't think that this situation was helped by the fact that she was the only girl in her family and that her father had indulged her as his little princess. She grew up having what she wanted when she wanted. I decided it was my job to bring her back to reality.

She would also spend a lot of money buying school uniforms and other outfits for the children. I used to say to her, 'How many uniforms do these kids need to go to school?' As well as the financial waste of buying new clothes all the time, there was also the issue of good taste. I was happy for Jennifer to look good, as she did on the first day we met, but I felt that as we were now man and wife and also parents it was important that she presented herself appropriately. As a successful businessman, I had an image to uphold.

Shortly after we had been married, I had taken her into the bedroom one day and had insisted that she throw out a lot of her clothes, particularly the ones that I felt were now demeaning for a married women to be wearing, such as the short skirts and the low-cut tops. I had laid them out on the bed to illustrate my point. 'When we go out to dinner with associates, I want you to be sociable, but not flirty,' I said.

I emphasised to her the importance of wearing sensible dresses, not provocative ones, and cutting back on the make-up so that she would not look cheap and draw the attention of other men. 'You looked beautiful the night we got married,' I would say. 'You hardly had any make-up on then.' This became something of a point of contention over the years. One night, when we were at a restaurant with Derek and a new client plus their wives, Jennifer excused herself from the table and returned from the ladies' room a few minutes later freshened up, her face caked with make-up and her lips a blaze of colour. It was that Poppy King cherry lipstick again. I was certain I had thrown every stick of it out of the house. This little rebellion only proved my point. The client sitting opposite her, who had up until then taken little notice of Jennifer, suddenly began to talk animatedly with her and she responded in kind. Before you knew it, her bubbly laugh had started to echo through the restaurant, drawing the attention of other diners. I was absolutely livid.

This forced me to excuse us early and head home on the pretence that the baby-sitter, a friend of a friend who had filled in at the last minute, needed to finish up at ten o'clock because she had school exams the next day. Driving home, it took all my powers of persuasion to convince Jennifer that doing something like that only made her look stupid and cheap and reflected badly on us as a couple.

'This does not help my business, do you understand?' I said. She folded her arms, angrily pushed herself back into the seat, and stared out the window. 'I was only trying to look good for you,' she said sourly. 'Besides, you must admit that it sparked up the conversation. That dead trout opposite me had said nothing up until then. Next time I'll flash my tits at him.'

I slammed on the brakes, pulled the car over to the side of the road, leaned across and put one hand around her throat. 'What a disgusting thing to say,' I said. 'You're not only trying to look like a slut, now you're sounding like one.'

'Stuart, I ...'

'Don't Stuart me!' I yelled, holding her throat firmly with one hand, while I wiped the lipstick off with the back of the other. 'See? All gone! No more cheap lipstick. Not now. Not ever!'

I let her go, got the car going again, and there was no further discussion as she sat hard up against the passenger door quietly weeping. After I had dropped her off and then driven the baby-sitter to her home nearby I returned to find that Jennifer had turned the bedroom light off and so I went downstairs and did some paperwork.

In the morning it was all I could do to get her to put the previous night's incident behind her and concentrate on our usual breakfast discussion of the upcoming day's activities, which we used to do in detail before I left for work. I appreciated her free spirit but as the ship's captain I did not want our boat to drift off course and crash on the rocks of marital misery through misinformation, indecision or lack of a clear plan. Or, worse still, rebellion. The insurance man in me insisted on taking action to prevent disasters before they occurred rather than having to clean up after they had happened. I knew all about the principle of the event after the fact. It's in the insurer's handbook.

That is why I used to phone her throughout the day. To make sure what we talked about actually happened and that she did not get distracted and do silly things or spend too much time with her friends. There was a joke in the family that you could tell the time of the day by my calls to the home landline or Jennifer's mobile.

There were four calls each day. I would ring as soon as I got to work, usually around ten past nine, just to let Jennifer know that I had arrived safely after the drive-and-park in the city and to see if the kids had got off all right to school. The mid-morning call, usually when I had a cup of coffee at 11.30 am, gave us a good opportunity to see how the day was panning out. I would then call at 2 pm. I always felt this was a good time. Lunch should be well and truly over by then and Jennifer should have had plans for dinner well in hand.

As well, I was always keen to know what Jennifer had achieved so far in terms of what we had discussed that morning and what else she had to do that afternoon. The final call at 4.55 pm was opportune because it usually confirmed that the kids were now well home from school and doing their homework and I could inform Jennifer that I was either on the way home for dinner, or staying back to do some work, or heading out to see a client.

I loved to hear the sound of her voice on the end of the line. When the children were really young it was great to get first-hand news on any milestones they might have achieved, whether that was saying a first word or taking a few tentative steps. I believed my role as captain of the ship became even more important as each child came along and the relationship between Jennifer and I changed.

Of course, I understood that the structure of a partnership must surely alter once the first flush of unbridled romance had passed. It modifies itself to the circumstances, each individual's strengths and weaknesses becoming apparent as challenges arise and trade-offs are established to keep things moving. What was once a partner's endearing peccadillo can easily, over a period of time, transform into a very annoying habit. I accepted all that and knew that I had to respond to those situations with a mixture of wisdom, diplomacy and the ability to take change on board. I couldn't afford to let things get out of control.

Jennifer's family might have tested my patience, but they provided me with a whole new world of business contacts and potential clients. Having spent more of my childhood out of the Ireland than in, I ended up speaking with something of an English accent, which didn't necessarily endear me to the more traditional Catholic community. I had to work harder than most to get business in that sector but having links with Jennifer's family, the doors started to open. Seamus and his sons might have enjoyed making life difficult for me on a social basis, but I was family, and in a business sense they proved invaluable.

I worked hard to create more personal wealth through commercial success to make things as comfortable and as best as I could for my family.

And what a time to do it. Other countries might have benefited from gold rushes or mining booms but Ireland had puttered along the poverty line until this economic rocket – the one the shark's teeth real estate agent had predicted that night at dinner – went off with a bang. Cash started flowing as employers and unions worked together, government investment boomed and women began to enter the workforce. After years of Ireland sending its people off to America, something finally began to drift back across the Atlantic – dollars.

To me, the Celtic Tiger was an odd name, taken from the Asian Tigers, such as Malaysia, Thailand and Singapore, who had their own economic miracles. Little old Ireland had never really had a 'tiger' feel about it. It had been a bit cranky at times. And physical, as seen on the sports field. And explosive, especially when old wounds re-surfaced. And dogged, particularly amongst the male population, to stick to a decision no matter how right or wrong it was.

But the Celtic Tiger it was, and how we benefited! Fitting in with my favourite credo – for every action there is an equal and opposite reaction – for every project there was an equal and appropriate underwriting. Our computer equipment had to be continually upgraded as the insurance contracts and paperwork flooded the system. Fortunately we never got into the really massive stuff such as insuring the construction of the new motorways that radiated out from the city and the giant buildings that dotted its skyline. But for a medium-size insurance agency, we flirted on the edges of the big time and some of the trailing commissions we picked up for not only insuring projects but also finding finance for clients were pretty impressive.

Our prize jewel was a project my friend Buchanan brought to our board one day, a sizeable development in Tallaght in south-west Dublin. It consisted of a four-star hotel, surrounded by luxury apartments, an entertainment complex, a lifestyle centre including swimming pool and gym, plus quality retail space. The figures looked excellent and the potential clients were blue chip, so we got involved both as insurers and, for the first time, as investors. We also encouraged some of our premium clients to put their money in. The city was awash with cash and even allowing for my inbuilt prudence on these matters, we lived very well indeed and the future could not have been rosier.

'Enjoy it,' I would say to Jennifer, when I would call her at precisely 9.10, 11.30, two o'clock and just before five. Every day.

Chapter 12

Anything I ever proposed, even if it seemed a bit tough, was always for the good of the family. So when Jennifer first spat the words 'control freak' at me I was absolutely shocked. I was reduced to silence for a moment and even after I had regained my composure all I could say was, 'What do you mean?'

'You look it up,' she yelled as she rushed across the landing at the top of the stairs before disappearing into the bedroom and slamming the door.

It was the climax to a rather unfortunate discussion. Robust interchanges were fairly rare around our house and I was taken by surprise. We had been invited to a party that night but the babysitter had pulled out at the very last minute. The phone call with the bad news came through just as both of us were coming down the stairs dressed for the party and awaiting her arrival. So I had decided that we would not be able to attend. But Jennifer insisted, pleaded, begged that she go, seeing as it was at the home of Pauline, one of our neighbours. 'It's just down the street, it's her fortieth birthday and it's a surprise,' she said. 'I'd just like to be there, even only at the start, just to see the look on her face. Oh, please, Stu.'

I said I didn't see how it was possible now that the babysitter had let us down at the eleventh hour, but typically Jennifer came up with a solution. 'What if I go down there now and see the first bit, the surprise part, and then I'll come back and then you can go down and we can take it in turns of looking after the children from there?'

I didn't like the idea of her walking up and down the road in the middle of the night and of us swapping roles and going in and out of houses. We would enjoy neither one nor the other. 'No,' I said, 'no.'

'Please, Stu,' she said, 'please. Rod has done so much to prepare this surprise for Pauline. He's worked so hard to keep it a secret. Besides, he's in your parish. And he *is* one of your clients.'

I thought about this for a while and finally concluded that maybe someone from the family being there wouldn't be such a bad thing after all. But to be truthful, I never really liked parties at the best of times. All that inane chit-chat about the weather, schools and property prices. Besides, I had noticed that there was a documentary on the Le Mans 24-hour race on BBC-2 and this would save me having to record it and try and find the time to watch it later. I agreed but told her not to worry about swapping over during the evening. 'I will stay home with the children for the night,' I said. I figured a quiet glass of red and watching the telly would be far more enjoyable than observing a bunch of childish forty-somethings getting screaming drunk.

'However,' I added, 'don't be late. Ten thirty at the latest.'

'Ten thirty?! But that's hardly any time at all,' she said, giving me her poor-little-me look with the girly green eyes.

'You heard. Ten thirty, that's enough time to party.'

As it turned out, staying home was a good decision on my part. I found a nice Chilean merlot at the bottom of the wine rack and the Le Mans doco was excellent. I didn't realise that Porsche had won it so many times.

But 10.30 pm came. No Jennifer. Then 10.35 and then 10.40. By 10.50, I was concerned. Not so much about her safety rather that Jennifer had made a promise and now she had broken it. This was typical. That insidious Wendy, her best friend, was probably down there at Pauline and Rod's, whispering in one ear about what she should do with her life while that pesky Karena, her so-called guru, would be telling her something else in the other. And who knows who else was slathering attention on her. I knew Rod's brother Alan would have been there – a dangerous individual at the best of times. He had a ramshackle marriage and was a notorious woman-iser, just the type that would start chatting up someone as pretty and vivacious as my wife and coaxing her towards a bedroom.

I disliked it intensely when other men started casting their eyes towards Jennifer. I knew what they were after. Fortunately I had insisted she dress demurely before she left. Although, you never knew, the minute she got out the door she probably slapped some of that red lipstick on and hitched her skirt up to show her legs. That's the sort of thing she would do. You could never trust her.

So, the appointed return time had come and gone, and no appearance. What to do? I decided I would give her half an hour's grace. But by 11.05 I had had enough of peering through the front window to see if she was coming home. After checking to see that all three kids were sound asleep, I marched briskly the eighty metres down the road to Rod's place. On the way I began figuring out a way to get Jennifer out of there quickly and without much fuss. I stood on the door-step and thought about it for a while before finally ringing the bell. I knew what I had to say.

Naturally enough, there was a great cheer from everyone when I entered. All the men kept slapping me on the back and offering me a pint or a whiskey. But the women, of course, knew immediately that my sudden appearance was not right. I was in charge of the children, so how come I had now turned up at the party without them? Had I somehow magically organised the impossible at that hour of the night – someone else to take over? Or had I done the unthinkable and left them on their own in the house? As I correctly assumed, when Jennifer made her way through the crowd, I knew that that thought would be foremost in her mind.

'What's the matter?' she said anxiously. 'The kids! Why aren't you with them?'

'It's Molly,' I said. Her face at once fell concerned.

'It's all right,' I quickly added. 'But she won't settle. She started crying just after you left and hasn't stopped since.' I looked downcast.

'Oh, you poor thing, Stu,' said Pauline, stepping forward and touching me lightly on the arm. 'Having to put up with that all night while we're down here having fun.' She looked around at the other guests. 'Isn't he wonderful, everyone?' I had found an ally amongst the enemy.

'Yes, yes,' came a smattering of voices.

'I didn't know what to do,' I added forlornly.

'Awww,' said my newfound audience.

'So I thought I'd best take the risk for just a few seconds and come down and get you, darling. She keeps saying she wants her mummy. You know how it is, Mam is number one.'

There were murmurs of both concern and approval, although out of the corner of my eye I detected that damn Wendy shaking her head. Someone produced Jennifer's coat and after a series of quick goodbyes – 'Let us know if everything's all right, Stu,' said Pauline – we headed quickly and silently out into the darkness and down the narrow footpath to our home. I opened the door and Jennifer raced in, cocking her ear for the sound of Molly as she headed for the stairs with me right behind her. 'I can't hear anything,' she said, stopping for an instant.

'No,' I said, grabbing her by the shoulder and turning her around to face me. 'She's been perfect all night.'

'What … what do you mean?'

I leaned forward, right into her face. I felt it was important that she understood how strongly I felt about this.

'When I say ten thirty, I mean ten thirty, okay?' I said. 'Not a minute more.'

'What? Is that what this is about?'

'Of course it is! I said ten thirty, didn't I? And now it is well after eleven. That is not good enough.'

'You made up that story to get me back here? You bastard!'

That was enough. I have never been so angry in all my life. No one speaks to me like that. I felt myself moving my hand from her shoulder around to her throat.

'Are you calling me a liar, now?' I said.

'No, no.'

'You just did.'

'No, I didn't, honestly, Stu.'

'Didn't you just say that I had made up a story?'

'Yes, but I didn't mean …'

I tightened my hand around her throat.

'You didn't mean what? To say that I was a liar? I think you just did,' I said, pushing her hard up against the wall. I felt it was important that she clearly understood that I was not happy with all this. First, she was late, now she was saying I told lies.

'Stuart, please, I was concerned about Molly. You said …'

'Hah! Molly! Your little princess. I knew that would get you out of there quickly, away from all those men hanging around leering at you. Would you have been so anxious if it had've been one of the boys? I don't think so.'

I banged her head against the wall. She winced as the back of it hit the solid plaster with a thump.

'Huh?' I demanded.

'Yes, yes, of course I would,' she said lamely. 'They're all important to me.'

'Now who's the liar?' I said. 'It's always you and Molly. Molly and you. That's all you care about. Apart from the little game Molly and I have together, that's it as far as I'm concerned. The pair of you have set up your own separate unit within the family.'

I felt that I had made my point so I let her go and she gasped for breath. 'Go to bed,' I said.

'Stu, please.'

'Go to fucking bed!!' I shouted. She put her head down, turned and walked slowly up the stairs.

'And don't dare do anything like this again,' I added, as she reached the landing.

It was then she turned and hissed, 'Control freak!'

I could not utter a word for a moment, I was so shocked that she would be so brazen. And even then, after I had regained my composure, all I could say was, 'What do you mean by that?' as she headed across the landing at the top of the stairs.

'You look it up,' she yelled, before disappearing into the bedroom, slamming the door. I heard the key turn in the lock. I was boiling angry and actually started up the stairs but I knew that it would be pointless going up there battering on the door and waking the kids. So I went into the front lounge, poured a whiskey, pulled out the divan bed and settled in for the night. It was a place I was getting accustomed to. Besides, I had a bit of research to do and it wasn't long before I found what I needed.

Amongst the shelves groaning with Jennifer's books on New Age philosophy, Eastern mysticism and God knows what else, I spotted a book on psychology that presumably one of her 'advisors' had given her. I scanned through the index and looked up 'control.'

'See "Emotional Abuse",' it said. I flipped through, found the page, sat down and began to read.

'Examples of emotional abuse,' it read, 'include when one person in a partnership, more often than not the male, unilaterally decides when and where the other person can go, who she can see and what sort of friends she can have. With the main aim of socially isolating her, he will disallow her from developing a support system by regulating who she can call on the phone or write to on email, as well as determining whether she can go out and get a job or not. This latter often includes selecting what type of employment. He will often scrutinise and make decisions on guests she invites into their home.'

Well, I thought, you couldn't blame me for that last bit, about who should be allowed into *my* home. Some of those women, particularly Jennifer's Buddhist gurus, were getting too influential for comfort as far as I was concerned and knew far too much about our lives. They acted like our place was theirs. I might have made it clear that I did not like them around. But did I stop them? Of course I didn't.

As for Jennifer getting a job, well we had both unilaterally agreed it was best that she be the manager of the home. And as for that other stuff about disallowing support systems and so on, well, as they said in the book, they were only 'examples'. Every home is different. When you are the captain, it is your duty to keep tabs on the crew so they don't get into trouble, lose focus or become rebellious. A good vessel only sails successfully if everyone clearly understands the captain's approach and does not deviate from that. You can't have it both ways. I used to try and explain to Jennifer that that was why we had such a wonderful family unit, lived in a lovely home in a beautiful suburb, had a sound financial set-up with excellent prospects and engendered the appreciation and envy of those all around us. 'You can't successfully establish that scenario when there is mutiny on board or people deliberately flouting the commander's orders,' I would say. 'That is why great skippers, like Admiral Nelson, achieved so much.'

I admired Nelson. He was one of my heroes. He was an inspiration to his men, dedicated to the cause and a leader who planned his tactics carefully. A very strong man that not even injury could stop through many campaigns. Even in death he was the victor.

I read on. There was more balderdash about emotional abuse and promoting lack of self-esteem. Something about 'death by a thousands cuts' and how things build up gradually over the years. 'Often, when the alienated person seeks help, she gives examples of what has happened. These, when isolated and mentioned by themselves, don't necessarily sound threatening. But when they occur continually over the years, and taken as a whole, they combine to create a fearful environment.'

There you go, I thought, that's exactly what I mean. These are all little incidents. Easily gotten over. Soon erased from the memory. Each individual situation should be taken on its merits. Something goes wrong, an inquiry is held, discipline is meted out, life goes on. End of story. Get on with it.

Just as I suspected, everything was quiet in the morning. Shipshape, in fact.

Chapter 13

Women actually talk to each other. Men don't. When women get together, they plumb the most personal of issues right down to the very depths. When men get together, we skim across the surface. We skirt around the issue, we talk about inanities, we only get to the point when we really, really have to. At a party, women will talk about the latest additions to their families, the progression of their children, the hot news on personal relationships, the impact commercial and government price rises are having on the household budget and what great bargains are going around. Men will discuss the English Premier League.

Under all our macho bravado and camaraderie, there is a lot of confusion, fear, loathing, mistrust and puzzlement between men. Women understand women; but men really do not understand men.

That is how I have found things in life, particularly in the club atmosphere. Clubs are good in that they provide an opportunity to network. You can set up business contacts, meet people in allied industries and cultivate someone who might prove invaluable down the track. So it is worth persisting with. But it is all so artificial.

One problem is the pecking order. Clubs tend to attract ego-tripping A-types who want to be the boss and push other people around. They see the club as theirs. So they take it over, re-fashion it in their own image and then insist that everyone fits into the environment that they have so graciously created. A new member has to go along with that agenda and play the game or otherwise he will quickly find out he is going to have a very quiet and quite possibly miserable time.

Jennifer's family introduced me to the golf scene and at first it seemed like a great idea. A nice game out on a beautifully manicured course. A few drinks with everyone afterwards. And above all, the opportunity to make contacts and connections to help grow the business. But it was not enjoyable; it was hard work. Even I, as a conservative man and a stickler for rules, found it stultifying, almost scary. Not only out on the course, where the draconian rules of the game made the insurer's handbook look like child's play, but in the clubhouse where the pecking order was at its worst.

I concentrated so hard on fitting in and not making a mistake that I never really relaxed and enjoyed it. I used to look at some of the older members slapping each other on the back and laughing at some lame joke and think, 'Will I ever get to the stage? Will I ever really enjoy myself here? Will I ever be accepted?' To succeed, it's as if you have to strip off the 'real you' at the front door and put on the cloak of the 'club you' before you walk inside.

When I played, my hands used to be sweaty throughout the round, particularly if it was some sort of four-ball competition and I had a partner relying on me. I bought the best clubs, listened attentively during my lessons and practised as much as I could.

On the practice range I could hit it straight as a die. But on the course, under the watchful eyes of others, I could rarely relax. I duffed shots, I hooked drives, I missed the simplest of putts. And when you do it once you get so down on yourself that it makes you more flustered and you commit more mistakes. Ones of the worst kind. Etiquette mistakes. 'Not your honour, old man,' they would say as I inadvertently teed up first. 'You grounded your club on the sand in the bunker, that's a two-shot penalty,' just as I was about to strike. 'Don't you remember, Stuart? The rule at this hole is, we mark our ball, step to the side of the green, call the next group on to play their tee shot and then we putt out. Right?'

In the clubhouse, certain people sat automatically at invisibly designated tables, rules of dress were severely followed, staff were treated with courteous disdain. For newcomers, the principal role seemed to be to pay homage to the older members. With my inability to quickly connect to people on a social basis, it was a long and painful process. One day, after realising that I had played the game for two and a half years and my handicap had barely improved and the Captain still did not know my name, I wrote out my resignation. But that evening with the letter still in my jacket pocket as I ordered a drink at the bar, a member who had never spoken to me before quietly sidled up and said, 'You're in insurance, aren't you? I've got some business I'd like to put your way.' He turned out to be one of my best clients and so I tore the quit letter up and never sent it.

Things improved. Connections lead to connections. Through one of the golf members I was lured into the service club scene. My experiences in the Lions ran somewhat parallel with what was happening on the golf course. I made a lot of money out of signing many a good Lion up for a policy but I was always on the fringe of the real club circle. I attended every meeting, drank cheap wine with the best of them and put on an apron and cooked at the Saturday morning sausage sizzle outside the local hardware store. I was an enthusiastic participant of every fund-raiser team and major project sub-committee.

At one stage I was even the tail-twister, the theatrical player in a sequence where members at the dinner meeting are dobbed in for tardiness, stupidity or poor performance. They are fined and have to throw a few coins into a money box. I tried to do this with the best of intentions and with as much humour and élan as I could muster. And I stuck with it for months, even after one night, when I went to the gents' toilet and was sitting in a cubicle and two others came in for a leak and one said to the other, 'That Stuart fellow. Did you see him tonight? He's a nice enough lad, but a bit of a try-hard.'

There are a lot of others who come up against this brick wall and who give it away. Me being me, inheriting some of father's military doggedness and having survived tough times at boarding college, I hung in there because I thought it was worth it business-wise, and therefore in the long term good for me, Jennifer and the family.

But in moments of self-realisation I knew that, even though I could hold up a reasonably good conversation on most topics, I did not have the required mental nimbleness and wherewithal to fully cope with these people, even when they were being overbearing and quite bullying in their superficial, polite, clubby way.

It dawned on me that I was surrounded by people, but I had no real friends; that I gave off the impression that I was a member of the A-team, but I was not even on the reserves bench; that I might be strong in my convictions, but I didn't have that upfront, blaggard persona to captivate a whole audience. I was more a one-on-one man. And apart from work, and perhaps on the church committee where most of the members were so old they hardly knew what was going on, the only place that I could confidently express my views and get what I wanted was at home. That was where I was the boss. Where I could exercise my authority. Where I could be in control. Home. That was my club.

Now, in my club, on my home turf, I will declare that I could be a bit insistent sometimes, occasionally demanding and sometimes over the top in my search for perfection. There were times that I regret that my anger spilled over. It was just that I wanted things to be 'right.' I would never mean to physically hurt Jennifer. That was the last thing on my mind. But there were moments, flash-points, when she would take me right to the edge. I had been originally attracted to her for, amongst many things, her beauty. But after we were married I didn't think that I should have to publicly share that beauty with others.

That is why I would get very cross with her when she wore dresses that were too short or tops that were low-cut, or when she applied heavy make-up or plastered on that bright red lipstick. Or when I detected her sending out the wrong signals to other men. I knew when she was doing it. I could tell. I felt she was doing herself and therefore me and the family a disservice, an injustice. She was better than that. I felt it was my duty to make it clear to her that she was only demeaning herself, and therefore me, by doing it. In outlining my view, perhaps I should not have physically intimidated her. I tried not to. But sometimes, when she was obviously not listening to what I was trying to explain, or showing signs of being resentful, or downright denying what was the obvious truth, I would suddenly find myself restraining her before I knew what I was doing. It was all so quick. The judo experience had sharpened my reflexes and trained me to take rapid action.

But sometimes she would deliberately push things too far and I would respond accordingly. It was just a natural response to strike her. Not premeditated. But I had to make my view on the situation clear. She knew the rules. It was up to her to conduct herself accordingly.

Anyone who has been down this path will tell you that pressures build up in marriages. External influences, elements that you don't even remotely consider in the first flush of warm romance, start to come into play and cause havoc. As each child comes along, the mother, the one bearing the brunt of the ever-growing domestic scene, gets more tired. Things like intimacy and love-making take a back seat. That was okay, I could understand that. I may have had a decent sperm count, I may have wanted sex more times than we actually did have, but don't forget I had endured a lot of years without a long-term partner. Or for that matter, any sort of girlfriend. So I was used to lengthy celibate periods.

Nevertheless, having now been married for some years, it could get very frustrating at times when the weeks went by and we never had sex. That was when the verbal spats would flare and I would, being so frustrated, take action. I would insist we make love for both my sanity and for Jennifer's too. Feeling the rigidity of her body I knew she was just going through the routine and waiting for it to finish. That only made me push harder in the hope that her resistance would somehow melt away and the joyous, cohesive love we used to make would magically return. Sometimes I used to think, 'If only she drank. A couple of glasses of wine, instead of that fucking fruit juice, and she might relax and be happy and enjoy it instead of being so damn uptight.'

I began to think, 'Could it be? That I have done the business, sired the children that she so desperately wanted and now she has cast me aside? That my services are not needed any more? That what is being left unsaid is, "Thank you Stuart, you've done a good job and you may now bugger off?"'

Then the other side of the argument would pop into my head. 'Surely that is not what has happened. That she targeted me solely for this role? She couldn't be that cynical, could she?' After a while, as things limped along, the thought began to eat into me that I was the innocent patsy in Jennifer's grand plan. A scheme of deception to achieve conception. Picking any bloke off the street to be the stud because all previous attempts had failed for varying reasons and she was fast running out of time. And I happened to be the one! Ultimately I began to think, 'Well, if that's what you've done and that's the way you want it, my dearest, then here it is.' And so our rare lovemaking became a dry, emotionless experience, a battle of wills, not much more than combat under the duvet. Usually very quick, often painful for both of us as I thrust in and out, hard and strong and angry, simmering with frustration, having to wear an infernal condom because she wouldn't take the pill. Goddam it, she could be so diffident, so difficult, so determined, when she wanted to be.

Often she would lay there with her head turned to one side, looking away from me, like an uninvolved prostitute waiting for the commercial transaction to conclude so she could collect her fee and depart. That's when I would turn her over and enter her from behind, which gave me some feeling of control, even though I knew that beneath me, on all fours, she would be staring into the gloom at the bed-head, waiting for it to end. Sometimes I did not know whether the moan she gave out each time I pushed was one of pleasure or pain. They always say there is a fine line between those two disparate sensations, but quite frankly I did not give a damn which one it was. I just wanted relief.

In post-coital coldness, as we lay next to each other staring silently at the ceiling, I used to think I would have been better off on my own with a copy of a men's magazine and a firm grip with my right hand, just like I had done when I successfully produced the sperm sample that proved our troubled baby-making experiences were not my fault. So, after a while, I started doing just that. 'Damn it,' I thought, 'she reduced me to doing that for her, when it was unecessary! So why not just do it for me? Everyone else around here seems to be looking after number one, so why shouldn't I?'

I had heard about the proliferation of pornography on the internet, even overhearing Buchanan telling one of his friends one day about how 'they do feckin' everythin' on those sites, those women, they take it every feckin' which way'. But being so useless with the computer and not having one in my study at home anyway, I opted for the more traditional method.

I began to quietly cruise my way through less than salubrious newsagents, ones that I would not normally frequent, discreetly buying magazines of that ilk and using them as a source of inspiration to relieve my frustration. To the casual observer, I suppose it would not be the most edifying image, that of the respected family man, successful business executive, pillar of the church and regular contributor of thoughtful correspondence to the letters pages of our better newspapers, hiding in his locked study, hunched over a picture of a naked spread-eagled woman, breathing heavily as he tugs rhythmically on his hardened penis, imagining that he is having sex with her, until he can no longer control himself and comes, spraying all over her picture, before collapsing back in the chair, replete with overwhelming physical satisfaction but racked with gnawing shame and embarrassment.

I had mixed feelings about it. Sometimes I felt awkward, sometimes I simply felt that it was the appropriate thing to do considering the circumstances, while at other times an exhilarating feeling of immense power would come over me and I would truly imagine myself having domineering sex with this dirty little slut spread out before me in full-colour gloss. 'I'm going to fuck you, you bitch,' I would moan quietly as I became more erect, even recalling the old play on words based on my surname that had dogged me in my younger days. 'Take this, you whore,' I would hiss. 'From one Hoare to another! Ha! How do you like that?'

I would have continued buying the magazines, but one day, as I was hovering around the mens' magazine section of a SPAR far away from home base, out of the corner of my eye I saw a parishioner I vaguely knew observing me. I quietly moved away from the racks, trying to give off the air that I had stumbled down the aisle by accident, and bought some bread and milk and exited casually, pretending not to see him. I think that I saved face, but it spooked me. What an embarrassment if that story had got around church circles.

One of my more successful techniques was to imagine that I did take up the offer made by the gorgeous Federica that night in the hotel in Dubrovnik, something that, as the gulf inexorably grew between Jennifer and me, I began to regret not doing.

The image would quickly come to mind of my Swiss love goddess lying naked on the bed beckoning me, her pure white skin glistening in the subdued light of the hotel room. Instead of fleeing, I could see myself confidently taking those last few steps across the floor to strip off and join her. As I would tug harder and get more excited and my mind would begin to race, I could almost smell her, feel her, touch every part of her fit, athletic body as we drove each other on to a crashing imaginary climax. 'Oh, Federica,' I would whisper in the darkened study. 'What a woman. What a lover. What an idiot I was to walk away from you.' I suppose the good thing was that after I came, the pressure valve was released and it calmed me down for days.

Other things also built up the tension, Jennifer's fascination with all things vegetarian proving to be particularly frustrating. I was brought up a meat-and-vegetables man and I will die one. That is the way my Mum cooked, that is what my Dad loved, and that is what I adored. To me, a nice piece of medium-rare fillet steak or some beautifully done pork chops or even grilled sausages along with potatoes in one form or other and some sort of vegetable, preferably peas, provided a good, sound, enjoyable diet. I have got nothing against lentils and hummus and fake curries made out of Brussel sprouts and all that other Asian malarkey, but it gets you down night after night.

One of the best release valves was when we would go down to one of the local restaurants at Dalkey and I could have a steak and a decent bottle of red. Things like that plus a nightly glass or two of a good single-malt whiskey by myself in my study, along with a vintage copy of *Hustler* or an imaginative creation of a wild night with Federica kept me going, made me think it was all worthwhile, helped me keep my sanity, stopped me from getting too serious and too over-bearing. And that was important to me.

Chapter 14

I absolutely, totally, firmly believe the entire blame for whatever friction or difficulty that erupted in our house should be laid directly at the feet of Wendy Cunningham.

Wendy was Jennifer's best friend. I was convinced she only developed the relationship to see what she could get out of it. Mainly my money. But Jennifer thought she was a wonderful person. They had met via the Buddhist movement and Wendy, who had built up a career as a personal development consultant and business coach, became not only Jennifer's pal but also her confidante and advisor. This annoyed me greatly.

Wendy was a New Zealander and, from what I could see, she not only came from a different country but another galaxy. She was tiny, with short-cropped dark hair, flawless olive skin and huge, saucer-shaped brown eyes that peered at you with an annoying glint that said, 'I-know-the-secret-to-the-meaning-of-life-and-you-don't.' Even though she was tiny she made up for her lack of size with her outfits, mainly voluminous caftans in layers of clashing reds, yellows, blues and greens. And the jewellery! She clanked and rattled wherever she went amid a sea of gold, silver and emeralds. Jangling bracelets on both wrists, chains around her neck, fingers covered in rings, giant hoop ear-rings you could throw a basketball through. Buchanan, long recognised in the industry for the accuracy of his valuations, reckoned she was lumping around approximately one-third of her own body weight in precious metals.

But while Wendy was the tiniest of persons, she made the biggest of impressions. She would turn up anywhere, whether in a private home or a public place, and float around like some sort of mystical goddess, her dress billowing in the breeze, her jewellery jangling and her mouth going non-stop. When I would walk in the door at home in the evening, I would immediately know if Wendy had been in the house sometime during the day. Even if she had left hours before, I could still detect the residue of that curious musk-like smell that always seemed to accompany those alternative types; that sickly-sweet aroma, like someone had lit a joss stick or smoked marijuana.

Wendy was the one who took over the production and sale of Jennifer's doleful little 'Inner Me' books and self-help camps, after I insisted that she give up that trite little business and concentrate on the important issue of solely running the house. As a result, the pair of them shared a very close bond, one that made me edgy, suspicious and occasionally angry. I often got the impression Jennifer would tell Wendy about things that she had planned for the family even before she would tell me. Sometimes Wendy would be there when I got home and you could tell from the smirk as she was leaving that she knew Jennifer was about to broach something with me. Some scheme or idea that the pair of them had hatched, and you could bet that she would phone Jennifer the next day to find out how I had responded to it.

Having arrived in Ireland from New Zealand in the late 1980s as a back-packer, Wendy had never left and had built up quite an operation advising clients, including business people, on how to improve their lives. As the Celtic Tiger flourished she had made a killing. Booming companies awash with cash would send their employees to see her with a view to improving their self-esteem, performance and organisational skills.

I used to laugh quietly to myself about that, because I knew that Wendy's own personal life was absolutely chaotic. She was typical of those types who got paid a fortune to tell other people how to run their lives and yet couldn't keep their own on track. She had been married twice, was estranged from her only daughter and was being sued for libel over one of her books. At one stage she had a restraining order placed on her then boyfriend, a moody, former Ukrainian soccer player she had met at a sports management conference in Kiev. Then typically she had the order taken off! I know that because she was at our home one day and her mobile phone rang and she went into another room and screamed down the line at him, threatening to hang up, although noticeably she didn't. Then, when he got in first and ended the call, she burst into tears and tried to phone him back.

That fraught, meaningless relationship raged for months until it reached its logical explosion. After she bawled on Jennifer's shoulder for a week, she suddenly brightened up, as she had found the next poor sap to go fifteen rounds with, a millionaire businessman with a yacht.

Despite the significant fees she pulled, although why people would pay to go and hear her speak I do not know, plus the sales of her books and DVDs, her finances were always in a mess. She was either flush with cash or desperately needing to borrow money in order to pay her bills, shore up an overdrawn account or stabilize a melting credit card. She swung wildly from total control of her affairs to sheer incompetence. While she was supremely confident in her own abilities, she was, as far as I was concerned, quite daffy.

I saw a bit of one of her presentations on video once, an eclectic and frequently bizarre ramble through where we were, where we should be and how to get there. She talked about releasing yourself from the shackles of life and following your whimsical spirit rather than any carefully set course charted by your strict moral compass.

She spoke in elliptical loops about personal development, individual growth and seizing the opportunity. She had every feel-good catchphrase down pat. I laughed out loud at one: 'To capture the delicate butterfly of life, you need to use the gossamer net of love.' She sold her books, videos, beads, bracelets, incense sticks and other tat from a little shop in south Dublin where she also ran workshops in a room up above.

A local lout sprayed graphiti over her shop front once, reading 'Buddhism – a big barrel of bollocks.' In typical style, Wendy said that if she found out who the perpetrator was she would counsel him, try and discover the deep-seated issue that was causing him such angst and present him with viable solutions. Jennifer said if she found him she would make him clean it off and then take him to a Buddhist temple for a peaceful interlude where he could rediscover his inner-self. I said that if I ever came across him, I'd pat him on the back and give him a tenner …

I used to say to Jennifer, 'Let me paraphrase Princess Diana. There are three people in this marriage – you, me and that bloody Kiwi friend of yours.'

There was a fourth person hovering on the edge, too – Karena, some sort of upper level member of the Buddhist movement. Somewhere along the line she had been appointed Jennifer's official guru. Apparently each member has one. As Buchanan said to me one day when they all traipsed out of the house, 'How many feckin' people do you need to tell you how to run your life?'

For someone like me who enjoyed following the simple directions supplied by our local vicar in his sermons and who took the Bible as Gospel – quote something to me out of the Good Book that you can genuinely prove is not relevant to today's society and I will give you a million euro – this was anathema.

At the end of the day Karena might have been a bit more professional than Wendy. She gave off the air of being more discreet and only taking on board the central core of the issue, out of which she would deduce a solution. But like Wendy she wheedled her way in and pretty soon knew practically everything about Jennifer, me, our relationship, our family and our hopes and dreams. I did not like that. I believed in what my father used to say in his typical military style: 'What goes on inside the barracks, stays inside the barracks.' As well, Jennifer used to pass business, personal and financial information on to Karena that I had given to her in private. This concerned me greatly. 'You don't know who she will tell!' I would say to Jennifer.

'Karena is a practicing, professional guru,' Jennifer would reply. 'She's sworn to secrecy. It's exactly the same as a doctor-patient relationship.'

'Don't make me laugh!'

'She's an acknowledged spiritual guide.'

'Ha! She's got a certificate from some witch doctor out of the Kenyan jungle, or wherever she comes from, printed off on a photocopier and stuck on her wall with Blu-Tack. I bet you she gets on the tom-toms and relays everything about us to her students and anyone else within earshot.'

Those conversations always resulted in Jennifer storming off in tears and it would take a while to placate her. Most times, it wan't even worth trying. It's just that I cannot stand self-appointed gurus. All they do is make the answers up as they go. They are gullible enough to believe that stuff in the first place then shrewd enough to recognise its opportunities and finally wily enough to set themselves up as high priests and lord it over poor devils who have not got the wherewithal to think for themselves. Jennifer virtually lay at her feet and hardly moved without her permission. 'What do you think about this, Karena? What do you think about that, Karena? What should I do here, Karena? Can I go and have a pee now, Karena?' Don't make me laugh. It was all a big con and people were stupid enough to buy into it.

In fact, I'm sure Jennifer discussed the most intimate of details of our relationship with Karena and Wendy, including our love-making - when it happened. One day when Wendy was there I dropped some papers on the floor as I came into the kitchen and uttered, 'Blimey.' Wendy burst into hysterical laughter. The look that flashed between her and Jennifer said it all.

I questioned Jennifer about it when Wendy was gone but she assured me that she had never told anyone anything about something as precious and personal as my response when I climaxed. Balder-dash. I knew she had. In fact, after a while I realised that Wendy was not the only one in on that little 'joke'. I came home early and unannounced one day – I used to do that occasionally just to see if everything was running smoothly – and Jennifer and her friends from the mother's group were in the kitchen down the back chatting over coffee. Just as I quietly slipped through the front door, one of them ended her sentence with 'Blimey' and they all burst into hysterical laughter. After I had put my briefcase down and hung up my coat and scarf and appeared at the kitchen door, the laughing suddenly stopped, there were red faces everywhere, and they all decided it was time to take their kids and leave. I heard a couple of them unsuccessfully trying to stifle giggles as they went up the hallway.

Jennifer's revelation of my personal traits made me very angry. I felt any other self-respecting husband would have been quite within his rights to be furious too.

When I asked her about it later that evening, Jennifer eventually admitted that, yes, she had told 'the girls', as she called them, a few 'little things' about our lives.

'But we all do!' she said. 'We all tell each other about our husbands and their endearing foibles. There's nothing wrong with that, it's all done with love.'

Love? I stormed off to bed and it was ages before we made that again.

Chapter 15

The death of the Celtic Tiger came so quickly it caught all of us on the hop. From riding an economic high one day, virtually the next day over-inflated prices were falling around our ears and the banks, including the Bank of Ireland and the Anglo Irish Bank, were revealing enormous debts. Even as a great supporter of the Government I had to admit that Fianna Fáil was tired and had been left stranded and flat-footed. I had always been a loyal follower of Bertie Ahern when he was Taoiseach, often showing my support by writing letters to the papers praising his efforts for 'conjuring up the great economic miracle that has transformed Ireland from a penniless country to a European powerhouse.'

But when the US merchant banks began to fold under the pressure of the sub-prime loan defaults and Wall Street crashed and our banks had the stuffing knocked out of them, the money dried up overnight. The cranes on the development sites suddenly stopped moving, no longer busily lifting the building materials up and down the multi-level projects that had mushroomed all over the country. This to me was the eeriest symbol of the bust. Silhouetted against the Dublin evening sky, they looked like giant mechanical giraffes stilled by some mysterious economic virus. A contractor told me it was cheaper to leave them there rather than take them down and return them to home base.

I started getting very anxious when the head-lines began blaring about the stock market collapse, the banks bordering on bankruptcy and the money drying up. I became even more concerned when it was obvious that this was impacting on property development all over Dublin. My fears reached an all time high when Buchanan rang me at home one evening, exceedingly agitated.

'I've just got off the phone,' he said anxiously. 'Work has stopped at Tallaght!'

'What!' I said. 'The whole fucking lot? You told us it was bullet-proof. The hotel, the entertainment, the leisure, the accommodation, the retail space. A great mix, you told us. It couldn't go wrong, no matter what else went belly-up.'

My hand started to tremble on the phone. 'Can we get this going again?'

'No,' came the voice. 'Not for the moment anyway. I spoke to Frank. He said he's got no money and can't pay the people we already owe, much less keep pushing on with the building. He locked the gate this afternoon and sent 'em all home. That's it, Stuart. Feckin' hell. I'm sorry.'

I mumbled thanks, told him we would have to meet in the morning to see what we could do, and hung up. The tears started to well in my eyes. What had I done? I may not have been lured into some foolish exercise like buying an investment holiday flat in Bulgaria sight unseen, like many other Irishmen riding the Tiger had, but I had poured a lot of money into this project. My own personal money.

It was all too much for me. I sat down, put my head in my hands and started sobbing. Hearing this Jennifer came into the room. 'What's the matter?' she said concerned.

I looked up at her, tried to open my mouth, but found it difficult to say anything.

'What is it?' she said anxiously, coming over to me. 'Something wrong with your Da?'

'No.'

'My Da, then? He hasn't got cancer or something?'

'No.'

'Well, what is it? Have *you* got cancer?'

I looked up at her sadly, trying to pick up my strength. I felt that there could not be anything harder for a husband to tell his wife than this.

'Tallaght. The project. It's stopped. We've lost thousands.'

'Oh! Is that all?' she replied immediately, her look of anxiety converting straight into one of relief. 'I thought it was something important, someone sick or something. But it's only about money.'

She put her arm around me. 'There, there. Don't worry, you'll get it back.' And she walked off! I looked up as she left the room, my mouth wide open, and shook my head. Her naïve reaction only made me feel more depressed. 'She just doesn't get it,' I thought.

I was still dispirited the next morning, but Buchanan was positively downcast because he knew it was on his recommendation that the firm should get involved in the development, not only as insurers, but also as investors. While he had to sort out how he was going to defend his position and salvage something of his reputation, the situation presented me with a big headache on three levels.

First, our company had provided the insurance on it. Now, with the developer almost certainly going bankrupt, there was going to be a lot of angst, paperwork, threats, writs and claims flying around. Fortunately we had hived a lot of it off to an insurance underwriter and the main damage to us would be a blow to our morale and a kick to our credibility. It's something you don't want to get involved in. I rang Frank, the project manager, hoping he might have some good news, but he was short, sharp and to the point. 'I'm lookin' for a new job meself right now, Stuart,' he said.

Second, I had encouraged some hand-picked, highly-valued clients of ours to invest in the project and would now have the difficult task of advising them that in all likelihood they would never see their cash again. Just like me. This was going to be a sensitive operation so I figured the best thing was that I should not take the brunt of it all. As he was the original proponent of the idea, I insisted Buchanan come along to the meeting so that they could crucify him.

He didn't exactly endear himself with his opening salvo, chucking aside the carefully written apologetic script that Derek and I had devised and instead going in boots and all. 'Well, no one, not even the best financial brains in the world, could have predicted this,' he roared. 'That sub-prime crap in

America has done us all in. You wouldn't think they would give loans to feckin' eedjits like that, would you? Most of the fat bastards couldn't get out of their own feckin' way, much less pay a mortgage, the lard-arses.'

Derek leaned forward and whispered, 'Jayzus, Buchanan, don't hold back will ya?'

And it was on. A man stood up and said, 'Don't try and make excuses, you feckin' thieves, we want our money back,' and a tirade of complaints hit us like a tornado.

'I'd prefer hot needles poked into my eyeballs than this,' Buchanan whispered as yet another aggrieved participant stood up at the back of the conference room to give us a blast, roaring that we had 'promised the world, but lost the lot.' Many of them were small investors, first timers, couples who had put in five, maybe ten thousand euro. They were extremely shocked and disappointed that their initial move into the exciting world of high finance had brought them only pain and loss, particularly as when they signed up the Tiger was roaring and the prospects for strong returns were excellent. 'It's not worth the damn paper it's printed on,' one wife said angrily as she threw down the beautifully-bound, four-colour prospectus which featured a photo of a yuppie couple lovingly walking across the designer square past a modernist fountain towards the smiling concierge at the revolving door of their chic apartment block. Fortunately I was able to calm many of them down and regain some trust by offering reductions on their next insurance policy premiums.

Third, there were the bigger investors to consider. They had split into two camps. The experienced 'old money' types who shrugged, patted me on the back and said, 'Bad luck, lad, not your fault,' and sauntered off into the evening air. They knew, as the old saying goes, never to put all your eggs in one basket. Always keep plenty in reserve to fight another day. That's why they have old money and plenty of it.

But the boots-and-all 'new money' tyros were not happy at the prospect of having to hand back the keys of the Maserati and down-sizing their luxury living conditions. They gave us a nasty pasting before they stormed out. Several threatened litigation including one who mentioned a notorious 'no-win, no-fee' Dublin barrister that he was going to hire to come after us.

'Good luck,' said Buchanan without batting an eyelid. 'He's gone to the wall, too ...'

But the worst part for me was that I had put my own money in and like everybody else, had to face up to the prospect of kissing it goodbye. When we had a chance to sit down together, I told Jennifer that it was a turn of events that no one could have predicted and that as a family we would now have to pull our collective belt in. I would have to trim back on her weekly domestic allowance, I told her.

The down-trodden, flame-haired, bog-Irish Catholic in her flared up like an aggrieved dragon. This, she considered, was very unfair. 'What's all this got to do with how we live?' she said. 'That was money I never saw anyway. It was cash you had locked up for years until you put it into this. So now it's gone, bad luck. You've still got your company and your car and your income and your commissions. And your house and your family! Why should the children and I suffer simply because of one business deal that's gone wrong?'

I tried to explain to her that it wasn't that simple.

'It's more complicated than that,' I said soothingly. 'You see, as you are not au fait with high finance ...'

'Oh, don't start that,' she interrupted. 'Don't give me that rubbish about me being the poor little housewife locked away at home who knows nothing about the big brave world of corporate business. I've got more degrees than you have, remember, and from a real university, too, not some tin-pot night school!'

'What? You be careful what you say, darling.'

'Careful? I've worked for bigger, more successful companies than your little operation, Stuart, and if I wasn't enjoying being with the kids, I'd have my own successful career.'

I was taken aback by her response. I could feel my face flushing red with anger. I tried to remain calm and reason with her.

'My so-called little operation provides a wonderful lifestyle for you and our children. And might I remind you that your much-lauded Cambridge degree is in law, Jennifer. Law, not economics! I was simply going to point out that the shockwaves from a collapse like this go all the way down the line, affecting everybody.'

'You mean straight to the kitchen,' she interrupted again. 'To me and all the other mums. What a joke.'

'Be that as it may, I'll forgive you your lack of financial knowledge.'

'Ha, you men, you got us into all this. You so-called experts. Your hero Bertie and now that gormless looking corpse that pretends to be leader, what's his name, Biffo? Hopeless, the lot of them.'

This was too much. 'Jennifer!' I shouted. 'That's outrageous. How dare you speak about good men like that. Ahern made this country great and now Cowen is trying to stabilise it after events over which he had no control have torpedoed all that was built up. He has to save the banks, otherwise we are all doomed.'

'Oh, brilliant. Throw more good money after bad. Make the people in the street pay. Have a bit of vision, why don't you? Think outside the square for once rather than coming up with the same tired old solutions.'

I moved in closer to her. I was getting angry. She was not only attacking my business acumen but the political party that I supported and which had served the country so well. I started to clench my fists.

She continued on. 'And now, after you've sat in your study and had a good cry like a baby, the family has to suffer.'

That was enough.

'Are you listening to me? Do you understand?' I hissed, moving up close to her, raising my hand.

'What?'

'Do you understand? I'm cutting your budget. Jennifer. Now, don't make me angry and force me to do something that we will both regret.' She looked at me blankly for a second and then stepped back. 'Do you understand?' I repeated.

'Yes, yes, I do, Stuart, I understand,' she said meekly.

'Good,' I said, dropping my hand. 'Just cut your cloth to suit, Jennifer, work within the budget that I set you and all will be fine.'

I left it at that and headed back to my study, moving slowly and deliberately, popping my head in the doorway of the lounge and saying a cheery 'Hi' to the boys, who were watching *The Karate Kid*.

As captain of the ship, I was angry that she should question my decision-making, but I was pleased that I had successfully put the mutiny down. 'Typical,' I thought, 'she not only knows nothing about high finance, but has no idea about real politics, as well.'

I did not raise the topic again, but I did notice that as part of the new regime, she started buying the cheaper brand of disposable razors and generic chocolate biscuits, so after a few weeks I quietly returned her allowance to its usual level and nothing further was said.

Things went back to normal on the home front. Or at least they did as far as I could see.

Chapter 16

Solid and reliable as I was, there was always one chink in my armour. The computer. It was not my scene. That's a terrible admission from a man who worked in an industry that was so dependent on it. But I had sales duties to undertake. I had managerial responsibilities to uphold. I had executive powers to wield. And I had Doreen to do my paperwork for me.

Doreen was my long and faithful secretary, my grand support, my indestructible, ever-present, wise and all-knowing angel. She could do anything. Some said she ran my department, if not the whole company. I think that was a bit over-stated. But she certainly was invaluable, as I knew very little about modern technology.

Her role included translating all my paperwork and correspondence onto the computer. Call me a Luddite, but I was a fountain-pen man. I did all my work with a gold-plated Parker 61 Stratus with a 14 carat medium nib. I enjoyed the atmospheric sound it made as it moved across the page. I also wrote everything on yellow sheets of A4, the old-fashioned legal pad, giving it a sense of authority. Whether it was the draft of a letter, the rough calculations for a project or the general outline for a proposal, to me it looked 'real'. The figures had a profundity about them, the writing an air of elegance. At a meeting, people would be impressed when I'd pull out the pen, do some rough calculations on the yellow sheets and hand them around. Afterwards Doreen would magically turn it all into a neatly-typed printout.

Even my Letters to the Editor that I enjoyed writing and sending off to the newspapers, preferably *The Independent* or *The Irish Times*, I always did in long hand. It gave me a great feeling of satisfaction, putting my thoughts about the economy or a social issue down on quality paper with real ink, placing it in an envelope and mailing it from the letterbox at the end of our street.

One of my few forays into the computer world was to get Doreen to show me how to access the Stock Market for a daily update on the share prices. Later I got her to show me how to access an email account, for viewing purposes only. Personally, I did not like email. I felt that important messages could disappear amongst all the rubbish that filled up the inbox every morning. I had heard of sales being lost and projects coming unstuck because an email that had been sent in time to catch the deadline had gone unsighted. I did not necessarily want to be shown how to use email. I just wanted to check Jennifer's every now and then.

I did not think there was anything wrong with that. I felt that having the occasional discreet peek at his wife's correspondence was a reasonable thing for a husband to do, in order to see if there was any message or subject that might cause concern or require action. It was important, so that everyone could move forward together with no secrets or hidden agendas.

I was always pleased to discover that whenever I got into her email account, with the obvious password of 'Molly', Jennifer's notes to her friends and family seemed straightforward and contained nothing untoward. There were no recipients that I did not know or had not heard of.

But I hadn't counted on Facebook.

Oh, I'd heard about it all right. Some sort of friendship site where people swapped messages and photos about what they were up to. Putting little quotes online about what they were doing at that precise moment and that sort of thing. What they were cooking, what they were wearing and where they had partied. I remember one day how one of the girls in Accounts was having lunch at her desk and she showed me her screen as I walked past. 'Look at this, Mr Hoare,' she said, 'this is really cool.'

Cool? Some character had written that he was 'feeling good' and 'might go shopping'. Another said that this year he would 'not live in a campervan'. A third wrote, 'I am a fan of duct tape'. Riveting stuff.

I concluded it was the province of the young – teenagers and twenty-somethings with not many brains and too much time on their hands – and dismissed it out of hand. I didn't realise that people of all ages used it, including those in their 30s, 40s, 50s and even older. I did not know that Facebook groups were formed of people interested in specific subjects, campaigns and movements, the recruitment often being quite vigorous. Above all, I did not have a clue that it provided an online opportunity for two people to talk to each other, discreetly and privately, in order to develop a relationship.

What a fatal error on my part. Especially for a man working in an industry where errors were inexcusable, who admired Horatio Nelson for his tactical ability and who had been brought up by a father who insisted on always knowing what your enemy was up to.

What I also did not know was that Jennifer had set up a separate email to accept the Facebook 'alert' notes that members got advising them that something had happened on their account. Jennifer later tried to tell me that she had done that for convenience because so many emails were being sent telling her that a comment had been posted or a message had been sent or a photo had been tagged and so on. I eventually found out that that was a lie. She had all along been deliberately hiding the content of that Facebook email box from me.

One day I arrived home at 5.27 pm as usual, and the house was in typical order. The kids were doing their homework, Jennifer was cooking dinner and all seemed right with the world. But it wasn't. She had a somewhat distracted look; an edgy visage, one almost of fear. She was slightly pale and a little jittery.

She jumped when I entered the kitchen and her kiss on the cheek was even briefer than usual. I noticed she didn't really give me eye contact. But I'm an understanding man, lots of things can happen to a busy mother during the day. Getting kids in and out of cars, doing pick-ups, tramping from the butcher to the grocer, it can all build up. Besides, when I questioned her, she assured me she was all right. 'I'm fine,' she said, 'how was your day?'

'Oh, okay, I guess. Not much joy. You know, it's like Thailand, that sort of thing ...''

She reacted nervously to that. 'What did you say?'

'I said, things are like in Thailand.'

'Thailand? Why did you mention that?'

'Well, Thailand was one of the original Asian Tigers, along with Hong Kong, Taiwan and the others. It was the first to go down the gurgler and that, to me, sums up where Ireland is heading now. Why?'

'Oh, nothing, nothing,' she said, looking a little more relieved and going back to her cooking. I studied her for a moment, then poured myself a glass of wine and was about to pursue the matter – why would the mention of Thailand unsettle her? – when the Angelus finished on the television in the kitchen and the news theme began blaring. I wanted to watch the bulletin because I had heard around the traps that some sort of new bank was in the pipeline to take on the toxic loans that were dogging the Irish financial institutions and which hopefully might ease things. As the Taoiseach made his announcement, I ruminated on the situation the country was in. What a mess. Economic doom, the Celtic Tiger shot down, the future looking gloomy.

So, Jennifer's uneasiness passed from my mind. But later that evening she got short with the children when she put them to bed, which was something she rarely did. And although she was watching the programs she liked on the television, including a travel program about Asia, she said very little about it and retired early. The only other thing I noticed was that she made a point of turning the computer off. She didn't necessarily always do that, something which annoyed me because I felt that leaving a computer on was not only a waste of power but also could damage components, lose data or spark a fire.

I was not too good on some of those things, but from my view at the doorway of the study as she stood over the desk and pressed the mouse, what I saw disappearing as the computer shut down was the blue and white colours of a website. I deduce now, long after the event, that it must have been Facebook. It still grieves me to realise that when I asked her what it was, she stood there and blatantly told me it was a buying group and she was having a look to see if there were any bargains. Impressed with her thrift, I blithely moved on, suspecting and knowing nothing.

What an idiot I was, I should have pressed the issue, looked for the signs, did a little snooping around. But why should I? Things might have been bad in Ireland and terrible in Thailand, but at least the Hoare family was standing strong and united, wasn't it?

Chapter 17

I never saw the next revelation coming at all. I never suspected for one minute that Jennifer, the person I had sworn my allegiance to by the banks of the Shannon on the eve of the summer solstice, would be anything other than faithful to me. I might have been a bit tough on her at times, but as I used to say whenever I made a decision that she did not agree with, 'It's for the good of the family, to keep us united and to protect our reputation.'

We had a successful marriage. We had a beautiful home. We had a lovely family. We had social currency and respect. Why would she want to jeopardize all that? I firmly believed that I was the captain of a good ship and that Jennifer and the children were an excellent crew despite she and Molly developing their own slightly mutinous group below decks. Surely no one in their right mind would want to send all that off course and condemn the whole thing to the bottom of the ocean?

She was the model wife. A bit scatty maybe, but a great mother to our children. Devoted to her own parents. And to mine, too. And as the years had rolled on, she never seemed to have deviated from that path. Never once did she give off a hint that something was going on. She maintained the same even-handed voice during my regular daily calls. She never used the house phone or her mobile for calls to strange numbers. I know that because I went through the bills with her every month and would immediately pick up on any new or unusual number. Her emails were clear and as far as I knew, Facebook was of little consequence.

I was so trusting that at one stage when Jennifer said, 'Can we get a laptop?' I acquiesced. She explained how the boys had a lot of homework and that having to share the home computer meant one of them might miss out and fall behind in his studies. That concerned me. She also pointed out that a laptop would be handy for her to help with the shopping and organising things. 'As well,' she said, 'one day soon I will be able to go back into the workforce, so it would be good for me to have my own computer.'

I had always made it clear that Jennifer was to never work again, even when the last of the kids started school. We had always agreed on our roles; I was the bread winner, she the home maker. But now, as things were getting tough, it didn't seem a bad idea to bring a little extra cash into the house. So I agreed, although rather than spend money on a new laptop, I brought home an old one from work which Doreen, my able secretary, assured me would function properly for years. It was perfect timing. I gave it to Jennifer for her birthday.

The laptop was easy enough to source as things were getting so tough at work that Derek and I had had to let a couple of salesmen go. The downsizing happened so quickly, I was soon able to bring another notebook home for the boys, too.

I started to realise that something was not right in the weeks after that evening when she had reacted so nervously when I mentioned Thailand. From that anxious moment on, a new Jennifer started to emerge. A slightly more self-confident Jennifer. Almost a disobedient Jennifer. She started chipping at me, firing back comments, ignoring my instructions. She started to display that oh-so-clever smile that her friend Wendy had perfected. And Wendy started to get more involved. Why, Wendy was even picking up the kids from school sometimes when Jennifer unaccountably found herself too late to be there. She started getting tardy about the meals, to the point of being careless about what the children were eating.

'Wait a minute,' I asked myself one day. 'What's all this about?'

Jennifer had never let the kids down, not once. I had, yes, I will freely admit that. Plenty of times I'd been late for concerts, missed soccer matches or tiptoed in at the back during the middle of a piano recital. Very often, at the most crucial of times when she needed my help most, I would not be there for her. Stuart Junior needs to be picked up from the dentist? I would be in an important meeting. Richard needs a lift to music? I would be at a business conference. Molly has to be taken to child care? 'Sorry, darling, I've got to drive over to Galway to stitch up a deal.'

I tried to participate as much as I could. But I was the money man, that was my job. Jennifer's job was to be the family woman. To stay home and look after the kids. We'd made an agreement that we would do it that way. Just as we had agreed to love, honour and be faithful to each other.

I was not the most sensitive of fellows, but after a while even I started to pick up the vibes from Jennifer. The nervousness, the belligerence, the cockiness, the tardiness. For a brief moment, I put it down to early menopause, but discarded that notion after I established that she didn't seem to be complaining of the other symptoms. Ironically, the subject of women's health came up when I found a packet of the pill in the bathroom, something she had not used for years, much to my obvious annoyance.

'What are these doing here?' I said. 'I know we hardly make love anymore. But when we do, you make me wear a condom. So, what's going on?'

She looked embarrassed and rather ruffled. She quickly and quietly took the packet out of my hand and regained her compsoure. 'I've been having women's troubles, darling,' she said blithely. 'Heavy bleeding. The doctor prescribed these to see if it will help.'

That threw me a bit. 'Are you all right?' I said.

'I'll be fine. We'll see how these work.'

I stared at her for a while, figured that that was fair enough and decided it would be best to leave an intimate matter like that alone.

However, from then on I began to quietly observe that Jennifer would become especially agitated, evasive and lose focus for three days in succession once a month. Always during the week, never the weekend. There appeared to be some sort of sequence, one which simply could not be put down to her menstrual cycle, the phases of the moon or even some of her more bizarre New Age theories.

Short of fronting her directly, I was struggling to find an answer, until one day, Doreen inadvertently provided the goods. Just before she was leaving work she said to me, 'I'm having dinner with someone special tonight.'

'Oh yes?' I said, a little surprised. This was indeed a turn up for the books. Doreen was only a couple of years younger than me, had never been married and had never indicated she was seeking a partner.

'I met someone on Facebook,' she said chirpily.

I looked at her stupidly. 'Doreen, with respect, what are you doing on something like that at your age? Isn't that for the young?'

'Oh, no, no,' she enthused. 'All sorts of people use it. Young, old, friends, family, husbands, wives, lovers ...'

'Lovers?'

'Yes, you don't have to make everything public, you know. You can talk discreetly, set up a whole romance, have a little tryst and no one will know.'

She giggled and looked to the heavens. 'Now that my poor dear mother has departed after years of sufferin' and I have the house to myself and all the time in the world, it's my chance for a bit of fun.'

I stared at her lamely as she picked up her coat and headed for the door. 'I'll let you know how I get on,' she said cheerily. I watched as she disappeared down the corridor. Then I looked down at her computer, then back at her receding figure and then at the computer again. I began to think, to link things together, to work elements through. Facebook. Discreet conversations. Lovers. I walked back into my own office, circled my desk a couple of times and then came back. Tentatively, I touched the space bar. Bingo. In her haste to meet her potential paramour, Doreen had not turned the computer off. The screen lit up to reveal the home page of Facebook. I tapped in Jennifer's email – the new one, the Gmail one that I had spotted on her laptop screen one night – and tried 'Molly' for the password.

The Facebook Home Page of Jennifer Hoare came up.

And so did he.

Right underneath her profile photo were pictures of six of Jennifer's friends. I knew the other five, including of course Karena and that damn Wendy. But not the sixth. Not him. Not this fellow. Not this, what's his name, let me see now? Tom.

I looked around the page using my limited skills with the mouse, flicking the cursor all over the place, scrolling things up and down, following the discussions between Jennifer and others – and him – on the screen. A lot of it was rubbish, but the more I read, the more I increasingly felt anxious, alarmed and finally sick to the stomach. You could tell from the energy and intimacy of the public dialogue between the two of them that something was going on. And if that was what they were letting anybody read, then God knows what they were saying to each other in private. Or, for that matter, doing.

I anxiously clicked at the buttons on the page with a clammy hand. Somehow, even with my computer incompetency, his profile came up and I read it quickly. I could see already from the picture what his genetics were. He was not pure Anglo Saxon, that was for sure. The colour of his skin and shape of his eyes attested to that. Now I read all about his background, where he lived, what he did for a job and some of his philosophical views on life. Ah-ha! Look at this. His mother was Thai! No wonder Jennifer went to water when I mentioned Thailand in the kitchen one night.

And there was the clincher. A little note at the bottom. 'Just to remind everybody I will be in Dublin from the 21st to the 23rd next month, as usual.'

I hastily cast my eyes around Doreen's well-organised desk and snatched up the calendar. My fingers were shaking as I flipped it over to the next month. The 21st to the 23rd. There it was. Three days in the middle of the week. The sort of time sequence each month when Jennifer would get unsettled. Just as I had worked out.

I have never been so furious, so angry, so riven with rage since that day at school when I snapped after years of being treated so badly by the in-house bullies. It was a level of anger that I had never attained since, a feeling that I had always success-fully subsumed when the pressure was on. But not this time. I could feel my cheeks burning with indignation.

I squeezed the calendar so hard that all the blood drained from my hand. I hurled it against the wall. I stepped back, stared at the smiling face on the screen and yelled. 'Arrrgggghhh!'

The cry of anguish and anger reverberated through the empty building.

My God! My wife was having an affair! With some character called Tom. A half-Asian Buddhist drummer living in some dive in the East End of London.

Chapter 18

I am not called Stu for nothing. I stewed.

I stewed and stewed every minute of every day over the terrible prospect that my wife was having an affair.

I stewed over it in the car on the way to work, I stewed over it all day at my office, I stewed over it in the car on the way home. I stewed over it in meetings, while standing in the ATM queue, even while sitting by the lake in the park eating my lunch-time sandwiches and solemnly watching the ducks.

Two conflicting arguments banged away in my brain. On the one hand, I was certain the bitch was doing it. I wanted to confront her there and then. Question her, interrogate her, get the story out of her. Use force if I had to. What a situation. Here was some jumped up little drummer having sex with my wife while I was going through endless periods of frustration or having to recourse to the demeaning solution of self gratification through fantasy. She was not going to get away with it. I fumed every time I thought about it.

On the other hand, I had no real proof. I was only guessing, surmising, extrapolating a devastating conclusion from a few scrappy comments I had seen on Facebook. What if I was wrong? What if they were just friends having a chat? What if I rushed in, starting shooting first and asking questions later, only to discover it was all innocent and above board?

Then the whole thing would have blown up in my face. I would have broken the bond between Jennifer and me, making myself look very foolish in the process.

'Stuart,' I would say to myself, 'you've constructed the worst possible scenario out of nothing.' It was quite possible. Even though I was from the 'old school', I had come to appreciate that the concepts of friendship, partnership and marriage had changed so radically that things were no longer clear cut. You were once able to say, 'This is my wife, now hands off,' and people would respect that.

But nowadays, people drift in and out of relationships, they become enamored with someone via all these modern technological devices, cyber-mating or something I think it is called, and nothing is ever set in stone or follows the old norms. You hear a couple explain, 'We've split up, but we're still good friends.' That is rubbish as far as I am concerned; ex-lovers cannot retain their friendship. Once it's over, it's over and they should never go near one another ever again. But in our brave new world, people believe that to end a relationship, take the sex out of it, and yet somehow remain firm friends is a tenable view.

So I stewed over both sides of the argument, especially at home. And particularly when Jennifer darted around the kitchen preparing meals, humming a little tune to herself. Or when she sat next to me in the lounge with the television guide in her hand asking me what I wanted to watch. Or when she greeted me with, 'How was your day?'

'How was my day?' I used to think to myself. 'How was my day, you ask? Fantastic, couldn't have been better. Here I am, up to my arse in work, trying to find ways to salvage the thousands we've lost while you're having it off with a layabout Asian percussionist. Great! Couldn't be better.'

Then I used to think, 'Hang on, it would be crazy saying that. Even if I am right, I'm just focusing on money. There's more to that than this. What about loyalty to each other? What about trust? What about being devoted to the family unit? Maybe those things don't mean much to her anymore.'

I would consider trying the placatory technique. I would imagine how I would put it: 'Darling, I realise that I have not been the best of husbands. I know our relationship has suffered, a lot of it being my fault through my devotion to work and rigid old-fashioned principles. I understand how you could be tempted to fall into the arms of someone else – not that I am saying you have, of course – but surely we can fix things before they get too bad?'

I used to think about how others would have approached it. The ice cool Derek, my business partner, would have calmly said, 'I've worked out exactly what's going on, I'm walking out, staying at a hotel, and a letter from my solicitor will be delivered to you in the morning.'

Buchanan would have given his wife the biggest bollocking, called her a 'feckin' slut,' reduced her to tears, then added that it was probably as much his fault as hers, opened a bottle of wine and tried to get her up to the bedroom.

But most of the time, I just seethed. I wanted to confront Jennifer, to say something, to elicit a response from her and gauge my next move based on what she said and, equally importantly, how she said it. Angry and furious as I was, I knew I really only had one shot at this and I used to think about every possible option as I paced up and down the lounge room late at night. I wanted answers, explanations, but I did not want to mess it up, to wreck everything, to destroy the lot. I had to be patient. As my father used to say about resolving issues, 'Be like an Army Court Martial, son. First, work out the result you want, and then set up the terms of reference to get it.'

I briefly thought about seeking more of Dad's wise counsel. But the Alzheimer's had chewed out his brain and he would have contributed little. My mother would have been of limited help, too, as she was now fully pre-occupied with Dad's illness. Besides, she and Jennifer had developed a very close relationship over the years and she adored the kids. I was sure she would have hated to see the family unit split, no matter how unpalatable the situation. How wrong that thinking proved to be.

I certainly did not want to consult Jennifer's family, either. They had a love/hate relationship with me at the best of times and the majority vote would have come down on her side, especially amongst her brothers. The general consensus, particularly endorsed by her father Seamus and her closest brother Kevin, would have been that I had been a poor choice in the first place and who could blame her for getting a bit of excitement on the side?

Besides, no matter who I would have carefully picked out from her family for a discreet discussion sworn to secrecy, the story would have spread around that sprawling, brawling bunch of ignorant Micks like wildfire.

There was only one way to find out. I hired a private detective.

Actually, he surprised me. I thought he would be wearing a pin-stripe, double-breasted suit and a grey Fedora hat, ceaselessly igniting cigarettes from a silver lighter that clanged loudly every time he shut it. But he was an ordinary man in ordinary clothes who could slip in and out of any crowd unnoticed. 'That's the name of the game,' he said.

He was very good at it, too, and the fifteen hundred euro that he charged, which I quietly slipped into the sundries column of the firm's monthly accounts, was well worth it. Distressing, but worth it. A picture of this Tom character entering a hotel in Dublin, followed by a snap of Jennifer entering a few minutes later. The third print, of them later fondly farewelling each other on the front steps, was enough to convince me. The closeness, the intimacy and the joy shown by their body language said it all. They had rekindled more than a friend-ship.

'I've got another shot here, taken with a long lens straight into the hotel window,' the investigator said, peering into a large envelope. 'It doesn't show them actually doing it, but you can see they're getting well prepared. I observed them for a little while, until the point where even I have to show a bit of discretion. Some sort of dance, preparing for intercourse, like a ritual.'

I held up my hands, palms out, and shook my head. Curious as I was, I declined to see it. I'd seen plenty and was outraged enough as it was.

That night when I came home from work, looked around and observed the state of the house, I knew I had to make a stand. Dinner had not been prepared, the place was in semi darkness, there was rubbish and toys and papers all over the place, the kids were all staring hypnotically at the television and Jennifer was in the study tapping away furiously on the laptop.

I pulled the photos out of my brief case, calmly walked into the room, immediately recognised from the blue and white page that she was on Facebook, strode up, grabbed the screen of the laptop and slammed it down. She only saw me loom over her at the last second and barely got her fingers out of the way as the lid hit the keyboard. She looked up at me, shocked. I think she knew what was coming, but was trying to act innocent.

'Stuart! What's the matter?'

I held back for as long as I could, staring straight into her eyes. The longer I sustained the silence, the more uncomfortable she became. I wanted her to think that the worst was going to happen – because it was about to.

Finally, I leaned right into her face, and spoke very slowly.

'Tell me about Tom,' I hissed.

'Who? How did you ...?' she gulped, before regaining a little composure. I could see her Irish Catholic butter-wouldn't-melt-in-its-mouth rat cunning working over time. 'Oh, why, Tom, he's just an old friend, from Cambridge days,' she said chirpily.

'And he's reappeared out of the blue, just like that?' I said cynically.

'Yes.'

'On the computer?'

'Yes, that's what happens on Facebook,' she said, nodding nervously towards the laptop. 'Friends from the past spot your name and get in touch. It happens all the time.'

I waited. She looked up at me for a moment and then looked down at the closed laptop again.

'And ..?' I said.

'And what?' she said, still looking down.

'What sort of friend is he?'

She clasped her hands in her lap and bowed her head further. When she replied, I could barely hear her.

'A good friend,' she whispered.

'How good?'

There was a long moment's hesitation.

'Just good friends, that's all,' she whispered.

I pulled the computer away from her and with both hands, lifted it high above my head and smashed it down on the corner of the antique hardwood desk. The thwack made her jump.

'Stuart!'

I leaned close into her face again. 'You're not telling the truth.'

'I am, I am! We're just friends from the past. His mother is from Thailand.'

'Oh, Thailand! Ah, now things are starting to become clearer. I mentioned Thailand in the kitchen one night and you nearly had a fit.'

She looked up, anxiously. 'Well ... there's the Buddhist thing ... we were both at Cambridge together, and after ...'

'After?'

'After, um, after ... a while, we lost touch.'

'But now you're back, as you so nicely put it, in touch, huh?'

'We're just friends! On Facebook.'

I slammed the notebook hard down on the desk again. A memory stick in a side port flew off with such force it bounced across the floor into the corner. The screen had started to fragment.

'You're more than friends, aren't you? Hey? More than friends?'

I hit the notebook down on the table again. Bang! The sound reverberated through the house. 'You've been seeing him!'

'No! No! I swear. Stuart, you're scaring me. There's nothing to this, we just talk on Facebook that's all.'

'Don't give me that crap.'

'Honest! We just chat on the computer. I haven't seen him. I swear!'

I threw the three photos down on the desk. 'Oh, yes?' I said. She gasped as I spread them out in front of her. Him going into the hotel. Her going into the hotel. The pair of them kissing as they left the hotel.

Her head jolted back in shock, her eyes began to glisten with tears, her bottom lip began to quiver.

'Well?' I continued. 'This is a nice little family photo album, isn't it? Huh? You say you haven't seen him, but there he is, in this picture. And there is you in that picture. Oh, and look at this, there you are in this one, together! He looks more than a friend in these, doesn't he? He looks very much part of the scene.'

'All right. Okay. We met just once, in the city, just to catch up. That's all. Nowhere else. There's nothing ...'

Before she could finish, a third voice intervened.

'Mummy ...' We both looked around. It was a tiny, subdued voice, coming from the doorway. The three kids had left the television and had come over to see what was happening, concerned and anxious.

'Mummy,' continued Stuart Junior, his voice a whisper. 'Does Daddy mean the man that was here one day when I got sick and stayed home from school ..?'

Chapter 19

It was a gut-wrenching, soul-destroying statement that Stuart Junior had so innocently uttered. The moment he mentioned 'the man' who had been in the house on the day he was ill, the memory started flooding back to me. How I had come back one afternoon to pick up some important papers that I had forgotten when I'd left home that morning. How I had stopped to talk to Pete the postman in the driveway. And how, when I had let myself in, Jennifer was washing up several dishes, including two coffee cups. This had seemed odd and when I questioned her, she made some excuse about her Mam being over for a chat that day. Normally I would have checked up on it, but I was so pre-occupied with the Tallaght disaster that I let it go. I should have discreetly asked her mother later whether she had been at our place that day or not.

Now, out of the mouth of an unknowing child, it was all becoming clear to me. That he – this monster, this home-wrecker, this Tom – was not only liaising with my wife in hotels but had been in our house, too! Why, that day that I had turned up unexpectedly, he must have been only a few metres away, hiding in another room while I was standing there chatting to my wife. The person who I loved, worshipped and trusted.

My mind started racing. What else had there been? Why, yes, of course. He was probably also there that time I rang Jennifer's mobile and she sounded quite flustered when she answered. She passed it off as being excited about one of the kids having had some success at school. But, my God, I now realised that she was probably in bed with him when she answered the phone. That's why she was so breathless and not making much sense. They had just had sex. He was lying next to her while I was talking to her on the phone. He would have had his dirty little drummer hands all over her, playing with her, smirking while she blatantly told me lies. The thought of that inflamed my brain.

Barely able to contain my anger, I remained calm enough to give the kids five euro and tell them to go down to the village to get an ice cream. Something like that, I can't exactly remember, anything to get them out of the way. 'Mummy and Daddy have something to talk about,' I said evenly.

I was livid, almost out of control. When the front door latch clicked, I leaned right into Jennifer's face and hissed:

'So, he *has* been here, then?'

'Ah ...' She dropped her head.

'Don't fucking lie to me, Jennifer!'

'Yes,' she whispered finally. 'Yes, he has.'

I wanted to explode. I wanted to hit her. I wanted to go and find the little bastard and kill him. But I also wanted to ask two more questions, get two more pieces of information, to confirm the depth of her infidelity.

'Be very careful about how you answer this next question, Jennifer. I will ask you just once. Did you have sex here, in this house?'

There was a long silence. Her head stayed down. 'Huh?' I barked. 'Answer me! Did you screw him here, in our house? The home we have built up together?'

Ater a few more seconds, she nodded her head imperceptibly and whispered, 'Yes.'

I stepped back, blinked and shook my head. I took a deep breath and leaned down close to her face again.

'So, was it in our bed? Hey? Did you fuck him in our bed?'

There was a long, long pause, as she struggled for breath. 'Yes,' she finally whispered. 'In our bed.'

'God damn it! You fucking slut!'

That was all I needed to hear. The Court Martial had sat. All admissions had been tendered. The defendant was guilty as charged. Sullying the matrimonial home with lust. Punishment was to be delivered. I punched her in the ribs. It was short, it was sharp, it was sweet. It was brutal. All those years of martial arts training melded into one stunning blow. My fist barely moved an inch, yet it connected with such force that I could hear the ribs crack as she doubled over in pain. I had not felt such a surge of unbridled power or such a release of deeply re-pressed anger since the day I snapped in the boarding school yard and pole-axed the college bully. And just like that day all those years before, once the flood gates were open, nothing was going to stop me. As Jennifer let out a piercing scream of pain, I punched her again, and again, and again, grabbing her by the hair with my free hand and pulling her face up towards me.

'You bitch,' I screamed. 'You fucking little bitch. So that's all you think of our marriage. Huh?'

She clutched at her ribs with her right hand and clawed for breath, slowly bringing her left hand up to her face to wipe her dripping nose with her sleeve. She dropped her head again, sobbing. 'Answer me, you slut!' I shouted, pushing my fist up close to her face. 'Fucking answer me or I'll ruin that pretty face forever!' At the sight of my raised fist, she began mumbling, incoherently at first, stumbling and mumbling and catching her breath, trying to get some words out. And slowly, piece by piece, little by little, her shoulders hunched and shaking, her head bowed so low it was almost touching the damaged noteboook keyboard, her eyes streaming with tears and her nose running, Jennifer told me all.

In little more than a whisper, with me prodding here every now and then and saying, 'Yes, and then what?', she related how she had studied with this Tom fellow in Cambridge, how they had been drawn together by Buddhism, how they had become great friends, and then, yes, how they had become lovers. How, with the energetic naivety of youth, they had tried to save the world by endeavouring to stop the French from testing their nuclear weapons in the Pacific. How his drumming skills had distracted him from his studies. How their romance, like many other glorious loves across the centuries, had dramatically collapsed and they had gone their own separate ways. How they had stayed totally apart, out of all communication, for twenty years or so until they were drawn back together again by a fluke of technology. Faceook. That damn Facebook.

Most of it I could handle. After all, Jennifer and I had not met each other until I was thirty-eight and she was thirty-one. You would have to be pretty naive if you thought that a person of that age had not experienced at least some real life adventures by then. Even someone from conservative little Ireland and from a super-protective family such as hers. You couldn't assume that she had spent her entire life wrapped in cotton-wool and had not ventured out into the real world and tasted its various delights including, of course, sex. Especially a woman as beautiful, vivacious and outgoing as Jennifer. She simply must have had a lover or lovers somewhere along the line. I'm not entirely worldly-wise but I'm not totally stupid either.

In our early days across the dinner table, she had obviously told me about her childhood and schooling, her university life, her career and some of the more personal, intimate background, including having had 'a couple of boyfriends.' But I now realised that I had been fed the sanitized version, one that in retrospect reeked of antiseptic that my lovelorn nostrils had not detected or had not wanted to detect. She had never told me about Tommy, now all grown up and known as Tom. Never once mentioned his name.

'Jennifer,' I said, as she finished her explanation and her voice trailed off, 'I have another question.'

There was another long pause. I grabbed her by the hair and yanked her head around to make sure she was facing me.

'You don't love this little drummer boy, do you?'

She took a deep breath, wincing in pain, and looked straight at me.

'Jennifer? You don't do you?' I demanded, shaking her head. 'You can't possibly? Not after what he did to you? Not after all we have shared together and built up?'

She peered into my eyes; she began to focus properly. She cleared her throat and her voice became a little stronger.

'Yes, I do.'

God damn! I pulled her hair as hard as I could, angrily spinning her head around in circles three, maybe four, times before letting go. I could feel a clump of her once radiant auburn crowning glory come away in my hands. Her head slumped forward. Her sobbing echoed through the room. I stepped back from her and readied my fist again. I figured it was about time those juicy lips of hers were made a bit fatter. I was about to grab her by the hair again and punch her in the face, when my eye caught the framed picture of our wedding on the sideboard behind her. She looked stunning on that night in her palest of green dresses. 'No, wait,' I thought to myself, 'don't smash up that beautiful face. People will notice.' Instead, I delivered another hard blow to the kidney area.

As she screamed and slumped forward in pain, gasping for breath, I concluded there was something better that I could do. Destroy their means of communication. Before her very eyes.

I unclenched my fist, picked up the laptop, raised it above my head, and smashed it once more on the solid hardwood table. I did it again. And again and again. It started to break into bits, the screen coming away in my hands and the keyboard falling onto the floor with a clatter as she shielded her eyes and continued whimpering, jumping involuntarily every time it banged on the table.

I thumped it again and again until, exhausted, I could do it no more. Then I staggered over to the window, opened it, and threw the screen out into the garden. Worn out by the exertion, I slumped in a chair in the corner, trying to regain my breath, my strength and my composure.

The sobbing continued for a few moments. Then she looked up, took a deep breath, and spoke quietly, albeit with some force.

'At least there was a real man in the bed,' she said.

'What?' I said. It was difficult to hear her as I tried to catch my breath. 'What did you just say?'

'I said,' she hissed angrily, standing up, bent over, clutching her ribs, 'at least there was a real man in the bed.' She picked up a shard of the broken laptop, summoned all her strength and, screaming in agony, hurled it at me. I ducked at the last second as it whizzed by and smashed into the wall. 'There hasn't been one in it for years,' she gasped as she struggled out of the room and headed for the stairs.

'Well, well, well,' I thought, 'there's no denying the guts of a feisty little Irish red-head. Down and out on the mat, but still cocky enough to stand up and give a bit of lip. No wonder they're always in fights.' I started to pull myself out of the chair to chase her, but I could hardly move, I was so emotionally and physically drained. She had half-crawled, half-walked up to the landing before I could get my aching body shifting with any speed. By the time I got some traction and climbed a few steps, she had staggered into the bathroom, slammed the door and locked it. I could hear her coughing and gasping for breath as she began manhandling a chest of antique drawers, the one we used to store towels.

There was a scraping sound as it was dragged across the tiles and a thump as it was wedged hard up against the door. If I was fresh and fit, I reckoned I could have run right through it and burst inside. But I was exhausted. I tried to crash it a couple of times with my shoulder, to no avail. 'You slut,' I screamed, banging on the door, before going back down stairs, rubbing my shoulder as I went. I picked up the keyboard of the dismembered laptop, went back up the stairs to the landing and hurled it at the bathroom door. 'There you go, princess,' I shouted as it bounced off the door and landed on the floor. 'See if you can chat to the little prick now!'

I went downstairs again and slumped in the chair. 'What a fool,' I thought. 'What an idiot I've been. I thought she loved me but now I know what I suspected was true all along. I was just the meal ticket, the bunny that appeared on the horizon when she thought all her hopes of marriage and children were gone. Last chance Stu. That was me. The provider of the cash, the sperm and the security. And once I'd done my job, she figured it was party time.'

After a while, I began to regain my strength, my mind began to clear and I worked out what I had to do. Wait. Just wait. She would have to come out of there some time and I could then reason with her, try and make her see what she had done, tell her to give up this nonsense and return things to the way they were.

That's it, I would wait. I sat in the chair, staring at the wedding photo on the other side of the room. Then my mobile rang. It was Buchanan, his normally cheery voice sounding exceptionally stressed. 'Stu, Stu, more problems at Tallaght,' he said. 'Some bastard is suing us. Can I meet you in the pub in fifteen, we need to talk.'

I let out a deep sigh. This was all I needed. More difficulties with that damn building project. Why, oh why, didn't I just stick to insurance? 'Sure, okay,' I said. 'In fifteen.'

The meeting only added to my stress; the situation was getting worse. When I returned that night, the boys were watching television but Jennifer was nowhere to be seen. She had taken Molly with her and gone over to her mother's. Any chance to try and reason with her had evaporated. We had moved into very dangerous territory.

Chapter 20

In the cool light of the next day, I began to think things through. 'Let's look at this carefully,' I thought. 'We are both adults. We are living under the same roof. We've built a lot up together. We both have responsibilities, particularly shared ones. There are three other very important people involved – young, innocent ones – plus the extended family.'

Even though I was furious, it made sense not to do something really silly over this one situation and throw everything away. So after all the tears and the admissions and the punching and the screaming and the throwing and the smashing had subsided, we met, we talked and we settled into a nice, simple compromise: I forbade her to see Tom again and she agreed that she wouldn't.

Okay, maybe that is not quite a compromise, more an instruction, a direct order from the captain on the bridge. Jennifer was the perpetrator and I was the humiliated, innocent and aggrieved party. End of story.

Admittedly it took me a while to get her to see the wisdom of my decision. Only consideration of the likely impact on our children made her see sense. 'Think about the kids,' I said. 'Look what happened to your brother's family after he got caught with his secretary.' That seemed to hit home. Following Patrick's indiscretion on his phantom golf trip to Galway, Kathy had been forced to go back to her home town of Tipperary and live the life of the single mother in a down-market flat. The kids, particularly the two in the sensitive early teenage stage, lost all interest in school and drifted into drugs, booze and strife. 'Besides, Jennifer,' I added, 'let me make it quite clear. If you go off with this Tom character, you will never see your children again. Never! Do you understand? Never!'

So, after some moody silence, Jennifer agreed to what I proposed and over the next few weeks life returned to something approaching normal. I was pleased that we had reached some sort of detente because things were really starting to bite at work. Money was even harder to come by and policies were not being renewed; with some clients, not even on their cars. When a recession hits, people start cutting corners and taking risks. Insurance is often one of the first aspects of their life that they abandon. We had to let more staff go and the Tallaght project had become a mess. We were one of the lucky ones in that the actual shells of the buildings had got to lock-up stage. But it was a very sad sight to see, with the rooms all empty, the wind whistling across the barren plaza and the tags of the graffiti louts all over the walls.

Angered by these so-called artistic endeavours of the disaffected youth, I dashed off a letter one day to *The Independent* proposing that anyone caught in the possession of a bag of those infernal spray cans should be immediately jailed for three months, no questions asked, no quarter given. Naturally enough, many of the published replies in the following days were from civil libertarian types castigating me for such a provocative proposal. But a reader from Sandyford, God bless him, said that I should stand in the next election on a law and order ticket and I would be guaranteed success.

Out of all this, the pressure was really on me and Derek to find new clients to keep the business afloat. But despite having to work even harder and trying to cope with the stress of it all, I still remained vigilant about Jennifer's movements. My trust had been broken once and it was going to take a lot of hard work on her behalf to go even a little way to restoring it.

I was starting to feel somewhat calmer during the following two months – particularly the time-frame when I knew that that loathsome little individual Tom would be in Dublin to record his tacky television program. It had some ridiculous name like *Who? When? What?* or something. But from what I could see, instead of chasing after Tom at that time, like she had done before, Jennifer stayed around the house. She seemed to be calm and content and not trying to get in touch with him. That was going to be pretty hard for her, anyway. I had not replaced the notebook that I had smashed and I had also banned her from using both the other laptop and the home computer to access Facebook. Regular checks, including rigorous examination of every number on the phone bills, convinced me that she was sticking to her promise.

But in the third month, when I knew Tom would be back in Dublin again, things began to go awry.

Throughout the Thursday, usually his last day in town for the recording, I could not contact Jennifer. She did not answer the home phone for my regular calls and her mobile was switched off. I rang a few of her friends, even that damned Wendy, who I hated talking to at the best of times, but they all said they knew nothing of her whereabouts. At least, that is what they claimed.

When I got home Jennifer said she had been out shopping for an outfit for Molly but had struggled to find something that would fit her because she was so tiny. More expense on clothes! And, she explained, her mobile battery was flat, and the house phone connection had been knocked out accidentally by the vacuum cleaner when she was cleaning that morning. And so on, and so on. Yeah, yeah, I had enough problems to worry about without being concerned with that sort of rubbish.

On the Friday, she was jumpy and anxious and I began to suspect something was up. I would have questioned her that evening but I had to go down to the church for an important committee meeting, which went on much longer than expected, and when I got home she was asleep.

On the Saturday, I followed my usual routine of rising early and taking the two boys with me to my weekly golf game, where they could caddy for me while I played and then practice a few pitches and putts under my direction after the match. When we came home from the course and entered the front door, to my amazement I was greeted not by my wife but my mother!

With a concerned look on her face, she pushed the boys into the lounge room, shut the door behind them, and then ushered me into the parlour on the other side of the hallway. She closed that door behind her and stared at me, shaking her head from side to side.

'Mum!' I said, 'what's going on? Is something wrong with Jennifer? With Molly?'

She looked straight at me with a strength and firmness I had never seen in her eyes before. 'It's the violence, Stuart,' she said. 'I put up with it from your father for years and I don't want Jennifer to have to suffer it like I did.'

I froze. She continued to stare straight at me. I didn't know which revelation shocked me more. That my father had been violent to her, something I had certainly never noticed in all the time I was at home – well, not anything that I would consider untoward – or that she considered my approach to Jennifer just as unacceptable.

'Mum, I never knew.'

'It happened,' she said. 'He used to try and pass it off as a result of his war days. But it was more than that. It was his way of controlling me. It wouldn't have mattered if he had been in the army or not, he still would have done it anyway.'

'But, Mum, me and Jennifer, I've never laid …'

'Don't!' she said, holding her hand up and stopping me. 'Don't lie to me, Stuart, I'm your mother. Don't try and defend yourself. She's shown me the bruises around the ribs, the bits of her pretty hair pulled out, the marks on her back. And when I was here one day and saw the pieces of that computer thing all over the garden and asked the kids what was going on, that was it.'

I could feel the anger welling in me. My ship was now under serious threat. Jennifer, my mutinous first mate, had been blabbing to everyone; even the children were proving a security risk.

'So, what's going on, then?' I said. 'What's this all about?'

'Stuart, she wants to be free of you. She's going to London to live with Tom.'

'Bullshit!'

'Stuart, please don't swear in front of me like that.'

'There is no fucking way my wife is leaving me and her children to go and live with that little prick.'

'She's not leaving all of the kids. She's taking Molly with her.'

I stepped back, my head spinning.

'What? Like hell she is! I'll soon sort this out.' I went to push past Mum and head for the door, but she stood firmly in front of me.

'Stuart,' she said resolutely. 'Just listen. You can see Jennifer in a minute, and tell her whatever you want, but please hear what I have to say first. You can't blame her for wanting a new life.'

'New life? She went off and …'

'No, no, wait, wait. She might have been unfaithful, but …'

'She certainly was!'

' … but that was after the event, Stuart. Did she ever bash you? No. Did she pull your hair out in clumps? No. Did she ridicule you in front of people, or insist on what clothes you wore, or check up on your every move, or complain when the meal was not right, or make sarcastic comments about the house-keeping? No, she didn't. She didn't do any of those things, Stuart, you did. *You* were the one who made *her* life miserable!

'I, ah …'

'And that is something that a mother is not proud to say about her son, I can tell you.'

'Oh, mum, I didn't mean …'

'You may not have meant it, Stuart, but it happened. You did it. Look, I know she has done a terrible thing to you and I know you are hurt and you feel betrayed.'

'I've got every right to feel betrayed!'

'But you instigated this, Stuart. You set up the division. You split her and Molly away from you.'

'I, ah …' I tried to respond, but nothing came out. I felt confused, hurt, deflated. Mum put her hand up and lightly touched my cheek.

'Look at it this way. You will still have the boys. That's a good thing. You love them and they love you. And Mary and I will help you with them. We'll make sure you get plenty of support with meals and pick-ups and all that sort of thing. You'll still be able to run the business and they will get on with their education and sport and whatever else they want to do in life.'

'Well, I guess …'

'Stuart, it will take all the sting out of the situation. All the heat and the argument and the unhappiness. I know this is hurting you now, but it will be best in the long run. You never know, she might even come back home to you one day.'

'If and when she returns to her senses,' I replied flatly.

'That's right! Come with me now, she's in the lounge. Come and say goodbye and wish her well and just let things rest. It's for the best.'

I looked down at Mum. She stared straight back at me, her soft blue eyes pleading, begging me to follow her wishes.

'Please, Stuart?'

'Okay,' I mumbled, 'okay.'

She looked relieved, gave a wan smile, grabbed me by the hand and led me out of the room. Still a little stunned, I obediently traipsed behind her as she crossed the hallway, opened the lounge room door and led me in. And there they all were. A blur of faces and bodies, variously sitting stiffly or standing awkwardly around the room, waiting in ambush. A whole group of them, family and friends, the stand-outs being Jennifer's mum, Mary, and her brother, Kevin, no doubt to provide a bit of muscle if things turned nasty. Perhaps he had heard about my judo triumph in Cork all those years ago.

I surveyed them all and took a deep breath. 'Ah, a welcoming committee,' I said, trying to break the ice.

Jennifer was at centre stage. Her skin was pale and tightly drawn and she was nervous, but I could see she was determined to make a stand.

'I've booked a flight to London,' she said.

'So I understand,' I replied. 'Mum told me.'

'I'm going with Tom.'

It suddenly dawned on me that the squeamish little bastard was standing opposite me. A fair distance away, I might point out. My mother might have told me some home truths and calmed me down and softened me up for this moment, but the mention of his name and the sight of him fired me up again. I started to move towards him. 'I'm gonna knock your block off,' I yelled. I reckoned I could have, too. He was much tinier than I had envisaged. 'You fucking little prick. She's my wife, not yours.'

You could hear the collective intake of breath, the murmurs of shock as I strode across the room, only to be blocked by Kevin. He had quickly moved across to stand between me and Tom. He folded his arms, set his jaw firmly and adopted a wide stance. It appeared he had acquired a few basic combat techniques while he'd been losing my money on the race track. I pushed him in the chest, but he remained solid.

'Kevin, my fight is not with you,' I hissed. 'Out of my way.'

'No can do, Stuart,' he said.

'Kevin, I do not want to have to hurt you.'

'Stuart,' came a pleading voice. It was Jennifer. 'Please do not make a scene.'

'A scene!' I said, turning around to look at her. 'Me, make a scene, for Christ's sake? You're the one that has set the scene, wrecking our family, pulling our lives apart.'

'Stuart, you started it all when you began to control me. To run my life, to insist that everything be done your way.'

'Jennifer, I was only doing the best for the family. To keep things on an even keel. You know how scatty you can get.'

'Scatty? Ha! Listen, I ran that house perfectly, all day every day, and raised three healthy, happy little kids, and all you did was turn up, eat, drink whiskey and whinge. If I ever appeared scatty it was my way of trying to be happy and making the best of the miserable life you chained me to.'

'Well, that's marriage for you, Jennifer. That's what it's all about. You have your ups and downs, your good days and your bad days. And you work through the bad stuff. You don't just suddenly walk out and end it all.'

'Well, I am. I've made up my mind. I've had enough of the pain and the misery and the beatings, and I'm going. Molly's coming with me and the boys can stay with you.'

I looked around the room. There were heads quietly nodding in assent everywhere.

She went on, spouting enthusiastically about how Junior and Rich would be happier and more secure with me, continuing to live in the same house, going to the same school, having the same friends, all that sort of stuff.

'And Molly will be better off with me,' she concluded. I looked across the room to see Tom step aside and reveal Molly who, up until now, had been standing behind him. My little girl took the loathsome individual's hand and looked up at me with a sad expression on her face, her little green eyes looking melancholy and confused.

'But, she's my daughter, too. You can't just …'

A voice suddenly came from the left of me, cutting me off. 'Let her go, Stu,' it said. 'She's made up her mind. You won't change it.' The jangle of jewellery and waft of perfume told me immediately who it was. I turned to confront Wendy looking relaxed, her red caftan flowing all over the lounge chair.

'You! You're the cause of most of this,' I said angrily. 'You and your bloody New Age garbage, filling her head with all those ridiculous ideas.'

She gave me that annoying smile, the one that said she knew something special that I didn't. 'And don't give me that smart-arse look,' I snapped. 'Just go back to fucking New Zealand will you and leave us alone.' I turned away from her and stared slowly around the room. 'I see,' I said, turning in a circle, staring at each stony face. 'It's let's get Stuart time, is it?'

'Stuart, we're all here to help,' said Mary.

'Ha! I know what you mean by help. Shaft me, that's what your idea of help is.'

Mary remained calm. 'I have always said, if you love something you should let it go free and then if it belongs to you it will return.'

'That's the sort of weird philosophical mumb-jumbo I would expect from you, Mary,' I snarled. 'A cart load of your Catholic crap mixed with a bucket load of your daughter's Buddhist bullshit.'

A quiver of fear spread through the group. They had never heard me attack anyone's beliefs with words like that before. I looked again at all their faces. I wanted to retaliate. I clenched my fists.

'You all make me sick,' I said. I looked directly at Jennifer. 'Especially you.'

'Stuart,' came a voice from the edge of the group. It was Tom.

'Oh, the big hero is coming to protect his girl!' I sneered. 'You stay out of this, you fucking prick. I know what you're after, you greedy little bastard.'

'Stuart, please,' chipped in Jennifer.

'He's after my money, that's what he is,' I declared loudly to the room. 'He's thinking that when the divorce goes through half of everything that I've spent my life building up will go to Jenny and he can get his grubby little hands on it. What a bonanza for a layabout musician!' I turned around and lowered my voice to a conspiratorial tone to emphasise my point, nodding towards him. 'None of these bastards ever do any actual work, you know.'

I moved towards Jennifer but Kevin stepped in the way again. I took a deep breath. I was furious. I wanted to smack him one, too. I always had, come to think of it, but the right level of passion and a definitive reason had never been quite in place before. Now I had a good one. However, deep down I knew there was no way around all this. I scanned their faces once more. The odds were heavily stacked against me. When it came to devising an ambush, Jennifer had certainly done her homework. Even Horatio Nelson would have been impressed.

Mary broke the silence. 'Moira and I will help you with the boys,' she said soothingly. 'We'll get through.'

Then came the killer blow. Mum stepped forward, put her hands out and covered my fists. 'Come on Stu, darling,' she said. 'We love you. And we love the boys. It's for the best.'

I could feel the warm, smooth skin of my mother's hands on mine. It felt good. Calming. Comforting. Like when I was a little boy after I had come home from yet another disastrous day in a new schoolyard. It made me feel like I wanted to be cuddled and protected again. I started to shake. The emotion of it all, the discovery of what was going on, the fights, and now the final betrayal, it was all too much. Tears trickled down my cheeks. I unclenched my fists and stepped back. People looked away as I tried to pull myself together.

Then, Wendy got up to leave. Now, there was a turn-up for the books. After all the years of unsuccessfully trying to force her out of my life, I now discovered that all I had to do was turn on the tears and she would have buggered off. 'I don't think it's my place to be here,' she said awkwardly.

'About time you realised that,' I grunted.

I took another deep breath and regained my focus. 'All right, everyone,' I said, 'I get the picture. I've made my bed and now I have to lie in it. Ho, ho, ho!' I giggled loudly, throwing my head back. 'A bit of a bedtime joke there between Jennifer and me.'

No one laughed. Jennifer moved forward. 'Stuart, we're leaving now. Tom and I and Molly are booked on a plane for London. We have to get going right away or we will miss it.'

'Right now? Wow,' I said as the enormity of it all began to hit home. 'Um, okay. I understand.'

I looked around. I could see people were starting to feel relieved that I wasn't going to try and get the drop on big Kev and little Tom and hurl them both through a window.

In the intervening silence, a thought suddenly came to me. I wasn't done yet. 'I'll drive you out to the airport, then?' I offered.

'What?' said Jennifer. I had caught her off guard. 'Ah, no, you don't have to do that.'

'No need, Stuart,' said Kevin, coming up close to me. 'I'm here to do the driving.'

I smiled. The ever-vigilant, ever-protective Kevin had finally found his moment in the sun. 'Ah, the dutiful brother,' I said, patting him on the shoulder. 'Good to see.'

I looked around at the faces and back to Jennifer. 'Well, can I at least go out there with you to say goodbye? Especially to Molly.'

Jennifer looked at her watch. 'We haven't got enough time!' she snapped.

'Please, especially as I won't be seeing her for a while.'

She looked anxiously behind her. Tom hesitated for a moment, then nodded his assent slowly.

'All right,' she said wearily. 'But it will mean we'll have to take two cars. Damn, I just want to get out of here.'

Despite the sparks between the two main protagonists, a sense of relief had come over the bit-part players. People started to relax, unwind a little, murmur to each other. We all went outside. Kevin jogged off down the street and re-appeared a few moments later at the wheel of a brand new BMW, one of those SUV things that lets you sit up high and lord it over all the other drivers. He had hidden it down the road so I would not be alerted to something unusual when I came home from golf. 'Nice car,' I said as I helped load the bags. 'Finally picked a winner at the Curragh, did you?'

'Mind the upholstery,' he barked, ignoring the jibe. 'I only picked it up yesterday.' He jumped into the driver's seat. Tom and Jennifer went to climb aboard with Molly, indicating that I would take the boys in the other car. My little daughter looked up at me, her face tired with anguish. The image came back to me! The painting of the sad green-eyed girl on the wall of the manor on our wedding night.

'Can I ride in the car with Molly?' I suddenly blurted. There was silence. I looked down at her gently. 'It would be nice to spend the last few moments with my little girl.'

Jennifer's eyes narrowed. She looked around at the others. Mary shrugged. Tom slowly and unhappily nodded.

'Well, okay, if you must!' snapped Jennifer. 'God, you *love* making things difficult, don't you?'

'What's that supposed to mean?' We were flaring at each other again. 'I've only ever done the best for the family.'

'Ha! Well, you'll have to come with us in Kevin's car. Molly's car-seat is strapped in it and we haven't got time to be mucking around.'

'Tom,' I said, turning to him and throwing him my keys, 'you take the boys and follow in our car. Then after you've flown out, I'll drive them home.' I climbed into the back seat of Kevin's shiny BMW, taking Molly with me. Jennifer, looking very put out, angrily hauled herself into the front passenger's seat next to Kevin. Tom slipped into the driver's seat of my Audi as the two boys scrambled into the rear seat. They both looked wary, perhaps a little scared, but seemed to have some sort of grip on what was going on. I think they figured that once all this drama was over, with Dad in charge of the domestic scene it would be fast food and *The Simpsons* every night.

After a wave of farewell hugs and kisses and streams of tears, Kevin carefully backed his gleaming new vehicle out and, unaccountably, turned left.

'What the hell are you doing?' snapped Jennifer, shocked. 'The motorway's the other way.'

'The M50's blocked,' he said. 'I heard it on the radio. Some eedjit's rolled his delivery van and there's a big game at Croke Park. It's jammed. I know a way to cut across and we'll pick it up further north.'

Jennifer looked at her watch, folded her arms angrily and pushed herself back hard into the plush leather seat. 'We're cutting it fine as it is! We don't want to miss our plane. I couldn't go through all this again.'

'Well,' I said, 'you don't have to, if you come to your senses.'

'Aggh!' she said. 'Kevin, just drive.'

I banged the back of her seat hard with my fist, and then leaned across and checked the seatbelt securing Molly into her booster seat. 'What have we got here?' I said soothingly, pointing to her Hannah Montana back-pack. She had books, games, a drink bottle. 'Goin' up in the sky on the big plane, hey?'

Molly looked up at me. Her eyes were sleepy, but she smiled. I had to look away for a second. It was the smile Jennifer first gave me when we met. She was the perfect replica of her mother. Pretty, bright, perky.

I could understand why Jennifer wanted to take her. They were made for each other. They laughed, giggled and played together. They told each other secrets. They cuddled each other when watching television. They were inseparable. Best mates. A unit unto themselves. Apart from our little game of Catch-Molly, they had all but locked me out. 'But,' I thought, 'she is not Jennifer's to take away like this. No, sir. Molly belongs in Dalkey with me, and with her brothers. And with her mother, too, if she chooses.'

I knew Jennifer loved the boys. What mother wouldn't? But boys return love in a different way. They take more than they give and see that as a positive. The fact that you are able to look after them is their own special gift to you. All things considered, it did make sense that they should stay with me. They were almost self-sufficient and with a bit of help from people around – apparently I was going to get the right assistance, according to Mary and Moira – I would be fine. Their lives wouldn't change too much.

But if Jennifer thought she was going to get away with this easily, she had another think coming. She had no right to break up a family. How dare she get involved again with this little jumped up Asiatic drummer boy. How dare she disobey my orders. How dare she organise a gang ambush in my own lounge. With my mother an integral part of the posse, too! What an embarrassing scene. This was humiliating. Well, if she wanted to play rough, then so be it.

Chapter 21

Determined to prove he had picked the correct route, and perhaps anxious to get Jennifer and me out of his new car as quickly as possible, Kevin drove with a combination of speed to get us to the airport on time and anxiety about not getting his pristine vehicle scratched on the way. In between moments of fuming silence, the pair of us bitched, bickered and screamed at each other, while he scurried along back streets, bounced over kerbs and took us up roads I'd never seen before; which was quite an achievement, because as an insurance salesman, I reckoned I had covered pretty much all of Dublin over the years.

We had barely got to the end of our street when she baited me. She turned around, her voice soft, a little smile on her face. 'Thank you for being so reasonable, Stuart,' she said soothingly.

Reasonable? It was all I could do to resist from leaning forward and grabbing her by the hair, pulling her head back and banging it hard against the seat. 'Bitch!' I hissed. 'It's nothing to do with being reasonable. You rail-roaded me!'

'God damn,' she said. 'See. I try and make peace with you and you still attack me.'

I leaned forward, close to her ear. 'You started all this, Jennifer. Or should I say Jobby?'

She turned around and pushed me in the chest, forcing me back into the seat. 'Go away, you horrible man. I'm glad I'm getting you out of my life.'

'Don't you dare push me around like that,' I snapped, banging on the back of her seat with my fist and making her head rock. 'Don't you worry, I'll still be around. You haven't seen the last of me yet.'

'Cut it out, you two,' Kevin barked suddenly. Jennifer looked at her watch and hissed something under her breath. I sat back. 'This is nothing to do with you, Kevin,' I mumbled.

As he gunned his shiny new toy down highways and byways, followed by Tom and the boys battling to keep up in our car, I stared out the side window, burning with anger. What was that patronising statement Mary had said back there? 'If you love someone, you'll let them go free'? Ha!

Before long, the hum of the car and the emotion of what had happened was too much for little Molly. She dropped off to sleep.

'Been a big day,' I said to Jennifer, nodding down at our little girl.

Jennifer turned around, looked down at Molly, then up at me and then turned back. 'Been a big day for all of us,' she murmured, staring forward.

The quicker Kevin drove, the more anxious Jennifer got. 'Kevin!' she screamed at one stage as we just squeezed through the ever-closing gap between a parked car and a rapidly oncoming plumber's white van. 'You want me to get you there on time, don't you?' he snarled.

'I don't know why you didn't take the motor-way,' she yelled.

'I told you, it was blocked and I'll pick it up soon.'

'He knows what he's doing!' I chipped in.

'Don't you back him up,' she turned and said to me. 'I just want to get to the airport and be out of here.' She turned back angrily, folded her arms, pushed herself hard back into the seat again and glared out the side window. 'We'll never make the plane now.'

I turned around and looked out the rear. Tom was really struggling to keep up. I looked down at Molly. She was sound asleep. I looked out the side window. And stewed.

'So,' I thought, 'it has come to this. I'm losing everything I have built up. My home. My family. My wife. Even my daughter.' Now, there was the irony. I loved Molly so much, I could barely bring myself to touch her in case she would break. Sometimes Jennifer saw this as an indication of a lack of feelings for her. That was not true. Our little game of me pretending to drop her and then catch her safely was my one display of affection. But it contained the greatest human element of all. Trust. And for me, trust was everything.

I began to think things through. Molly was as much part of me as the boys were. She was my little girl and I loved her. Yet Jennifer had kept diverting her away from me so that they could form their own little two-person tribe. 'Why should Molly be subjected to all this?' I thought. 'To be made the pawn, the hostage, in Jennifer and Tom's little game?'

I leaned over towards Jennifer.

'You know what?' I said. 'That cocky little smart-arse back there is not Molly's father. I am! I'm her Da! I know what's best for her. And what I say, goes. I'm still the decision-maker. I'm still the captain of the ship!'

'Yeah, well, we're abandoning your precious ship!' Jennifer said. 'I hope you sink in it.'

'That's enough, you two,' yelled Kevin. 'We're almost to the M50.'

I looked out the window to see that the road was beginning to widen and the houses had been replaced by landscaped concrete walls. 'See,' said Kevin triumphantly. 'The motorway's up ahead. I've just got to cross it on this flyover, go down the other side and pick it up.'

He gunned the car up the ramp but as we reached the top and levelled out, there was a mighty screech of brakes and we came to a halt, an anxious Tom pulling up right behind us. 'Feckin' hell,' Kevin muttered. I could barely hear him over the roar of the motorway below. A car up front had stopped and both its front doors were open. The middle-aged driver and his wife were out of their vehicle, bending down anxiously. 'The silly old fecker has hit some eedjit on a motorbike,' hissed Kevin, banging the steering wheel in frustration with his hand. Peering between Jennifer and Kevin, I could just make out the shattered bike and crumpled leather-clad body sprawled across the flyover, blocking our way. The motorcyclist was screaming in pain.

Jennifer turned to Kevin and hit him hard on the arm with a clenched fist. 'I told you to go on the motorway from the fucking start!' she screamed.

'Jennifer!' I said. 'There's no need to swear.'

She turned. 'You! You keep out of this!' she yelled. 'You're the cause of everything. I finally get a chance for freedom, and here you are, sitting right behind me, still bullying me!'

It was her use of the word 'freedom' that really got to me. Everyone was getting their freedom out of this, except me. I would be directly responsible for the boys, with Mary hanging around making sure I did it properly. Not much freedom there. You could bet Kevin and Seamus and the rest of them would be putting their oar in, too. Not much freedom there, either. Not forgetting the input of my mother. Say no more.

Freedom? What a joke. Then it came to me. The only person who truly deserved to be free was Molly. She shouldn't be dragged off to live a miserable life with these two scheming liars. She should be allowed to enjoy growing up with her brothers in her real home. And if not, then she should be allowed to fly free like a little bird. Mary was right – if I love this little one, then I should give her her freedom. The question was, how?

I leaned forward and tapped Jennifer on the shoulder.

'I want to know,' I asked. 'Where are you going to live in London?'

'What's it to you?'

'It's very important to me!' I flared. 'I want to know what situation my daughter is going to end up in. She's being taken away from her beautiful home in Dalkey, so are you going to get a place in Kensington or somewhere decent like that?'

'Well, if you must know, until things sort themselves out, we're moving into Tom's place in Barking Road.'

'Fucking hell, what sort of a life is that? Stuck in some grimy little East End flat with a handful of second-hand toys while you two won't be able keep your dirty hands off each other.'

She turned around angrily. 'Stuart, how dare you!'

'Well, it's true. You're only doing this so you can fuck each other senseless. For the first few months, anyway, until the passion subsides.'

'You bastard!'

'And how will it be for Molly having a drummer for a substitute father?'

'What do you mean? He has a career, he always has plenty of work.'

'Ha! They're notorious those fellows! Their way-out lifestyle. He'll be unreliable, selfish, in and out of work, on the road, a spendthrift. You just see.'

'I trust him.'

'Trust him?! Jennifer, he's let you down once already. Very badly, too. What he did to you when you were young ruined your life for the next twenty years.'

'But he loves me for who I am and wants me for me.'

'Christ almighty, grow up. He wants my money, that's what he wants. And I can tell you, whatever money you do get out of this, sweetheart, and believe me, there won't be much because I am going to fight you to the bitter fucking end, will be gone in a minute on cigarettes and drugs and booze and then you'll be out in the street.'

'I don't want your stinking money, Stuart,' she screamed. 'In fact, I don't want anything from you!'

'Right then! That's a deal,' I hissed, furiously punching the back of her seat. The impact made her head jolt forward and the noise made Molly stir. 'I'll make sure you get nothing at all, Jennifer,' I yelled. 'In fact,' I said, looking down at the sweet little face, 'I'll make sure you lose everything.'

In one quick movement, I leaned across, unbuckled Molly's belt and smoothly lifted her tiny body out of the booster seat. 'Daddy, daddy, what?' she mumbled, still half-asleep.

Without a break, I opened my door and stepped down from the SUV, landing lightly on the flyover, Molly cradled limply in my arms. 'Daddy?' she said drowsily. I looked down at her beautiful face, which started to slowly come alive as I took a couple of steps. 'Are we playing our game?' she said.

Jennifer screwed her head around to see what I was up to, anxiously pushing at the buttons on the unfamiliar console until one finally wound down her window. She stared at me, puzzled, concerned. 'Stuart,' she said very evenly, as if saying it loudly or in a hurried tone might panic me. 'Stuart. What are you doing?'

I stopped, turned around, and stared straight into her eyes. 'You've taken something very special from me,' I said slowly. 'My trust. You found me, used me, and now you're getting rid of me. So now it's my turn to take something special from you.'

'Daddy,' said Molly, 'are we playing Catch-Molly?'

I looked down at her angelic face. 'Yes, darling,' I said, 'yes, we are.'

'Stuart!' screamed Jennifer, as she wrestled with the door handle. 'Stuart!'

'Jennifer,' I said evenly, 'everything comes at a price. Especially freedom.'

I turned away and walked over to the barrier, and with the screams of Jennifer and the roar of the thundering traffic in my ears, lifted Molly high and held her over the edge, like an offering to the gods. She smiled gently up at me, in her trusting little way, as I dropped her. 'Fly free, little bird,' I whispered. 'Fly free.'

Amid the sound of screeching tyres and metal crashing on metal coming from below, I calmly turned around, stared at Jennifer and then at Tom. Then with a military precision that my father would have been proud of, I turned on my heel and started striding briskly away, down the flyover.

As Jennifer's screams pierced through the wall of noise and confusion erupting from the motorway below, my thoughts were quite clear.

'Freedom? Let them enjoy their freedom now.'